THE LONGEST DAY

THE LONGEST DAY

(ARK ROYAL, BOOK X)

CHRISTOPHER G. NUTTALL

The characters and events portrayed in this book are fictitious. Any similarity to real persons, living or dead, is coincidental and not intended by the author.

ISBN 13: 9781548520052
ISBN: 1548520055

http://www.chrishanger.net
http://chrishanger.wordpress.com/
http://www.facebook.com/ChristopherGNuttall

Cover by Justin Adams
http://www.variastudios.com/

All Comments Welcome!

HISTORIAN'S NOTE

The Longest Day is set during the Earth-Tadpole War, at roughly the same time as the latter half of *The Nelson Touch*. However, it is designed to stand alone.

PROLOGUE

Tadpole Prime

No human had ever visited the Heart of the Song. No human ever would.

The Tadpoles - as their human opponents had termed them - didn't really believe in cities. It wasn't *necessary*, under the waters, to live in a compound, let alone sacrifice some of their freedoms to convenience. Even the giant factories they'd built, first on the surface and then in orbit around Tadpole Prime, felt profoundly unnatural to them. Something was lost, they thought, even as their race advanced into space. Ideas - the currency of their society - were slowly giving way to a bland uniformity that was as unnatural as the cities themselves.

It was something that disturbed them, although they would never have admitted it. Their whole society was based on freedom of movement and association. The disparate factions lived or died, stood alone or amalgamated, based on their ability to attract new voices and adapt to new circumstances. Being trapped in an echo chamber, where no new ideas could germinate and grow, was their racial nightmare. And yet, as they clawed their way into space, it seemed to be on the verge of coming true. They knew it...

...And yet, they didn't know how to deal with it.

The Heart of the Song was the closest thing their race had to a genuine capital city, hundreds of metres below the waves. It was holy ground, sacred to a race that had never really developed anything resembling a religion. A human would have wondered at the lack of opulence, but the Tadpoles cared little for grandeur. All that mattered was that the area possessed excellent acoustics. All the factions could send representatives, if they wished, and be heard. And then a consensus would be reached.

Hundreds of thousands of Tadpoles floated in the water, adding their voices to the song as it rose and fell. Millions of seedlings rushed through the liquid, unnoticed by their older brethren. The Tadpoles knew - and accepted - that most of those seedlings would never grow to maturity, never claim the intelligence that was their birthright. It was the way of things, as unquestioned as the laws of physics themselves. Children only had value when they reached an age to join their voices to the song.

The war had not gone as planned, the Tadpoles acknowledged. It was...*frustrating*. They'd spent a great deal of time studying their enemy, since First Contact, yet they clearly hadn't learnt everything they needed to know. The song - the consensus - admitted those points, then moved on. There would be time for recriminations and improvements later, after the war. Their enemies had proven themselves adaptive, alarmingly adaptive. It was not a pleasant thought.

The original plan has failed, the voices urged. *Let us take the offensive directly to their homeworld.*

The song echoed backwards and forwards for hours. There were advantages to taking the offensive, but there were also disadvantages. And yet, did they dare wait? They'd determined that they shared a region of space with an aggressive, ever-expanding race. Much of the material they'd captured had been incomprehensible - and their alien prisoners very *alien* - but it was clear that humanity had practically exploded into space. It was sheer luck, the song acknowledged, that they'd encountered humanity when the Tadpoles held a tech advantage. A decade or two later and it might well have been the other way round.

They are already learning to adapt our technology to serve themselves, the voices insisted, grimly. *Time is not on our side.*

Then we should speak to them, other voices injected. *Try to convince them to share the universe with us.*

The song wavered for a long moment. Not *all* the factions had been keen on war. Wars were risky, they'd insisted. There was no way to know if humanity would fight like the Tadpoles of old or something different, something not bound by the song. But human history seemed to be one continuous liturgy of war. The Tadpoles didn't understand the *reason* humans had put so much energy into warring amongst themselves - the captured files were readable, yet incomprehensible - but they were frightened. It was impossible to avoid the belief that the galaxy, the utterly immense galaxy, might not be big enough for both races, even though they could have shared a hundred worlds without problems.

They are inventive, the war factions said. *Let us dictate terms to them after we have won the war and removed all danger to ourselves.*

They are too dangerous to exist, another faction added. *We must destroy them before they destroy us.*

The song hissed with indignation. Humans were an *intelligent* race, the only other intelligent race known to exist. They did not deserve to be exterminated. And yet, the risk of leaving them alive had to be admitted. The Tadpoles were creative, but far - far - less innovative than their opponents. It was all too easy to believe that the humans might come up with something that would tip the scales decisively against them. And then... human history was full of examples of what winners did to losers. If they were prepared to crush people who were their biological identicals, the Tadpoles asked, what would they do to *aliens*?

Let us win the war, the song said. *We can worry about the aftermath afterwards.*

New ideas flooded through the gathering. An offensive, targeted directly on the human homeworld. It might not succeed in occupying the system - the Tadpoles admitted that the system was heavily defended, even if the human factions didn't work very well together - but it would devastate the human industrial base. Follow-up raids could target their remaining colony worlds, crippling their space navies for lack of spare parts and maintenance. And then the war would be over, bar the shouting.

And then we can dictate peace terms, the factions said.

It would be risky, the song agreed. But there was always an element of risk in war. They'd thought they'd prepared for everything, but the humans had surprised them. Losing so many carriers to a single ancient ship - a ship so old it had never registered with them as a potential threat - was galling. It was also a grim reminder that, for all of their technological prowess, they could still lose the war. The song was unanimous. They had to win. They didn't dare lose.

And if the offensive fails? A lone faction asked. *What then?*

It will not fail, the war factions sang. *The fleet will be strong enough to retreat, if necessary.*

The lone faction was unimpressed. *And what if you're wrong?*

Then we will deal with it, the song insisted. The decision had been made. A thrill of anticipation ran through the gathering. *Until then...we must win this war.*

CHAPTER ONE

RFS *Brezhnev*, Deep Space

Captain Svetlana Zadornov slept with a gun under her pillow and a knife hidden by the side of her bunk.

It was, she felt, a reasonable precaution. Mother Russia expected her womenfolk to be *mothers*, not starship officers and commanders. There were only a handful of women in the Russian Space Navy and almost all of them had been harassed - or worse - during their careers, even though they'd all been officers. Svetlana's uncle, Sasha Zadornov, was a high-ranking member of the Politburo and even *his* name wasn't enough to deter the troglodytes who resented a woman intruding into what they saw as a purely male sphere. It was sad, but true - she'd discovered as her career progressed - that her skills in starship command and maintenance were less impressive than the ability to injure or kill someone who thought a mere woman couldn't possibly offer any resistance to him. Knifing two officers and one rating had done more for her reputation than winning a coveted gunnery award.

And then they sent me to Brezhnev *anyway*, she thought, coldly. Her lips quirked into a nasty smile as she lay in her bunk, half-asleep. *And didn't that come back to haunt them?*

It wasn't a pleasant thought. Everyone conceded - officially, at least - that Svetlana was qualified to command one of the *Rodina's* starships. But there had been no question of giving her a carrier command, let alone one of the modern destroyers or survey ships. She was a woman, after all.

They'd given her *Brezhnev*, a destroyer so old that she'd only been refitted with artificial gravity two years ago. Giving the ship to *anyone* would have been a calculated insult, but giving *Brezhnev* to her...it galled her, sometimes. She knew her scores were higher than those of half her classmates at the academy.

But if I'd been on one of the modern ships, she reminded herself, *I might have died at New Russia.*

Her intercom pinged. "Captain?"

Svetlana snapped into full wakefulness. One hand gripped her pistol, automatically. It wasn't *likely* that the message presaged an assassination attempt - or worse - but she hadn't survived so long without taking a few basic precautions. "Commander Ignatyev?"

"Please can you come to the bridge, Captain," Commander Misha Ignatyev said. "Long-range sensors have detected something you need to see."

"Understood," Svetlana said. Ignatyev was nearly thirty years her senior and bitterly resentful at having been passed over for command, again. He wouldn't call her to the bridge unless he had a very good reason. "I'm on my way."

She swung her legs over the side of the bunk and stood, feeling the gravity field wobbling around her. *Brezhnev* hadn't been designed for artificial gravity and it showed. Her cabin, so tiny she could barely swing a cat, looked oddly slanted to her eyes. Half the lockers were embedded in the bulkhead, high enough to make retrieving anything on the top shelves very difficult. But the design would have made perfect sense, she knew, if the ship hadn't had a gravity field of its own. There were times when she seriously considered turning the gravity generator off and keeping the crew in zero-g.

Which wouldn't please the engineers, she thought. The engineering crew weren't much better than the *rest* of her crew, although they'd fallen in line after she'd proved she knew what she was talking about. She pitied the poor butterflies who concentrated on acing the political reliability courses at the academy rather than learning how starships actually worked. A hint of technobabble and they'd be drowning helplessly, unable to make a decision. *And the engineers would take ruthless advantage of them.*

She reached for her jacket and pulled it on, then inspected herself in the mirror. Her blonde hair was cut short, a mannish hairstyle that gave some of her aunts fits of the vapours every time they looked at her. They twittered endlessly about how *poor* Svetlana would never get a man, let alone fulfil her duties to Mother Russia. She pursued her lips in annoyance, silently cursing the old biddies under her breath. They *knew* she was sterile, damn them. Children were simply not a possibility.

And it isn't as if we are still facing a demographic crisis, she thought, as she strapped her pistol into place. *We don't* need *every woman turning out four kids before she turns thirty.*

She glared at her own reflection. Her face wasn't as sharp as she would have liked, but she was mannish enough not to seem automatically female in male eyes. Most men, she'd come to realise, looked past hints of femininity as long as the woman in question behaved like a man. Sharing crude jokes and defending her territory - with a gun, a knife or her bare hands - wasn't pleasant, but it was the only way to get respect. And while she doubted she would ever see a carrier command, she knew she'd done well. *That* was all that mattered.

Opening the hatch, she stepped into the command corridor and walked down to the bridge. A pair of armed spacers stood guard - no naval infantry on *Brezhnev* - and saluted her as the hatch hissed open. Svetlana made no response. Instead, she stepped through the hatch and onto the cramped bridge. It felt uncomfortably warm. The temperature regulators were probably on the fritz, again.

"Captain," Ignatyev said. He was a short, dumpy man with a white beard, easily old enough to be her father. His competence was unquestioned, but he lacked the connections to rise any higher. "Long-range sensors picked up hints of turbulence in the distance."

Svetlana sucked in her breath, sharply. The Earth Defence Organisation had been holding an exercise designed to get the various national navies used to working together, but - as far as she knew - none of the planned operations were taking place anywhere near *Brezhnev's* patrol route. *Her* ship hadn't been invited to take part, of course. The Russian Navy considered the ninety-year-old destroyer an embarrassment, even though she was a near-contemporary to the British *Ark Royal and* she'd been kept in active service all that time. But most of *Brezhnev's* systems were still outdated...

Her armour isn't outdated, Svetlana thought, coldly. *Brezhnev* and her sisters had been designed for a very different environment. *And that might give us a fighting chance.*

There were no holographic projectors on *Brezhnev,* of course. She bent over the tactical officer's console, examining the very vague readings. They were faint, faint enough to make her wonder if *Brezhnev* was seeing things. Space wasn't *quite* as dark and silent as civilians believed and her sensors were old enough, despite the refit, to pick up on something that wasn't actually there. But she *had* heard about the alien tramlines. The mysterious contact - if it *was* a contact - was on a vector that suggested it *might* have come from the closest tramline...

"Keep us in stealth," she ordered. "Helm, inch us towards the contact."

"Aye, Captain," the helmsman said.

Svetlana glanced at Ignatyev. "Send a FLASH message to Putin Station and Pournelle Base," she ordered. "Inform them that we have detected a contact and are moving out of position to attempt to pin it down. Attach a full copy of our sensor log too."

"Aye, Captain," Ignatyev said. He lowered his voice. "The Kremlin may not be pleased if we abandon our patrol route. Or if we alert Pournelle Base."

"We have standing orders to investigate all sensor contacts," Svetlana reminded him, fighting down a flicker of annoyance. She didn't mind having a lively debate with her XO, but not where her crew could hear. "And the Kremlin ordered us to copy all alerts to Pournelle Base."

She sat down in her command chair and strapped herself in, then keyed her console to bring up the latest set of standing orders. Ignatyev might well have a point. The Kremlin *might* be unhappy if Pournelle Base was alerted ahead of time, even though she had standing orders to do just that. But she also understood the reasoning behind the standing orders. The human race was at war and, like it or not, the defence of the solar system and Earth herself was being coordinated through Pournelle Base. They *had* to be informed of any prospective threat to humanity's homeworld.

A low rumble ran through her ship as the drives picked up speed. Svetlana glanced at the readouts, hoping and praying that the sensors *hadn't* decided to start seeing things. She had enemies back home - her *family* had enemies. Moving out of position to investigate a sensor contact that turned out to be nothing more than a random energy flicker could be made to look bad, if the wrong people got hold of her sensor logs. And, in the constant battle for patronage that defined modern Russia, it was a given that they *would* get hold of it.

We don't need an external enemy, she thought, sourly. *We're perfectly capable of fucking things up for ourselves.*

But we do have an external enemy, her thoughts reminded her. *And so does the rest of the human race.*

She sighed, inwardly. Eighteen months ago, alien forces had attacked Vera Cruz and a handful of other colonies along the rim of explored space. Aliens! Svetlana hadn't believed it at first, not until her uncle had confirmed it. The entire human race was under threat! She'd been concerned, when it finally sank in, but everyone had believed that the space navies could handle the threat. The Multinational Force assembled to cover New Russia, the largest and most powerful formation assembled by the human race, was invincible. Twelve fleet carriers and over fifty smaller ships, as well as New Russia's formidable defences. The aliens should have hit the defence and bounced...

Instead, they'd blown it to hell. Svetlana still couldn't believe it, even though nearly a year had passed since the battle. The aliens hadn't just beaten the fleet, they'd destroyed it. Sixty ships, including twelve fleet carriers, wiped out in less than an hour. The panic had been overwhelming, when the news had finally sunk in. If the British hadn't had a single ancient carrier that had been able to stand up to the alien weapons, the war might already be over and humanity would have lost. Svetlana had no idea what the Tadpoles - as the British had termed the aliens - had in mind for a defeated humanity, but she doubted it would be particularly pleasant. Human history showed everything from enslavement to outright extermination.

And we have armour too, she thought, glancing at her status board. Half the icons were dark...she hoped that meant the computer nodes were having problems, again. She was fairly sure they were. *Brezhnev* was tough, but she'd be in real trouble if she'd lost *all* of those systems. *We might be able to take one or two blows from the aliens before they finish us.*

"Captain," the tactical officer said. "The turbulence is getting stronger."

"Slow to full stop," Svetlana ordered. It was an old rule of thumb. Anyone she was close enough to see was close enough to see her too. "Passive sensors?"

"Picking up flickers of power distortion," the tactical officer reported. He looked up, his pale face suddenly paler. "Captain, power distribution is very similar to the alien masking field reported at New Russia."

"Then we're too close," Ignatyev said.

"Perhaps," Svetlana agreed. She studied the readouts for a long moment. There was *definitely* something out there. Something *big*. If she'd had a proper tactical expert...she buried the thought with all the other resentments. The Navy had sent its finest people to take part in the defence of New Russia, where most of them had died. "Tactical, keep probing for insight."

"Aye, Captain," the tactical officer said.

Svetlana leaned forward. Ignatyev was right. They were already *far* too close to the unknowns for anyone's peace of mind, let alone hers. But they did have some advantages, ones she wouldn't dismiss in a hurry. The unknowns couldn't risk using their active sensors without risking detection - the solar system was seeded with listening stations and scansats - and *Brezhnev* was radiating almost nothing. It was unlikely, highly unlikely, that the aliens would get a sniff of her presence, unless they had some piece of tech that the human race had never heard of.

And that isn't entirely impossible, she reminded herself. She'd seen too many images of plasma bolts tearing through carriers as though they were made of paper. *If they can see through their own stealth fields, we may be in some trouble.*

"Contact," the tactical officer hissed. His display filled with red icons. "Captain, I have thirteen - perhaps fifteen - carriers and over a hundred smaller ships."

Svetlana felt her heart sink as she studied the readings. The carriers were all too familiar now, their elegant lines a silent mockery of crude human ships. She'd seen too many images of the alien ships to mistake them for anything else. There were no deployed starfighters, as far as her sensors could tell, but it hardly mattered. The aliens had arrived in force. And if they couldn't be stopped, Earth would fall.

She kept her voice steady with an effort. "Launch two probes on ballistic trajectories," she ordered. "I want them to pass through the middle of the enemy formation."

"Aye, Captain," the tactical officer said.

Svetlana looked at Ignatyev. "Do a course projection," she ordered. She suspected she already knew the answer, but she needed to check. "Where are they going? And when will they arrive?"

Ignatyev bent over his console. "Earth, Captain. They'll be there in less than five hours unless they reduce speed."

Shit, Svetlana thought.

She'd assumed as much. Earth was still the centre of the human sphere, still home to seventy percent of the entire human race. The industrial nodes orbiting the planet *couldn't* be replaced in a hurry, even if the remaining colonies pooled their resources without the normal human bickering. God knew that New Russia had already been lost to the enemy. And who knew what was happening there? Svetlana knew better than to believe everything she heard on the datanet - the Russian media parroted the government's line, unlike its western counterparts - but *some* of the horror stories might have some basis in fact. The Tadpoles *might* be enslaving the entire population.

"Send another FLASH signal," she ordered, curtly. There *was* a risk of detection, but it had to be borne. Earth *had* to know what was heading its way. "Scatter the message - I want a copy sent to every naval base in the system. Inform them of our contact, then attach full copies of our sensor records."

"Aye, Captain." Ignatyev didn't argue. That, if nothing else, indicated just how serious matters had become. "Signal sent."

"They're ignoring us," the tactical officer said. The alien ships were flowing past *Brezhnev*, seemingly unaware of her presence. "They didn't even pick up the drones!"

"It looks that way," Svetlana agreed, dryly. It was good news, she supposed. The drones were sending a constant feed of information back to their mothership, telling her things she hadn't wanted to know about the enemy fleet. Earth would have some warning of the oncoming storm. "When they pass us, bring the ship about. I want to shadow them all the way to Earth."

"Aye, Captain," the helmsman said.

Ignatyev shot her a questioning look. Svetlana ignored it. She didn't have time to explain her reasoning, not now. The alien ships were still too far from Earth to be tracked by the orbital defences, let alone the starships that made up the combined Home Fleet. *Brezhnev* had to stay close to them, whatever the risk. If the fleet split up under stealth, Earth wouldn't have the slightest idea that anything had happened until it was too late. Humanity's homeworld was a pretty big target, but it wasn't the only one.

Long-range kinetic strikes on the Jupiter Cloudscoops or the asteroid mining colonies will do a great deal of damage, she thought. *Maybe not enough to cripple us, but enough to make it harder for us to recover.*

"Launch a relay drone," she added. "Once it's in place, establish a relay laser link. I don't want them getting a sniff of us."

"Aye, Captain," Ignatyev said.

Svetlana's lips twitched. If the aliens detected *Brezhnev*, the ship would be blown away before her crew had a chance to take any sort of evasive action. She didn't dare make any radio transmissions when the signals would be passing *through* the alien formation. *That* would be pushing her luck too far.

Another shiver ran through the ship. "We're moving into position, Captain," the helmsman reported.

"Laser link established," Ignatyev added. "Captain, the time delay..."

"I know," Svetlana said, sharply. It would be at least an hour before her alert reached Pournelle Base. Earth's defenders wouldn't have *that* long to prepare to defend the planet against the oncoming storm. "It can't be helped."

She shivered, a cold sensation running down her spine. To her, it was a tactical problem; to Earth, it was life or death. Mother Russia was about to face its most severe threat since Hitler's invasion or the Central Asian Wars. And so was the rest of the planet. Humanity's *homeworld* was about to be attacked.

And they don't even know the enemy is on the way, she thought. Her messages were speeding towards Earth, but they wouldn't have reached their destination. There would be people sleeping on Earth, or going to work or school or whatever they did all day...utterly unaware of the nightmare bearing down on them. *They don't have the slightest idea what's coming.*

Her blood grew colder. *They'd know soon,* she told herself. *The entire planet is about to go to war.*

CHAPTER
TWO

Sin City, Luna

"Welcome to Sin City," the speaker blared, as the underground train finally came to a halt beside a garish platform. "Where everything that happens in Sin City *stays* in Sin City!"

Brian Wheeler pursed his lips together in disapproval as the passengers scrambled to the doors, fighting to get out. It wasn't as if the doors were going to slam shut and deny the slower passengers the chance to enjoy themselves, was it? The Management wouldn't permit *that*, not when there was a chance to make money from the guests. It was far more likely that the doors would be kept open until the last of the guests had departed, then a security team sweep the train for surveillance devices before allowing it to take on new passengers.

He picked up his briefcase, walked through the doors and headed up the stairs, keeping an eye on his fellow passengers. Half of them seemed to be naval cadets and crewmen from Britain and America, laughing and chatting nervously as they passed through the security gate. The remainder appeared to be civilians, although a handful were probably military contractors. He caught sight of a warning notice, informing all travellers that there were strict limits to what could be brought through the gates and into Sin City proper. The colony guarded its secrets well, he knew from prior experience. No one was allowed to bring recording or surveillance equipment to Sin City. The potential for blackmail was too high.

Sweat prickled down his back as he reached the security gate and pushed his ID chip against the reader. It was possible, quite possible, that he'd been blacklisted. Sin City ran automatic checks against security and criminal databases before allowing newcomers to pass through the gates... if they had a record of him, they could deny him entry or force him to wait for a decision to be made at a higher level. Brian would have been tempted to do just that, if he'd been sure of the outcome. But too much was at stake to take foolish chances.

The gate hissed open. He smiled as he walked through, heading down the corridor and into the giant complex. Flickering holograms and wall-mounted billboards greeted visitors, offering them pleasures beyond imagination...some of which were illegal almost anywhere else. Gambling, sex, VR adventures...the possibilities were endless. You could find anything in Sin City, he'd been told...the only real danger was becoming addicted to the pleasures and never wanting to leave. Or being caught with traces of illegal drugs in one's bloodstream. Brian had never been a naval officer, but he'd been told that drug tests were mandatory after personnel returned from leave. He believed it.

Sin City was a vast complex buried beneath the luna soil, he recalled as he studied the holographic display. The upper levels were devoted to gambling and other mainstream pleasures, places where first-timers were separated from their money as quickly and efficiently as possible. Brian couldn't help wondering if the games were rigged, although the Management had been quick to deny the possibility. People did win and win big, they pointed out. It just didn't happen very often.

Finding the security office on the chart, he turned and walked down towards the stairwell. A dozen topless girls walked past him, laughing and joking as they made their way to a burlesque show. Brian took one look at bare breasts bobbing in front of his eyes, then told himself to keep his mind on the job. He couldn't afford to let himself be distracted. The girls giggled as he passed, but he ignored them. They'd have no trouble finding clients when the time came.

More advertisements bombarded him as he reached the stairwell and made his way downwards, deeper into the colony. He could enter a fantasy world and have adventures, or a harem, or...he couldn't help a smile as a list of possibilities appeared in front of him. Most of them were pathetic and *none* of them were real. He didn't care to pretend to be a secret agent for a day, let alone some of the weirder options. It would have surprised him if they had any customers...

People always want to indulge their fantasies, he thought, wryly. *And it certainly beats spending years developing one's skills if all one wants to do is have fun.*

He glanced into one of the casinos as he reached the lower levels. Hundreds of men - serious gamblers, judging by the chips on the tables - were playing for very high stakes. The waitresses were topless, again, but none of the men were paying attention. Brian rolled his eyes, remembering some of his older cases. The girls would make hundreds of pounds - perhaps more - in tips, while the house would take its cut of the winnings. And they didn't even have to do much, beyond keeping glasses filled.

The surroundings changed as he reached the lowest level. It felt almost as if he was walking into a prison, or into the real world behind the facade. The walls were cold grey, the ceiling so low he felt as though it was brushing the top of his head. Two security guards eyed him warily, shifting slightly to expose the weapons at their belt. They looked overdressed, Brian decided, but he knew better than to underestimate them. Sin City's Management recruited from the ever-growing pool of ex-military personnel, particularly Special Forces. The guards might well have more training than himself.

And they probably get paid better too, he thought, without heat. He'd read hundreds of stories from close-protection details around the world, but never anything from anyone who'd worked in Sin City. They were paid very well to keep their traps shut. What happened in Sin City stayed in Sin City. *God alone knows how much has been covered up over the years.*

The lead guard moved to block his path. "Yes?"

"I need to speak to Chief Patel," Brian said. He held out his ID chip. "Please inform him that I am here."

The guard eyed him for a long moment, then took the datachip and ran it through his portable reader. Brian frowned, bracing himself. It was quite possible, despite everything, that Chief Clancy Patel would order him unceremoniously deported from Sin City. Or even take more unpleasant steps to deal with the intruder. Technically, Brian was breaking several regulations just by entering the city without permission. But Patel would know that, Brian reasoned. The man he remembered would wonder why Brian had revealed himself so openly.

"Wait," the guard said.

He stepped back, then started subvocalising into a mouthpiece, sending a message to higher authority. Brian waited, telling himself to be patient. Chief Patel *would* want to see him...surely. And if he didn't, there were other ways to accomplish his mission. Rumours aside, he doubted the Management would order his immediate execution. They'd never be *certain* that Brian didn't have friends who knew where he'd gone. Sin City rested on thin ice at the best of times. They wouldn't want the Luna Federation to start taking a harder look at them.

"The Chief will see you," the guard said. "You will accompany me."

Brian nodded, then followed the guard through a pair of solid airlocks. The interior *definitely* resembled a police station, right down to a handful of people in handcuffs. Brian glanced at them - a trio of naval ratings and two young women, one of whom had a nasty bruise on her face - then looked away. Sin City had a good reputation for protecting its guests. A hostess who'd decided to pickpocket would be lucky if she wasn't immediately returned to Earth.

And they won't want that, Brian thought, as they passed a handful of other guards. *They probably escaped from the security zone.*

The guard led him to a door, knocked once and opened it. Brian stepped inside without waiting for orders, looking around with interest. It was definitely more homely than the rest of the complex, right down to a photograph of Patel's wife and children on the desk. The man himself sat behind the desk, eying Brian with interest. Brian looked back, silently cataloguing the rest of the oversized office. There were files, folders and knickknacks everywhere. Patel had always been a magpie, but it hadn't been until recently that he'd had a chance to indulge his obsession.

"Brian," Patel said. He rose to his feet and held out a hand. "Long time no see."

Brian shook his hand, firmly. Time hadn't been kind to his old friend. Patel looked older - and stouter - than he remembered, his hair thinning on top. Working in Sin City was worse than being on the beat, Brian had heard. Disturbances had to be handled as quietly as possible, apparently, and troublemakers had to be removed without delay. The guests could not be allowed to think that they were unsafe in Sin City.

"You too," he said. "How are the children?"

Patel shrugged expressively as he motioned Brian into a seat, then sat down again behind the desk. "Coping," he said. "Luna is a better place for them than London, these days. Mia got my father's skin colour and so..."

Brian nodded in understanding. Patel was clearly *not* of British blood, even though his family had been in Britain for generations. Looking East Asian after the Troubles was *not* an advantage, although the photograph on the desk showed a very beautiful young girl. Mia would be nineteen or twenty now, if he remembered correctly. She'd find Luna much more congenial than Britain.

"I assume this is not a social call," Patel said, after his secretary had served them both foul-tasting coffee. "What do you want?"

Brian placed his briefcase on the table and opened it, removing a paper folder. He would have preferred a computer file, but experience had taught him that they could be hacked from a distance. It was unlikely that anyone would expend so much effort on him, yet taking precautions was second nature after ten years on the force. Some of his cases - before and after he'd retired - had had a political dimension. This one might have a political dimension too.

He opened the folder and passed Patel a photograph. "Abigail Swansong, fifteen years old," he said, as his friend peered down at the image. Abigail was blonde and beautiful, but her face seemed set in a permanent scowl. "Daughter of Timothy and Maria Swansong, CEOs of Swansong Enterprises. You may have heard of them."

Patel's face went blank. "Vaguely."

Brian snorted. Timothy and Maria Swansong might not have been the richest people on the moon, but they were definitely in the top ten. And they were *connected*. Swansong Enterprises did a great deal of work for the Royal Navy, as well as the United States and the Luna Federation. They were not the sort of people one wanted as enemies. They'd built their company up from the ground, punching their way through obstacles with a thoroughness Brian could only admire. It was a shame that their daughter was such...such a brat.

"She had a fight with her parents, three weeks ago," Brian said. "Screaming, shouting...I believe the words 'you'll be sorry' were mixed up in there somewhere. She went to a friend's house to cool down, then vanished. It took two weeks of detective work to trace her route to Sin City."

"Getting through the security gates would have posed a challenge," Patel observed, studiously.

"Her friend had a dealer who supplied her with - among other things - fake ID cards," Brian said, with heavy patience. "The police interrogated him at some length" - he removed another folder from his briefcase and passed it over - "and he was kind enough to provide full details of the fake. We do not believe the silly girl has left Sin City."

"Unless she went to Russian or Chinese territory," Patel commented.

Brian met his eyes. "Do you really believe that?"

Patel shrugged. "It wouldn't be the first time someone tried to defect through Sin City."

"Bullshit," Brian said. He tapped the folder. "If either of them knew who she really was, they'd be trying to make use of her. And if they didn't, they'd have passed her back to us by now. They don't have her, Clancy. She's somewhere within Sin City."

There was a long pause. "I'll choose to assume you're right, for the moment," Patel said, stiffly. "However, we cannot take action..."

Brian met his eyes. "Can you afford *not* to take action?"

"We have very strict secrecy policies," Patel countered. "The people who come to Sin City wouldn't come if they thought their...indiscretions... would be broadcast on the nightly news or splashed all over the datanet. This girl deserves the same secrecy as every other visitor."

"Bullshit," Brian said.

"The rules cannot be changed," Patel said. "I..."

Brian cut him off. "Let's discuss this, shall we? Abigail entered Sin City using a false ID, which - I believe - is one of your dealbreakers. God alone knows what she's been doing since then, because she probably didn't have very much cash with her. I doubt she brought enough money to rent an apartment for very long. She certainly hasn't made any attempt to access her credit balance.

"And she's *fifteen*. I was under the impression that the minimum age to pass through the security gates was *eighteen*."

"Sin City cannot be blamed if she uses a false ID," Patel snapped. "We do not make a habit of checking and double-checking every ID that passes the first scan."

"Perhaps you should," Brian said. "The point is this - Abigail's parents are rich, powerful and *very* influential. They want their daughter back, alive and intact. They're prepared to go to the Luna Federation and demand action, Clancy, and you *know* just how fragile Sin City's position is. Too many people want you shut down for good."

Patel glared at him, but said nothing. Brian wasn't particularly surprised. The Luna Federation - Sin City was an associated member - had never been keen on strong-arming its member states, but Sin City had always been beyond the pale. Illegal drugs and other forbidden pleasures...yes, there *were* people who wanted Sin City raided and then closed down permanently. Given a fig-leaf to justify it - and Brian couldn't think of anything better than a missing young girl - the Luna Federation would probably have to act.

"On the other hand, we agree that this is a difficult position for you," Brian added. "If you help us clear it up now, I'm sure the family won't push for sanctions."

"Hah," Patel said. "Can you guarantee it?"

"No," Brian said, honestly. "But I *can* guarantee that there *will* be a scandal if they *don't* get their daughter back. You know as well as I do that Sin City isn't completely independent from the outside universe. And principle counts for nothing when your opponent has the better cause and bigger guns."

He leaned forward. "Come on, Clancy. What would you do if it was *Mia* trapped here?"

Patel scowled. "I need to consult with my superiors," he said. He jabbed a finger at Brian's chest. "Wait here. And don't touch anything."

Brian watched him go, then leaned back into his chair. He didn't really blame his old friend for wanting to pass the buck. He'd always disliked politics back when he'd been in the police, when doing the right thing could become the wrong thing very quickly if it upset the wrong person. But Patel and his superiors were caught between a rock and a hard place. If they cooperated, they risked their reputation; if they refused to cooperate, they risked everything. The scandal would be immense.

He kept an eye on his watch as the seconds ticked by, waiting. The longer it took, he knew from experience, the further the buck had been passed. No one was *entirely* sure who ran Sin City - their names had been carefully concealed - but he doubted they were blind to the danger they were facing. Their privacy had only been tolerated because various governments had chosen to tolerate Sin City. That might change in a hurry.

Patel returned, twenty minutes after leaving. "They've authorised me to tell you where to find her," he said. "You can ask her to leave with you, if you like. If she chooses to go, you can take her to the station and depart at once; if she refuses, we'll honour her decision."

"You do realise her *parents* won't honour her decision?" Brian rose. "And she's certainly too young to be here, whatever else she is?"

"That's what I was told to do," Patel said, curtly. "Norma Lee - sorry, *Abigail Swanson* - is working at the Skittles Bar, on Level Five. Do you need an escort?"

Brian pursed his lips. He'd hoped for better. But it would have to suffice.

"I believe I can find my own way there," he said, shortly. Level Five... it could have been worse. "Once I convince her to leave with me, I'll take her straight to the station."

"We'll confiscate her fake ID before you leave," Patel said. "We clearly missed a trick when *this* one got through."

"There's no central database," Brian reminded him. The Luna Federation had never liked the concept of centralising everything. Too many of the smaller colonies had bitter memories of hard times on Earth. "This one...I think it *was* official, from Dylan. The forger just bribed them to insert a few more names onto the rolls."

"Joy," Patel said. "Good luck, Brian."

"Thanks," Brian said. He didn't blame Patel. It wasn't his fault. "And give my best to the kids."

CHAPTER
THREE

Woking, United Kingdom

Molly Schneider took a long breath, then removed her robe and stood naked in front of the mirror.

Her reflection looked back at her, seemingly displeased. Molly pursed her lips in annoyance as she examined her appearance with a critical air. Her figure had never been quite the same since she'd had two children - and age was taking a toll, no matter how many rejuvenation treatments she took - but it wasn't a *disaster*. She and Kurt might not have made love in weeks - they'd hardly made love since their daughter had been born - yet she still looked attractive. Kurt had told her so, the last time they'd kissed before he'd headed back to his damned ship. She couldn't help thinking he loved space - and his starfighter - more than he loved her.

And if he were here, I could have shared this with him, she thought, bitterly. *But he's not here and I am.*

Her eyes travelled up and down her figure, picking out the small imperfections that loomed larger and larger every day. Her bright red hair was darkening, forcing her to decide between dying it or letting her hair turn grey. Faint spots, barely visible to the naked eye, revealed where she'd dabbed concealment scales on her skin. Her breasts were still firm, but she knew it was only a matter of time before they began to sag; her thighs and buttocks were slowly putting on weight, no matter how much hard work she put in at the gym. Childbirth had *definitely* ruined her figure, even though it had given her two beautiful children. But neither of them really appreciated how many sacrifices their parents had made for them. Molly had given the best years of her life to them and they rewarded her with more and more demands.

Sighing, she turned to the bed and opened the new box. The dress inside came directly from Middleton, one of the most famous dressmakers in London. Princess Elspeth *herself* bought her dresses there, according to the promotional materials. Kurt would faint, Molly knew, if he ever realised just how much she'd spent on the dress. And yet, she needed it. The material flattered her figure, showcasing her curves, but any ordinary dress could have done that without spending quite so much money. It was a *Middleton* dress that would showcase her wealth, giving her access - finally - to the higher social circles. It would give her the life she'd thought she was getting when she'd married Kurt.

She donned her underwear - pricey too, but necessary - and then pulled the dress over her head. It fitted perfectly, thankfully. She'd invested so many of her hopes in the dress that she thought she would have broken down and cried if it *hadn't* been perfect. She moved from side to side in the mirror, making sure that everything was held firmly in place, then turned to check her handbag. Her small collection of everything from breath mints to perfume and birth control pills was where it should be, waiting for her.

The door opened. Molly jumped.

"You look nice, Mum," Penny said. "Are you going somewhere *fun?*"

Molly gritted her teeth. Penny took after her paternal grandmother, rather than either of her parents. Her hair was blonde, her face was narrow and her eyes...her green eyes were all she'd inherited from her mother. Molly didn't pretend to understand how the genetics had worked themselves out, but it didn't matter. Penny was her daughter and *that* was all that mattered, even if she was being a right little brat as she grew into adulthood.

"None of your business," Molly snapped. "What are you doing here?"

Penny smirked. "I heard that some of the boys at school were selling fake bags on the online marketplace," she said. She nodded towards the bag on Molly's bed. "Do you think *that* one might be fake?"

Molly gritted her teeth. Surely *she* hadn't been so unpleasant to *her* mother when she'd been a teenager...she *hoped* she hadn't been that unpleasant. Penny was going through a rough patch, made worse by her father's prolonged absence and constant fights with her teachers at school. She'd brought home more pink slips than *Percy* and *Percy* was a boy! Molly's own brothers had been right little hellions until they'd been conscripted into the Home Guard and knocked into shape by unsympathetic drill sergeants. Penny was damn lucky *she* wouldn't be conscripted.

"I bought it from a verified dealer," Molly said, tightly. She didn't like the suggestion she wouldn't know a fake from a *real* bag, even though she suspected it might be true. There were some *very* skilled counterfeiters out there. "It has a certificate and everything."

Penny smiled, lazily. "That's my point," she said, in a tone that would have earned her a slap if she'd been standing any closer. "The fakers can fake the certificates, too."

Molly forced herself to calm down. It was an important evening, perhaps the most important of her life. She couldn't afford to allow her daughter to put her in a bad mood before it had even begun. Penny was still a child, even though she wore adult clothes and affected adult airs. She didn't have enough experience to know what she was talking about... even if she *was* more aware of modern technology than her mother. But then, that had been true of Molly and *her* mother too.

"I told you not to interrupt me," she said, as she turned back to the mirror. "What do you want?"

"Gayle is downstairs," Penny said. She didn't *sound* pleased. "I think she wants a word with you before you go."

"I hope you let her in this time," Molly said. Penny had talked her older brother into leaving Gayle ringing the bell until Molly had come down to open it herself. The poor babysitter had been furious, of course, and only the promise of a major raise had been enough to get her to stay, let alone come back. "You did, didn't you?"

"She's in the living room," Penny said. She looked downcast. "I think she brought some work too."

"You could learn from her example," Molly said, firmly. "Your father would agree with me, if he were here."

"He's *not* here," Penny said. "And he would agree with *me*."

Molly gritted her teeth, again. A headache was beginning to pound behind her skull, growing more and more painful with every heartbeat.

Penny had a nasty habit of picking fights with her teachers, then refusing to do the work they assigned. If Kurt hadn't been in the navy - if there hadn't been a law that forbade expelling the children of military personnel - Penny would probably have been expelled by now. As it was, she was well on the way to setting a record for the number of disciplinary actions.

She'd probably be proud, if she knew, Molly thought, sourly. *And act up even more to ensure she actually took the goddamned record.*

"Your father would tell you to study hard," Molly said. "And you know it."

She glared at her daughter, daring her to disagree. Kurt had worked hard - very hard - to put Penny in an expensive private school, instead of a state school. It would give Penny a chance to enter society *without* having to start at the bottom, if she worked hard. But none of it would matter if she got expelled or simply failed all of her exams. She'd be lucky if any of the state-run schools took her, with her permanent record. Molly had no idea just how many of the horror stories about borstals were true, but she doubted her daughter would last a year if she was exiled to one of *them.* Jail would be kinder.

"I miss him," Penny said. "I wish...when will this war be over?"

"I have no idea," Molly told her, bluntly. She wanted Kurt home and she *didn't* want him home. Kurt at home would mean putting an end to her new life. "I'm sure he'll be home soon."

"Hah," Penny said. She looked up at her mother. "Why are you even going out? You *shouldn't* be going out."

Molly reminded herself, sharply, that her daughter was no longer the tiny babe she'd birthed...had it really been sixteen years ago? She'd instructed Penny not to date - she didn't want to see her daughter make the same mistakes as herself - but she doubted Penny had listened to her. She was old enough to find young men interesting and too young to understand the potential dangers. No doubt she knew - or guessed - what her mother was doing. But how could Molly tell her daughter that her relationship with her husband had long since lost its spark?

You can't, her own thoughts answered. *She doesn't need to know.*

"Mind your own business," she snapped, instead. "Go downstairs. And behave!"

Penny shot her a sharp look, then turned and hurried out the room before Molly could give vent to an increasingly unpleasant series of threats. The wretched girl seemed to be completely immune to discipline, even being grounded and denied access to the datanet...there was no way Molly would dare leave Penny without adult supervision, even though Percy was technically an adult. Penny was far too good at running rings around her elder brother.

Putting the thought out of her mind, Molly checked her appearance in the mirror one last time and then pulled the coat over her dress. She would have preferred to wear something more comfortable for the drive, but she doubted there was anywhere to change in Penzance. There was no way she was changing in a toilet, even a clean and private one. And besides, Thomas Garrison would probably appreciate the view.

She sagged, just for a moment. It was the life she wanted, yet it came with a price...and a risk. Being caught would get her in *real* trouble, if Kurt decided to make an issue of it. She was cheating on a husband who'd gone to the wars, a husband who could make a strong claim to everything she owned...and the children. Kurt would be hurt, very hurt, if she was caught. And yet, it was the life she wanted. Pulling her coat around her, Molly walked through the door and locked it behind her. Penny had raided her wardrobes before and Molly was damned if she was letting the little brat do it again.

The sound of an argument was already echoing up the stairs as she hurried down. Percy didn't seem to dislike Gayle - Molly was sure he had a crush on her, although Gayle was five years older than him - but Penny picked fights with everyone these days. Except her father...Molly made a mental note to report Penny's latest transgressions to Kurt, then dismissed the thought. Kurt was a million light-years away. There was nothing he could *do* about it until he came home, by which time there would no doubt be a few thousand *other* problems.

"I'll be leaving in five minutes," she said, checking her smartphone. Garrison was already on the way, of course. The man was nothing if not efficient. "Gayle, Penny has some work to do" - she ignored her daughter's muttered curse - "and I expect it to be done before she does anything else. You can unlock her codekey to the datanode after the work is completed."

"Yes, Mrs. Schneider," Gayle said.

Molly nodded in approval. Gayle knew how to work hard, which was more than could be said for Penny. Molly paid Gayle well, but still... she wished, suddenly, that Kurt had allowed her to hire a live-in maid. Constant supervision would probably be good for Penny, particularly if the supervisor was tough enough not to let Penny's barbs get under her skin. It was just a shame *Molly* didn't have the time to do it herself.

"You have permission to use whatever forms of discipline you think are appropriate," she added, curtly. "And she is to go to bed at ten."

Penny gasped. "Mother!"

"At ten," Molly repeated. Penny would probably consider it outrageous, but Molly found it hard to care. "She has to be up bright and early for school tomorrow."

She met her daughter's eyes. "And I expect you to behave yourself," she added. "Or else."

"Hah," Penny muttered.

Molly swallowed several nasty responses as she turned and walked out onto the street. The car was parked several houses down, just to make it harder for the gossiping hens to notice that she was getting into a stranger's vehicle. Molly didn't *think* they'd tell Kurt, when he returned home, but there was no point in taking *too* many chances. She risked social death - perhaps even criminal prosecution - if she was caught cheating on a deployed military officer.

And that is half of the thrill, she thought, as she opened the car door. *The prospect of getting caught.*

Thomas Garrison smiled at her as she sat down and closed the door. He was ten years older than her, handsome in a dark way...she rather thought he had some Italian or French blood in him somewhere. Perhaps something from even further away, although it was considered rude to ask about *that* so soon. His face was hard and angular, his dark hair so dark that she honestly wondered if it was dyed. And his clothes were so expensive that she could have bought a new family car for the same amount, if she wished.

"Molly," he said. As always, his accent thrilled her. He spoke like a London-born aristocrat. "I trust that all is well?"

"It is," Molly said. She tried to keep her impatience out of her voice. "We can leave as soon as you want."

Garrison smiled, then keyed a command into the dashboard. The car hummed to life, moving out of the parking space and heading down the road. Molly watched, openly thrilled. Kurt had never allowed her to buy a self-driving car, even though it would have made life easier - and safer. Garrison, on the other hand, had bought the latest model to go on the market. It had cost him more than Molly cared to think about...

She leaned back in her chair. "Do you have an updated guest list?"

He gave her a sultry smile. "Lady Penelope Ward will be hosting, of course," he said. "And a number of others have confirmed that they will attend. It should be an interesting night."

Molly nodded. Lady Penelope Ward was *famous* for throwing parties. According to the datanet - and tabloids - it was all she *ever* did. And yet, she'd somehow turned her parties into *the* premier social event outside the London Season. Molly wanted to know how she did it - and burned with envy, every time she thought about it. Some people had all the luck.

I'm making my own luck, she thought. Garrison was a catch. A wealthy lawyer with aristocratic connections...if she scratched his back, he'd scratch hers. He couldn't take her all the way, not when they couldn't get married, but he could get her started. *And when he dumps me, I'll have a place of my own.*

"The Prime Minister apparently declined," Garrison added, after a moment. "But Lord Campbell said he would probably be attending."

Molly lifted her eyebrows. "Probably?"

"If his wife can't convince him to change his mind," Garrison said. "She's having a feud with Lady MacDonald and *she's* going to the party. It should be amusing if they actually *meet* each other on the dance floor."

"Very amusing," Molly said. She took every titbit of gossip he gave her and stored it away at the back of her mind. Someday, she would find a use for it. She was sure she would. "And are there any other scandals likely to explode?"

"Apart from us, my dear?" Garrison gave her another smile as he reached out to stroke her cheek. "I do not know. But not knowing makes it fun."

Molly winced. She'd taken lessons in graces and etiquette, but she knew she didn't know enough to navigate the social minefield. Who should she curtsey to? Everyone? Or just the lords and ladies? Lady Penelope had a habit of inviting people from all walks of life, as long as they were British. Garrison had probably piqued her interest at some point.

"You can keep me advised," she said. His touch felt cool against her skin. "How long until we get there?"

"Around two hours, once we hit the motorway," Garrison said. He tapped a button, tinting the windows. No one could see in or out. "It will give us some time for fun."

He wrapped an arm around her, holding her tightly. Molly hesitated, torn between two conflicting impulses as his fingers probed her neckline, trying to undo her coat. She wanted - she needed - to keep him sweet, yet...yet she didn't want to ruin the dress. She didn't even know if there was a place to clean up a little before they hit the dance floor...if they ever did. He'd ruined one evening by insisting on finding a hotel rather than going to their destination.

"It will," she agreed. She kissed him on the lips. He kissed her back, but it felt odd. She couldn't help thinking that he was out of practice. "But should we not wait until after the dance?"

"It's two hours," Garrison said, sardonically. His voice was bland, but there was a hint of ice in his tone. She knew he wasn't someone to push lightly. He was used to getting what he wanted, when he wanted it. "What do you want to do until we arrive?"

Molly sighed and surrendered to the inevitable.

CHAPTER

FOUR

Pournelle Base (USA), Earth Orbit

Admiral Jonathan Winters hadn't slept well since the news had come in from Vera Cruz.

It wasn't something he'd expected, even though he'd acknowledged the possibility of alien life years ago. The civilians could talk all they liked about crashed alien starships to vague sensor contacts at the rim of explored space, but Jon had risen high enough to know that *no one* in authority had known the Tadpoles were out there. There certainly hadn't been any *real* preparations made for alien contact. The United States Navy had skirmished with China and Russia - and fretted over colonial issues on a handful of settled worlds - but no one had seriously expected all-out war. There was just too much at stake.

Sure, he thought, rubbing his forehead as he tried to concentrate on the meeting. *That's what they said back in 1914 and 2020 too.*

"It could have gone better," Admiral Henri Guichy said. "But it could have gone worse too."

"I don't think we can afford another failure like that," Admiral Cathy Mountbatten said. The British officer scowled. "Exercise BRAVE DEFENDER was an exercise. What happens if we have to do it for real?"

Jon nodded, curtly. Cathy Mountbatten - she was apparently related to *the* Mountbatten - was an aristocrat, something that offended his meritocratic principles, but she was more than merely competent. He'd been worried, at first, when she'd been assigned to the Earth Defence

Organisation as one of his Chiefs of Staff, yet he had to admit she'd worked out well. And yet, she had almost no experience in interstellar warfare... *none* of them had any real experience in interstellar warfare. No one had *really* considered a long, drawn-out war that would be fought outside the various Solar Treaties.

Which was a failure of imagination on our part, he told himself. *We're going to have to do better in future.*

He pushed the thought aside, looking from one to the other. Admiral Henri Guichy was a political appointee, but - thankfully - he was genuinely competent too. His brown hair and faint smile masked a tactical mind that Jon admired, sometimes. The French had won the right to name the second-in-command of Earth's defences and they hadn't abused it. Beside him, Cathy Mountbatten was tall and blonde. They both stood in odd contrast to Jon's black skin and blacker hair.

"The exercise is now winding down," he said. "I have no doubt the analysts will murder thousands of innocent databytes to tell us what we should be thinking about it, but...before the politicos get involved, what do you think?"

"We haven't *quite* mastered the art of cooperation, even after New Russia," Cathy said, bluntly. "Linking our command datanets together was quite hard enough, but convincing our personnel to work together was even harder."

Jon nodded, sourly. American and British personnel worked together regularly, but none of the other Great Powers had such a close working relationship. The Chinese and Russians were only close because they hated the idea of standing alone against America and Britain, while the French tried to navigate a course between two factions and the smaller powers worked hard to keep from being assimilated. Hell, the Great Power system itself had been steadily unbalancing for decades. Jon privately suspected that it was - that it had been - only a matter of time before one of the smaller powers insisted on being treated as a Great Power.

Japan, India...even Brazil and Turkey, he thought. *They're all building up their space fleets now.*

"That's something we are going to have to address when the other representatives return," he said. The Chinese and Russian representatives had been assigned to monitor BRAVE DEFENDER from the participating starships. "If nothing else, we don't know *what* will happen now the Tadpoles have been rocked back on their heels."

He closed his eyes for a long moment, remembering the recordings from New Russia. The aliens had slaughtered nearly a hundred starships, including twelve fleet carriers, then proceeded to occupy the system itself. There was no way to escape the conclusion that the Tadpoles possessed far superior weapons technology, as well as a drive system that was far more flexible than anything humanity had devised. *Ark Royal* had captured an alien ship - largely intact - and *that* would make it easier to unlock the alien secrets, but he knew it would take time to put anything more significant than the plasma cannons into production. Hell, producing as many plasma cannons as possible carried its own risks.

"They might talk to us," Guichy said. "Has there been any progress with the prisoners?"

Jon shook his head. The alien prisoners seemed happy enough, as far as anyone could tell, but talking to them was impossible. Some of the more paranoid members of the Oversight Board were demanding enhanced interrogation, yet it seemed pointless. Asking questions was impossible when one couldn't put them in the right language.

And we don't know how they'd react if we started torturing their people, he thought. *But after what we found on Alien-One, some people have stopped giving a fuck.*

He pushed the thought aside. "It's been a long day," he said, nodding towards the giant holographic display. Earth was surrounded by a small galaxy of tactical icons, ranging from tiny single-shot weapons platforms to giant industrial nodes and asteroid settlements. It looked invulnerable, yet he hadn't needed New Russia to know just how vulnerable it really was. "Perhaps we should continue this discussion tomorrow."

Cathy shot him a sympathetic look. "Politics in Washington?"

"Yeah," Jon said. He was lucky he hadn't been called in front of a Senate committee exploring just *what* had gone wrong at New Russia - again. Losing three fleet carriers had been a nasty shock for the United States Navy. Nearly seven thousand crewmen had died with them. The inquest was *still* going on as midterm elections approached. "Are they any better in Britain?"

"*Ark Royal* gave us a much needed boost," Cathy said. "But people are still scared."

Jon had to smile, humourlessly. In hindsight, decommissioning and breaking up America's armoured carriers had been a serious error. Sure, they'd been costly and slow and unprepared for a modern combat zone... but they would have been able to stand up to the aliens. Bolting extra armour on modern carriers wasn't the same. The flimsy ships just didn't have enough protection to give them a reasonable chance against alien starfighters.

"I don't blame them," he said. "But at least we know the aliens are not invincible."

He rose. "Get some sleep," he ordered. "We'll reconvene tomorrow morning."

"Yes, sir," Cathy said. "Make sure you get some sleep too."

If I can, Jon thought. He'd lost friends at New Russia. *And if something doesn't come up that only I can handle.*

He scowled at the thought as he headed for the hatch. There had been a time when he'd thought he had a real career, back when he'd boarded his first command. He'd climbed the ladder step by step, careful not to make any missteps that would see him condemned to an asteroid mining settlement or the Mexican Wall, but when he'd reached the top...he was no longer in command. He held meetings and talked to politicians - he was their whipping boy - and yet it seemed he did nothing of value. Unless one counted shielding the juniors from their political masters...

Pournelle Base hummed around him as he walked into his suite. It was immense, easily large enough for two or three senior officers. But Pournelle Base had been built on a grand scale, ensuring that there was plenty of room for its command staff. Personally, Jon would have preferred extra starfighter launch racks, but that hadn't been an option. The USN *had* wanted a large base, after all.

He removed his shoes, then climbed into bed and closed his eyes.

The alarms howled, seconds later. Jon sat up, cursing under his breath as he fumbled for his console. Had he slept at all? It felt as if he'd barely closed his eyes before the alarms howled. And yet...what was happening? He keyed the console and the alarms fell silent, at least in his quarters. Moments later, Captain Mike Hanson's face appeared in front of him.

"Admiral," he said. His face was ashen. Jon knew what he was going to say before he opened his mouth. "We've had a report from one of the picket ships. An enemy force has entered the system."

Jon felt his blood run cold. No one had ever seriously considered a conflict in the solar system, certainly nothing much larger than tiny settlement wars in the asteroid belt. The Solar Treaty, the one international treaty that all the spacefaring powers took seriously, forbade it. There was just too much at stake...

The Tadpoles never signed the treaty, he thought, numbly. *And why should they?*

"I'm on my way," he said, scrambling out of bed. "ETA?"

"Two hours," Hanson said. "Unless they start taking pot-shots at us with a mass driver, of course."

"Of course," Jon said. Mass drivers weren't exactly *banned*, but the Great Powers had worked hard to discourage their use. Another mistake, in hindsight. "Do they know they've been detected?"

"Not at last report," Hanson said, as Jon pulled on his jacket. "But that could have changed by now and we wouldn't know."

"No," Jon agreed. "Have some coffee sent to the pit. I'm on my way."

He hurried out of the cabin and down into the giant Combat Information Centre. A massive hologram was floating above the central console, showing the solar system and every known human installation in exquisite detail. He felt his heart sink as he looked up and spotted a cluster of red lights advancing steadily towards Earth. Smaller windows, opening below the main display, told him things he didn't want to know about their firepower. This was no mere raid, not like the escort carriers humanity had dispatched to keep the enemy off balance. This was an all-out invasion.

His steward met him at the command chair, holding out a mug of coffee. Jon took a swig absently, keeping his eyes on the display. Deliberately or otherwise, the Tadpoles had timed their invasion well. Two-thirds of humanity's forces were out of position, finishing BRAVE DEFENDER. It would take time, time he didn't have, to concentrate his forces. He hoped that meant the enemy had the system under covert observation. If Lady Luck - or God - had deserted the human race to *that* extent...

"Two hours," he mused. The display was already outdated, of course. A set of conical vectors showed where the aliens *should* be, unless they had somehow managed to improve their drive systems still further. "Or less, perhaps."

He looked at Hanson. "Do we have a ship count?"

"*Brezhnev* reported fourteen fleet carriers and one hundred and seven smaller ships, as of the last update," Hanson said. He took a breath. "Sir, she's an old ship. Her sensors might have missed something. It was sheer luck she even spotted the bastards."

Jon nodded, curtly. Perhaps God hadn't abandoned humanity after all.

"Send a planetary alert," he ordered, putting the thought aside. There would be time to think about it later. "Inform the EDO that I am assuming command of all mobile forces and fixed defences, in line with the EDO Treaty. Make sure you copy the message to all planetary governments. They'll have to start their civil defence procedures."

"Aye, sir," Hanson said. "Two hours...it's not very long."

"It will have to do," Jon said. The aliens hadn't landed on New Russia, according to the last set of updates. Earth was a bigger target. But the planet wasn't the *main* target. "Once that's done, copy the message to every starship and fixed installation within the system. Make sure they understand that the EDO Treaty is now in effect."

"Yes, sir," Hanson said.

Jon sat down, thinking hard. Hopefully, there wouldn't be any real objections. The prospect of being hanged *did* tend to concentrate the mind wonderfully. But he knew it wasn't going to be easy. They'd assumed, even after New Russia, that they would have more warning, more time to work the kinks out of the system. *That* assumption had been a mistake. He couldn't help wondering just how many *other* mistakes they'd made.

They timed it very well, he thought, sourly. *If I don't concentrate the fleet, they can defeat us piece by piece; if I do concentrate the fleet, I run the risk of letting them do a great deal of damage before they can be stopped. I might win a tactical victory and lose on a strategic scale.*

He felt his heart sink as he contemplated the possibilities. There was no way to be *sure* that the attack force *Brezhnev* had detected was the *only* attack force. Space, even interplanetary space, was vast beyond imagination. The Tadpoles could hide another invasion force within the interplanetary void, if they wished. And he wouldn't know until it reached its destination and opened fire.

A human admiral wouldn't be keen on splitting his fleet, he reminded himself. *But would the Tadpoles feel the same way?*

It wasn't a pleasant thought. He'd assumed he'd be leading the navy into battle against the Russians or Chinese, if the diplomats didn't manage to smooth over whatever crisis had sparked the war. And *they* would have been *human* foes, their logic understandable...their tactics predictable. But his true opponent were aliens, aliens who might have their own ideas about how to fight a war. They might consider splitting their fleet to be a smart move.

Then we'll teach them better, he told himself.

He glanced at Hanson. "Any word from the ground?"

"Nothing beyond a brief acknowledgement," Hanson said. "But the world is going dark."

Jon nodded, shortly. *That* was planned, at least. One thing they'd learnt from New Russia was that the aliens had no hesitation in dropping KEWs on radio sources. Or light sources, perhaps. The civilians would howl if they were denied access to the datanet, but it might just keep them alive. Unless the aliens *did* intend to scorch the entire planet. America's population was more dispersed than it had been for centuries, but he knew better than to think it would be enough to protect them. Rendering Earth uninhabitable shouldn't pose any serious problems to the Tadpoles. Their technological base was more than capable of producing the required weapons.

He leaned back in his chair, feeling the weight of the world - of the solar system - fall onto his shoulders. Years of extensive political micromanagement had led him to believe that that would never change, even though the EDO Treaty placed command authority firmly in his hands.

And yet...he pushed the thought out of his head. He couldn't go to his political superiors and beg them to share the responsibility. The buck stopped with him.

Which won't stop them from complaining, afterwards, he thought. A nasty thought struck him and he went cold. *If there's anyone left to complain.*

He cleared his throat. "Record for Admiral Robertson, *Enterprise*," he said. Admiral Robertson had been in command of BRAVE DEFENDER. He waited for the nod, then went on. "Thaddeus, the system has been invaded. You are ordered to concentrate your forces at Point Asimov, along with other forces I will dispatch to you, and then advance against the enemy fleet. By that point, I imagine, they will have already attacked Earth."

The words caught in his throat. A human admiral would seek to bring the enemy fleet to battle...he'd certainly *want* to bring the enemy fleet to battle, although he would also be aware of the importance of devastating the enemy's industrial base. And yet, the mobile fleet couldn't be replaced in a hurry...which way would the aliens jump? Admiral Robertson might find himself the target of concentrated alien malice.

"If they do so, you are to trap them against the planetary defences," he ordered. "If they attempt to engage you, you are to evade them as long as possible and then fall back on Earth so you can be supported by the planetary defences. I expect you to use your own best judgment in deploying your forces against the enemy."

He took a long breath. The next set of orders...he didn't want to issue them, but he had no choice. All contingencies had to be prepared for. "In the event of both Pournelle Base and Nelson Base being destroyed, you will assume command of the remaining military installations within the system. Give them hell."

"Good luck."

He glanced at Hanson. "Send the message," he ordered. "And then inform all mobile fleet units within the Earth-Luna region that they are to prepare to leave orbit within thirty minutes."

"Yes, sir," Hanson said. He paused. "If we lose them, we'll be dependent on our fixed defences."

"I know," Jon said. He bit down the flash of annoyance. Hanson was doing his job, pointing out potential flaws with his superior's orders. "But they don't add *that* much to our firepower. Admiral Robertson is going to need them."

He leaned back in his chair. The orders had been given. His subordinates were rushing to their stations, preparing themselves for the prospect of a sudden and violent death in the next few hours. And yet...all he could do was wait for the aliens. There was nothing he could do until they reached engagement range.

The prospect of being hanged concentrates the mind wonderfully, he quoted mentally. He couldn't remember where the quote had come from, but it had struck him as important years ago. *But it concentrates the mind on the fact that it is going to be hanged.*

It wasn't a very reassuring thought.

CHAPTER

FIVE

Ten Downing Street, London, United Kingdom

"I think we're done here," Prime Minister Andrew Davidson said. The Cabinet Office was feeling oddly oppressive as night fell slowly over London. "Unless there's anything that should be raised now?"

"Well, the economy is starting to fray," the Secretary of State said. Anita Jordan was too much of a politician to be blunt. "Realistically, Prime Minister, there's very little we can do about it."

Andrew nodded, impatiently. Late-night meetings were *always* bad. Everyone wanted to go to bed, but everyone *also* wanted to make sure they had the last word. It was frustrating as hell, particularly for him. His cabinet ministers wanted to ensure that they promoted their own careers as well as serving in his government, preparing themselves for the inevitable faction fight that would follow his resignation or his electoral defeat. And while he understood the importance of keeping them hungry, he couldn't help finding it irritating too.

"Let us hope that things get better," Andrew said, although he knew they wouldn't. The British economy was slowly shifting onto a war footing, causing massive dislocations throughout society. Thankfully, they'd managed to paper over the worst of the cracks in the system, but it had been too long since large sections of the population had been forced to sacrifice for victory. "And that the Opposition remains quiet."

His lips quirked in grim amusement. The Opposition had been relatively quiet since the war had begun, surprisingly. But then, the government *had* had a stroke of good luck when *Ark Royal* proved she could fight the Tadpoles on even terms. The Opposition politicians could merely gnash their teeth and wait for an opening they could use to criticize the government without facing a major backlash. Thankfully, they'd been too stunned to capitalise on the Battle of New Russia before *Ark Royal* had given the Tadpoles a bloody nose.

"There have been some industrial disputes," Neddy Young said. The Home Secretary looked tired and worn. "So far, mainly just grumbling... but that will change."

"Probably," Andrew said. He shook his head. "And I *definitely* think we're done here. I'll see you all in the morning."

He leaned back in his comfortable chair and watched as his cabinet rose and hurried out of the chamber. They'd be driven back to their apartments in the Secure Zone, where they would get a few hours of sleep before they would have to return to their desks. Andrew was too much of a cynic to believe that their presence was *truly* important to their departments - the cabinet ministers were all political appointees - but hopefully the general public would believe the government was on top of the situation. The last thing Britain needed was another round of unrest and ethnic conflict.

There was a knock on the door. "Coffee, Prime Minister?"

Andrew looked up. A young maid was standing there, looking uncertain of herself. Andrew didn't really blame her. The housekeeping staff were supposed to be neither seen nor heard, particularly by the politicians they served. He'd thought it was an archaic policy when he'd first heard of it, but he had to admit it did have a point. Too many government ministers had abused their positions before the Troubles.

And they still do, he thought, crossly. *It's just that we're better at dealing with it now.*

"No, thank you," he said, rising. "I'll go back to my office."

He walked past the girl and strode down the corridor. None of the other staff were in evidence, although it was clear that *someone* had swept the passageway in the last couple of hours. They'd have heard him coming and scattered to get out of his way...he shook his head, silently promising himself that he'd do something about it. The housekeeping staff didn't have to run and hide like mice fleeing the cat, did they? But it was very much a minor issue, compared to the problems that were turning his hair grey. He didn't know if he'd ever have time to handle it.

Ten Downing Street had been severely damaged during the Troubles, he reminded himself as he walked past a long line of portraits. A truck bomb had exploded in Whitehall, killing hundreds of government officials and wounding hundreds more. The building had been rebuilt with increased security - the government wouldn't have left the area in ruins, even though some people had wanted a more flamboyant centre of government - but Andrew couldn't help wondering if something had been lost. Some of the faces looking down on him - Prime Ministers through the ages - would not have approved of modern-day Britain. Others would have thought it a dream come true.

We do the best we can, he thought. *And sometimes we just force ourselves to keep going until the problem goes away.*

He sucked in his breath as his eyes moved from face to face. Winston Churchill, Margaret Thatcher, Tony Blair, Charles Hanover...he'd read hundreds of books discussing their strengths and weaknesses, trying to see if there was an ideal. But there wasn't, as far as he could tell. Even Churchill had had to play to the backbenchers. Only Hanover had had a considerable degree of freedom and *he* was perhaps the most controversial figure in British history. A saint or a sinner...no one really knew for sure. There were no balanced biographies of him, as far as Andrew knew. His death had either been a tragedy for his country or a very lucky escape.

We'll never know, Andrew thought, walking into his office. *And perhaps we should be glad of it.*

He sat down at his desk, eying the pile of folders that had somehow materialised on the table while he'd been gone. He'd delegated as much as he could to his staff, but there were still far too many issues that required the Prime Minister's personal attention. The Civil Service could and did carry out orders, shaping governmental intentions into something practical, yet they didn't run the country. Andrew knew, all too well, that the buck stopped with him.

Damn it, he thought. *I...*

An alarm rang. Andrew froze in his seat, shocked. He'd never heard *that* alarm outside drills, drills they'd only just restarted. An attack...Ten Downing Street was under attack? It *had* to be a drill. No one could have sneaked through the ring of steel protecting the centre of London, no one...

He jerked to his feet as two burly men crashed through the door and into his office. One of them grabbed him, yanking him away from the desk; the other opened a hidden door, revealing a gravity chute. Andrew had no time to protest before the first man hurled him down the chute, then jumped after him. It felt like forever before he hit the antigravity field at the bottom of the chute and stopped. A hand grabbed him and pulled him out of the field, holding him steady. Andrew's stomach heaved, as if he were going to be sick. He swallowed hard, reminding himself that he'd taken the chute before. But he'd had plenty of time to prepare himself, last time.

"Prime Minister," a calm voice said. "Welcome to the bunker."

Andrew brushed dust off his sleeves, taking the opportunity to concentrate his mind. His stomach was still churning. And yet...he looked up at the speaker, forcing himself to match the name to the face. General Peter Templeton, one of the duty officers who rotated through the Whitehall Bunker. Andrew didn't know him that well - he hadn't had time to meet and greet *everyone* who worked in Whitehall - but Templeton would be competent. He wouldn't be manning the bunker if he weren't.

"Thank you," he said. "What happened?"

Templeton looked grim. "The orbital defences sounded the alert, Prime Minister," he said, as he motioned for Andrew to follow him into the bunker. "An enemy fleet is heading directly for Earth."

Andrew felt his blood run cold. He'd assumed, despite himself, that Ten Downing Street had become the target of a terrorist attack. There hadn't been a major terrorist attack in over a hundred years, but that proved nothing. The security services had made it clear to him, when he'd moved into Downing Street, that the odds of preventing terrorist attacks completely were very low. There were more guns on the streets, these days, than there had been before the Troubles. And obtaining explosive materials wasn't *that* difficult.

He shuddered. A terrorist attack might have been preferable. Security officers were trained to assume the worst and get the principals to safety as soon as possible, rather than hoping for the best. Throwing him down the chute had been unpleasant, but necessary. He understood that too.

"Crap," he said. "How long do we have?"

"Assuming the enemy's speed remains constant, somewhere around two hours," Templeton said. He led the way into the bunker. "They're moving at a pretty fair clip, Prime Minister, but they will have to slow down before they reach Earth."

Andrew nodded as he studied the central hologram, wishing he could understand it. He'd visited the Whitehall Bunker twice, shortly after his election, but he hadn't bothered to bring himself up to speed on the installation. The bunker was fully staffed, ready to take command of Britain's military and security forces if the shit hit the fan. He'd thought he hadn't needed to know much more, back then. In hindsight, that might have been a mistake. He hoped Templeton and his staff wouldn't hold it against him.

"So far, the enemy appears to believe that they remain undetected," Templeton said, nodding to the display. "We believe they'll drop their sensor masks at some point within the next hour or so. They would be fools to assume they'll remain undetected until they enter weapons range."

Andrew nodded. Earth was protected by more fixed defences - and sensor nodes - than any other planet in the human sphere. The sheer multitude of defence systems alone would make spoofing them very difficult, although he knew better than to think that was a certainty. He supposed it didn't matter, in any case. The aliens would realise, sooner rather than later, that the human defenders were reacting to *something...*

He pushed the thought aside. The defence of Earth was out of his hands. *His* responsibility was his country and people.

"The media will be watching," he said, slowly. "Do they know what's happening?"

"The first reports came in less than ten minutes ago," Templeton said. "However, it will not be long before the media realises that something *is* wrong. And then..."

"Panic," Andrew said. There had been panic in the streets after New Russia. Everyone had expected the aliens to punch straight through to

Earth before the human forces could adapt to their weapons. "There'll be anarchy."

He sucked in his breath. He'd seen a multitude of plans for every contingency, from a Great Power conflict to outright civil war and *none* of them had made reassuring reading. Britain was a more unified country than some of the other Great Powers, but a combination of alien attack and governmental collapse would bring out the beast in everyone. The planners had been pessimistic. It remained to be seen if they were actually wrong.

"I understand that we have a contingency plan for this situation," he said. "Is that correct?"

"Yes, Prime Minister," Templeton said. He spoke from memory. "We'll alert military bases and police stations first, then inform the general public once the security forces have been deployed. Martial law will be declared. All reservists who haven't already been called up will be ordered to report to their nearest base, while the remainder of the civilian population will be instructed to stay put and wait. We anticipate that most people will obey orders. Those who don't will be arrested and detained until the emergency is over."

Andrew swallowed. It was late, thankfully. *Most* civilians would be at home, he hoped. They'd be safe, for a while. But that wouldn't last. The government had advised everyone to stock up on food and water, when the war had begun, yet he had no idea how many people had actually followed the government's suggestion. If food distribution services started to break down, millions of people would starve. Some of them would go looking for food elsewhere.

And they might be shot, he thought, grimly. The police had strict orders about dealing with looters. *And won't that come back to haunt us?*

He pushed the thought out of his head. "Make it so," he said. "I'll address the nation once the first alerts have gone out."

"Yes, Prime Minister," Templeton said. He paused. "We also require your permission to deal with the media. They *cannot* be allowed to cause a panic."

Andrew sighed. Even now, the media wielded considerable power. He'd be Public Enemy Number One after the crisis...if, of course, the crisis ended. His party would certainly pay a high price during the next election. But if the crisis didn't end, the next election would be the least of their worries. He had no idea what sort of government the Tadpoles would impose on Earth - if they didn't simply eradicate the human race - but he doubted it would be one most humans would find congenial.

"Do it," he said. Perhaps he could resign, afterwards. It might salvage the party's chances in the General Election. "And make sure they know it was my decision."

He took a chair and forced himself to think, dragging up details from half-remembered briefings. The Whitehall Bunker was *deep* under Whitehall, deep enough that nothing in humanity's arsenal could destroy it without doing immense damage to London. It was linked to an entire network of bunkers and storage depots around the country, allowing the government to keep functioning even if the country itself was invaded. The cynical side of his mind wondered if there would be any point - any survivors above ground would not be pleased to see the government after the war - but it didn't matter. It was their *duty* to rebuild the country after the war.

The red icons on the display didn't seem to be moving. It took him several minutes to work out that the display itself was shrinking as the alien ships moved closer and closer to Earth, gliding into position to threaten the entire planet. The bunker staff spoke in hushed voices as they struggled to coordinate a national response to a planetary threat, snatches of conversation echoing in Andrew's ears as they worked. Many of them seemed to be dealing with officials who didn't quite believe the news.

We should have held more drills, Andrew thought. *But we always considered them too disruptive.*

It was a frustrating thought. The country hadn't held national drills since the Troubles. Even the annual military exercises hadn't involved more than a tiny fraction of the population. He couldn't help wondering just how people were going to react, when the news finally crashed into their minds. There would be panic, then chaos. He had no doubt that thousands upon thousands of people would rush to buy food and arm themselves, despite the order to remain at home. There was always *someone* who thought the rules didn't apply to them.

"The King has been informed," a voice said. "He's staying in London."

Andrew nodded to himself. The Royal Family didn't have any power of its own - the Houses of Parliament were united on that, if nothing else - but it did have symbolic value. King Charles IV could encourage the population to work together to overcome their problems, although the cynic in Andrew suspected his words would fall on deaf ears. What did a man who had grown up in Buckingham Palace know of the common man? The Royal Family's true role was to distract the public from power. There would be little cause for *that* if the Tadpoles won the war.

Templeton walked back over to where Andrew was sitting. "The datanet is already flooding with alerts," he said. "Someone in America or France let the cat out of the bag."

Andrew glanced at his watch, then winced. Barely twenty-seven minutes had passed since he'd entered the bunker. The police and military would do all they could, but they simply hadn't had time to prepare for either riots or enemy landings. There was no way to keep the word from spreading, too. The datanet was meant to be carefully monitored, but hackers had been exploiting flaws in the system for years. It hadn't been seen as a major problem, as long as they stayed out of government systems.

"Alert the population," he said, finally. "Better they hear it from us than anyone else."

"Yes, Prime Minister," Templeton said.

Andrew sighed. The British public maintained a healthy scepticism of anything that came out of a politician's mouth. It was hardly a surprise - British politicians had done a great deal of damage because they'd lost touch with reality, before the Troubles - but right now it was a major headache. Andrew liked to think that his honesty ratings were higher than his predecessors, yet that meant nothing. The person sitting in Ten Downing Street was a liar, as far as most of the population was concerned. They never had to deal with the compromises Andrew had to make every day.

"Keep it as truthful as possible," he said. He'd have to address the nation. There were a number of emergency speeches in his desk drawer, but none of them really fitted the situation. "And make sure they know to stay indoors."

"Yes, Prime Minister," Templeton said.

Andrew leaned back into his chair, gritting his teeth. It wasn't going to be pleasant. Even in the best case scenario, hundreds of thousands of people were going to be seriously injured - or die. And yet, there was no choice. His country was about to be attacked.

And we'll beat them off, he told himself. *We will.*

But he knew, all too well, that *that* was out of his hands.

CHAPTER
SIX

Sin City, Luna

There was definitely something *darker* in the air, Brian decided, as he made his way up the stairs and onto Level Five. The wild parties were still going on - he ducked as a piece of underwear flew over his head - but there was an *edge* to the air that worried him. He glanced at his watch, deciding that time had to be running out for most of the guests. They'd be in deep shit if they failed to catch the last train back to their destination.

"Banned in Boston, sir," a young waitress said, holding out a set of datachips. "Yours for a hundred credits."

Brian rolled his eyes as he took in the titles. Semi-legal porn, probably already pirated and uploaded to the darker corners of the datanet. They probably *would* be banned in America - the social conservatives had been fighting a war against datanet porn for years - but that probably meant nothing to anyone who actually *wanted* it. There was no shortage of ways to get around datanet restrictions with the right tools and knowledge. Besides, the porn flicks weren't banned in Britain.

"No, thank you," he said, tersely.

The girl shrugged and headed on to the next potential customer. Brian rather doubted she'd have better luck. Smuggling datanet porn into a military base could get someone in *real* trouble, although there was always some idiot who thought he could get away with it. No doubt the idiot would have plenty of time to reflect on his stupidity in the brig. He glanced at the string of adverts on the walls, then walked down to the bar. It looked to be heaving with customers, the waitresses carrying vast trays of drinks from the bar to the tables. Brian couldn't help thinking that the clientele didn't look very savoury. Most of them were either merchant spacers or military types.

Many a foul crime has probably been planned in here, he thought, as he walked into the bar and looked around. *Or tips shared on how to evade anti-smuggling patrols.*

He gritted his teeth as the music started to pound, a dull throbbing beat that was supposed to be popular...somewhere. A line of naked dancers appeared on the stage, shaking their breasts and kicking their legs in a manner that made Brian roll his eyes. He liked the female form as much as any other straight male, but there were limits. The blatant sexuality was more disturbing than enticing. But it didn't seem to be a problem for the drunkards in the front row. They were hooting and hollering as the dancing became more and more obscene.

A waitress, her skin as dark as the night, appeared in front of him. "Table, sir?"

"Yes, please," Brian said. He passed her a tip, watching with admiration as she made the coin vanish before any of her superiors noticed it. The bar looked to be the sort of place where tips were expected to be shared. "Can you give me somewhere away from the stage?"

"Of course, sir," the waitress said. "If you'll follow me...?"

Brian followed her, his eyes moving from waitress to waitress as he searched for his target. *None* of the waitresses looked particularly happy to be there, although some were clearly better at hiding it than others. A handful of girls had nasty marks on their skin, utterly unconcealed. Abuse was technically forbidden in Sin City, but the girls were probably not in any position to make a complaint. Their visas would be cancelled if they couldn't find replacement positions after they were fired.

Poor bitches, he thought. *But where is Abigail?*

He was tempted to ask his escort as she offered him an empty table and waited for his order, but he suspected it would be a bad idea. It was unlikely that anyone at the bar knew who 'Norma Lee' really was, yet if they did...Brian wasn't in the mood for a fight. God alone knew what Sin City's Management would do if the shit really *did* hit the fan. They'd have to be insane to pick a fight with Abigail's family, but their reputation for secrecy was important to them. Sin City would lose half its customer base if secrecy was no longer an option. He ordered a pint, then leaned back to watch the waitresses. He'd just have to keep his eyes open and wait.

The dancing finally came to an end, the dancers bowing obscenely before marching off the stage. Thankfully, Abigail didn't seem to be among them. Brian kept looking, silently praying that Abigail hadn't thought to change her looks. He'd seen videos of the girl, but he knew better than to think that he'd recognise her if she cut or dyed her hair. Facial identification software might not even be able to pick her out from the crowd.

Perhaps I'll have to ask after all, he thought, as he sipped his beer. *Someone might tip her boss off if Clancy screws the pooch.*

A new set of waitresses appeared, looking worn down by life. Brian studied them, but...his eyes almost flickered *over* Abigail before he spotted her. She hadn't changed much, yet...she looked different. She looked beaten down by life. There were no visible bruises, but that meant nothing. Brian was old enough to know that there were plenty of ways to hurt someone that left no visible trace. Naked threats and intimidation of someone who was very much a fish out of water would probably be enough to do the trick.

He watched her carefully, waiting for the moment he could signal her. Abigail looked *young*, painfully young. Surely *someone* would have noticed she was *too* young. But he doubted Abigail's boss would have looked any further than her fake papers. They'd gotten her into Sin City, so there was nothing wrong with them. And if there was, Brian knew, it wouldn't be the boss's fault. He caught her eye, just for a second, and waved. She hesitated, looking as though she wanted to send someone else, then slowly made her way to his table. Brian couldn't help thinking she looked as though she was walking to her own execution.

"Abigail," he said, quietly. "I'm here to help."

Abigail's eyes went very wide. "Who are you?"

"Sit down," Brian said, quietly. The music was drowning out every conversation, as far as he could tell, but he knew better than to count on it. Someone with a focused mike would probably be able to hear every word. "Your parents sent me to get you home."

Abigail swallowed, hard. "I don't want to go home."

Brian studied her for a long moment. He didn't have daughters, but he'd seen his fair share of teenage suspects. They'd often been pushed into doing more and more stupid things until they attracted the attention of the law, then wound up in cells waiting for transport to the nearest borstal. They tried to sound prideful, they tried to sound grown-up, but most of them knew they were in deep shit. Abigail sounded just like the ones who wanted to call their parents, yet were too stubborn or too afraid to make the call. They were the ones who could be helped, once justice had run its course. The ones who couldn't were probably already doomed.

He sighed, inwardly. Kids grew up too fast, these days.

"You shouldn't even be here," Brian said. "Do you even *want* to be here?"

He saw the answer in her eyes and nodded to himself. Abigail might be trying to put a brave face on it, but she was terrified. *Someone* had found her work, then taken a share of her salary...perhaps *all* of her salary. It was hardly an uncommon problem, even though it was technically illegal. God knew the Management would turn a blind eye as long as it didn't become a major problem.

"Your parents aren't mad at you," he reassured her. "They just want you home."

"They think I'm a baby," Abigail whispered.

"They know better now," Brian said, seriously. Teenage runaways weren't *that* common on the moon. Most children grew up fast when they were raised in a lethal environment. "Let me take you home."

"I owe money," Abigail said, quietly. "I..."

"Don't worry about it," Brian said. He'd seen shitty contracts before. The chances were good that the whole system was rigged. Abigail would get her salary, then be billed for everything from her food and drink to her outfits. She'd wind up more in debt than ever before. "I can take you out of here."

He watched her for a long moment, silently praying that she'd take the opportunity. There was no way he could drug her and carry her out, not when the security forces might turn on him. And if she refused...someone might ask her a number of very pointed questions about just why her parents had sent a private detective after her. Most runaways didn't have wealthy parents.

"I can't leave," Abigail said. "They need me..."

"They don't," Brian said, firmly. "There is no shortage of girls like you."

"Fine," Abigail said. She sounded torn between hope and fear. "I'll get my coat and..."

Brian met her eyes. "Do you have anything with you that can't be replaced? If so, come with me now."

Abigail nodded and rose. Brian rose too, one hand dropping to his pocket as he quickly swept the bar for potential trouble. Ideally, he'd just take Abigail and walk out before anyone could react, but her employer might not take kindly to it. Several potential excuses ran through his mind, yet all of them would be chancy. Abigail probably wasn't allowed to leave the bar, even when she wasn't on duty. Who knew what might happen if she found a terminal?

And the bar patrons aren't exactly the nicest people, he thought, wryly. *They might join in a fight for the sheer hell of it.*

The waitress at the door looked worried, then alarmed. Abigail gulped. Brian braced himself as he turned around, somehow unsurprised to see a giant slab of muscle ambulating towards him. The bartender - Abigail's employer, he assumed - was a misshapen parody of a man, his arms and legs bulging with exaggerated muscles while his chest, neck and head seemed inhumanly small. His piggish eyes glared suspiciously at Brian, as if he suspected Brian of kidnapping a waitress. The outfit he wore hid nothing, not even the bulge between his legs. Brian hid his disgust with practiced ease. *Smart* people knew better than to have their bodies enhanced in back-alley cosmetic surgeries. The side effects were almost always unpleasant.

"And where," he demanded in a nasal whine, "do you think *you're* going?"

Brian contemplated a number of options, then decided on the truth. "I'm returning this girl to her parents," he said, firmly. He had no intention of telling the whole truth, if it could be avoided. "I'm sure you'll have no trouble finding a replacement."

The piggish man glowered at him. Brian heard Abigail whimper and felt a flicker of annoyance, mixed with anger. The bartender probably *would* be intimidating to someone without combat training. Brian had met worse people in military bars near Catterick, back during his probationary period. Wrestling half-drunk squaddies wasn't a sport for the faint of heart. But the bartender was nowhere near as tough. Brian would have bet good money the bastard simply couldn't move very fast without toppling over and hitting the ground.

"She owes me money," the bartender said, finally. "Seven thousand credits, counting interest."

Brian did the calculation in his head. Seven thousand Luna Credits was roughly five thousand pounds. He rolled his eyes at the conceit. He had no idea how much debt Abigail might have incurred, but he was fairly sure it wasn't *that* high. Her outfit probably wouldn't cost more than fifty pounds at the local store.

"I rather doubt it," he said, sharply. He removed a card from his pocket and held it out. "If you have a genuine claim, submit it to this address. I'll see to it that your claim is taken into consideration."

The piggy man's glare grew darker. "I'll take it out of your hide," he said, cracking his fists loudly. "I won't let anyone steal from me..."

Brian briefly considered drawing his shockrod and jamming it into the man's groin. The screaming alone would deter anyone from following them, at least long enough for Brian and Abigail to put some distance between themselves and the bar. But it would also draw a great deal of attention. He didn't want to have to deal with that.

He leaned forward, instead. "The girl's fifteen," he said. "Do you *really* want to argue it with the Management?"

There was a long pause. Brian tensed, bracing himself for an attack. Sin City *did* have a strict age limit. The bartender would be in deep shit if he were caught violating it, even if Abigail's papers *had* passed muster. The smart thing to do would be to let the matter - and Abigail - go, but Brian didn't dare *count* on the man being that smart. He'd either not noticed Abigail's age or chosen to ignore it.

"I'll send a bill," the man warned. "And I expect it paid at once."

Brian shrugged. "Come on," he said, to Abigail. "We have to go."

He led her out of the bar and down the corridor. Abigail followed, her eyes flickering from side to side as if she expected an attack at any moment. Brian had seen prisoners - freshly released from jail - showing the same reaction. Prisons were meant to be safe, but somehow vast numbers of weapons and illegal drugs were smuggled past the guards. A prisoner who couldn't stand up for herself was in deep shit.

"Thank you," Abigail said, softly. "I..."

Brian looked her up and down. "What happened?"

Abigail swallowed, hard. "Is Terry in trouble?"

"I imagine he's been grounded for a few decades," Brian said, dryly. He had no idea what Abigail's parents had done to her friend, but he doubted it was anything *pleasant.* God knew Terry's parents would be pissed too. "What happened to you?"

"I thought no one could follow me if I came here," Abigail said. "I...I didn't think to take any money. I...I trusted the wrong people. They...they told me I had to work, or else...or else they'd hurt me and...they didn't *listen* to me."

"I imagine they wouldn't," Brian said. He thought, fast. There would be a medical centre nearby. He could have Abigail checked for any immediate problems before they boarded a train to Luna City. But he wanted to get her out as quickly as possible. The bartender probably had friends. "Are you in pain now?"

Abigail shook her head. "Just...just scared."

"We'll get you out of here in a jiffy," Brian told her. He studied her for a long moment. She didn't seem to be hurt, as far as he could tell. But she was shaking...it looked as though she was torn between clinging to him and running as fast as she could. "And then you can go home."

"My parents will kill me," Abigail said, as they resumed their walk. "Are they...are they really mad?"

"They're not *pleased,*" Brian said. They reached the stairwell and started heading up. "But I think they're more shocked than angry."

"That'll change," Abigail predicted, darkly. "They never *listen* to me."

"A common complaint," Brian said. "I..."

He broke off as the alarms started to howl. Abigail caught his arm, her entire body trembling like a leaf. Brian reached for his shockrod, then stopped himself. That wasn't the intruder alert siren, he thought. It was the emergency alert.

"ATTENTION," a voice blared. "THIS IS AN EMERGENCY SITUATION. ALL GUESTS ARE ADVISED TO MAKE THEIR WAY TO THE NEAREST SHELTER AS QUICKLY AS POSSIBLE. I SAY AGAIN, ALL GUESTS ARE ADVISED TO MAKE THEIR WAY TO THE NEAREST SHELTER AS QUICKLY AS POSSIBLE."

Brian blanched. An attack? There *was* a war on - he *knew* there was a war on - but he hadn't really expected an attack on Sol itself. Perhaps the war had been going badly, worse than the media claimed. God knew no one in their right mind would take *any* government's word for granted. And an attack meant that Luna might be attacked. *Sin City* might be attacked. Or it might be something as simple as an air leak. Better to assume the worst...

He caught Abigail's hand. "We have to go to the nearest shelter," he said. The tube network would already be shutting down, if he recalled correctly. There was no way to leave Sin City without it, unless they rented a shuttle. "And then we wait."

Abigail glanced back down the stairs. "What about...what about *them*?"

"Right now, we have other problems," Brian said. He led her down the corridor. A handful of other guests were making their way to the shelters, but most seemed determined to remain in the casinos. Some of them were even arguing with the staff. Brian understood their logic - they thought that a major attack on Sin City would kill everyone, in or out of the shelters - but he didn't agree with it. If there *was* an attack, they had to do everything they could to stack the odds in favour of survival.

Which won't help a bit if someone nukes the place, he thought, as they reached the shelter hatch. It looked grim inside, as grim and desolate as an airport passenger lounge. The handful of inhabitants looked scared. *We'll be dead before we know what hit us.*

He kept that thought to himself as he found a seat. There was no point in scaring Abigail.

She looked at him. "How long do we have to stay here?"

"As long as it takes," Brian said. He drew his terminal from his belt and opened it, trying to access the local datanet. "Get some sleep. It might be quite some time."

CHAPTER

SEVEN

Ward Mansion, Penzance, United Kingdom

Molly stumbled into the bathroom and bent over the washbasin, feeling sick.

She hadn't really expected the party to be quite so...*intense.* They'd been late, largely because Garrison had been intent on showing her that he was still in good shape for an older man, but that wasn't the problem. She'd had a chance to clean her dress and redo her makeup before going onto the dance floor. The *real* problem was the number of young and beautiful people she'd met at the party. Indeed, women had outnumbered men two to one. She couldn't help thinking that Garrison had been attracted to quite a few of them.

It isn't fair, she thought, bitterly. *It just isn't fair.*

She swallowed, hard. She'd been to quite a few formal parties since they'd come into money, but this was different. She felt terribly out of place. The chatter was all about people and places she didn't know - and would probably never know - while the food and drink were utterly unfamiliar. She was tempted to think that Garrison was probably playing a joke on her, when he'd told her that Lady Penelope's food was to die for. Her stomach churned, mocking her. Expensive food just didn't agree with her, it seemed.

The dress felt clammy against her skin, despite the promises in the brochure. Perhaps there was something in the air...or perhaps it was just her sweat. She looked down at her hands, remembering what she'd been doing before they reached the hall. Did everyone *know* what she'd been doing? She couldn't help feeling that everyone was laughing at her, behind her back. She didn't know how to *talk* to the upper crust, she didn't know how to dance, she didn't even know how to fake it...what *was* she, really? What did she have that the younger girls *didn't* have?

No one had been rude to her, openly. No one had cut her dead on the dance floor. But they *knew* she wasn't one of them. They'd watched her muff the dances and make a fool of herself...God knew what *Garrison* thought, damn the man. Perhaps he was already planning to make her take a taxi home while he went off with one of the younger girls. Could she even *get* a taxi all the way to Woking? She wasn't sure. It was already far too late to guarantee finding a driver...

She forced herself to think. Perhaps she could just go. It wasn't as if she needed anything beyond her bag and coat. She could call a taxi...she might have to spend more money than she cared to think about, but she could just go. And then...she looked down at the sink, fighting the urge to retch. All of her dreams would turn to powder if she just abandoned Garrison and Lady Penelope.

And Kurt will be furious, she thought, bitterly. Why hadn't he been the sort of man she wanted? She'd certainly thought he had good prospects, back when they'd married. But he wasn't inclined to spend money on parties and fancy dresses and...she swallowed, again, as her gorge rose in her throat. *What the hell am I doing?*

Her smartphone bleeped, loudly. Molly cursed, almost stumbling as she reached for the wretched device. She'd drunk far too much, part of her mind noted. She wasn't thinking clearly. There weren't many people who had her number, which meant...Gayle? Or one of the kids? Or...or Garrison? Perhaps he thought she was taking too long in the bathroom. She opened the phone and stared at the display. A red message was blinking on the screen.

Molly stared down at it. EMERGENCY ALERT. EMERGENCY ALERT. ENEMY FORCES HAVE ENTERED THE SOLAR SYSTEM. ALL CIVILIANS ARE ORDERED TO...

Her mind spun as she read the entire message. The solar system was under attack...it was impossible. Wasn't it? The war was thousands of light years away, right? She swallowed, hard, as the news sunk in. The solar system was under attack and she was over four hundred kilometres from her children. She flicked through the rest of the message, cursing under her breath. Civilians were ordered to remain where they were and await further instructions.

She clicked the phone, trying to call Gayle. But nothing happened. There was no signal, something she'd been told was impossible. Britain had the most advanced datanet in the world and yet...and yet there was no signal. Had the aliens already taken it down? Or...she cursed, again, as she realised the truth. The government had probably taken the network down, just to make sure the civilians couldn't jam up the system. Or to keep them from spreading panic...

Molly checked her appearance in the mirror, then hurried back outside. The dancing seemed to have come to a sudden end, with half the dancers streaming through the doors and down towards the car park. The others were milling around in confusion, muttering to each other as they checked their smartphones time and time again. It wasn't a joke, Molly noted as she searched for Garrison. The planet really *was* under attack. She heard the sound of cars moving out of the parking lot and glanced through the doors, just in time to see a string of fancy cars leaving the hall. No doubt the drivers believed the curfew didn't apply to *them*.

I have to get back to the kids, she thought, grimly. *I can't afford to follow the curfew either.*

Garrison was standing next to two men she didn't recognise, chatting with them. He'd warned her never to interrupt a private discussion, but this was *important*. One of the men huffed in annoyance as she caught his attention, while the other looked oddly relieved. Molly made a mental note to work out what that meant later, if she ever cared enough to do it. She had other problems at the moment.

"This had better be important," Garrison said. He sounded irked. "I was on the verge of closing a very important deal."

Molly swallowed a number of very nasty remarks as she held out her smartphone. The emergency alert was still on top, blinking constantly. No doubt the government could update her at any moment, if it wished to do so. God knew she got enough messages from people she didn't know, trying to sell her shit she didn't want. Garrison lifted his eyebrows as he read the message, then shrugged.

"We'll have to stay here," he said, calmly. "We've been ordered to stay off the roads."

"I need to get back to the children," Molly snapped. She fought down the urge to slap him, hard. "Take me back."

"There'll be a room for you here, if you want it," Garrison said. He sounded faintly bored, as if the fate of Molly's children didn't bother him. It probably didn't. "You can stay until the all-clear is sounded."

Molly clenched her fists. "And how long will that be?"

"I have no idea," Garrison said. "But if you can't go on the roads, how do you expect to go home?"

"Give me the keys," Molly said. "I'll drive myself home."

"You need me," Garrison said. "The car won't accept any other driver."

"Then take me home," Molly snapped. "Now!"

"You are in no position to make demands," Garrison observed. He turned, surveying the handful of people who'd remained in the hall. "I do not..."

Molly leaned forward and caught his arm. "You are going to take me home," she snarled, angrily. God! Was this what he was *really* like? Or was he panicking on the inside, just like her? She found it hard to care. The asshole clearly didn't give a damn about her. Perhaps he'd just brought her to the party to humiliate her. He'd certainly indulged his pleasures on the trip to Penzance. "Now!"

Anger gave her strength. She dragged him down towards the doors, holding him tightly. He was probably stronger than her, normally, but she was a mother...a stab of guilt tore through her heart as she realised just how blatantly she'd abandoned her children. Gayle would be with them, but Gayle wasn't much older than her charges. She certainly didn't know how to take care of them for more than a day or two. Did she even know where the food was hidden, under the stairs? Molly couldn't remember if *Percy* knew.

The cold air snapped at her as they walked down to the car park. She looked up, half-expecting to see a giant invasion fleet high above her, but there was nothing. The lights she knew to be space habitats and industrial stations were still there, twinkling faintly against the night sky. Kurt had told her, once, that the stars shone constantly in space, but she hadn't believed him. Now...now she didn't know *what* she believed.

"This is completely ridiculous," Garrison said. "Do you know how hard it will be to reach Woking?"

"I don't care," Molly snarled. In the distance, she could hear the sound of helicopters. She told herself, firmly, that they were *human* helicopters. But that proved nothing...did it? She couldn't help remembering a handful of alien invasion movies where the aliens had taken over innocent humans and turned them into living weapons. "We are going to Woking."

Garrison opened the car door and pressed his hand against the sensor. It should have turned green as the engine came to life. Instead, a red alert blinked up on the dashboard. Molly read it, torn between the urge to start crying and a madcap desire to giggle like a schoolgirl. GPS OFFLINE, it read. CAR NAVIGATION SYSTEM DISABLED.

"Start it up," she snapped. "Now!"

"I can't," Garrison said. She thought she heard a hint of panic in his voice. "I don't know how!"

Molly stared at him. "You bought an expensive car you don't know how to drive?"

"The computer does the driving," Garrison insisted. "It's just...it's just been *disabled*!"

"...Fuck," Molly said. All of a sudden, she understood *precisely* why Kurt had refused to buy a self-driving car. Garrison had spent shitloads of money on a car that could be remotely disabled. She couldn't keep a giggle from escaping her lips, despite the situation. Garrison's car was now nothing more than an oddly-shaped piece of metal. "You...you spent all that money on a useless car?"

"It isn't funny," Garrison snapped. It didn't sound as though he liked her mockery. Most men disliked being mocked. "Think of everyone who was on the road!"

Molly leaned against the car door, staring up into the night sky. He was right. If a car could be remotely disabled, everyone unlucky enough to be on the road might have had their trip brought to a sudden end. She had a vision of countless cars stopped on the motorway, unable to proceed to their destination. And yet...surely that would block the roads. She doubted the government would want to disrupt the motorways *that* much.

She looked around, desperately. Most of the cars were gone. The remaining cars looked far too much like Garrison's to give her any confidence that their owners could drive them without the computers. And that meant...she looked eastwards, cursing under her breath as the problem sank in. Four hundred kilometres wasn't *that* long a journey, in a modern car, but it would take her *days* to cover on foot. She touched her smartphone, trying to place another call. Nothing happened. The network was still down.

There are boats on the water, she thought. She could see their lights, glimmering in the darkness. *I could take one...*

Cold logic caught up with her. *And go where, dumbass? Woking's inland.*

Garrison caught her arm. "Come back to the hall," he said. "We'll see what we can do there."

Molly gritted her teeth as she pulled her arm free. The hall was the *last* place she wanted to go. But where else *could* she go? They were several miles outside Penzance...she could walk *there*, she supposed, but what then? A hotel? Or a taxi...she doubted she could find a taxi driver willing to violate the curfew. Garrison had connections, but a random stranger on the street probably wouldn't.

"Fine," she said, softly. "But we're not staying."

Garrison said nothing as they made their way back up the garden path. The hall looked eerie in the semi-darkness, the lighted gardens she'd admired already cloaked in shadow. A handful of servants were cleaning up the buffet, while two more were keeping a wary eye on a portable terminal. A talking head was blathering about nothing while alien warships were closing in on Earth.

"I need to speak to Lady Penelope," Garrison said, once they were inside. "Coming?"

Molly shrugged and followed him up the stairs. The interior of the building felt eerie too, like a movie stage that had suddenly been deserted. Molly recalled seeing hundreds of servants manning the building, but most of them appeared to have vanished. She couldn't tell if they'd gone to be with their families or been assigned to other jobs. The estate was large, larger than she'd realised. She couldn't imagine being in charge of it herself.

Lady Penelope was sitting in her office, talking on an old-style telephone. Molly felt a spurt of hope - *she* could use the telephone - which died as Lady Penelope put down the handset with a curse. Landlines had gone out of fashion *years* ago, at least for modern houses and settlements. Her home didn't even *have* a landline. She might be able to use the handset to call someone in Woking, but probably not her family.

"The landline is down," Lady Penelope said, glaring at the handset. "I couldn't even call my family."

"I can't contact mine either," Molly said. She held out her handset. "Do you have a vehicle that can take me home?"

"Not at the moment," Lady Penelope said. She jabbed a finger at the display. A line of prisoners were being marched into a police van. "Do you *want* to go into a detention centre?"

Molly stared. "They can't do that!"

"The government has invoked the Security and Defence of the Realm Act," Lady Penelope told her. She sounded distant, as if her mind was occupied elsewhere. "You do *not* want to be caught on the streets, not now."

"...Shit," Molly said. She flushed. "Begging your pardon, My Lady."

"I understand the impulse," Lady Penelope said. "But you do *not* want to mess with the police, not now."

Molly nodded. It had been *years* since she'd taken Modern Studies in school - the courses were mandatory - and she'd forgotten much of it, but some things had stayed with her. The Security and Defence of the Realm Act, passed during Charles Hanover's second year as Prime Minister after a particularly unpleasant terrorist atrocity, had granted the government incredibly wide powers to fight terrorism and terrorists. The act had been hugely controversial at the time, even though the population was still reeling after the slaughter of hundreds of children. On one hand, it had given the police and security forces a free hand to go after terrorists; on the other, it had made a joke of civil liberties and put thousands of innocent people behind the wire. Even one hundred and fifty years after the Troubles, the act was still controversial...

And still on the books, she thought, numbly. *I could go straight to jail.*

"I don't know what to do," she confessed. "What *should* I do?"

"Nothing," Lady Penelope said. "Stay here. I'll have the staff make up a bed for you."

"Can they get me a sober-up too," Molly said. She looked down at her dress. "And some proper clothes?"

"If they have something in your size," Lady Penelope said. "I think..."

She broke off and nodded to the terminal. The Prime Minister was giving a speech. Molly couldn't help thinking he looked tired, even though he *was* in London. She had no doubt that *his* family had already been rushed to safety. The surge of bitter envy shocked her more than she cared to admit. She'd always thought of herself as upper middle class. But now... now, she was cut off from her children, unable even to call them. What could she do?

"...Country faces its gravest test since the Battle of Britain," the Prime Minister said. He sounded tired too. "The aliens have entered our solar system and are advancing on our homeworld. It will not be long before they open fire."

There was a long chilling pause. "Years ago, a great politician insisted that Britain would never surrender. He said that we would fight on the beaches, we would fight on the landing grounds, we would fight in the fields and in the streets, we would fight in the hills; we would never surrender. I say that to you now - we will fight in space, we will fight on the land...we will fight until we drive the invader from our system.

"Today, humanity stands as one, united against a common foe. Be of stout heart. Humanity will win this war. We will drive the enemy back into deep space, then counterattack until our world - our *worlds* - are safe once again."

"Pretty words," Garrison said.

"And cribbed from Winston Churchill," Lady Penelope added.

Molly shrugged. She didn't care about who'd written the original speech, let alone who'd modified it for the Prime Minister. Perhaps he'd done it himself. There was a rawness about it she'd never heard from his more polished political speeches.

"Fine," she said. "What do we do now?"

"The only thing we can do," Lady Penelope said. "We wait."

CHAPTER
EIGHT

Carrier 05/RFS *Brezhnev*, Deep Space

The humans had noticed them.

It was not unexpected, the combat faction noted. The human star system *teemed* with activity, with hundreds of starships and spacecraft making their way between worlds or heading directly to the tramlines. They'd known there was a very good chance of being spotted sooner or later, although they'd hoped to get closer before they were detected. It was... awkward.

The discussion raced backwards and forwards as more and more data flooded into the sensor datanet. The timing was *definitely* awkward. A number of human warships were pulling away from their homeworld, either fleeing or aiming to link up with other human units outside sensor range. The factions paused, momentarily unsure which way to go. Destroying the human carriers would cripple their ability to take the offensive - although the armoured carrier was nowhere to be seen - but wiping out their industrial base would finish the war, if the humans couldn't muster a counterattack before it was too late. Isolating and destroying a human sub-unit would be greeted with complete satisfaction, yet if there were other human ships out there...

The planet remains the priority target, the faction decided. New orders raced through the datanet, reorganising the flotillas. *Their industrial base must be targeted and destroyed.*

The Song grew louder as the fleet dropped its sensor mask. There was no point in trying to hide any longer. The humans had already seen them. Besides, it soaked up energy at a terrifying rate. The fleet adjusted course slightly, preparing to launch starfighters once the first set of targets were isolated. Humanity's homeworld would be heavily defended, of course. The defences would reveal themselves soon enough. And they would be destroyed before they could tip the balance in humanity's favour.

One squadron altered course, preparing to intercept and shadow the human ships as they powered away from Earth. Two more readied themselves to detach from the fleet and engage the human positions on Earth's satellite. The moon was unusually large, the Tadpoles noted, although that meant nothing to them. A star system that had birthed intelligent life was already a rarity. There were only two such stars within explored space.

Almost as an afterthought, the fleet brought its active sensors online. There was no point in denying themselves their most powerful systems any longer. Their positions were already noted and logged. Besides, their human opponents were still out of range. Better to learn as much as they could about the defences before they had to fight. If the humans were trying to lure them into a trap...

We can evade if necessary, the combat faction stated, silencing the doubters. *And we can outrun them if we are forced to retreat.*

"Captain," the sensor officer said. "They're bringing their active sensors online."

"Hold us steady," Captain Svetlana Zadornov ordered, coolly. She'd expected it for several minutes. The Tadpoles had already dropped their sensor mask. They probably already knew they'd been detected. If her puny sensors could pick up Earth's defences hastily preparing for war - and they had - the aliens would have no trouble doing the same. "Don't let them get a hint of our presence."

She braced herself as the aliens swept nearby space for trouble. They *might* not have detected *Brezhnev* - they would have blown her out of space if they had - but that might change the moment they used active sensors.

Brezhnev was far too close to the edge of their formation for comfort, precisely where a covert shadow would *want* to be. She'd practiced sneaking up on carriers before - modern starships had a sensor blindspot directly to the rear - but there were just too many ships in the formation to make it easy. One ship could keep an eye on another's blindspot. Assuming, of course, the Tadpoles *had* blindspots. The reports from previous engagements had been inconclusive.

We're about to find out, she thought, grimly. She had no doubt of their fate if the Tadpoles spotted them. *Brezhnev* was faster than their carriers, but she wouldn't have a hope of outrunning either missiles or starfighters. *If they see us, we're dead.*

"Updating fleet tallies now," the sensor officer said. "I have a complete list..."

"Forward it to Pournelle Base," Svetlana ordered. Earth could see the incoming fleet for itself now, but there was no point in taking chances. The Tadpoles were flying in tight formation, clearly trying to confuse the defenders. That, if nothing else, suggested they didn't know about her ship. "Helm, reduce speed a little. Let them get ahead of us."

"Aye, Captain," the helmsman said.

"We should prepare to take evasive action," Ignatyev muttered. "Captain, if they see us..."

"We're dead," Svetlana confirmed. She shrugged. There was no point in making preparations. *Brezhnev* could not *hope* to evade whatever the enemy threw at her, once they realised she was there. "It doesn't matter."

"Captain," the sensor officer said. "They're detaching a fleet group - seven starships, all destroyers!"

Svetlana narrowed her eyes. "Destination?"

"Unsure as yet, Captain," the sensor officer said. "But they're definitely pulling away from the main body."

"I see," Svetlana said.

She ran through the potential vectors in her head. The alien ships probably *weren't* coming after her. They didn't *need* to play games if they wanted to smash *Brezhnev* out of existence. But where were they going? Concentration of force was the first lesson in the tactical handbooks she'd read during basic training. Mother Russia's tacticians had learnt, the hard way, that dispersing their force across the battlefield led to defeat. And yet, seven destroyers weren't going to make a significant difference. Unless, of course, the aliens had come up with something new.

"Alert Pournelle Base," she ordered. The alien vectors were sharpening now, heading directly towards the human ships. A picket force, then. Their sensors must be better than hers, she decided. They clearly didn't feel they'd lose track of their targets. "Inform them that the aliens are watching them."

"Aye, Captain," the communications officer said.

Svetlana leaned back in her command chair, careful to project an aura of calm confidence as she contemplated her options. *Brezhnev* had received no further orders since detecting the alien fleet, although *that* wasn't surprising. The Americans were notoriously careless about communications security, but even *they* understood the dangers of sending messages to a starship so close to the enemy. It was unlikely that the Tadpoles could decrypt humanity's encryption codes, at least quickly enough to matter, yet even they would wonder who was supposed to *receive* a message they intercepted. And that meant she had freedom to act as she saw fit.

As long as I do my duty, she thought, wryly. *And that means staying close to the aliens.*

She looked at her XO. "Keep the alpha crew on duty, but send the beta and gamma crews back to bed," she ordered. The engagement would probably be a long one, unless it turned out to be as one-sided as New Russia. "I want them refreshed for when the shit hits the fan."

Ignatyev nodded, curtly. "Aye, Captain."

Svetlana returned her attention to the display. The main body of the alien fleet was slowing, unsurprisingly. Launching starfighters at a respectable percentage of the speed of light would be a major headache, although human carriers had done it *in extremis*. It was good to know that the aliens had some limitations too. The detached squadron, on the other hand, was picking up speed as it hurried away from the main body. She couldn't help wondering if whoever was in command of the detached ships wanted as much independence as possible. It was certainly something *she'd* want, if she were in command.

They're aliens, she reminded herself. *They won't think like us.*

"We could alter course to track the detached units, Captain," Ignatyev suggested. "The main body is not trying to hide."

Svetlana fought down a flicker of annoyance. The detached units might pose a problem, but they lacked the firepower to be a real threat. It was the main body of the alien fleet that needed to be tracked, even though it was *definitely* not trying to hide. Sensor nodes right across the system were already tracking the aliens as they approached Earth. It was possible that the main body of the fleet was a diversion - she had to admit it was possible - but she doubted it. Ignatyev was trying to get her in trouble. It wouldn't take much to convince her superiors that a woman had no place on the command deck.

She gritted her teeth. The hell of it was that she would never *know* if he was trying to trick her...or if he was trying to offer sound advice. She didn't dare trust him, she didn't dare trust *anyone*. Her uncle's political enemies would want to take her command just to spite him, while the sycophancy of his allies was almost worse. But then, she couldn't help wondering if a sycophant might actually be useful. She wouldn't need to keep guarding her back against the knife.

"We need to keep our eyes on the bigger formation," she said, firmly. "We'll hold our current course."

Ignatyev didn't look pleased, but he said nothing else. Svetlana watched him as he turned away, wondering if he would try to cross the line from offering alternatives to insubordination and outright mutiny. She had legal authority to execute her crewmen if they turned against her - or for anything she considered reasonable grounds for a hasty court-martial and execution, but she knew it would be dangerous. Ignatyev didn't have the sort of connections that would save his ass - or fry hers, if she killed him anyway - yet it would send a bad message to the crew. No one had ever *proved* that a couple of captains had been murdered by their crew - the official reports stated that both cases were accidents - but she'd heard the rumours. Crewmen who thought they could be killed on a whim were likely to try to find a way to strike first.

And you wanted to be on the command deck, she reminded herself, dryly. *Stop whining and get on with it.*

Svetlana tapped her console, bringing up the sensor reports. The alien fleet looked twice as ominous, now it was revealed in all its malevolent glory. So far, it hadn't launched starfighters, but it didn't need them. There was nearly an hour to go until it was ready to engage Earth's defences, unless Home Fleet mounted a counterattack ahead of time. She hadn't seen the plans, but she doubted it. Home Fleet needed to concentrate its forces before moving out to engage the enemy.

Bastards got lucky with the timing, she thought, sourly. *Or was it really a coincidence?*

Her face darkened as she remembered her last lunch with her uncle, shortly before returning to her command. A number of ships *had* gone missing in the months before the Battle of Vera Cruz, ships that could easily have been captured or destroyed by the Tadpoles. And it *was* clear the Tadpoles *could* speak to humans, even though they rarely bothered. Could they have made contact with dissident human factions? Could they have placed spies within the Kremlin? It didn't seem likely, but that hadn't stopped the KGB from cracking down on dissidents all over the Russian Federation. Mother Russia had thousands of enemies. Some of them were even inside the walls.

And it made a nice little excuse for a crackdown, she thought. *And round up quite a few people who thought themselves untouchable.*

It was a sobering thought. She had few illusions about her government, even though she loved her country. Russia had always been ruled by the knout, even if the justifications changed over the years. Dissidents could not be tolerated, not within the walls. Their selfishness would bring the country to its knees, if given the chance. Better to crack down on them before it was too late.

She allowed herself a cold smile. She'd seen the list of purged men and women - most of whom had been sent to Siberia rather than simply executed - and several had been quite familiar. One of them, a professor who'd expected her to service him in exchange for a good grade, deserved far worse than spending the rest of his life counting trees. Svetlana wouldn't waste her time feeling sorry for him. He'd probably spend far too much time on *his* knees once he reached the gulag. The nasty part of her mind wondered how he'd enjoy playing the girl.

It's all about power, her uncle had said, months ago. *And about never letting a crisis go to waste.*

"The enemy ships are repeating their sensor scans," the sensor officer reported. "So far, they haven't seen us."

"Keep us steady," Svetlana ordered. *Brezhnev* was within the turbulence zone. There was a good chance that anyone who caught a sniff of her presence would put it down to the turbulence instead of a prowling human starship. But she knew better than to take that for granted. The aliens knew they'd been detected, after all. "Keep forwarding our sensor readings to Pournelle Base."

"Aye, Captain."

Svetlana nodded curtly as the seconds ticked away. Earth wasn't *that* far away now...she wondered, grimly, just what was happening on the streets of Moscow. Schoolchildren were taught what to do, if the alarms sounded, but she had no faith in the system. The shelters had been designed for terrorist bombings, not for alien invasion. All the official dogma about how Mother Russia's vast size worked in her favour didn't apply to an enemy who controlled the high orbitals, ready and willing to drop KEWs on anything that moved. She knew just how effective orbital firepower had been against insurgents, during the later stages of the Age of Unrest. The barbarians simply hadn't realised just how advanced technology had become, nor how effective it could be when its users were no longer concerned about collateral damage. Every young man in Russia was expected to join the militia - if they weren't conscripted into the military - but she had no idea how they'd stack up against the aliens. There just wasn't enough data from New Russia on how the Tadpoles intended to treat humanity's homeworld.

"Captain, we have received a message directly from Pournelle Base," the communications officer said. "They're ordering us to remain where we are and prepare for fire-control duties, if necessary."

Svetlana tensed. "Was that message relayed through the drone?"

"Yes, Captain," the communications officer said. "But the aliens might have gotten a sniff of the original message."

"Understood," Svetlana said. "Send back an acknowledgement, then wait."

She kept her face impassive, even though it was bad news. If the aliens *had* picked up the original message, they might wonder who had *actually* been intended to receive it. Perhaps they'd dismiss it - humanity's home-world practically radiated with radio signals heading in all directions, most of which would be utterly incomprehensible to alien minds - but she didn't dare take it for granted. The aliens knew they'd been detected. It wasn't *that* much of a jump to think they might have accidentally crossed paths with a stealthed picket ship.

"Fucking Americans," Ignatyev growled. "They could have *killed* us!"

"Perhaps," Svetlana said. She watched the alien ships for a long moment. It didn't *look* as though they were preparing to blow *Brezhnev* into space dust, but that meant nothing. Her ship was far too close to them for her peace of mind. "But the aliens don't seem to have noticed."

She silently promised herself she'd file a complaint later, if there *was* a later. It would probably come to nothing, but it *might* give Uncle Sasha leverage in the ongoing Great Power negotiations. She had no doubt that her family would praise her achievement to the skies, particularly if she lost her life during the battle. They'd always found her more of an embarrassment than she knew they cared to admit. She couldn't help wondering if one of the reasons she'd been assigned to *Brezhnev* was her family hoping it would keep her out of sight and out of mind.

"The alien fleet is reducing speed again," the sensor officer reported. "They're launching sensor probes towards Earth."

"Watch for them sending anything to the rear," Svetlana ordered, curtly. "Helm, reduce speed to match."

"Aye, Captain," the helmsman said.

Svetlana nodded, then turned her attention to the in-system display. The system was going dark, hundreds of radio sources snapping out of existence as the alert raced across the solar system. Asteroid miners, freighters...they were trying to hide in the vastness of space, trusting that the aliens wouldn't be able to find them easily. Svetlana hoped they were right, although she feared the worst. The aliens had had plenty of time to note the locations of each and every radio source before they'd been detected.

And the planetary colonies couldn't hope to hide, she thought, grimly. If the Tadpoles won the coming battle, they'd be able to destroy the colonies, asteroid habitats and industrial nodes at leisure. *They'll be easy to find, once the aliens start looking.*

"They'll see us, sooner or later," Ignatyev warned. His face was very grim. He looked like a man in desperate need of a drink. "And then we're dead."

"I know," Svetlana said. The closer they got to Earth, the harder it was to justify sticking so close to the aliens. They were far too close for comfort. "But we have to keep an eye on them."

Her lips quirked into a cold smile. Ignatyev might be right. But if he was right, he'd be too dead to say he'd told her so. They'd all be dead.

And as long as we die bravely, she thought, *we might as well die for something.*

CHAPTER
NINE

Pournelle Base (USA), Earth Orbit

"We're picking up messages from across the system, sir," Captain Mike Hanson said. "The entire system is going dark."

"Very good," Admiral Jonathan Winters said, coolly. "Are the emergency procedures in place?"

"Yes, sir," Hanson said. He paused. "I don't know how effective they will be."

"Of course not," Jon said. "We never actually *tested* them, did we?"

He pushed his annoyance aside with an effort. The alien fleet had reduced speed twice, either preparing to launch starfighters or deliberately trying to lure him into sending Home Fleet to engage the enemy in interplanetary space. *That* would be a mistake. Home Fleet was stronger, numerically, but the alien technology gave them the edge. There was no way he could risk committing Home Fleet to battle until it was concentrated and, ideally, the alien forces had been worn down a little.

"Mars, Venus and the smaller colonies are activating their emergency procedures now, sir," Hanson said. "The asteroid miners should be able to avoid detection indefinitely."

Jon shrugged. He wasn't that concerned about the asteroid miners. The technology used to mine the asteroids, from tiny one-man ships to giant mobile refiners, was hardly difficult to replace. He was a great deal more concerned about the industrial nodes and the cloudscoops orbiting the gas giants. Losing the cloudscoops alone would do immense damage to the planetary economy. There *were* stockpiles of HE3 across the system, but he doubted they could meet demand until the cloudscoops were replaced. If Earth ran out of fuel...

"We'll worry about it later," he said. "Time to engagement?"

"Thirty minutes, unless they reduce speed again," Hanson said. He nodded to the display. "They're trying to keep us guessing."

"Or force us to put wear and tear on our equipment and personnel," Jon said. "Clever of them."

He rubbed his forehead as he contemplated the problem. Naval doctrine called for launching starfighters and bombers as quickly as possible, but *that* would tire his pilots before the battle even began. And yet, *not* getting them out into space risked losing them if the aliens took out their bases. The Tadpoles knew to go for the carriers. They could probably also guess which orbital installations carried starfighters of their own. They'd certainly seen orbital defence installations at New Russia.

"Order the CSP to remain on alert, but hold back the remaining starfighters," he ordered, grimly. "Have we primed the remainder of the defences?"

"Yes, sir," Hanson said. "All orbital installations have been alerted. Automated systems are coming online now, while missile pods are being deployed and linked into the planetary defence datanet. We'll be at peak readiness within twenty minutes."

"Let us hope so," Jon said. He frowned as another report came in from the long-range sensors. The detached alien squadron was heading straight for Home Fleet. "And the fleet?"

"Readying itself, sir," Hanson said. "The main body of the fleet will be concentrated in forty minutes, save for the Mars and Io detachments. They were caught out of position and will require more time to join the fleet."

Jon nodded, tersely. It was unfortunate, but it couldn't be helped. A civilian would probably have asked why the remaining detachments couldn't hit the enemy ships from the rear, yet anyone with any grounding in space combat would know the answer at once. Coordinating a battle on an interplanetary scale would be an absolute nightmare, even if spreading out his forces in the face of the enemy hadn't been a spectacularly *bad* idea. He'd seen a handful of fleet exercises where the planners had tried to be clever, but almost all of them had ended badly. A handful of the groundpounders had even had the nerve to accuse the umpires of rigging the game against them.

Their grand plans won't be workable until we find a way to send messages at FTL speeds, he thought. It wasn't something he'd wanted, when he'd stood on a command deck, but he saw the value of it now. Real-time updates from his detachments would be very useful, even if it would allow him to nag his subordinates. *And then the politicos will use it to micromanage.*

"Inform me when they finally link up with Home Fleet," he ordered. "And then start launching long-range probes towards the alien fleet."

"Aye, sir," Hanson said.

Jon studied the display, thinking hard. On one hand, the aliens had dropped the sensor mask, revealing their presence to anyone who cared to look. Cold logic told him that they'd seen his ships departing orbit and drawn the right conclusion. On the other hand, the aliens were flying in such close formation that they *had* to assume he couldn't pick one ship out from the others. If he hadn't had *Brezhnev* in position, they would have been right.

They don't think like us, he reminded himself, sternly. *They might not have any problem revealing themselves at this stage.*

Hanson coughed. "A shame we sent *Ark Royal* away, sir."

Jon shrugged. They'd made the best call they could with the information they'd had at the time, although he didn't expect the politicians to understand *that.* There would be recriminations aplenty after the battle, if there was anyone left to recriminate. Taking the offensive - hopefully knocking the aliens back long enough for humanity's space navies to adapt to the new reality - had seemed a good idea at the time. And pinning humanity's one major combatant that had a hope in hell of *hurting* the bastards, to a single planet, would have cost them the war. He had no doubt that the Tadpoles were adapting their tactics too.

"We'll have to cope without her," he said, dryly. "And I'm sure we will."

He leaned back in his command chair and took a sip of his coffee, trying to appear calm and composed even though his heart was beating like a drum. The defence of the solar system rested in his hands. *Earth* rested in his hands. If he failed, billions of humans would either be enslaved or killed. The Tadpoles would devastate the orbital industrial nodes, if nothing else. They weren't *that* alien. They'd know that destroying humanity's industrial base would be enough to win the war.

Hanson cleared his throat. "The Japanese and Chinese squadrons are finally ready to launch, sir," he said. "Two officers have apparently been removed by their direct superiors."

"Understood," Jon said.

He sighed, inwardly. There was a war on...and the various Great Powers were still playing games. But then, if a Chinese or Russian officer had been in charge of the planetary defences, he rather suspected that America would have qualms too. Hell, even getting an American to take command had been a political nightmare. The only officer who enjoyed universal support was Theodore Smith and *his* record was decidedly mixed.

But he did give us our first victories, Jon thought. *And that definitely counts for something.*

"Keep me informed," he said, putting the thought aside. "We have to be ready when the hammer comes down."

———

"They want us to stay here? Are they mad?"

Captain Ginny Saito kept her expression under tight control, even though she privately agreed with Lieutenant Bush Williams. The starfighters were lethal in space - all the more so now the squadron had been refitted with plasma guns - but they were utterly vulnerable as long as they remained in the station's launch bays. Hell, the fighter pilots themselves were sitting in the ready room, rather than manning their craft. She understood the logic - starfighters simply *didn't* have very long endurance - but she also understood the frustration. Her pilots *wanted* to get out there and start tearing into the enemy.

"The CO has issued his orders," she said, sharply. "And we will obey them."

She sat back in her chair, keeping her private frustration off her face. She'd been in the military long enough to know that you *never* bad-mouthed your seniors to your juniors, even if you thought it was just a harmless griping session. It was bad for discipline, if nothing else. *And* she did understand the orders they'd been given. Better to take the squadron directly into battle rather than risk running out of life support midway through the engagement.

"I'm just saying we're sitting ducks," Williams insisted. "What happens if they start throwing rocks at us?"

Ginny shrugged. "Sit down and shut up," she said, firmly. "We'll launch when we are *told* to launch."

She looked from face to face, silently gauging their feelings. The squadron had been on active duty *before* the war, but an assignment to home defence meant that they wouldn't have a chance to actually engage the enemy. Or so they'd thought. The big display was showing a host of red icons descending on Earth with murderous intent. God alone knew what the aliens would do, when they entered orbit, but she doubted it would be pleasant. She'd seen speculations of everything from a negotiated surrender to the complete destruction of humanity's homeworld.

And we lost friends at New Russia, she thought. She'd known a number of pilots who'd died in the brief, one-sided engagement. *We all want a little revenge.*

She forced herself to sit still, despite an overwhelming urge to get up and pace. *That* would have upset her squadron...she wondered, suddenly, if she had any paperwork she needed to do in a hurry. But that probably didn't matter. She'd seen too many of the reports from New Russia - and *Ark Royal's* engagements - to have any doubt about just how powerful the aliens actually *were*. The odds were stacked against any of her squadron surviving to see the end of the war.

"I knew I should have rewritten my will," Lieutenant George Faulkner said, suddenly. "That bitch in Los Angeles is going to get my pension, I know it!"

"Then try not to die," Williams advised. "You don't have time to write your will now."

Ginny rolled her eyes. Faulkner had been married twice and both relationships had been disastrous. Honestly! She didn't understand why he hadn't gone to Sin City on his last leave and spent some time in the brothels there. Or simply picked up a girl or boy in one of the bars that sprang up like weeds around military bases. It wasn't as if starfighter pilots, male or female, had any trouble finding company for the night. A flightsuit was just as good as a pheromone-tinged perfume for attracting the opposite sex and it had the advantage of being legal. But she supposed some people were eternal optimists. She wouldn't consider marriage herself until she left the service or took a desk job.

When hell freezes over, she thought, darkly. *If I survive long enough to say no when they offer it to me.*

She winced, inwardly, as she remembered her last...chat...with her parents. She'd come from a military family, but her father and grandfather had never quite reconciled to *Ginny* joining the military. She knew they meant well - she knew they didn't want to lose her - yet she still found it annoying. She'd joined the USN and worked her way through the hellishly tough starfighter training course. She'd *earned* her wings.

Although I also earned the chance to get my ass shot off, she reminded herself, wryly. *And that might have been a mistake.*

She didn't regret anything, really. And it wasn't as if she *intended* to remain single for the rest of her life. She'd have access to rejuvenation treatments when she retired, assuming she survived long enough *to* retire. There would be a husband, children...her father would have grandchildren, eventually. He'd just have to be patient.

I just wish I could message him one more time, she thought. *Just to say goodbye, just in case.*

She shook her head. She'd fallen out of the habit when she'd enlisted, knowing her father would do his level best to convince her to leave the training program. Anyone else who left, she was sure, would be called a quitter...at least by her father. Did he *want* his daughter to be a quitter? She smiled at the thought, although she knew it wasn't really funny. He'd find a way to rationalise it somehow, she was sure. Now...she wasn't sure if he'd be proud of her or if he'd be terrified. Perhaps it would be better to call him *after* the battle.

And besides, I might not be able to get a message out, she thought grimly. *The main communications network is down.*

A low hooting echoed through the ready room. The pilots looked up, then grabbed and donned their helmets as they prepared themselves for action. Ginny put her maudlin thoughts aside and checked her own helmet, bracing herself. They'd be launching in ten minutes, perhaps less. And then...

Williams cleared his throat. "Let all who go to don armour tomorrow," he announced dramatically, "remember to go *before* they don armour tomorrow."

Ginny face-palmed as the rest of the pilots snickered. "It was a mistake to let you watch that show, wasn't it?"

"I'm afraid there's going to be a certain amount of...*violence,*" Williams agreed. He put on a smarmy look that made Ginny want to hit him. "But at least we know it's all in a good cause, don't we?"

"Yeah," Ginny said. She made a mental note to find whoever had introduced William to *The Black Adder* and do something thoroughly horrible to him. Something lingering in boiling oil, perhaps. "We do."

Admiral Thaddeus Robertson had the uneasy sense that he was sitting on top of an unexploded bomb. It wasn't a sensation he liked - and he kept telling himself that he was being silly - but it refused to fade. USS *Enterprise* was the largest and most powerful carrier in human space...or she had been, two years ago. Now, she might as well have been made of paper for all the protection she'd give her crew if the aliens caught them. The engineers had bolted on great slabs of armour when the USN had realised just how vulnerable the carrier was - slowing her effective speed more than he cared to think about - but he had no illusions. A concentrated attack would be lethal.

He sat in the CIC, watching as Home Fleet gathered around the flagship. It was the largest fleet humanity had ever assembled, consisting of every warship in the system, yet he knew - all too well - that it had its flaws. The starships hadn't been *designed* to stand up to plasma fire, half his starfighters didn't have plasma cannons of their own and the crews just weren't *used* to working together. Everyone spoke English - it was the standard language outside the upper atmosphere - but they simply didn't have much else in common. And the international rivalries...

"The enemy squadron is approaching us," Commodore Jack Warner reported. "They'll be within engagement range in twenty minutes."

Thaddeus shrugged. He would have been astonished if the enemy squadron actually *attacked*, although he knew from bitter experience that the damned aliens had quite a few surprises up their sleeves. If the politics had worked out, *he* would have been in command at New Russia...and he knew, even if he didn't want to admit it, that it wouldn't have made a difference. The squadron approaching his ships might not be able to punch through his defences and inflict real harm before they were stopped, but it didn't matter. What *did* matter was that their presence would make it impossible to hide his movements.

"Order the fleet to engage stealth protocols," he said. It probably wouldn't fool the aliens for long, if at all, but it might keep them guessing. He'd take anything he could get. "Time to full concentration?"

"Thirty minutes," Warner said, slowly. He looked down at his datapad, then back at his commander. "Unless we wait for the Io detachment. That would add an extra twenty minutes to the wait."

Thaddeus considered it, briefly. Humanity knew *some* of the alien tricks - now - but he didn't dare assume that they knew *all* of them. Concentrating his entire fleet was obviously a good idea, yet...how long would it take? And how much damage would the aliens do to Earth in the meantime? There was enough firepower bearing down on the planet to give the combined fleet a very hard time. God alone knew just how many carriers and starfighters the aliens had. There was no way to tell just how badly they'd been hurt after each engagement.

"We'll move without them," he ordered, finally. It was a gamble, but the Io detachment wouldn't add *that* much to his firepower. "We cannot let them punch through to the high orbitals."

"Yes, sir," Warner said.

Thaddeus nodded, curtly. What would the aliens *do*? What were they planning? A smash and run raid, or an actual occupation? Did they even know themselves? A *smart* planner would have contingency plans for both, depending on how the battle went. For all he knew, they were planning to smash Earth to rubble and then spend the next few weeks hunting down every last settlement in the solar system. If that happened...

We'll just have to make sure it doesn't, he told himself, firmly. *And get to Earth as quickly as possible.*

He winced. His crews - *all* of his crews - would do everything in their power to get Home Fleet moving as quickly as possible. They were already cutting corners he knew they'd pay for, sooner or later. And yet, it would still take time to get the fleet on its way...time Earth didn't have. The aliens were already beginning their final approach.

And, until his fleet arrived, Earth would have to stand alone.

CHAPTER

TEN

London, United Kingdom

"They'll be within engagement range soon," the First Space Lord said, quietly. "It's out of our hands now."

Prime Minister Andrew Davidson shot him a sharp look. "You can't take command?"

"Admiral Winters is in command," the First Space Lord said. He sat facing Andrew, his face calm and composed. "And I'm on the ground. Admiral Cathy Mountbatten has already moved to Nelson Base. She'll take command if anything happens to Pournelle Base."

Andrew looked down at his hands, feeling helpless. He'd never really understood just how Churchill, Thatcher and Hanover must have felt, not until now. Countless British spacers were going into battle and he could do nothing, but wait for the results. He could issue orders, if he wished, yet it would be pointless. The fate of Earth was about to be decided and he could do nothing.

"Understood," he said, grimly. He looked at General Peter Templeton. "Are we ready for this?"

Templeton cleared his throat. "Almost certainly not, Prime Minister," he said. He spoke - again - from memory. "Military bases are on alert - mobile infantry units have been dispersed, in case the enemy takes control of the high orbitals. Political figures are currently being scattered around the countryside, where they *should* be relatively safe unless the aliens intend to scorch the entire planet. The command and control network is up and running, allowing us to keep in touch with our national units. If worse comes to worst, Prime Minister, our bases have orders to act on their own if they lose contact with London or Britain One."

Andrew met his eyes. "And what will they do?"

"What they see fit," Templeton said. "It's never been tested in real life."

"I know," Andrew said.

He'd taken a moment to review some of the contingency plans, but none of them had been designed for alien invasion. An all-out Great Power war had seemed far more likely. None of those plans had made reassuring reading, either. The planners had warned that orbital and nuclear strikes would probably be directed against Britain, both to wear down the ground-based defences and cripple the government and military infrastructure. Their worst-case scenarios had been the stuff of nightmares.

He forced himself to think about something else. "And the general public?"

"There have been...*incidents*," Templeton said. He looked down at the table. "Panic-buying, a handful of riots...we've deployed riot control units to deal with them, under the Security and Defence of the Realm Act. Several thousand rioters are now in a number of makeshift detention camps, awaiting processing. It's sheer bloody good luck that this happened so late at night."

Andrew nodded. The thought of hundreds of thousands of people trying to get home, blocking the roads and arguing with police officers, was chilling. It would have been an absolute nightmare. Hell, it was *still* going to be a nightmare. Far too many people probably *had* been caught away from home. Sorting out the mess would take weeks.

"Remind the policemen to be as gentle as possible," he said, softly. "We're not talking about insurgents or traitors here."

Templeton frowned. "With all due respect, Prime Minister, keeping the motorways clear is an absolute priority. We *have* to be able to move men and equipment around the country as quickly as possible. And frankly, we *don't* want looters on the streets. We'll need to make sure that food is distributed as fairly as possible."

Andrew scowled. "You mean, *useful* people get fed first."

"Yes," Templeton said. He didn't bother to try to deny it. "We will have to make hard decisions in the future."

"I saw those plans too," Andrew said, sharply. He wondered, briefly, if *he* counted as a useful person. Right now, his position seemed meaningless. "It won't be easy, will it?"

"No, Prime Minister," Templeton said. "But we do have matters under control, for the moment."

"That won't last," the First Space Lord warned. "The aliens will engage Earth's defences in the next ten minutes."

Andrew looked at him. He knew he was clutching at straws, but he had to try. "Did you not attempt to communicate?"

"We tried," the First Space Lord said. For a moment, he looked older - far older. "We planned for this, Prime Minister. We sent messages in everything from plain English to mathematical concepts. We *know* these bastards understand us; they're just not interested in *talking* to us."

"Some people need to be smacked around a bit before they pay attention," Templeton said.

Andrew frowned. "Is that what they taught you at Catterick?"

"At Kendrick Borstal," Templeton said. "I'd already mastered the art of listening when I went to Catterick."

"Oh," Andrew said.

He looked up at the display. Hundreds of starfighters were already visible, settling into formation as the alien starships made their final approach. Behind them, the planetary defences were preparing to fire. A handful of smaller displays simulated the battle, showing everything from a costly victory to a total defeat. Andrew knew better than to believe the simulations - long experience had told him that they couldn't be trusted - but one thing was clear. It was going to be a long and bloody engagement.

And there was nothing he could do.

He could go to bed, he knew. The Prime Minister *did* have a suite of rooms in the underground bunker. Indeed, it might be the *best* thing he could do. He'd be needed after the battle, although he had no idea - yet - if he'd have to offer surrender or start reconstruction. But he couldn't just go to bed, even though he was tired. He eyed the empty coffee mug balefully, wondering if he was on the verge of caffeine poisoning. Whoever had stocked the bunker had gone for potency over taste.

"Tell me something," he said, quietly. He wasn't sure which one he was addressing. "How did you cope? When you sent young men out to die?"

"It never gets any easier," the First Space Lord said, equally quietly. "You just learn to compartmentalise your feelings until afterwards. And then you deal with them in private."

Stiff upper lip and all that, Andrew thought. His tutors had believed, firmly, that all the troubles Britain had faced over the last two hundred years had come from a *lack* of stiff upper lip. They might have been right, he conceded privately, although he hadn't forgiven some of them for how they'd treated the students in their care. *Better a boy dies like a hero instead of living like a coward.*

He pushed the thought aside. "Do whatever you need to do," he said, quietly. "I'll be here."

"Yes, Prime Minister," the First Space Lord said.

Andrew watched them go, then keyed his terminal. The BBC was broadcasting a series of updates, all carefully bland and stripped of any useful data. But then, there were censors in the broadcasting offices now, making sure that nothing leaked out that might cause panic on the streets. Andrew had his doubts - the public was unlikely to believe bland reports once they saw lights in the sky - but there was no choice. A real panic would be utterly disastrous.

He looked around the conference room, feeling...old. The bunker was safe, unless the enemy knew where to find it *and* were prepared to drop heavy weapons on London. *He* was safe, while his people were suffering. Or would be suffering, once the aliens started dropping bombs on the planet. He'd pay a price for that, during the next election. If, of course, there *was* a next election. He doubted the Tadpoles cared one whit for democracy.

They can't be attacking us for nothing, he thought, desperately. *What do they want?*

He shook his head. There was no answer. And there was no choice, but to fight.

"RETURN TO YOUR HOMES! I SAY AGAIN, RETURN TO YOUR HOMES!"

Police Constable Robin Mathews braced himself as the police line formed at the end of the road. Hundreds of men and women were gathered outside the shops, forcing open the doors and windows as they tried - desperately - to stock up on food. None of them seemed to be paying any attention to the policemen, even though more and more police vehicles were arriving at any moment. They were too concerned about grabbing enough food to stay alive.

Stupid idiots should have stocked up while they could, he thought, darkly. The police line grew stronger by the minute, but he wasn't looking forward to wading into the crowd. *They really should have bought the damn food when they were told to buy it.*

He shook his head inside his helmet. *He'd* stocked up on food - his partners and he had shared the cost - but not everyone could afford it. And far too many people didn't really believe in the aliens. Who *would* have believed in them? The war had been hundreds of light years away. They didn't really want to believe it could come to Earth.

His earpiece buzzed. "We're going to have to clear them," the captain said. "Get your shockrods ready."

Robin muttered a curse under his breath as he drew his shockrod from his belt and activated it. The device glowed blue, something he'd been told was intended to intimidate anyone who wanted to pick a fight with the police. He had to admit it worked, but...he wasn't too keen on it. The police might have been armed for the last two hundred years, yet it wasn't something they *liked.* He'd always felt that there were times when it was better to keep the weapons out of sight.

And not to attack people who are scared, he told himself, curtly. *All hell is about to break loose.*

"THIS IS YOUR FINAL WARNING," the captain said, over the megaphone. "DISPERSE NOW AND RETURN TO YOUR HOMES. THERE WILL BE NO FURTHER WARNING."

Robin braced himself. Mobs were always dangerous. People were smart, but a mob was a dangerous beast. His eyes moved from person to person, silently noting the ones who were trying to slip away and contrasting them to the idiots who were urging the others on. Once the mob reached a certain level, it wouldn't need any encouragement any longer. Everyone would be swept up in the violence until they were shocked out of it.

"Shit," someone muttered, as the first beer bottle flew through the air and smashed on a riot shield. "Someone's been drinking."

"Here they come," someone else said.

The mob lunged at the police line, shouting and screaming. Robin held up his shockrod as the mass approached, then started striking people when they got too close to him. But the mob was too strong. The police line wavered as the rioters slammed into their shields, forcing some of the policemen backwards. Robin felt sweat trickling down his back as the shouting grew louder. He'd shocked a dozen rioters, perhaps more, but the rest of them just kept coming, shoving their stunned comrades up against the shields. Some of them were going to be seriously injured or worse. He'd seen rioters trample their former comrades during rugby matches.

"Brace yourself," the captain snapped. He sounded grim. "Screamers incoming!"

Robin resisted an insane urge to drop his shockrod and cover his fragile ears as the screamers flew overhead. Strobe lights flared, his visor darkening automatically to block out the worst of it. The sound was terrible, even through his earpiece. He had to fight to keep from turning and fleeing like the rioters. There was something about the screamers that unmanned everyone unlucky enough to be caught without protection. Using them on a riot...the captain had to be desperate. There would be hell to pay, afterwards. Questions would be asked in Parliament.

Darkness fell like a hammer. Robin blinked hard as his visor cleared, swallowing hard as he saw the remains of the riot. Some of the rioters had managed to escape, but the remainder were lying on the ground, covering their ears or rubbing their eyes. Most of them looked to have been sick, or lost control of their bowels. Guilt stabbed at him, even though he knew the rioters had been on the verge of smashing the police line. He hadn't become a copper for *this*!

"Anyone who wants to run, let them," the captain said, over the intercom. "The remainder...cuff them and get them in the vans."

It was hardly proper procedure, Robin knew, but no one seemed inclined to care. The majority of the rioters would run back home, where - hopefully - they'd stay until the crisis was over. If it was ever over. Robin was only a lowly constable, but he'd overheard a couple of senior officers discussing the possibilities in low voices. The entire planet was under attack and London, one of the most important cities in the world, might be among the first targets.

I should have taken the post in Cardiff, he thought, as he removed a collection of zip-cuffs from his belt and walked forward. *But I just had to go to London, didn't I?*

He reached the first rioter, a man who would have been intimidating if it wasn't clear he was wearing a pair of soiled pants. He'd probably been far too close to one of the screamers when it lit up. Robin checked his condition, just to be sure, then snapped on the cuffs. The man was burly, but offered no resistance. Robin wasn't too surprised. There was definitely *something* about the screamers that made it impossible to continue the fight. A handful of others moaned at him, but didn't resist. He allowed himself a sigh of relief as back-up finally arrived, carrying or dragging cuffed rioters to the vans.

"This one is dead, sir," Lieutenant Ryman reported. "Poor bitch had her head stamped on."

Robin looked, then swallowed hard to keep from throwing up. The girl's head had been smashed like an eggshell. Someone - probably several someone's - had crushed her during the riot. Her body was so heavily mutilated that he wouldn't have been sure she was female, if he hadn't been able to see breasts. She'd been young, he thought, probably in her early twenties. And now she was dead. He couldn't help wondering what she was *doing* on the streets. Was she desperate for food or had she scented excitement and rushed to the scene?

He pushed the thought out of his mind. There was nothing that could be done for her, even with modern medicine. She was just the first - one of the first - to die. If the aliens started raining rocks on Britain, she'd be the first of many. He muttered a brief update into his mouthpiece, then continued cuffing rioters too slow or too stunned to escape. Slowly, but surely, order was restored to the streets. The prisoners were handed over to the vans, who took them to a nearby stadium. It would serve as a detention centre until something better could be arranged.

"They stole a lot of food and drink," the captain said, as the police regrouped. A number of officers looked battered. Robin winced. The rioters had managed to get through the line in places, then. "And several of them stole more expensive shit too."

Robin wasn't surprised. There was always someone willing to take advantage of a crisis to enrich themselves. He was surprised there hadn't been *more* rioting, particularly in London proper. The capital never slept. Normally, hundreds of thousands of bright young things would be on the streets, drinking, dancing and trying to forget their lives for a few short hours. And yet...

He looked around, feeling a shiver running down his spine. The streets were eerily quiet. London normally never slept, but now...the underground was still, the streets were closed and most of the population safely behind closed doors. The only vehicles on the street belonged to the police, the military and various government officials as they struggled to prepare for the impending invasion. A line of army lorries rumbled past them, carrying tough-looking soldiers from the nearby barracks. They headed onto the bridges, narrowly missing a pair of diplomatic outriders escorting a diplomat to Whitehall. Robin was surprised the foreigners hadn't hunkered down in their embassies. He'd pulled guard duty at the French embassy, a couple of years ago. The building looked as if it had come straight out of the Sun King's France, but it was more heavily fortified than any of the police stations in London.

Maybe they have plans for future cleverness, he thought, as he helped pick up the handful of bodies and bag them up. There was nothing that could be done for them until after the crisis was over, when they'd be identified and the next-of-kin informed. *Or maybe they think they'll be safer out of the city.*

It was a tempting thought, he had to admit. A number of policemen hadn't reported for duty when the alert had gone off, even though they *should* have done. The streets were closed, but a savvy person could grab a boat and head upriver if they wanted. Or drift down to the sea...Robin would have been tempted himself, he admitted privately, if he hadn't believed firmly in his duty. And yet, the urge to grab his partners and just run from London was almost overwhelming. There were plenty of potential targets in and around London, but if he went further away he should be safe...

His earpiece buzzed. "Report to Alpha-Nine," a voice said. It took Robin a moment to place the speaker. One of the emergency staff from New Scotland Yard...the man who'd briefed them on the crisis. "Time is short. I say again, time is short."

Robin felt his blood run cold. The aliens were arriving. Their time was about to run out.

And no time to run, he told himself. *Whatever happens, we'll be here for it.*

CHAPTER
ELEVEN

Near Earth/Earth Orbit

The humans have established mass drivers on their satellite, the combat faction announced, bluntly. A ripple of unease ran through the Song. *This must be handled promptly.*

The combat faction steadied itself as more and more data flowed into its nexus. Mass drivers were not unexpected. The humans had used them to great effect in some of the more significant engagements. Indeed, the *real* frustration was that the factions responsible for designing and producing weapons hadn't thought of them before it was too late. Programs were already underway to copy and hurry ship-mounted mass drivers into production, but it was quite possible that workable hardware wouldn't be deployed until after the war.

They will have to be careful where they place their shots, tactical sub-factions noted. *A projectile that strikes their planet will do considerable damage.*

There was a hum of consensus. The fleet was already altering its position randomly, making it harder for the humans to get a solid lock on its hulls. There was no way to keep the humans from firing into their general vicinity, of course, but they'd have problems actually scoring hits. Indeed, counterbattery weapons were already primed to intercept the projectiles when they came screaming into range. And the humans *would* have to be careful not to strike their own homeworld. Even a relatively small projectile would be disastrous, if it struck the planet at a respectable fraction of the speed of light.

Redeploy formations to engage the lunar defences, the combat faction ordered. The closer they came to Earth, the greater the chance of the enemy scoring a lucky hit. *And prepare to launch starfighters.*

The planet is heavily defended, another sub-faction stated. *It is impossible to separate military installations from civilian.*

Another ripple of unease ran through the Song. Earth was *surrounded* by installations, everything from asteroid habitats to industrial nodes and defensive stations. It was hellishly impressive, particularly as the humans *hadn't* been out in space for *that* long. The various sub-factions couldn't help agreeing that there would have been trouble, sooner or later, even if First Contact hadn't gone so badly wrong. Humanity...was advancing into space at a terrifying speed.

The fleet altered course again, detaching three squadrons to attend to the lunar defences. The remainder of the fleet continued on a direct route to Earth. So far, there seemed to be no reason to be concerned. The human fleet was a potential danger, but the humans were trying to concentrate their forces before making a move to take the offensive. There would be a window to engage the planet's defences before their fleet entered the fray.

Launch starfighters, the combat faction ordered. New orders raced through the command network. *Prepare to engage the enemy.*

Captain Svetlana Zadornov hadn't dared leave the bridge since detecting the alien ships, even though part of her body cried out for rest. She'd already taken two stimulants, even though she knew from bitter experience that they weren't always trustworthy. The production factors prized speed over efficiency, often diluting the drugs or replacing them with water just to meet their quotas. There was no way to be *entirely* sure what she was shooting into her bloodstream.

I should have bought some of the American shit for myself, she thought, resisting the urge to rub her eyes. She didn't *think* her XO would try to relieve her in the middle of an engagement, but there was no point in taking chances. Showing weakness on the command deck was never a good idea, even for male officers. *But they'd catch up with me later.*

"Captain," the sensor officer said. "Two - no, *three* - enemy squadrons have detached themselves from the main body. They're heading to the moon."

"Update Pournelle Base," Svetlana said, automatically. Given how close they were to Earth, the enemy movement would be detected within minutes. They certainly wouldn't be able to materialise in the lunar skies and take the defenders by surprise. "Can you confirm their destination?"

"They're on a least-time course for the moon," the sensor officer said. He paused. "They may be deploying ECM drones."

"And the rest of their force is still heading for Earth," Zadornov commented. "Why aren't they moving to be out of Luna's range?"

Good question, Svetlana acknowledged. The Tadpoles were at the extreme edge of effective mass driver range, but it wouldn't be *that* hard to put Earth between their fleet and Luna. God knew the mass drivers couldn't shoot *through* the planet. *Are they desperate to do as much damage as possible before Home Fleet intercepts them or are they prepared to soak up a number of casualties to continue with a pre-planned offensive?*

She contemplated the problem for a long moment. Mother Russia knew *all* about sacrificing vast numbers of soldiers to push through enemy defences and claim victory, even though all the old tactics had long since gone out of fashion. Russia simply couldn't afford, even now, to trade thousands of lives for relatively small gains. Besides, replacing damaged or destroyed starships took time. The British or Americans might be able to produce a fleet carrier in nine months, assuming there were no unpleasant surprises, but Russia couldn't do it in less than twenty-two. Even *that* was far too optimistic for her taste.

"Let's not complain," she said. She wasn't blind to the dangers of hundreds of unguided projectiles racing through the enemy formation - passing far too close to her position - but there was nothing she could do about it. "Keep forwarding targeting data to Pournelle Base."

"Aye, Captain."

The tactical console bleeped an alert. "Captain, the enemy ships are launching starfighters," the tactical officer reported. "They're funnelling down towards Earth!"

Svetlana sucked in her breath. Two years ago, she'd *known* that individual starfighters didn't pose much of a danger to her ship. *Bombers* were the real problem, back then. But now, plasma cannons had turned starfighters into serious threats. A single pass, cannons blazing, had been more than enough to take out an entire fleet carrier. She had no illusions about the outcome if a squadron of enemy starfighters came after her ship. She'd only be able to hope that she managed to kill a handful of them before they blew her to atoms.

"Alert Pournelle Base," she ordered. "And keep a careful eye on their CSP."

She settled back into her chair, watching the blood-red starfighter icons as they streamed towards Earth. The Tadpoles didn't *seem* to have deployed a CSP, but that wouldn't last. If they thought anything like humans, they'd probably decided to keep the CSP back until the human defenders mounted a counterattack. Their starfighters *did* seem to have more endurance than their human counterparts, but they couldn't be *that* superior. Or so she hoped.

And if they come prowling up here, we're dead, she thought. She had no illusions about that, either. *But we'll stay here as long as we can.*

———

"The enemy ships are launching starfighters," Captain Mike Hanson reported. "They're coming straight for us."

Jon nodded, tersely. "Do we have a solid count?"

"No, sir," Hanson said. "There are too many of them for us to get a solid count. At least five hundred, perhaps more."

"Probably," Jon said.

He would have been surprised if there were *just* five hundred starfighters bearing down on the defenders. There were *fifteen* alien fleet carriers approaching Earth. It was impossible to be sure, but post-battle analysis from New Russia suggested that an alien carrier could deploy at least a hundred starfighters. They had it easier in some respects, he admitted. Their starfighters had a uniformity he could only envy. They certainly didn't have to refit launch decks to handle both starfighters and bombers.

And they can cram three extra squadrons into their hulls, he thought. *It gives them some additional punch.*

"Order our starfighters to launch," he said. He studied the display for a long moment, considering his options. "We'll proceed with Deployment Beta."

"Aye, Admiral."

Jon couldn't help feeling a flicker of relief, even though he knew it wasn't a good thing. The waiting was over. The engagement had finally begun. And yet, he knew he'd be glad to be bored again when it was all over. Far too many people were about to die.

The display updated rapidly as green icons poured out of their launch platforms and into interplanetary space. Two-thirds fell into CSP mode, patrolling the orbitals; the remainder boosting out of orbit and heading directly for the alien swarm. New alerts flashed up in his display, warning him that the bombers were arming for an anti-shipping strike. They'd be dispatched as soon as possible, once the alien starfighters were engaged...

They're going to take a hellish beating, Jon thought, numbly. The bombers were far too vulnerable to enemy point defence, even though humanity *had* come up with a few tactics that *should* deny the aliens some of their tricks. *God help us.*

"Admiral, the Luna defences are requesting permission to engage the enemy," Hanson said, looking up from his screen. "Should I clear them to fire?"

"As long as there's no real prospect of hitting Earth," Jon ordered. The enemy was clearly already aware of the potential danger. Three of their squadrons were on a direct course for the moon. "Order them to fire at will."

He sighed, inwardly. The odds of scoring a direct hit were very low. *Ark Royal* had fired at *much* closer ranges, aiming at an enemy who didn't appear to have *considered* building mass drivers of their own. It would require a freakish stroke of luck to score even one hit. And yet, it wasn't as if the mass drivers were short of raw material. Even *one* hit might tip the balance in humanity's favour.

"Signal sent, sir," Hanson said.

Jon nodded. There was little left to do, now. His subordinates had their orders. They knew what to do. And all *he* could do was wait and pray.

———

Captain Ginny Saito gritted her teeth as her starfighter was launched into space, keeping one eye on her defences. The cockpit was wide enough for her to see Earth as she spun the starfighter around, but she knew better than to waste time enjoying the view. Knife-range starfighter engagements were rare, although they'd become more common since the aliens had announced their presence. There was certainly no way she could steer her starfighter through visual input alone.

"Form up on me," she ordered, as she took in the situation. A swarm of alien starfighters - she could think of no other word that fitted - were racing directly towards Earth, bringing death in their wake. *Her* orders were to scatter the alien craft before they reached the high orbitals, a standard tactic she doubted would be wholly effective in this setting. The Tadpoles simply didn't deploy massed rows of bombers. "Prepare to engage the enemy."

She silently tallied the replies as more and more data flooded into her HUD, then led the squadron directly towards the enemy ships. This time, thankfully, there had been no equipment failures to ground one or two of her pilots. It had happened several times before as starfighters had been brought out of storage and reactivated, despite the best effort of the flight engineers. Then, it had been embarrassing and the unfortunate pilots had been the butts of hundreds of jokes; now, it would have trapped a couple of her pilots on the station, sitting ducks if - when - the aliens attacked. She wouldn't have wanted to be there, even if the odds of survival weren't in her favour. She didn't like being a sitting duck.

A civilian would have called her formation ragged, if they called it anything at all. Her pilots jinked from side to side automatically, as if they were already evading incoming fire. It looked as though she had no control at all. But a military officer would know better. A randomised formation would make it far harder for the enemy to predict their course and put a railgun pellet in their path. Ginny knew *precisely* what would happen if she struck a tiny pellet at high speed and it wasn't pretty. She'd be insanely lucky to survive.

Fancy formations are for President's Day, she thought, wryly. *Survival beats formation flying any day.*

She tapped a command into her console, bringing the plasma guns online. It felt warmer all of a sudden, as if she was sitting on an engine, even though she *knew* it was all in her imagination. She'd heard too many horror stories about early plasma weapons overheating and exploding, taking their starfighters and pilots with them. Even now, after the alien weapons had been reverse-engineered and put into mass production, there were too many problems with the plasma guns for her to feel comfortable *using* them. But she knew, all too well, that without the plasma guns they wouldn't stand a chance.

"On my mark, break and attack," she ordered. The alien starfighters were drawing closer, ducking and weaving in their own version of the human formation. She wondered, grimly, if any of the pilots facing her had been at New Russia. Killing *those* aliens would be very satisfying. She *wanted* some payback, damn it. "Prepare to move..."

She leaned forward, bracing herself. "Attack!"

Her starfighter twisted as she opened fire, shooting a stream of super-hot plasma towards the nearest alien starfighter. The alien formation came apart, then reformed into a very different hunting formation...part of her mind admired their skill, even as they started to return fire with savage intensity. Either their plasma guns were still better, she noted, or they weren't particularly concerned about the risk. They were firing madly, shooting even when there was only a faint chance of actually scoring a hit.

An alien starfighter loomed in front of her. She snapped off a shot, blowing the alien craft into a fireball, then evaded as another starfighter targeted her. Lieutenant Powers blew it away seconds later, only to die himself as a third alien craft blasted him in the back. Ginny avenged him, then spun her starfighter like a top as three more alien craft appeared, firing madly. It looked, very much, as though they'd set their plasma guns to auto-fire.

"I can't shake him," Lieutenant Yu snapped. His voice was composed, but she heard an undertone of panic. "Help!"

"On my way," Ginny said. Yu was twisting and turning desperately, but the alien pilot chasing him seemed to have no trouble keeping up with him. "Fly straight, just for a second."

She smiled, savagely, as the alien fell into a predictable firing position. The enemy pilot was focused on his prey, *too* focused. He - or she - didn't even notice Ginny before she slipped right into his blindspot and blew him away. It was a very *human* problem, she noted as she twisted her starfighter through space. And yet...the thought that she might have something in common with her enemies disturbed her. She'd always assumed she'd face Chinese or Russian pilots in combat, yet...

We can talk to them, she thought. She'd enjoyed some of her chats with Russian and French pilots, although the Chinese and Japanese had been more standoffish. *And these bastards refuse to talk to us.*

She broke through into a patch of clear space and hastily checked her HUD, trying to get a sense of the overall situation. A third of the alien starfighters seemed to have stayed behind to dogfight with her and the rest of the squadrons, while the remainder were still heading directly towards Earth. The CSP was already moving to intercept, the automated weapons platforms turning to provide last-ditch back-up. She wondered, suddenly, what would happen to the missile pods. Firing *now* ran the risk of wasting them - the alien point defence was far too good - but holding them back gave the aliens a chance to pick them off before they could be deployed. She hoped the admiral made the right decision when the time came to act.

An alien starfighter dropped into attack position, right behind her. Ginny cursed and kicked the drive forward, spinning her craft through a series of evasive manoeuvres. The bastard kept on her tail, following her with all the persistence of a half-drunk suitor too stupid to realise that he'd already been given an answer. She felt a flicker of admiration, mingled with cold hatred. The alien pilot *had* to have real experience. No simulator ever designed could teach pilots *all* the tricks of the trade. And that meant he'd been on New Russia.

Her thoughts were cold and hard. *Tell me, who did you kill? Which of my friends died at your hands?*

She braced herself, then yanked her craft around until she was racing directly *towards* her pursuer. The alien seemed to flinch - although it could have been her imagination - and then opened fire, spraying plasma bolts like machine-gun fire. Ginny jammed her finger on the firing key, returning fire as the range closed with terrifying speed. A bolt of plasma passed so close to her starfighter that she saw it with her naked eye, a second before the alien craft was blown to dust. She flew right through where the alien starfighter had been, wishing she had time for a proper victory roll. But the fighting was still going on.

"The enemy carriers are still closing," the CAG noted. New updates flickered to life on her display. The enemy didn't *seem* to think their carriers were also battleships - in that, if nothing else, they agreed with their human enemies - but they did pack some considerable firepower of their own. "Prepare to regroup."

Ginny sucked in her breath as the starfighters raced back towards Earth. She'd lost four of her pilots, *four*. And the other squadrons looked to have been hurt just as badly. And the battle had only just begun...

CHAPTER
TWELVE

Near Earth/Earth Orbit

The Combat Faction tallied the aftermath of the first strikes with a profound sense of displeasure.

Losses had been higher for the humans, the various sub-factions noted, but their own losses hadn't been *small*. The humans had upgraded their weapons - one analysis faction claimed that the humans must have captured a starfighter at some point, although the others insisted that that was suspiciously optimistic - and their tactics had clearly been improved too. Their defences had been weakened, but...*insufficiently*.

We cannot withdraw now, the faction announced. *We must deploy missile strikes at once.*

The Song shifted as new voices demanded to be heard. On one hand, deploying the missiles might just weaken the human defences; on the other hand, the risk of accidentally striking the human homeworld could not be ruled out. Some of the factions didn't care - the only good human was a dead human - but the others overruled them. Genocide - deliberate or accidental - could not be tolerated. The humans would certainly retaliate in kind, once they realised their homeworld had been depopulated. And it was a great deal easier to wreck a world than occupy it.

The enemy defences are holding their own, the faction concluded. The Song rose to a crescendo as consensus was - once again - formed. *We must increase our attempts to weaken them before it is too late.*

There was a pause as new orders were formulated. *Launch missiles.*

————

"Admiral," Hanson said. "The enemy starships are launching missiles."

Jon turned to the display, gritting his teeth as the red icons appeared. The aliens were firing at long range...*far* too long range. His defences would have plenty of time to come to grips with the missiles, which meant...either the aliens were being stupid or they had something hidden up their sleeves. Perhaps it was a diversion. But if it *was*, he'd expect to see something else...

"Order the point defence to engage as soon as possible," he said. "And alert the starfighters to engage the missiles as they pass."

"Aye, Admiral," Hanson said.

The missiles picked up speed rapidly, pushing their drives to the limits. *They* didn't have to worry about crew who'd be squashed flat if the compensators failed...and yet, they weren't *that* fast. His point defences were already tracking them, preparing to engage with plasma cannons and railguns. The aliens wouldn't even get *close* to his facilities before they slammed into the point defence. Unless that was what they *wanted* him to think.

He switched his attention back to the starfighters. A mass of alien craft had entered orbit, firing madly at everything within range, but they'd done relatively little damage. The panic after New Russia had done *some* good, he conceded reluctantly. Mounting weapons on everything from commercial relay satellites to asteroid habitats ensured that the enemy starfighters had to run one hell of a gauntlet before they reached the *real* targets. A great deal of equipment would have to be replaced, after the battle was over, but that wouldn't be a problem. He'd be glad of it, as long as they soaked up missiles and plasma fire that would otherwise be aimed at something vital.

And our own starfighters have held up well, he thought. *They're not being brushed aside by superior firepower and speed.*

"Admiral," Hanson said. "The alien missiles are *still* picking up speed."

Jon bit down a curse. The alien missiles were the fastest things in known space, showing an acceleration curve that was frightening as hell.

No *manned* ship would be able to hit that speed unless there was a revolutionary compensator breakthrough...he pushed the thought aside, hard. The missiles were far more of a threat than he'd assumed.

"Order the point defence to engage," he ordered, sharply. The original calculations would have to be tossed out the airlock. Thankfully, there should be enough time to redo them before it was too late. "And then alert their potential targets."

He cursed the aliens under his breath. *Regular* missiles would be going ballistic by now, falling onto predictable trajectories. But the aliens...even if they'd just over-engineered the missiles, they'd thrown all his calculations for a loop. He didn't even have a definite idea of what they were targeting, although he had some suspicions. The aliens had to be able to pick some of the more important targets out of the halo of installations surrounding Earth.

Including Pournelle Base, he thought, numbly. *They might target us.*

———

"Jesus Christ!"

Captain Ginny Saito barely heard the curse as she tried to jockey her starfighter into an interception position. The speeds the alien missiles were pulling were terrifying, even though she *knew* they weren't aimed at her starfighter. She was used to flying the fastest thing in space and the alien missiles threatened to outrace her easily.

The fastest manned *thing in space*, she corrected herself, as she shifted her plasma guns to automatic. No human could hope to react in time to engage the missiles with guns. *I couldn't hope to catch up with the missiles if I had to give chase.*

Her guns opened fire a second later, spewing plasma fire into the void. A missile vanished from the display, followed by two more as they flew too close to the rest of the squadron, but the remainder flashed past them and continued to roar towards Earth. The squadron had just been caught out of position, utterly unaware that it would need to adjust course to intercept the missiles...there were other starfighters, nearer the planet, but they'd have the same problem. She could only hope that the missiles weren't aimed at the planet itself. A single hit at *those* speeds would be utterly disastrous.

And they might not even be aiming *at the planet,* she thought. *They might miss their targets and slam into the planet instead.*

Her threat receiver bleeped as an alien starfighter locked onto her. She threw the starfighter into an evasion pattern, trying to dodge a hail of plasma fire before it was too late. There was nothing she could do for the people closer to Earth, not now. All she could do was fight to survive...

...And hope there was a planet left, after the battle was over.

—————

"A handful of the missiles were taken out," Hanson reported. "Two more appeared to self-destruct."

Jon frowned. It *was* possible that the Tadpoles had overpowered the missile drives to the point where a single disharmonic flicker was enough to rip the entire drive unit to atoms. A brute-force solution *might* be workable, although he was all too aware that the cost would be staggering for very little return. Long-range missiles had been on the drawing board for years, but no one had been able to make them workable. The Tadpoles might have punched their way through a few of the issues, yet the rest remained.

"Let us hope the others go the same way," he said. The missiles were entering terminal attack range now, their targets suddenly becoming very clear. "Or that we manage to take them down before it's too late."

—————

"I can't see the fucker," Lewis Dennison said. "I can't..."

He cursed as he manoeuvred the worker bee around Tidemark Asteroid. He'd never expected to be on the front line of a war, not when he'd accepted the job of maintenance worker on an asteroid crammed with the rich and powerful. It was the ultimate gated community, he'd thought when he'd seen the job advertisement, but it came with plenty of benefits for a retired asteroid miner and his family. Hell, the school on the asteroid was so vastly superior to anything on Earth that he'd been determined to do whatever it took to keep his kids on the asteroid, even if it meant taking a pay cut. But now...

I should have taken them out to the belt, he thought. It wasn't as if there weren't plenty of independent, semi-independent and corporate asteroids that had schools of their own, although they were intensely focused on space-based technologies and jobs rather than anything more interesting. *But I had to stay here, didn't I?*

He swallowed, hard, as the alien missile came closer. The damned thing was moving at a terrible speed, fast enough to leave his worker bee in the dust. Lewis didn't have the slightest idea who'd thought it was a good idea to stick a pair of lasers on the tiny craft and call it part of the asteroid's defences, but he would have loved to meet the idiot up a dark alley one night. Dealing with space junk was one thing, dealing with incoming missiles was quite another. The lasers weren't even that powerful.

The lasers fired. Lewis thought, just for a second, that they'd actually hit their target, but the alien missile appeared unaffected. It was still coming...he stared, then jammed the worker bee forward, intending to put it between the missile and its target. But the goddamned craft was too slow. The missile raced past him and slammed into the asteroid, punching through the rocky exterior. A second later, it exploded.

Lewis could only stare in horror as the asteroid shattered, pieces of rocky debris flying out in all directions. His kids had been on the asteroid, his kids and his wife...*hundreds* of families had been on the asteroid...all dead. Tidemark Asteroid had shelters, of *course* it had shelters, but they weren't designed to survive a missile strike. The nuclear blast had not only smashed the asteroid, it had destroyed the shelters as well. His kids...

The radio hissed at him, barking orders. Lewis could barely hear it over the ringing in his ears. His kids were dead. Pieces of debris were falling into the atmosphere now, some of them easily large enough to cause real trouble if they hit the surface. Others...he hoped, with a vindictiveness that surprised him, that an alien ship crashed into a piece of rock and was smashed to rubble. He wanted to throw his tiny craft directly into their formation, to ram one of their carriers for himself, but he knew it wouldn't solve anything. Even if he made it through their point defence, he doubted he'd do more than scar their hull. It wouldn't be enough to pay them back for what he'd lost.

Tears brimmed in his eyes as he keyed the radio. Orders popped up a moment later, telling him to keep the debris from falling into the planet's atmosphere. Lewis almost laughed at the sheer absurdity of the orders. What the hell did they think he was flying? A heavy-lift tug? A worker bee barely had enough thrust to move under its own power. God knew he'd never win any goddamned races in his little craft. A starfighter would outrace him in seconds...

He forced himself to remain calm as he looked around for a piece of debris he could push into a stable orbit, but there were none. Most of the bigger pieces were heading down - Tidemark Asteroid hadn't been the *only* target, he noted - and there was no way he could stop them. He didn't want to *think* about what would happen when they hit the ground. Some pieces would break up, he was sure, and others would be smashed by the defences, but...

His kids were dead. And there was nothing he could do.

A piece of debris flew past him. He steered the worker bee after it, knowing he'd be lucky if he managed to catch up before the rock fell into the atmosphere. But what else could he do?

———

"Seven asteroids and five industrial nodes have been hit," Hanson reported. "Death tolls..."

"Save it," Jon growled. The industrial nodes had been evacuated, when the alien fleet arrived, but there had been no time to evacuate most of the civilian asteroids. *Some* people had made it out...he shook his head. In hindsight, the asteroids should have been evacuated long ago. "Have the ground-based defences been alerted?"

"Yes, sir," Hanson said. "They're already engaging pieces of falling debris."

"Order the orbital defences to engage as well, if they're not otherwise occupied," Jon said, grimly. "And prepare the bomber flight to launch."

"Aye, sir," Hanson said.

Jon nodded, grimly. The alien fleet had done immense damage...there was no way to avoid it. It could be repaired, of course, but not quickly. Losing so many civilians would probably have bad effects too. Earth's asteroid halo played host to some of the most powerful people in the solar system. Now...he didn't want to know how many of them had died. The halo's reputation for safety - established during the later years of the Age of Unrest - had drawn hundreds of thousands of people to orbit.

He pushed the thought aside. Most of the falling debris would either burn up in the atmosphere or be blown to bits before it reached the ground, but *some* pieces would get through. His orbital defences had too many alien ships to engage, while there were places that *couldn't* be defended by the planetary defence centres. A large chunk of debris that fell into the Pacific Ocean would send tidal waves racing across the globe. Hundreds of thousands of people would die.

And we can't do anything about it, he told himself, grimly. *We just have to keep fighting and hope for the best.*

He looked at his aide. "What's the latest update from Admiral Robertson?"

"Home Fleet will be ready to move into position to engage the enemy in twenty minutes, once they've completed their concentration," Hanson said. "They're currently preparing their counteroffensive."

"Good," Jon said.

He was tempted to order Hanson to tell Admiral Robertson to expedite, but he knew it would be pointless. Home Fleet would be moving as fast as possible. He contemplated the vectors for a long moment, wondering if it would be worth advising Admiral Robertson to try to pin the aliens against the moon. If the lunar mass drivers survived that long, the aliens would be in some trouble. Maybe they'd underestimate the threat. So far, the mass drivers hadn't struck a single target.

The display updated again, warningly. A dozen pieces of rock were going to strike the surface, despite the planetary defences. And that meant...

All hell is going to break out down there, Jon thought. It had been *decades* since the last major terrorist attack...and *that* had been several orders of magnitude smaller than a single asteroid strike. *There will be utter panic.*

"Admiral, they're launching another set of starfighters," Hanson reported. "And recalling their first squadrons."

"I see," Jon said. It wasn't the pause in the storm he wanted, but it would have to do. "Order the starfighter squadrons to regroup and reform, then deploy half of them to cover the bombers."

"Aye, sir," Hanson said. "The bombers will take heavy losses."

"I know," Jon said, sharply.

He closed his eyes for a long moment. On the display, the alien squadrons were approaching the moon.

At least we have a decent chance of blasting them with the mass drivers, he thought. *But they'll be shooting back at us all the time.*

———

Lily had been told, time and time again, that when the emergency alarms sounded, she had to go straight to the nearest shelter and hide there. Eight-year-old girls weren't meant to do anything else, she'd been told. If her parents weren't there, she was to speak to the nearest adult and get them to report her presence...once she was in the shelter. Going to the shelter was *important*. But the handful of adults in the shelter didn't seem to have any time to help her, if they'd even *noticed* her. They were panicking, shouting words Lily had been told never to use. And the lights were flickering...

She told herself, firmly, that she needed to be grown-up. She wasn't a *baby*. Her parents trusted her. But she wanted them, desperately. She wanted to be told that everything would be fine. And yet...she'd never seen the lights fail before. The asteroid was safe. Her parents had told her so many horror stories about Earth that she had no intention of ever living there.

The floor shook under her feet. She checked her suit quickly, silently grateful that her parents had forced her to learn how to put it on without help. Whatever was going on, it had to be bad. The grown-ups were looking around, frantically. The gravity seemed to grow stronger for long moments, then weaken until they were almost in zero-g. Lily wished, desperately, that her parents were there, but they were...doing something. If she'd stayed with her friend...

A long rumble echoed through the air. The gravity failed completely. She looked up, just in time to see pieces of dust and stone falling from the ceiling. The grown-ups screamed at her to put on her helmet, an instant before the shelter shattered around her. Air rushed past her, snatching her helmet out of her hands and tossing it...tossing it into space. Earth glowed below her, blue and green against the darkness of space. There were...*things*...nearby, falling towards the planet...she felt herself moving, an instant before *someone* grabbed hold of her leg. She twisted, just in time to see one of the grown-ups pulling her back. He was holding a life-support bubble in one hand, the device automatically inflating. She tried to remember how to use it as he pushed her into the bubble, an instant before he lost his grip and plunged up - or down - towards Earth. And then the bubble itself started to move as a piece of...*something*...slammed into it.

Lily started to scream. But it was already far too late.

CHAPTER
THIRTEEN

Ward Mansion, Penzance, United Kingdom

"Nothing useful on the BBC, of course."

Molly nodded, tersely. Lady Penelope seemed to want Garrison and her to stay in the main room, even though she would have preferred to wait somewhere else. But the hall was quiet, now that two-thirds of the staff had left to see to their own families. Molly wished she'd thought to see if one of them had a working car before they'd gone, but she'd been too busy trying to draw something - anything - off the datanet.

"Of course not," Garrison said. He sat on a comfortable chair, drinking a glass of wine. "The BBC never tells us anything useful."

"There'll be people in the offices, making sure that nothing inconvenient gets out," Lady Penelope said. "Like the truth, for example."

Molly shook her head in grim disbelief. She'd grown far too used to modern telecommunications. A few hours ago, she'd been able to talk to someone on the far side of the planet - or even the moon - without any significant delays. She certainly hadn't been more than an hour or two away from home. But now her world had shrunk and the distance between Penzance and Woking seemed insurmountable. She remembered rolling her eyes, in history class, at just how small Britain had been in the past. Now, she understood just how many limitations her ancestors had faced. They'd certainly never been able to fly to France, let alone halfway around the planet, for breakfast.

She glowered at the television set. It wasn't telling her anything *useful*, beyond vague reports of troubles on the streets and - once again

- incoming alien ships. There was certainly nothing she wanted to hear, starting with when the curfew would be lifted. She'd checked the phone every twenty, but the network remained down. There was no way she could send a message to her children.

"Sit down," Lady Penelope said. She indicated the drinks cabinet. "Have a drink?"

"No, thank you," Molly said. She just didn't *want* to drink. Alcohol led to bad decisions, in her experience. God knew she'd already drunk far too much. The sober-up had cleared her system, but left her feeling weak at the knees. She really needed to get some rest. "I don't know what to do."

Garrison eyed her, blearily. "There's nothing you *can* do," he said. His voice was very flat. His hand shook as he poured himself yet another glass. "I think we should go to bed."

Molly scowled at him. To think she'd thought highly of him, once upon a time. She felt sick when she remembered what they'd been doing in his car. To think she'd...she felt her gorge rise and suppressed it, ruthlessly. She was *not* going to throw up on Lady Penelope's carpet, whatever else she did. Knowing her luck, the carpet was worth more money than her entire family would see in their entire life.

"I can't sleep," she said, crossly. She hoped he'd take the hint. He was already half-drunk. If he decided to push his claim on her, she'd have to knee him in the groin and hope she didn't wind up being arrested for assault. She doubted the charges would stick, but it would reveal to *everyone* what she'd been doing. "Go to bed if you want."

She wandered over to the drinks cabinet and inspected the contents. As she'd suspected, everything was expensive beyond belief. There were no non-alcoholic drinks, no energy drinks...she was tempted to ask for a glass of water, but she had no idea if there *was* any water. The nasty part of her mind speculated that Lady Penelope might not even know how to work the tap! No doubt she had a servant who turned the water on and off for her.

The thought saddened her, even though she knew it was probably nonsensical. Lady Penelope - and Garrison - had grown up in a world of utter privilege. They'd been surrounded by servants from birth to...to now. And it had warped them beyond recognition. Garrison had considered himself entitled to her - probably *still* considered himself entitled to her - but he didn't even know how to drive a car! She'd wanted to move into the upper crust, yet...had it really been a good idea? What would happen to her children if they were raised amongst the nobility?

"Ah," Lady Penelope said. She jabbed a finger at the screen. "This might be more interesting."

"...Enemy forces have engaged Earth's defenders," the BBC talking head said. He sounded flat, utterly atonal. "Fighting has spread through the orbital defences..."

Garrison looked up. "We should be on the roof," he said. He stood, picking up the bottle as he moved. "Let's go."

Molly exchanged glances with Lady Penelope, then followed Garrison up a tiny stairwell and onto the roof. Some of the party had been held there, she recalled, although she hadn't had a chance to see for herself before the alert had sounded. Now, there were a handful of tables scattered around the rooftop, covered with the remains of a buffet. Molly wondered, as she looked up, just how much food had been wasted. She had a nasty feeling they'd come to regret the loss in the next few days.

"My God," Garrison said.

Lights flickered, high overhead. Molly stared, unable to look away. She'd never seen the halo, but she'd heard Kurt's stories. Hundreds of asteroids, thousands of industrial nodes, defence stations and...her imagination failed her. She'd vaguely considered trying to find a home there, once upon a time. But Kurt had never been interested in moving and the idea had died, back when they'd both taken their marriage seriously. Now...

She watched lights twinkle into existence, then vanish into the darkness. It was hard to believe, as the lights grew brighter, that there were living people up there, fighting to survive against a merciless onslaught. She wondered, grimly, if the lights were starfighter pilots dying...she'd met a few of Kurt's buddies when they'd been dating, years ago. If Kurt had been called back to service, how many others had been recalled too? Did she *know* anyone up there?

The sound of helicopters echoed through the night. She looked north, realising - for the first time - just how dark the landscape had become.

Lady Penelope's hall didn't seem to have lost power - it was possible that there was a generator in the basement - but the remainder of the country was chillingly dark. Or maybe there was no one out there...she couldn't recall if there were any small towns or villages close to the estate.

She turned and looked west. Penzance was still visible, a faint glimmer of light against the darkness. The power wasn't out, then. Or perhaps the government felt it needed to keep the cities lit up. She wondered at it for a long moment, as she peered towards the distant waters. There were fewer lights on the sea than she recalled, but they were still there...

A cold wind blew across the estate. She shivered, wishing she'd thought to bring a proper coat. The one she had brought was good enough to protect her dress - although the dress itself was in pretty poor condition - but not good enough to keep her warm. She shivered again as she looked up, watching the lights dancing across the sky. It was almost beautiful, in a way. And yet, she knew there were men and women dying up there.

"Remarkable," Garrison said. He held out the bottle. "Would you like a drink?"

"No, thank you," Molly said, tartly. "Put the bottle down and *watch*."

Garrison ignored her, lifting the bottle to his lips and taking a swig. Molly sighed and turned her attention back to the skies. Pieces of fire seemed to be dipping into the atmosphere, falling like fireworks and petering out somewhere high overhead. She shivered, once again, as she realised what it meant. The orbital defences were taking a beating and the debris was falling from the skies...

"You're cold," Garrison said. He stumbled up next to her and wrapped an arm around her shoulders. "Let me warm you up."

Molly gritted her teeth as his fingers started to fiddle with her coat, trying to open the way to her breasts. She had no idea if they could repair their relationship - she had no idea if she *wanted* to repair their relationship - but right now she felt nothing but utter revulsion at the thought of him touching her. His fingers kept probing...she stepped back, then pushed him away as hard as she could. Garrison stumbled and sat down hard. The bottle of alcohol crashed to the ground and shattered, spilling everywhere. He stared at her as if he couldn't quite believe what had happened.

"That...that was a '66 Claret, you...you *peasant*," he managed. He definitely *sounded* drunk. Molly hoped he'd forget everything after a long night's sleep. "You..."

"I suppose I should stick to the gin," she said, tartly. She'd *definitely* gone off him. "And perhaps a little beer, when I'm feeling frisky."

A light blazed, high overhead. She looked up, just in time to see... *something*...burning through the upper atmosphere, followed by several more. A handful seemed to vanish - she thought she saw beams of light touching them - but the others kept going until they fell over the horizon. She stared, feeling oddly uneasy. There was something about it that nagged at her mind, something important...

There was a brilliant flash of light, just over the horizon. Molly covered her eyes as night turned to day, too late. Moments later, there was a long roll of thunder. The sound was so loud that she dropped to the rooftop, covering her ears as best as she could. And then silence fell so sharply she could hear birds hooting in the trees. They must have been woken up by the thunder.

"...Fuck," Garrison managed. He stumbled onto his knees, looking unsteady. "What was that?"

"I don't know," Molly said. She vaguely recalled seeing *something* that looked like it, but she couldn't remember what. "I..."

Her smartphone bleeped. She jumped, then reached for the device. She'd assumed it was useless, now the network had been deactivated. And yet, an emergency message was blinking on the display, warning her to seek high ground. She stared down at it, unable to comprehend what she was seeing. High ground? Why?

Something...*shifted*...in the air. She turned and looked east, suddenly *certain* that something was out there in the darkness. And yet, there was nothing...she looked from side to side, trying to see what might be lurking there. She wished, suddenly, for a pair of night-vision goggles, something that would help her see in the dark. Kurt had loved to buy little devices like that, when they'd had the money. She knew where they were. She'd just never thought to bring them with her.

"The boats," Garrison said. "*Look!*"

Molly followed his pointing finger. The lights on the waters were *rising* into the air...she stared, unable to comprehend what she was seeing. How could a boat rise into the air? She'd seen seaplanes - she'd even seen a couple of luxury yachts that doubled as airplanes - but why would they be flying now? And then it dawned on her. The *water* was rising...

"My God," she breathed.

A great swell of *darkness* was rushing towards them at terrifying speed. Whatever had hit the water had started a *tidal* wave...she stared, transfixed. She wanted to turn and run, but where could she go? There was nowhere to hide, as far as she knew. They were already on the highest part of the estate. She wished, suddenly, that she'd started walking as soon as they discovered the cars were useless, but...she would have been caught on the roads. The water would have crushed her like a bug.

She could hear it now too, a roaring thunder that chilled her to the bone. Penzance went dark, the lights vanishing into nothingness...she said a quick prayer for the citizens, many of whom wouldn't have the chance to escape before the water crashed over their home. And then it dawned on her that the waters were going to rush over the estate...the waves were losing power fast, but not fast enough.

"Get down," Garrison snapped, as the roaring grew louder. "Hang on for dear life!"

Molly threw herself down, unsure what to grab...the hall was solid, but was it solid enough to withstand such an impact? Her fingers found a hatch in the rooftop and clutched tight, just as the water slammed into the building. The hall quivered - it suddenly felt chillingly fragile - and water showered down over her, smashing the remains of the tables and destroying the buffet. Molly yelped as ice-cold water drenched her skin, trying desperately to hold on...

The water drained, slowly. Her entire body was trembling, helplessly, as she forced herself to stand up. The coat was waterlogged...goosebumps rose on her skin as a cold wind followed the tidal wave, mocking her. She tore the coat off, ignoring just how much the dress clung to her curves now it was wet. The tidal wave seemed to have vanished in the darkness, but...

She forced her way to the railing and looked down. The estate had gone completely dark, but she could hear water splashing below her. Her feet felt oddly unsteady, as if the building was suddenly a boat...she wondered, as she looked up, just how much damage the water had done. Penzance was still wrapped in darkness...she couldn't see the boats any longer, let alone anything else. Even the birds were silent. It was easy to believe, all of a sudden, that she was the last person on Earth.

"Dear God," Garrison said. He sounded sober, all of a sudden. His clothes dripped water too. "What was that?"

Molly hugged him, tightly. It wasn't lust, not really. It was...it was the sheer relief of knowing she was *not* alone. Her body started to respond, but she choked it down hard. She didn't want anything right now, apart from a hot bath and a warm bed. But she had the feeling she wasn't going to get either of them right now.

She took one last look towards Penzance - or where Penzance had been - and then followed Garrison down the stairs. Water had washed into the house, turning the tiny steps into slippery nightmares. The emergency lights had come on, but half of them were dim and the other half had failed. She had to struggle to keep from slipping and falling as they reached the lower floor and headed down to the study. Doors and windows had been blown open, water flooding into the giant building...she looked into the library and almost cried when she saw the piles of sodden books on the floor. There was no way any of them could be recovered in time.

"Lady Penelope," Garrison said. He stopped outside her study, then ran inside. "Shit!"

Molly followed him. Lady Penelope was lying against the far wall, utterly unmoving. She checked the woman's pulse automatically - she'd picked up *some* first aid in school, although she'd never used it - but found nothing. The older woman was dead. Molly looked down at her for a long moment, then glanced around the room. The water must have poured in and slammed Lady Penelope against the wall before she could escape. Her feet squelched as she walked back to the door. She didn't have the slightest idea what to do.

The emergency lighting flickered. Molly tensed. There was no way she could get out of the building if the lighting failed completely. And yet...she looked at Garrison, seeing the fear in his eyes too. They were trapped in a crumbling building, perhaps unable to do anything to save themselves...

"The building itself appears to be stable," Garrison said. He glanced around. "If there's someone left, we can ask for help."

Servants, Molly thought. *Did they survive?*

She took one last look at Lady Penelope, then followed Garrison out of the room. The hallway had been utterly trashed; paintings had been yanked from the walls and dashed to the floor, pieces of artwork had been smashed to rubble, puddles of water lay everywhere...they'd been lucky, very lucky, that they'd survived. She glanced at the walls as water dripped down, working its way through the building. If a water leak could do real damage to an otherwise perfect building, she dreaded to think what an entire *flood* could do.

There was no sign of any of the servants. The kitchens were empty - and flooded. A handful of rooms that Garrison thought probably belonged to live-in maids were also empty. Outside, there was nothing, but utter darkness. Molly was tempted to suggest they sleep in the car - even if they couldn't do anything else with it - yet...she had no idea where the car actually *was*. If the wave had picked up a number of boats, what could it do to a *car*?

"We should be able to sleep in the lobby," Garrison announced, finally. "It should give us enough shelter for the moment."

Molly shrugged. She'd have to look for some new clothes, if nothing else. The damp dress wasn't doing her any favours. And then...she shook her head. Technically, they should report Lady Penelope's death to some-one, but all the landlines were down. She wasn't even sure if there was anyone left alive...could the wave have reached Woking?

No, she told herself. *My kids are still alive. I just have to get to them.*

But, as she hunted for clothes and bedding that weren't impossibly damp, she found it hard to convince herself that that was true.

CHAPTER
FOURTEEN

London, United Kingdom

"What the hell is happening?" Andrew stared at the display. "Are they attacking us?"

"Not directly, Prime Minister," General Peter Templeton said. "They hit a number of orbital installations. Pieces of debris are falling out of orbit and plunging into the atmosphere."

"Where they will hit the surface," Andrew finished. He'd watched several movies that featured an asteroid habitat being knocked out of orbit. They'd been banned, when he was a child. The government had felt they would upset people. "Where...where's going to be hit?"

"We're not sure just how many pieces will make it through the atmosphere and the defences," Templeton told him. His eyes never left the display. "One large piece looks as though it will come down in the Atlantic, west of Britain; several smaller pieces are scattering over Europe and North Africa. There may be another crashing down in the Indian Ocean, but the Indian defences *may* be able to take care of it."

"Because there are no defence installations in the Middle East," Andrew finished. The whole area had been isolated for years, tin-pot warlords and religious fanatics rising to power and then falling just as quickly. "How many of them are going to die?"

He pushed the thought to the back of his mind. "How many of *us* are going to die?"

"Unknown, Prime Minister," Templeton said. "We cannot even *begin* to make a workable set of predictions."

Andrew looked at him, then at the display. More and more pieces of debris were falling into the atmosphere, a handful vanishing as they were picked off by the defences or burnt up before they reached the ground. It looked like a computer simulation, utterly unconnected to reality. And yet...and yet he knew, all too well, that there were real people underneath the falling debris. British basements and bomb shelters wouldn't provide any protection to someone unlucky enough to have a piece of debris come down on their heads.

Templeton swore. "We have an impact," he said, as the display updated. "One large chunk came down in the Atlantic. There'll be tidal waves up and down the west coast. And Ireland too."

"Warn the Irish," Andrew said. Ireland *should* have access to the live feed from orbit, but it was better to make sure they actually got the warning. "Is there anything we can do to stop it?"

"No, Prime Minister," Templeton said. "Local military and police units have already been alerted, but the best they can do is hunker down and send out alerts. Anyone along the coastline will have to fend for themselves."

"...Shit," Andrew said.

The display updated again. "Two more impacts," Templeton reported. "Both in the North Sea..."

Andrew felt cold. The damage was steadily mounting. Reports were coming in from all over the world. Something large had come down far too close to San Francisco for comfort, while the remains of an industrial node had crashed on Russia. So far, the Japanese appeared to be lucky - their defence grid had destroyed a handful of pieces of debris - but he knew it wouldn't last. Tidal waves were already spreading in all directions.

Templeton frowned. "Penzance has gone dark, Prime Minister," he said. His fingers danced over the control panel. "We've lost touch with the Regional HQ."

"Do what you can," Andrew said.

He looked down at his hands, feeling utterly helpless. Britain hadn't lost so many lives since the Troubles...no, even the *Troubles* hadn't killed so many people. The display kept updating, showing him tidal waves marching inland...hundreds of thousands of people would be drowned or rendered homeless if they survived. Modern buildings were built to last, but he doubted they'd stand up to a tidal wave. The carnage would make the Iranian Civil War looked like a playground spat. It looked bloodless, on the display, but he knew it was real. Britain...Britain would never be the same again.

"I've got staffers trying to find someone still linked to the military net," Templeton said, grimly. "Right now, none of our hardened systems appear to be working. The entire region's gone dark."

He swore, softly. "And there are waves rushing up the Thames too," he added. "The water level is rising sharply."

Andrew fought the urge to give in to despair. There was nothing he could do. How could someone fight something on such a scale? He could issue orders all he wanted, but...but they wouldn't be enough. The command and control network was breaking down...or the people on the far end were dead. His position as Prime Minister was worthless in all, but name. London was about to be drenched - or worse - and there was nothing he could do about that too. He didn't even know if the *bunker* was safe. It should be, but...

You should share the risk, he told himself grimly. *The people up there have no bunkers at all.*

Templeton frowned. "We're trying to get people away from the coasts now," he added. "But it might already be too late."

"Of course it's too late," Andrew snapped. "I..."

He shook his head. "Do what you can," he said, again. "We have to keep fighting, don't we?"

"Yes, Prime Minister," Templeton said. He tapped a key, altering the display. "I believe Admiral Winters is trying to mount a counterattack now."

"Let's hope so," Andrew said. He studied the display for a long moment, trying not to think of just how many millions of people might have died. "I don't know how much more of a battering we can take."

"We may be about to find out," Templeton said. Red icons flared up on the display. "They just hit another installation."

"Shit," Andrew said.

————

Major Toby Griffins, London Home Guard, had never seriously expected to be called out, let alone ordered to take command of a planetary defence station. He'd only joined the Home Guard because the reservist bonuses and benefits had made it easier to buy a house. A weekend every month on a military base, keeping his skills sharp, or taking part in an exercise hadn't seemed a bad idea. His wife had certainly made approving noises every time he'd come home, drenched in mud and sweat. But even that had started to pall as he grew older. His wife had openly questioned the wisdom of running around with the younger men.

"You're not as young as you used to be," she'd said, poking him in his ample belly. "And you really *are* putting on weight."

Toby wasn't sure, in all honestly, *why* he'd stayed with the Home Guard. Reservists didn't have the social cachet of *real* soldiers...and besides, his wife wasn't wrong. He *had* been putting on weight. Scrambling up ropes and charging around with the young bucks wasn't on the cards any longer, not for him. These days, trying to climb into a hovering helicopter would probably cause the helicopter to crash. He certainly didn't live up to the ideal squaddie, let alone the Special Forces. But being in the Home Guard *did* bring some status of its own...

And if I'd known there was going to be an actual war, he thought as he studied the display, *I might have kept myself in better shape.*

"I've got three more pieces of debris de-orbiting into our AOR," Lieutenant Kathy Roberson said. "They're entering range now."

Toby nodded. "Take them out."

He wished, suddenly, that the plan to produce ground-based mass drivers had come to fruition. The heavy lasers at his disposal were powerful enough to vaporise an incoming missile - or anything else stupid enough to fly through the UKADR without permission - but they hadn't been designed to deal with falling rocks. It required a steady bombardment to take out even one chunk, which ran the risk of allowing dozens of others to hit the planet while the station was dealing with just one. He'd have sold his soul for missiles or even railguns. But there just hadn't been enough of them to make a real difference.

"One down," Kathy reported. She looked odd, to his eyes. Women weren't *that* common in the combat arms, certainly not one with long hair and a pretty face. But she was good at handling the firing system and that was all that counted. "Targeting the second one now."

"See if you can break it up, then move to the third," Toby ordered. "Let the smaller pieces burn up in the atmosphere."

"Aye, sir," Kathy said.

Toby nodded, keeping his eyes on the display. Most chunks of debris definitely *would* break up in the atmosphere, but it was hard to be sure *which* chunks would die. A giant cluster of debris didn't even fall a kilometre before it burned up and vanished; a smaller piece fell through the atmosphere and crashed somewhere in France. Toby didn't like the French very much - the Home Guard had often joked that the French were the only ones who wanted to invade Britain - but he couldn't help feeling sorry for anyone close to the blast zone. The piece of debris had been larger than a standard KEW. It would have caused immense damage...

"Shit," Kathy snapped. A red icon flashed up, then vanished. An impact in the English Channel, far too close to the mouth of the Thames for comfort. Powerful waves would already be rolling out in all directions. "Sir, I..."

"Remain focused," Toby said. His wife was safe, he hoped. He'd sent her to stay with his parents in Bolton, north of Manchester. She should be safe as long as none of the falling rocks came down anywhere near her. "Keep striking the larger pieces before they get too close."

Kathy swallowed. "Aye, sir."

Toby turned away from the screen, blinking hard. The darkened chamber suddenly felt oppressive beyond belief. There were no windows in the tiny compartment, nothing to show the outside world. They were quite some distance from the nearest town. Apart from the three platoons of Home Guardsmen under his command and the handful of operations staff, they were alone. And yet...

He wished, suddenly, that he'd stayed with his wife. It wouldn't have been *hard* to arrange a post closer to her, although - as a Home Guardsman - he was expected to remain in his hometown. Or maybe he could have retired before the war...

I have my duty, he thought, as he turned back to the screen. *And I have to carry it out.*

It was a sobering thought, but not one he could avoid. He'd taken the King's Shilling long ago, never really expecting that his country would call in the debt. It had seemed a reasonable calculation, back then. What sort of modern war required the reserves to be called up, let alone deployed? The Home Guard certainly wasn't supposed to be deployed outside the country...

He shook his head. Whatever else happened, he knew he should be grateful. He was on a military base, surrounded by armed men. Others would not be so lucky.

And if they do take the high orbitals, this place will be smashed, he thought, tersely. *Fuck.*

———

"Put out that light," Sergeant Collins muttered.

Police Constable Robin Mathews rolled his eyes as the three policemen made their way along the embankment. It was almost eerily quiet in Central London. No planes flew overhead, no taxis or cars made their way up and down the streets or over the bridges...even Big Ben, normally sounding out the time, was silent. The Houses of Parliament were illuminated, but much of the remainder of the city was dark. Robin couldn't help wondering, cynically, if someone was hoping that that Houses of Parliament would draw alien fire.

Not that they'd have any trouble picking out London from orbit, he thought, as he glanced at his watch. It was just past midnight. Normally, his duty shift would have ended long ago and he'd be tucked up at home, trying to get some rest before he had to make his way back to the station. *The bastards will have no trouble finding the city if they want it.*

He glanced towards the darkened waters, carefully picking out the handful of boats moving covertly up and down the river. People trying to get out of the city, he guessed, even though the government had told everyone to stay put. There was no point in trying to stop them, not now. He just hoped they didn't get in the way of any military boats. The wet-navy had been sending troopships up and down the river all day. No doubt they'd been moving government personnel and paperwork out of the city too.

A light flickered at the far end of the eastern bridge. Someone shouted. Robin glanced around, one hand dropping to the pistol on his belt. He had no intention of shooting looters if it could be avoided, but he did have legal authority to shoot if necessary. And anyone looting now, with the battle clearly visible high overhead, would be willing to shoot back. He looked at his comrades, then jumped as his radio hissed an alert. It was...

"The river," Collins said. "*Look!*"

Robin stared. The Thames was rising, rising with terrifying speed. For a moment, he honestly didn't believe what he was seeing. The darkened waters were rising so rapidly that it was already threatening to break over the embankment. In the distance, he could hear boats hooting their horns...and a dull rumble of something that sounded like thunder. A flash of light, in the distance, caught his eye for a second. When he looked back, the river had burst its banks. Water was rushing rapidly towards them. There was no sign it was going to slow down.

"Run," he snapped.

Collins grabbed his radio and babbled out a report as the policemen fled up the road towards Trafalgar Square. The water followed them, splashing and crashing its way through the parked cars and buses. Robin glanced from side to side, hearing alarms sounding from all directions. The row of expensive hotels probably wasn't deserted, he thought. God knew the government had tried to keep things as normal as possible. There were probably hundreds of rich tourists in the city, caught by the curfew.

They reached Trafalgar Square, nearly running into an army patrol. The waters raged towards them, constantly rising; Robin scrambled up the steps, hoping desperately that the flow would stop before it was too late. They weren't *that* close to the sea, not in Central London...it dawned on him, suddenly, that it must be far worse downriver. The flood barriers had to have broken, shattered under the impact. What the hell had happened?

The waters gurgled, slowly coming to a halt. Robin breathed a sigh of relief, which died when he heard the screams. The waters were still moving, pouring into drains and smashing into buildings and shops. A coffee shop on the near side of the square - he vaguely recalled it had a large basement - seemed to be attracting a great deal of water. He hoped - desperately - that there was no one inside. Did the staff live over the shop? It didn't seem likely.

"There," Collins said. He jabbed a finger back down the road. "Look!"

Robin swore. Two youngsters - a boy and a girl - were caught in the waters. He kicked off his shoes and ran down to the water. It was bitterly cold, but he forced himself on anyway as the waters started to flow back to the sea. Pieces of debris - everything from leaves to sewage - drifted past him. Collins followed as he threw himself forward, splashing through the water. Hundreds of other people were staring out of windows or hurrying up to the rooftops.

"I've got you," he said, as he caught hold of the girl. Collins grabbed the boy a second later, yanking him towards a lamppost. "Hang on tight!"

The waters picked up speed. Robin gripped the girl's hand as tightly as he could as the water dragged him back towards the embankment. It was deeper than he'd realised, but that wouldn't last. Cold ice ran through him as he remembered the cars and buses that had been buried under the waves. There was a very good chance they'd hit something that would do them a serious injury...or be dragged over the embankment and into the Thames. He doubted they'd have a hope of hell of surviving...

"Don't let go," he said, as they were dragged past a fence. "Keep hold of me."

He caught hold with one hand, holding the girl with the other. He heard her scream as the waters moved faster and faster, a deafening roar echoing in his ears as they plunged back into the river. He'd heard some of the river policemen talk about the river being a living thing, but he'd never really believed them until now. The water seemed to want to kill them both...

The level dropped, sharply. He lowered them down as quickly as he could before it was too late, landing on the wet pavement. The dark river rolled and seethed under his gaze, as if it was biding its time before raging back through London again. He looked west and shivered helplessly as he saw the darkened city. The lights illuminating the Houses of Parliament had vanished. The entire city seemed to have plunged into darkness.

"Thank you," the girl managed. She was freezing, her teeth chattering frantically. "I..."

"We'll find you some dry clothes," Robin promised. There would be something for her to wear in the hotels, wouldn't there? He didn't expect ambulances, let alone reinforcements, to show up in a hurry. The emergency services would have worse problems to the west. "And then..."

He sobered as he saw the body, lying by the side of the embankment. Whatever had happened, whatever had caused the flood, had been bad. And it was just the beginning...

"Come on," he said. He shivered as a cold breeze struck him. It smelled of the sea. "Let's find you something to wear."

CHAPTER
FIFTEEN

Near Earth/Earth Orbit

The human installations have been severely damaged, the analysis sub-faction declared, coldly. *However, many installations remain.*

There was a long pause as the various sub-factions bickered, briefly, over how to proceed. The missiles had worked well, but there weren't enough of them left for a second barrage, not now the humans knew what they faced. It was...*frustrating.* Several factions did not hesitate to state their opinions. The offensive should have been delayed several months, just to ensure enough missiles were available to inflict far greater damage. And yet...

The Combat Faction brushed aside the argument. *The enemy starfighters are being worn down,* it stated. *We are pushing them hard.*

Another update flickered into their collective awareness. The enemy starfighters were rallying, moving out towards the carriers. More and more updates followed, tallying the enemy starfighters. Half of them were *designed* to take on capital ships. It was odd, but understandable. Human technology hadn't reached the point where they could build multi-role starfighters, although *that* was already changing. A number of their starfighters were armed with plasma guns...

The Combat Faction hesitated, rapidly assessing its options. A third of its starfighters were deployed to cover the carriers, but the humans would have a numerical advantage. It might amount to nothing - the carriers themselves mounted plenty of point defence - yet it was a concern. But if they called back the other starfighters, the human defences would have a chance to rearm *their* starfighters and repair some of the damage. And yet...

Recall the starfighters, the Combat Faction ordered. It didn't dare risk losing too many carriers. The shock of losing several fleet carriers in quick succession had sparked a new flood of construction, but it would be months before the new ships were ready for deployment. *Point defence, prepare to engage the enemy.*

———

"This is a death ride," Lieutenant Bush Williams commented.

"Be silent," Captain Ginny Saito ordered, although she was tempted to agree with him. The hasty reorganisation had dumped three Chinese pilots and a lone Japanese into her squadron, although - thankfully - none of them seemed inclined to dispute her authority. She was much more concerned about their ability to work with her pilots. "Concentrate on your task."

She gritted her teeth as the alien carriers grew closer, their CSP forming up in front of the onrushing human squadrons. Her pre-war training insisted that the aliens were being stupid by giving the humans a chance to blow through them, but actual combat experience told her that they knew what they were doing. Their carriers bristled with plasma guns...she'd even heard a couple of analysts insisting that their carriers had the ability to shoot plasma from anywhere on their hull. The pilots had joked about the whole concept, but it was no laughing matter. It would be incredibly difficult to get into attack position without being blown out of space.

"Your targets are the flattops," the dispatcher said. "Ignore the smaller ships as much as possible."

Ginny nodded, tersely. She knew they were going to take a beating. The enemy's cruisers and destroyers packed plenty of point defence themselves. They'd stop trying to hold something back to cover themselves once they realised they were being ignored, allowing them to devote everything to protecting the carriers. And yet, those carriers had to be taken out. They were the *true* danger threatening her homeworld.

Their images grew sharper on her display as they flew closer. The alien ships didn't seem *that* different in concept from their human counterparts, but there was something oddly *organic* about their hulls - as if the ships had been melted slightly - that made them look very alien. And yet, they had an understated elegance to them that none of the human carriers could match. Ginny had served on *Enterprise* and *Kennedy* before being transferred to Pournelle Base. She'd liked both carriers, but she couldn't deny they were ugly as sin. Their boxy hulls were just .. *crude.*

She pushed the thought aside as the alien starfighters loomed in front of her. "Break and attack," she ordered, uncovering her firing key. "Cover the bombers as much as possible."

The aliens opened fire at the same moment, spitting streams of plasma towards her starfighters. They didn't *look* as though they wanted a dogfight, but they swiftly realised they had no choice. Holding a single position - even while moving in a randomised pattern - was asking for certain death. Ginny smiled as she vaporised an alien pilot, then took out two more in quick succession. *This* batch didn't seem to be quite so well trained.

"Watch your rear," the dispatcher warned. "They're recalling the remainder of their starfighters."

Ginny nodded, grimly. The alien starfighters were fast, but it would take them several minutes to catch up with the human craft. Their pals would have to hold the line until then...it wasn't going to be easy. An alien craft lunged at her, only to be blown away by one of her wingmen. The others reformed, then flashed towards the bombers. Ginny kicked her starfighter into high gear and gave chase. The bombers were already making their steady way into attack range.

"Pournelle Base has authorised missile launch," the dispatcher said. "Try not to fly into one of the missiles."

Asshole, Ginny thought. Of all the ways to go, dying by accidentally colliding with a missile - or another starfighter - would be amongst the most embarrassing. Normally, the odds would be against it, although now...there were so many starfighters in a relatively small region of space that she supposed a collision might be possible. *And...*

She gritted her teeth, pushing the thought aside as the alien starfighters tried to engage the bombers. She couldn't fault their bravery, even though their training wasn't up to par. They didn't seem to have realised that their carriers were already spitting plasma bolts in all directions. The bombers were going to fly through a holocaust into firing range.

Which is why the missile pods were finally allowed to open fire, she thought, as she killed another alien pilot. *They wouldn't normally have a chance to punch through the enemy defences, but now...they might just make it.*

———

The timing, the Combat Faction acknowledged, was unfortunate. Deliberately or otherwise, the humans had caught them with half of their starfighters out of position. Worse, a number of human *missile* pods had opened fire. The human missiles didn't have the sheer acceleration necessary to match the missiles the Combat Faction had deployed, but they had numbers *and* they had a distraction. Choosing to deal with one set of threats might easily lead to the *other* punching through their defences and inflicting real harm.

More attention should have been paid to human installations, one of the sub-factions noted, grimly. *We didn't realise what the missile pods were until it was too late.*

The Combat Faction signalled its agreement, then dismissed the matter. One way or another, the human missile pods no longer mattered. They'd expended their deadly cargo already, rendering them valueless. They could be broken down later, once the high orbitals were secured. Right now, there were other - more important - matters to attend to.

Adjust point defence, the Combat Faction ordered, as the human missiles roared into their engagement envelope. They didn't seem to be capable of taking evasive action. Indeed, a handful were already burning out and going ballistic. *Target the missiles...*

And then it all went to hell. The human missiles multiplied rapidly, doubling and tripling the size of the barrage in seconds. For a long second, the Combat Faction was utterly dumbfounded. The Song itself fell silent. Consensus was gone. It was impossible...it was obviously impossible. Those missiles couldn't be there, yet they were...weren't they?

Sensor ghosts, a sub-faction stated, coldly. New analysis updates flooded through their awareness. *Some of those missiles are designed to mislead our sensors. Careful analysis will allow us to pick out the real missiles from the fakes.*

The Combat Faction had no time for careful analysis. *Target all incoming missiles*, it ordered, sharply. It didn't want to find out that a given missile was real when it slammed into a starship hull. *And order the starfighters to engage the enemy bombers.*

Captain Jean-Paul Foch braced himself as he led his flight of bombers directly into the teeth of the alien point defence. The alien carriers were incredible, practically glowing with light as they spat fire in all directions. He couldn't help a flicker of envy as he silently catalogued all the advantages the aliens held, even though the French Navy was duplicating them one by one. His bomber would have been far more deadly if he'd been given a set of plasma guns of his own.

He threw his craft through a series of evasive manoeuvres as he prepared to launch his torpedoes. He'd trained for this - they'd all trained for this - and yet the aliens had managed to throw them a loop. The first engagements fought according to pre-war tactical doctrine had been failures so horrific that the tactical manuals had been discarded with almost indecent speed. Not that Jean-Paul cared much about *that*. He would sooner go back to the beginning and go through basic training again than get his ass blown off because he refused to adapt to the new reality.

"Fall into attack pattern now," he ordered. He flew straight for as long as he dared, around two and a half seconds. The alien carrier was already zeroing in on him and the rest of the squadron. Their computers would have no difficulty calculating his trajectory and putting a plasma bolt in his path. "And...*fire!*"

The bomber jerked as she launched both of her nuclear-tipped torpedoes at the nearest alien carrier. Jean-Paul yanked the bomber to one side as a plasma bolt shot through where he'd been, two seconds ago, then turned away from the alien carrier. The remainder of the squadron followed suit as the aliens refocused their attention on the torpedoes. Three more squadrons added their torpedoes to the barrage, giving the aliens hundreds of tiny targets to destroy. The alien carriers were tough, but nowhere near as tough as *Ark Royal*. A handful of hits would be enough to mess them up...

He watched, just for a second, as the first bomb-pumped laser detonated. A beam of ravening force stabbed deep into the alien hull. Three more followed in quick succession, knocking the alien carrier out of formation. For a second, he thought the carrier was going to survive, despite the atmosphere streaming from a dozen hull breaches. And then the giant craft exploded into a ball of plasma. Jean-Paul whooped in delight...

...And never saw the alien starfighter that killed him.

———

"Scratch one flattop," a voice carolled. "Scratch *two!*"

Ginny smiled, despite herself, as she blasted another alien starfighter. The dogfight had turned into a nightmare: the starfighters trying desperately to keep the aliens distracted while the bombers ran for home. But the aliens were *mad*, some of them practically ignoring the human starfighters and going after the bombers. She supposed there was a method in their madness - the human bombers were a real threat, if they had a chance to rearm - but it annoyed her. God knew the starfighters were threats too.

Be glad of it, she told herself. Another alien starfighter flashed past her, but evaded the stream of plasma she fired in its direction. *They might turn their attention to you soon.*

She broke into clear space and took a second to assess the situation. Two alien carriers were gone, two more were heavily damaged. A handful of smaller ships had also been destroyed or damaged. She was mildly surprised the alien commanders hadn't ordered the damaged ships to retreat back to the tramlines, although Home Fleet *was* out there somewhere. Killing a crippled carrier might seem unfair, but it was *practical*. She didn't have any real objections to smashing a helpless ship that might come back to haunt her if she left it alone.

"Cover the remainder of the bombers," the dispatcher ordered. New updates flooded into her system. She gritted her teeth in annoyance as she realised the dispatcher was trying to update on the fly. It wasn't the smartest thing to do when there was a good chance that some of her new subordinates would die in the next few minutes. "And then get back to Earth."

"Understood," Ginny said. The Tadpole starfighters didn't seem inclined to break off the pursuit. "We'll get right on it."

Her body ached as she pushed her starfighter back into the fire. It felt like hours since the engagement had started, hours in her cockpit...she wondered, suddenly, if she should take a booster. She was pushing her body to the limits. But she knew better than to take them if there was any other choice. An hour or two in the quick-sleep machine would be lovely, but...she shook her head as her craft started to gain on the alien starfighters. She just didn't have time.

And we'll be facing worse, once the aliens regroup, she thought. She took a quick sip of juice as she targeted the nearest alien craft. *If they weren't mad at us before, they sure as hell are mad at us now.*

———

The Combat Faction seethed with cold annoyance as the Song rose and fell. It hadn't expected a bloodless conquest, but losing two fleet carriers to inferior ships was...frustrating. The damaged carriers were in no state to recover and rearm starfighters, let alone launch them back into the fray. Worse, they could barely keep up with the remainder of the fleet. Once the humans realised they were sitting ducks, their mass drivers would be turned on them. They had yet to be silenced.

It contemplated a number of options, one by one. Pushing the offensive against Earth would wreck the remaining infrastructure, as well as letting them take shots at bases and industrial nodes on the ground. But the human fleet was already reforming. The Combat Faction didn't *want* to be trapped against the wretched planet. The humans had *some* planetary defences. Maybe not as dangerous as their mass drivers, but dangerous enough to give the faction pause.

And yet...the other possibilities weren't much better. It was starting to look as though actually *taking* the system was no longer an option, certainly not without expending too much of the fleet. *That* was a significant problem.

If the first objective can no longer be met, one sub-faction said, *we should attempt to meet the second.*

The Combat Faction could not disagree. Punching its way through to Earth would be satisfying, but of limited value. The human fleet would either force them into an engagement or remain intact, giving the humans options for retaliation. That fleet was now the main target. It had to be destroyed before the Combat Faction withdrew from the system.

Complete the destruction of the orbital installations, it ordered. Starfighters could do that, if nothing else. Long-range kinetic strikes would make life harder for the defenders. It wasn't something they'd prepared to do, but it was time to be a little adaptable. *And then prepare to meet the enemy fleet...*

A shock ran through the command network as a mass driver projectile slammed into one of the crippled carriers. The giant starship disintegrated, plunging its surviving personnel into space. A handful of starfighters tried to locate survivors, but found none. Exposure to naked vacuum was almost always fatal.

Continue with the offensive, the Combat Faction stated. It had expected to lose the cripples, but that didn't make it any easier. *And order the detached squadrons to increase speed.*

———

"Scratch a *third* flattop, sir," Captain Mike Hanson said. He sounded pleased. "The mass drivers on the moon scored a direct hit!"

"On one of the cripples," Jon said. There was no way to be *sure*, but long-range sensors had definitely suggested that the crippled carriers were *hors de combat*. They hadn't been trying to surrender, unfortunately, but they hadn't been launching or recovering starfighters. "But a good shot, none the less."

He pushed his sour thoughts aside as he contemplated the losses. His bomber crews had paid a staggering price for their success, losing nearly a fourth of their number. They'd lose more too, he was sure, when they launched the next strike. He didn't have any more missile pods he could deploy to cover their backs. The only good news was that the new ECM drones mixed in with the missiles seemed to have worked. The alien craft had been distracted long enough to let the bombers slip into attack range.

Better we lose the bombers than the remaining installations, he thought. It wasn't a pleasant thought, but bombers were relatively cheap. Replacing the craft and their pilots wouldn't be *that* tricky. *Or let them start dropping rocks on Earth.*

He'd done his best not to watch the updates from the surface, but he knew it was bad. Pieces of debris had fallen everywhere, despite the best efforts of his people. He'd refused to *look* at the live reports from San Francisco, let alone the rest of the west coast. Giant tidal waves had been pounding the coastline ever since the first piece of debris had hit the ocean. It would only get worse, even though the ground-based defences were doing better at taking out the really dangerous rocks.

"Admiral, their lunar squadron is entering attack range," Hanson added.

Jon nodded. The mass driver installations on the lunar surface had their orders. They knew what to do.

And they've plenty of experience by now, he thought, numbly. *They're going to need it.*

CHAPTER
SIXTEEN

Luna Defence Installation #17/Sin City, Luna

"They're coming into attack range, sir," Lieutenant Adam Selene said. He looked far too young for his role - his brown hair made him look as if he hadn't left his teens - but people grew up quickly on the moon. "Orders?"

Commander Garcia O'Kelly nodded, curtly. He'd always assumed - the Luna Federation had always assumed - that they'd have to assert their independence against the Great Powers. It would have been a nightmare - the network of independent settlements on Luna were matched by dozens of settlements belonging to the Great Powers - but they'd been prepared to fight. They'd built something new on the moon, a melting pot of settlements that had flourished away from the semi-fascism of Earth. The idea of actually fighting *beside* the Great Powers had never crossed anyone's mind until the Battle of New Russia.

"Switch targets," he ordered. The alien squadrons were the real threats now. Hitting a carrier was all very well and good - he was fairly sure *his* crews had scored the direct hit - but far too many of the nearby settlements were easy targets. The aliens were probably madder than a taxman from Earth after discovering that the Luna Federation felt no obligation to share its tax records with anyone else. "Prepare to open fire."

"Targets locked," Selene said.

Garcia smiled, grimly. The closer the aliens came, the easier the shot - and the harder it would be for them to take any kind of evasive action.

They *were* running their ships through a series of evasive manoeuvres, even though the mass drivers hadn't tried to engage them yet, but they weren't altering their courses *that* much. Taking them down should be relatively easy.

Of course, they'll be firing back at us too, he thought. *That might get interesting.*

"Fire," he ordered.

He heard the mass driver *thrum* as it launched the first projectile towards the alien ships, followed by three more in quick succession. The mass drivers were designed for rapid fire, allowing the Luna Federation to impede travel between Earth and Luna if necessary. Indeed, the facility had practically been shut down before the war had started...he wished, suddenly, that the plans to build entire *fortresses* on the lunar surface had been put into production. The mass driver was far too fragile for his peace of mind.

"The enemy ships are launching missiles," Lieutenant Tracy Combs reported. Her black hair fell over pointed elfin ears as she glanced at him. "Half of them appear to be targeted on the defence stations, the remainder appear to be targeted on signal sources and settlements."

They must have some rough idea where our settlements are, Garcia thought, as the display updated. There were a handful of point defence stations scattered around the surface, but not enough to take down *all* of the missiles. *They probably probed the system before showing themselves.*

"Direct hit," Selene called. "One of the cruisers has been blown to shit!"

Garcia smirked. All of the mass driver stations were shooting now, throwing hundreds of rocks into a relatively small region of space. As he watched, another alien craft vanished from the display. He slapped his fist into his palm in silent exultation. He'd wondered, when the news first came in from Vera Cruz, if the Great Powers had done something to offend the aliens. They certainly didn't bother to show any consideration to any of the minor powers in the human sphere. But now...humanity had to stand together or die...

"Direct hit, Runnymede Colony," Tracy reported.

"Shit," Garcia muttered. He had no idea what sort of weapons the aliens were using, but the vast majority of colonies were alarmingly fragile. A nuke would be more than enough to do real harm. "Pass the alert up the chain."

He watched as another alien craft exploded, the crew blasted to dust before they realised what had hit them. The Luna Federation had plans to assist colonies that ran into trouble, but they'd never prepared for anything on such a scale. How *could* they have? He doubted it would be particularly safe to move around on the surface, at least for a little while. The aliens seemed to be targeting signal sources in particular.

A pity we didn't know that in advance, he thought. *We could have covered the entire surface in radio transmitters.*

"Mycroft reports three alien craft heading for farside," Tracy added. "Central Command is asking us to adjust our targeting."

"See to it," Garcia ordered.

"Aye, sir," Selene said. "I..."

The ground shook. "Impact, one kilometre away," Tracy reported. Her face paled as she worked her console. "I think it was a nuke, sir, but it was embedded in the soil when it detonated."

"Probably a penetrator warhead," Garcia said. The alien targeting seemed to have gone funny, unless they'd thought they were aiming at a hidden installation. There was nothing closer to the blast zone than themselves. "They might have thought they'd trigger off an earthquake and take out the base."

"Perhaps, sir," Tracy said. She swore, loudly. "Sir, they're striking at Rivendell!"

Garcia winced. He'd been to Rivendell a couple of times - the founders had been far too obsessed with Middle-Earth for his peace of mind - but Tracy had grown up there. It was a minor miracle she'd escaped with such a normal name, unless she'd changed it once she left the colony. Perhaps she had. The Luna Federation rarely cared what its citizens did unless it presented a clear and present danger to everyone else. But she had kept the ears...

"Warn them," he said. Rivendell rarely paid much attention to the outside world, but even *they* knew there was a war on. Didn't they? "And then alert the point defence."

He turned his attention back to the display, just in time to see the alien craft launch yet another spread of missiles. Their targeting was getting better, he noted, or perhaps they were just throwing everything they had at the mass drivers. They probably wanted to suppress them before it was too late...

"Direct hit, Rivendell," Tracy said. Her voice was broken. "They used a nuke."

"Concentrate," Garcia snapped. He didn't have *time* to let her have a breakdown, even though he understood. God knew *he* wouldn't have reacted well if his parents and childhood friends had been killed. "Cry later!"

Tracy glared at him, then looked down at her console, tears running down her cheeks. "New targets," he said. "Molina, Balamory and...and Sin City."

"That'll piss everyone off," Selene predicted.

"Pass the warning," Garcia said. He didn't think Sin City was heavily defended, even though it was a wretched hive of scum and villainy. "Tell them...tell them to take cover."

———

"How long do we have to stay here?"

"Good question," Brian said. It had been nearly two hours since they'd entered the shelter, shortly before the hatches had slammed closed. He wanted to scold Abigail for asking questions he couldn't answer, but she was doing better than most of the others. Half of them jumped at the slightest sound, while the others seemed inclined to try to open the door and escape. "I don't know."

He glared down at his terminal. Sin City's datanet wasn't *that* advanced, compared to the datanet on Earth, but whoever had designed it had made the system damn near impossible to crack. Nothing he did seemed to work. It made perfect sense - anyone who *did* hack the system would have access to the security cameras, allowing them to cheat at cards or spy on guests - but it was frustrating as hell. *Anything* could be happening out there and he wouldn't know about it.

Not until it is far too late, he thought, grimly. *Anything could be happening out there.*

He glared at the hatch, then back at his terminal. He'd wondered if Abigail's former employer had somehow triggered the emergency alert, just to trap them, but so far it seemed unlikely. The Luna Federation had strong laws against crying wolf. Chief Clancy Patel and his men would arrest anyone stupid enough to trigger the alarms deliberately, just so the Management could make a horrible example out of them.

"Perhaps there's been an air leak," one of the other people offered. He was a young man, alcohol on his breath. "The entire colony could be in vacuum by now."

Brian shook his head, curtly. The telltales on the near side of the hatch were still glowing green. There *was* air - breathable air - on the far side. Besides, Sin City would have the same precautions built into its tunnels as every other colony on the moon. An air leak would have been detected: hatches would have slammed down and emergency crews would have been dispatched. Hell, most children received training in how to patch tiny air leaks at school; adults got far more intensive training. He couldn't imagine something that couldn't be fixed quickly that *hadn't* taken out most of the colony.

He stared at the hatch, then at the collection of emergency equipment and supplies. They *could* get out, if they wished, but what would they find? He had no idea. Perhaps there had been a terrorist attack or an armed robbery, although he couldn't imagine either getting very far. There had never been a terrorist attack on the moon - even when the Luna Federation was girding itself to stand up to the Great Powers - and armed robbers would run right into one of the most well-organised private security forces on the moon. Brian had no difficulty imagining what he might want to steal, but securing it and getting out would be damn near impossible. Perhaps there was a hostage situation...

Abigail caught his arm. "How long do we have to stay here?"

"I don't know," Brian said, as patiently as he could. It was hard to keep the irritation out of his voice. He'd prefer to be on the way himself, but that was clearly impossible. "Perhaps if you could..."

His terminal bleeped, loudly. An alert flashed up, warning of incoming attack. Brian gaped at it in honest shock. Incoming attack? From where? The Luna Federation? The Great Powers? He scrolled through the alert, then swore. The entire solar system was under attack!

"That's impossible," one of the guests said. He was a heavyset man, wearing a shirt that was a size too small for him. "The aliens wouldn't attack Earth, would they?"

"It seems as though they are," Brian said. He kept his voice calm, even though part of his mind was panicking. He knew from bitter experience that panic was contagious. "We're in the shelters. We should be safe."

Unless they start throwing nukes at us, his thoughts added, silently. He told that part of his mind to shut up as he tried, once again, to break into the local datanet. Next time - if there was a next time - he'd ask his friend for security clearance. *We wouldn't know what hit us until it was far too late.*

He forced himself to think as he paced the shelter, checking the emergency supplies. Sin City wasn't a military target. He hadn't heard anything to suggest that the aliens went after non-military targets, although it was possible they wouldn't *know* Sin City was a civilian installation. But there were no weapons mounted on the colony, he thought. Sin City probably had laser installations - most colonies did, in case there was a runaway shuttle - yet the aliens probably wouldn't notice them unless they opened fire.

Which they might, if the surface is attacked, he thought, numbly. *The Luna Federation was supposed to have linked all the ground-based installations together.*

Abigail caught his eye. "What does it mean if the system is attacked?"

Brian shrugged. "It depends on the outcome," he said. He turned to face her. "We might get out of here, only to discover that the system had been occupied. Or..."

Another alert flashed up on his terminal. IMPACT IMMINENT. Brian stared at it for a long moment, then shouted at everyone to get down on the ground. The aliens were attacking Sin City? It was impossible, yet... yet it was happening. Abigail hit the ground next to him, then caught hold of his hand. He hesitated, then let her hold his hand as the terminal started to bleep louder and louder. Someone whimpered, a second before the ground heaved. The lights dimmed, then recovered. A low quiver ran through the shelter, then nothing.

Abigail coughed, loudly. "Was that it?"

Brian rolled over and checked his terminal. The link to the datanet had vanished. He hastily checked around, but there didn't seem to be any working processor nodes within range. Even the emergency system was down. The lights flickered again, worryingly. He stared at them for a long moment, trying to decide what it meant. The Management might well have skimped on the shelters. Perhaps they hadn't bothered to keep them in good condition after all.

He sat up and peered at the airlock hatch. The telltales were slowly turning to red. Brian sucked in his breath, resisting the urge to curse savagely. Outside, the atmosphere was gone. And that meant...he stood and walked over to the life support system. It *looked* as though it was working, but he had no idea how long it would last. If the atmosphere was leaking out of the colony, and it certainly looked like it was, it was quite possible that the rest of the emergency systems were in a pretty poor state too.

"Someone will come to rescue us," the heavyset man said. "Won't they?"

Brian kept his thoughts to himself. The solar system was at war. Sin City wasn't *that* important, not in the short run. And besides, the aliens were probably shooting at anything that moved. God alone knew how long it would take Home Fleet to drive the aliens away...if they *did* drive the aliens away. Brian had followed the news as best as he could - too much had been censored - and he knew, all too well, what had happened at New Russia. Home Fleet might have already been destroyed.

Abigail poked his arm. "How much oxygen do we have?"

She was raised on the moon, Brian reminded himself. *She knows the importance of air.*

"I'm not sure," he admitted. "If the recycler is working, we'd be able to stay here indefinitely - at least until we run out of food and water. If not" - he checked the system, carefully - "we have somewhere between six to eight hours."

"That's long enough," the heavyset man said. "Isn't it?"

"I don't know," Brian said. "There's a war on. It might take far too long for someone to come looking for us. They might not even know we're here."

Abigail paled. "They would, wouldn't they?"

Brian shrugged. "I don't know," he repeated. "They might not have alerted the SAR network before all hell broke loose."

The heavyset man didn't look any better. "What do we do?"

Brian looked at the emergency supplies. "I think we wait long enough to see if the Management manages to reseal the colony," he said. "And if we don't hear from them, we leave the shelter and try to escape."

"We'd die," the heavyset man said. He was definitely panicking. "Do we have enough air to go somewhere else?"

"I don't know," Brian said, suddenly feeling very tired. If only they knew more about the situation outside the hatch! "But if we stay here, we will die."

———

"Hits confirmed," Tracy reported. A new string of updates flowed into the defensive station as the Luna Federation's decentralised command network struggled to cope with the situation. "Sin City and Balamory have gone off the air. Even landlines are down."

"Crap," Garcia said. There was nothing he could do about any of it. "I..."

"Incoming fire," Selene snapped, loudly. His voice hardened as new alerts appeared in front of him. "They're targeting us specifically!"

"Switch the lasers back to point defence mode, then put the mass driver on rapid fire," Garcia snapped. The aliens had already taken out two other mass drivers. If they shot out a couple more, they'd have a window to land troops on the moon. If, of course, they *wanted* to actually invade the moon. Their first set of attacks showed a frightening lack of concern for civilian casualties. "And alert our back-up. They may have to take command of this sector."

"Aye, sir."

Garcia leaned back in his chair as the wave of missiles and KEWs came closer. The aliens had clearly learnt a few things during the battle, even if it was just to use KEWs to weaken the point defence long enough to let the missiles slip through and strike their targets. Selene could take out one set of incoming weapons, but the second set would hammer the base to rubble.

Building those damn fortresses would have been a very good idea, he thought. Half the incoming missiles vanished from the display, but the remainder kept coming. A proper fortress could probably have taken a KEW hit and survived. *I...*

The ground shuddered. "They took out the mass driver," Selene reported. Another earthquake followed, shaking the entire base. "Sir..."

Garcia let out a breath. He'd known death was a possibility. The moon was a harsh mistress, after all. She didn't show mercy to those who flouted her rules, who ignored the dangers, who...making a mistake, deliberately or otherwise, was lethal on the moon. It was a truth that few Earthers understood. Those who did chose to live in space rather than planetside.

"It's been a honour," he said, quietly. He'd never see his wife and children again. He just hoped they knew he'd died well. "I thank you."

He closed his eyes and waited for death.

CHAPTER
SEVENTEEN

Near Earth/Earth Orbit

"Damn you," Ginny swore. The alien pilot was twisting and turning like a corkscrew as she chased him through the remains of an industrial node. "Hold still!"

The alien craft spun around and started to spit plasma death at her. Ginny evaded, firing back with savage intensity. The alien pilot avoided the first set of plasma bolts, but one of the later ones struck his craft and blew it to atoms. Ginny yanked her starfighter away from the orbiting debris and glanced around, trying to assess the situation. The combat datanet was badly disrupted. Deliberately or not, the aliens had taken out a number of the relay nodes.

Probably deliberately, she thought, as she watched the next wave of alien starfighters roaring towards Earth. It looked as though they'd managed to refresh their pilots, probably by holding a number of craft in reserve until the bombers had forced them to deploy everything they had or face destruction. *They may not look like us, but their tactics aren't that different.*

"Rally at Point Delta," the dispatcher ordered. A new note of intensity had entered his voice. "Enemy craft are on a direct course for Pournelle Base."

Ginny felt her blood run cold as she kicked her starfighter into high gear. Pournelle Base had backups, of course, but losing one of the major orbital bases would weaken the defences quite badly. Losing *all* of them would be disastrous. None of the starfighters could make it through the atmosphere, which meant they might run out of life support before Home Fleet's carriers arrived to recover them. And she hated to imagine trying to run the battle from the ground. Whoever took over after all the major orbital bases were destroyed wouldn't be able to see *everything* that was going on.

"Form up on me," she ordered, curtly. She'd been lucky. Six of her subordinates were still alive. The remainder had been rapidly reassigned to her by the datanet, after their original squadrons had been temporarily disbanded. "Try to draw them onto us instead of the base."

The alien formations didn't waver as they approached Pournelle Base, the defenders fanning out to meet them. Ginny sucked in her breath, silently admiring the enemy starfighters' discipline. She'd been right, it seemed. Whoever was directing the battle seemed willing to soak up a number of casualties so they could stick with the original plan. It struck her as faintly absurd, but the Tadpoles might not consider themselves individuals in the sense that humans did. Besides, there wasn't any shortage of human militaries prepared to spend hundreds of lives just to secure a relatively minor target.

And there's nothing minor about Pournelle Base, she thought. *It doesn't matter if they know what they're targeting or not. If they take it out, they put a major crimp in our defences.*

Her HUD updated, showing that seven other squadrons had been assigned to the defence force. Ginny bit her lip as the alien starfighters came closer, bracing herself to return to the fray. Committing so many fighters to defending the base would highlight its importance to the aliens, but it couldn't be helped. The aliens were *already* targeting Pournelle Base.

"Give them hell," she ordered, as she pushed the firing key. Her target exploded, but the other alien craft didn't seem inclined to break and attack. It was odd. They returned fire, but didn't break formation. Five more starfighters died in quick succession. "Reverse course and attack."

She braced herself as she chased the aliens towards Pournelle Base. The base's point defence grid was already online, firing on the alien craft as they approached. Ginny hoped the IFF system was working, although she knew from grim experience that it was somewhat unreliable at close range. There just wasn't time to assess all the incoming targets properly before opening fire. The Tadpole starfighters were too dangerous to take lightly.

Two more alien starfighters died, but the remainder kept moving, ducking and weaving in an evasive pattern that was disturbingly human-like. Ginny snapped off a shot whenever she could, yet it was hard to get a solid lock. The aliens bored towards their target until they entered weapons range, then opened fire. Brilliant streaks of light shot towards Pournelle Base, smashing into the base's makeshift armour. It held, for the moment. Ginny knew it wouldn't last.

"Pournelle Base is losing point defence," the dispatcher warned. "Move to cover the base..."

Ginny gritted her teeth. "What do you think I'm *trying* to do?"

The alien craft darted around the giant installation, pouring fire into every weak spot they found. Ginny saw dozens of point defence weapons and sensor blisters blasted off the hull, airlocks smashed open and venting atmosphere until inner hatches slammed closed. She said a silent prayer for her friends as one alien pilot crashed into a starfighter launch tube, setting off a chain of explosions that threatened to destroy the entire base. Another pilot made a suicide run, only to be picked off a handful of seconds before he would have rammed the base. Ginny cursed, savagely. There was no way the base could endure for long.

"Incoming friends," Lieutenant Bush Williams carolled. "Try not to shoot them!"

Ginny snorted as the French and Chinese pilots slammed into the alien squadrons, driving them away from the base. It didn't last. The aliens regrouped, then launched yet another attack on Pournelle Base. A large chunk of armour came free, blasting out into space with immense force. The alien craft whipped around it and positioned themselves to pour fire into the station's vitals. Ginny and her squadron raced to drive them away, but she knew it was too late. Pournelle Base was doomed.

She picked off two alien starfighters in quick succession, then dodged as their comrades came at her. She couldn't tell if the aliens were trying to distract her or believed they'd already succeeded, but it hardly mattered. They had to protect the base long enough to get the rest of the personnel evacuated. And then...

I had personal stuff in my locker, she thought, numbly. An alien pilot made a mistake and exposed himself. She killed him without thinking. *I'll never see it again.*

"The bombers are heading out again," Lieutenant Williams reported. "Maybe they'll distract the aliens."

Ginny shook her head. The second bomber strike had been completely ineffective, save for one fleet carrier that had taken a beating. There was no reason to assume that the *third* bomber strike would be any better. Hell, the aliens didn't have to worry about missile strikes either. They could concentrate on slaughtering the bombers...

And then come back and slaughter the rest of us, she thought. Her body ached. It felt like hours since she'd taken her starfighter out into space. *They might wear us down on points alone.*

————

"Switch direct command to Nelson Base," Jon ordered, tersely. A low rumble ran through Pournelle Base. "And then order half of our defending starfighters to escort the bombers."

"Aye, sir," Hanson said. He paused as the giant installation shook again. "Sir, this base is no longer tenable."

Jon nodded. Pournelle Base hadn't been designed to stand up to plasma guns. The armour the USN had hastily bolted onto the base's hull, when they'd realised that the threat environment had changed, wasn't *that* much of an improvement. They'd really needed to rebuild the entire base and *that* hadn't been in the cards, not when building new carriers and armoured warships was far more important. It was something for his successors to worry about, after the war.

More red icons flared up on the status display. The lower starfighter tubes were gone...it was sheer luck that the chain reaction hadn't spread to the upper levels. Thankfully, the designers had anticipated an explosion in the starfighter bays and planned accordingly. But there was a gaping hole in their armour and it wasn't going to be repaired in a hurry. It was only a matter of time before the aliens hit something vital, no matter how desperately the defending starfighters fought to drive them off. There were already fires on a dozen decks.

"Order all hands to abandon the base," Jon ordered. He hoped his people wouldn't be jumping from the frying pan into the fire. The Tadpoles didn't make a habit of shooting at lifepods, but there was too great a chance of the tiny craft being mistaken for something dangerous or merely being targeted by accident. "And inform Cathy that she's in tactical command."

Until Nelson Base gets targeted, Jon thought. He wasn't sure if the aliens knew that Pournelle Base was the heart of the enemy defences or not, but it hardly mattered. The defences would be thrown into confusion until Admiral Mountbatten managed to take command. *If they worked out that we were commanding the defences, they can pick Nelson Base out too.*

The thought nagged at his mind as he keyed commands into his console. Pournelle Base was obviously a naval installation - the Tadpoles could hardly have missed the starfighters launching from the base's tubes - but it wasn't so obvious that it was the command hub. It certainly wasn't the *only* large naval base in orbit. Why Pournelle Base instead of Nelson or Foch? Had the aliens managed to track human communications through a network of relay stations or had they merely gotten lucky? There was no way to know.

He opened a hidden compartment in his command chair and toggled the switches inside, ordering the station's datanodes to begin their self-destruct sequence, then rose. The rest of the staff were already making their way through the hatches, heading down to the lifepods on the far side of the hull. There was no sign of panic. Jon felt a flicker of pride as he grabbed a facemask, holding it tightly as the gravity started to fail. Another series of rumbles ran through the station, the lights flickering and fading. Emergency lighting came on a second later, casting the corridor into gloom.

They'll keep attacking until the base is destroyed, he thought, grimly. He could smell burning plastic in the air. The aliens were ripping the base to shreds. *And the remains showering down onto Earth.*

"This way, sir," Hanson called. The remainder of the staff were already climbing into lifepods. "We have to move!"

Jon nodded, feeling a flicker of claustrophobia as he jumped through the hatch and into the lifepod. The lifepods were tiny, barely large enough to hold a dozen grown men. He'd never liked them. A second later, the hatch slammed down and he felt a lurch as the lifepod launched itself into space. He wondered, grimly, if the automated systems would try to get them down to the planet or keep them in orbit. Staying in orbit might be the smartest choice, but...

If we fall through the atmosphere, we may be taken for an enemy attack and vaporised by a ground-based laser station, he thought. The ground-based defences weren't very trusting at the best of times. Now, with pieces of debris raining down all over the planet, they'd shoot first and not bother to ask questions later. *But if we stay in orbit, we might be picked off by an enemy starfighter.*

Hanson was peering through the hatch. "Sir, the base is exploding."

Jon nodded, shortly. That added another danger, didn't it? The life-pod was too fragile to remain airtight if a piece of debris slammed into it at speed. And there would be thousands of pieces of debris in the same general area as themselves...he sighed, strapping himself into his chair and placing the facemask on his lap. There was no point in worrying about it now, he told himself firmly. Either they survived long enough for a SAR shuttle to pick them up or they died. They should have enough air to remain in orbit for several days.

And then we'll have to risk re-entry anyway, he thought. *And who'll be in command of the system then?*

"Sit down," he said. He glanced from face to face. Five staffers, all suddenly isolated - and helpless. There was nothing they could do, if a marauding starfighter decided the lifepod was a threat and blew it out of space. They didn't even have access to the command datanet any longer. "All we can do now is wait."

———

"There she blows," Williams said, quietly.

Ginny watched, wordlessly, as Pournelle Base disintegrated. The alien craft scattered as a series of explosions tore the base apart, throwing pieces of debris in all directions. None of the chunks *looked* large enough to make it through the atmosphere and cause damage on the ground, but she kept an eye on them anyway. Her sensors picked up a number of lifepods, all trying to remain unnoticed. She hoped, grimly, that the Tadpoles didn't decide to use them for target practice.

All my gear is gone, she thought. She travelled light, like most starfighter pilots, but she'd kept some souvenirs with her. *And some of my photographs...*

"Admiral Mountbatten has assumed command," a different dispatcher said. The voice caught her by surprise for a moment, before she remembered that the old dispatcher and his staff would have been on Pournelle Base. She hoped they'd managed to get off before the base exploded. There was no way to know. The Tadpoles had torn up the base's interior pretty good before finally blowing it to atoms. "Prepare for new orders."

"And keep shooting at the aliens until we *get* the new orders," Ginny muttered. The aliens were already racing away from the remains of the base, thankfully not hanging around long enough to start shooting at the lifepods. They didn't *need* to shoot at the lifepods - or the remaining starfighters. They'd already accomplished their goal. "Squadron, form up on me."

She forced herself to survey the battlefield as the command network struggled to update itself. There was always some confusion if someone new assumed command in the middle of a battle - she knew that from grim experience - and it would cost lives. All the emergency drills they'd done since the war had begun had left out the emergency. She'd never met Admiral Mountbatten, but no one - not even Grant or Sherman - could have taken over smoothly. The confusion wouldn't abate in a hurry.

The alien starfighters were racing to catch up with the bombers, while their CSP was moving to confront them. Ginny winced. The bomber pilots were going to get caught between two fires, forced to blow through the CSP with the remainder of the enemy starfighters breathing down their necks. And yet...she spun her starfighter around as a trio of alien craft flashed past her, heading towards a smaller industrial node. The aliens hadn't recalled *all* their starfighters. They'd left enough behind to deter the remaining squadrons from racing after the retreating craft.

We can't go on like this, Ginny thought numbly, as she threw her starfighter after the alien craft. She needed a shower and a few hours sleep - even one hour, in the sleep machine. She was pushing the limits of what she could inject into her bloodstream to keep reasonably alert. *They'll grind us down if we don't manage to get some rest soon.*

She eyed the alien carriers on the HUD, holding position far too close to the planet for comfort. They *had* to be forced away, somehow. Where was Home Fleet? What were they doing? Jerking off while the aliens systematically wrecked Earth's defences and industrial base? How many people had died on the planet while Home Fleet concentrated its forces and prepared to move?

"Prepare to engage the alien carriers," the dispatcher said, finally. Updates flashed up in front of her, providing precise targeting orders. Hitting an alien carrier with plasma guns *might* be effective...she supposed they were about to find out. "New squadron orders..."

Ginny nodded, feeling sweat trickling down her back as the dispatcher rattled off a new set of makeshift formations. If nothing else, the battle had concentrated a few minds on the importance of working together. Pilots flew with whatever wingmen they could find and to hell with national formations. But it was starting to look as though they'd hang together and get hanged anyway.

"Understood," she said, when the new formations had assembled. Only four of her friends had survived long enough to join her new squadron. The remainder were all strangers to her. But they were starfighter pilots and they'd have to do. "Let's go."

There wasn't enough data to be sure, the analysis sub-factions reported, but it *did* look as though the human command-and-control network had been thrown into brief confusion. The starfighter installation the Combat Faction had marked down for destruction might actually have been more important than they'd realised at the time, although the humans were clearly already recovering from the chaos. If they'd known in advance what they were targeting...

The Combat Faction dismissed the thought as it studied the endless series of updates. The raid on the lunar installations had been largely successful, silencing most of the lunar mass drivers. The remainder were still a problem, but they could be handled. And *that* meant that it would be easier to bring the fleet closer to Earth, allowing them to accelerate the destruction of the human industrial base. Taking and holding the high orbitals would be difficult, as long as the human fleet remained in being, but they would weaken the humans to the point where further resistance was impossible.

And then we can put an end to the engagement, the Combat Faction stated. The Song rose again as the various factions rededicated themselves to their task. There was consensus, once again. *And the war itself will soon be won.*

And then the *next* set of updates arrived...

CHAPTER
EIGHTEEN

Sin City, Luna

"There's been no response to any of my pings," Brian said. Nearly thirty minutes had passed since the colony had been attacked. The telltales on the hatch remained red. "I think we have to assume that no one is coming."

He glanced around the compartment. It hadn't been easy to assume command - damn civilians kept wanting to argue - but it *had* managed to keep everyone from arguing. And yet, half of them wanted to stay where they were and the other half wanted to move. The only one who hadn't expressed an opinion was Abigail and she'd grown *up* on the moon.

"We can slip through the hatch without venting the air," he added, after a moment. "Anyone who wants to come with us is welcome."

The heavyset man - whose name had turned out to be Paul Farrakhan - frowned. "Can you guarantee finding a way to the surface?"

"Of course not," Brian said, dryly. "But if they don't even know we're here, they're not going to come looking for us."

He kept the rest of his speculations to himself. Sin City was not a military target. If the aliens were willing to target non-military colonies and installations, it suggested that the *military* installations might have already been taken out. And *that* meant that there might be no one left to help them, even if they *wanted* to help. He had no idea what they would find, when - if - they reached the surface, but he knew they couldn't *rely* on finding help.

"We'll get ready now," he said, reaching for the spacesuits. A couple looked to be about the right size for him; one *might* fit Abigail, although it would be a little loose. "If any of you want to stay here, we'll try and send help back for you when we reach the surface."

Abigail donned her spacesuit with practiced ease. Brian eyed her carefully - she looked bored, rather than frightened - and then checked her life support system. Everything *looked* to be in order, although he wasn't sure how far he trusted the city's spacesuits. Sin City clearly *hadn't* spent as much money and time on their safety precautions as they *should* have done. The Luna Federation would be pissed, if there was still a Federation left. They took safety precautions *seriously*.

"I'll come," Farrakhan said. He glanced at his wife. "I'll send help back for you, all right?"

"You'd be better coming with us," Brian said. He pulled his own spacesuit on, then waited while Abigail checked the telltales. "We don't know how long it will be before help can be organised."

He picked up a set of emergency equipment and dropped it into a bag. Hopefully, they wouldn't have problems reaching the lunar surface, but he knew better than to assume anything. They weren't on the uppermost level. If the colony had vented completely, *all* the airlocks and hatches must have failed. Or...something had punched right through several layers of rock and concrete. He wasn't sure which option bothered him the most.

"I'm ready," Abigail said. She paused. "Shouldn't we carry weapons? We might run into aliens up there."

Brian shrugged. He had a shockrod, but it wouldn't be any use against an alien in powered combat armour. Or even a man in a spacesuit. Projectile weapons weren't exactly banned on Luna, but it was unusual for a civilian to carry one. The risk of someone putting a shot through the dome and causing a leak was too high. Brian doubted it was *that* high, but it hardly mattered. Projectile weapons wouldn't make much of a difference either.

"I don't think they'll pay much attention to this colony," he said, finally. "There's nothing here they'll want."

"Wine, women and song," Farrakhan commented. He seemed to be having problems with his spacesuit. "They might want to take some time off to relax too."

"Hah," Brian said. He doubted the Tadpoles would be particularly interested in what the human race considered relaxing. They were hardly *human*. "Lean over here. I'll check your suit."

He glanced at Abigail as soon as Farrakhan was suited up, then looked at the others. "Keep a sharp eye on the air gauge," he ordered. "If it drops too low, suit up yourselves and follow us."

The airlock opened at his touch, somewhat to his surprise. He knew it was designed not to open *both* doors at once - that feature was engineered into all airlocks, wherever they were - but he'd expected to have to crank the hatch open so they could walk into the chamber. He walked inside, checking the hatch carefully, then pulled his helmet over his head. The short-range transmitter seemed to work perfectly, much to his relief. At least they could *talk* once they were through the airlock. The hatch hissed closed behind the others, once they joined him. Brian let out a sigh of relief, then started to work on the outer hatch. It opened, allowing the chamber's air to vent into Sin City. He suddenly felt very cold.

"No atmosphere," he said. He'd half-hoped the telltales were lying. Some of the civilian models were so over-engineered that they reacted badly to even a minor drop in the local atmosphere. "Keep your helmets on at all costs."

"I grew up here," Abigail said, tartly. "I know what I'm doing."

"Good," Brian said. He looked down the corridor. "Stay behind me."

The main lighting had failed, he noted grimly. Emergency lighting had come on, thankfully, but it was flickering alarmingly. Either the power distribution net had collapsed completely or the Management had skimped on the system. Dark shadows flickered at the corner of his eyes as the lighting dimmed still further, worrying him more than he cared to admit. The chances were that anyone not in a shelter was dead, but...he knew he couldn't take that for granted. Someone *might* have managed to get into a suit or a life support bubble before it was too late.

He inched down the corridor, checking the channels one by one. His suit was sending out an automatic distress beacon, but there was no reply. There weren't any other beacons either, as far as he could tell. The local datanet seemed to have failed completely. He gritted his teeth as he reached the door and peered into the casino, then swore. The room was a nightmarish horror show. Dead bodies lay everywhere: on the floors, on the tables...gathered around the rear hatches, as if they'd open and provide succour. Men and women, young and old...they were all dead.

"My God," he said. He fought down the urge to throw up. A modern suit was designed to cope with vomit, but he had no idea how the older design would cope. "How many people died here?"

Farrakhan moved up behind him. "There were ten tables in the room," he said. "Each of them had seven players and dozens of spectators..."

Brian shook his head as he looked around, treating the room like a crime scene. The position of most of the bodies suggested a panicky flight to safety, wherever *that* was. There didn't look to have been *any* safety...the damage to the bar and tables suggested a major impact, but not one big enough to knock the light fittings from the ceiling. He looked down at the closest body and shivered. The poor bastard hadn't had a chance to grab a facemask, let alone a spacesuit, before he'd died.

You have to be near life support gear, his instructor had said years ago, when he'd talked about dealing with explosive decompression. *If you're not, you're dead.*

"Stay back," he ordered, tersely. He hoped Abigail wouldn't throw up, when she saw the bodies. "I just need to check around."

He left the two of them behind as he circled the room. The rear hatches remained solidly closed, even when he banged his gauntlet against them. Someone might be alive in there - it was the logical space for an airtight compartment - but there was no way to be sure. It certainly didn't look as though anyone was interested in opening the hatch. He checked behind the bar, silently noticing the number of shattered bottles and glasses on the ground, then walked back to the others. There was nothing left for them in the casino, but death.

"They could have run to the shelters," Abigail said, plaintively. "Why *didn't* they run to the shelters?"

Brian shrugged. It was clear that no one, up to and including the Management, had taken the crisis seriously. Sin City wasn't a military target, *ergo* it wouldn't be attacked. And that had been a disastrous mistake. His thoughts raced, churning in circles. Why *had* Sin City been attacked? It had no military value whatsoever...hell, it had no *industrial* value either.

The death of so many guests *might* have an economic effect, but he couldn't imagine the Tadpoles caring about *that*. Besides, it would take longer than a few hours for it to take effect.

"I imagine they just wanted to keep gambling," he said, finally. "Let's move on."

They made their way slowly towards the stairwells, glancing into each chamber as they passed. Some were as nightmarish as the first - dead bodies littered everywhere - and others seemed abandoned, as though the inhabitants had been smart enough to run for cover before the hammer came down. The damage was getting worse, too. Two corridors were blocked by cave-ins, forcing them to find alternate ways to reach the stairwells. Brian didn't like the implications of *that*. A kinetic strike or a tactical nuke? If the latter, they might be walking through a radioactive field. His skin crawled, although he knew it was psychosomatic. If they were at risk of radiation poisoning, they wouldn't know until later.

The lights were growing dimmer as they finally reached the stairwell and looked up. Brian swore, inwardly, as he saw the stars high above them. There shouldn't have been any breach in the colony's dome, which meant...something had punched through and detonated inside the colony. Or maybe just punched though...he felt a wave of relief as he realised that it had been a kinetic strike. There was no real risk of radiation poisoning.

And we're going to have trouble getting up, he thought. There was just too much damage to the stairwell. The piles of rubble suggested that the stairwell's upper layers had been smashed. *But we don't have a choice.*

"Follow me," he said, softly. "And don't look back."

Farrakhan coughed. "What about my wife?"

"We have to get to the top if we're going to call for help," Brian said, patiently. He checked his radio, again. Still nothing. That worried him, more than he cared to admit. Luna wasn't Earth, but there was normally enough bandwidth to let him establish a solid connection to the datanet anywhere on the surface. If the orbiting relay satellites and ground-based nodes were out...he didn't care to think about the implications. "If you want to go back to her, go back."

He half-wished the man *would* go back, even though he knew it was wrong of him. An untrained civilian wasn't exactly *helpful*, was he? And yet, Farrakhan had done reasonably well so far. Brian felt his lips twitch in cold disapproval. Perhaps he was just being an ass. Besides, he had the feeling he'd be glad of Farrakhan's help when the shit hit the fan.

"Come on," he added, looking at Abigail. "Let's move."

He walked up the stairwell, feeling pieces of glass and plaster shatter under his feet. The impact had done a *lot* of damage, smashing roofs and destroying airtight chambers closer to the surface. No *wonder* so many safety precautions had failed. A system designed to seal off a single venting compartment wasn't designed to deal with a disaster on such a scale. Add poor maintenance to the list of problems and they were lucky *they* had survived.

And the rest of the shelters might be full too, he thought. *But they won't know what to do either.*

He reached the top of the stairwell and looked up. There were two more levels to go, but the stairwell was in utter ruin. He looked down a darkened corridor and shook his head in grim disbelief. The lights had failed completely. There had to be other stairwells leading up to the surface, but where were they? He had no idea.

"I never saw them," Abigail said, when he asked. "I used the lifts."

"Good thought," Brian said. "We should check out the lift shafts."

He led the way down the corridor, shining his suit's flashlight ahead of him. If he recalled correctly, the Luna Federation mandated that lift shafts *had* to be used for emergency evacuation if necessary. It wasn't something he cared to do, particularly in utter darkness, but he didn't see any choice. Clambering up the remains of the stairwell would be damn near impossible without proper equipment, which they didn't have. The snide part of his mind pointed out that there were probably ropes in the bondage suites, if they had time to look, but he wasn't sure how much time they actually had. They'd start running out of air sooner or later.

"That's the lift door there," Abigail said. "I don't know how to open it."

"Brute force," Brian said. The door was slightly ajar. He took one side and motioned for Farrakhan, then tugged the heavy door as hard as he could. The door wobbled, then slowly inched open. Brian pushed it as far as he could, looking around for something they could use to lock it in place, but there was nothing. "We'll have to be very careful."

He shone his torch inside the shaft. There *was* a ladder, set into the metal. He looked up, trying to determine where the lift itself actually *was*, but he could see nothing. At least the uppermost levels of the shaft didn't seem to have been exposed to vacuum. He looked down into the darkness, then sighed. They'd just have to take their chances.

"I'll go first," he said, positioning his torch on the suit. "Abigail, you follow me once I reach the top. Paul, you bring up the rear."

Farrakhan looked nervous, although it was hard to be sure with his face half-hidden behind the helmet. Brian didn't really blame him. Climbing up a lift shaft in semi-darkness, unsure if the lift was going to come plummeting down at any second...it was enough to unnerve anyone. He told himself to get on with it before he had an attack of nerves and reached out, taking hold of the rungs. They felt solid, thankfully. He forced himself to swing out and start climbing up before it was too late. The darkness ebbed and flowed around him like a living thing as he scrambled up and...

He bumped his head into something, hard. His hands unclenched, automatically. It was all he could do to catch hold again before he plummeted down the shaft. He cursed, a second later, as he realised what had happened. The lift had been secured at the top of the shaft, blocking his way. He hadn't even *seen* it before bumping his head.

Fuck, he thought. He reached up, trying to find the bottom hatch. There should be a way to climb into the lift...unless, of course, the Management had skimped on that too. He wouldn't care to bet, either way. *Ah!*

He opened the hatch and pulled himself up into the lift. The doors were open, revealing the uppermost level. Stars shone down, unblinkingly, through the gashes in the dome. He keyed his radio, calling for Abigail to follow him, then helped her into the cab when she reached the top. The lift quivered under him as she climbed inside. Brian cursed, hoping it would remain stable for a few minutes longer. Farrakhan was already climbing up to them...

The lift shuddered, then started to move. Brian threw himself out of the doors a second before it was too late, shouting a desperate warning. But Farrakhan had nowhere to hide. The falling lift slammed into him, knocking him down the shaft. Brian rolled over and peered downwards, hoping desperately for a miracle as the lift hit the bottom. But it was hopeless. His imagination filled in the details all too well. Farrakhan would have been crushed to a pulp under the lift, his body trapped right at the bottom. Even if he'd avoided *that*, his suit wouldn't have stood up to the impact.

"I'm sorry," he said. "I..."

Abigail caught his arm. "What now?"

Brian looked around. The railway station was to the north, but he doubted the trains would be running on time. There was a shuttleport - he had a rough idea where it was - yet flying a shuttle through a war zone was asking for trouble. Besides, he didn't know how to *fly* a shuttle. That left...

"The garage," he said. He keyed his radio, once again. Still nothing. He was starting to suspect the entire colony was dead. Anyone in the shelters was probably waiting, expecting to be rescued at any moment. "If we're lucky, we can find a buggy of some kind."

Abigail looked at him, suddenly. "What...what if my parents are dead?"

Brian hesitated. He hadn't considered *that*.

"I don't know," he said. He'd accepted a contract to return Abigail to her family, but...who would pay him if her parents were dead? He shrugged. He couldn't just abandon her. "We'll find out when we get there."

"If the aliens hit this colony," Abigail mused, "they'll hit other colonies too."

"Don't worry about it," Brian said. The last thing he wanted was her dwelling on the possibility of being an orphan. Besides, they really didn't have *time* to worry about it. "I'm sure they're still alive."

CHAPTER
NINETEEN

Near Earth/Earth Orbit

"Targets locked, sir," Commodore Jack Warner said. "The starfighters are ready."

Admiral Thaddeus Robertson nodded, grimly. Home Fleet had sat on the sidelines for *far* too long. Delay had followed delay, keeping his formation out of the engagement while Earth's defenders stood alone. No longer, he promised himself, as a low rumble echoed through *Enterprise's* hull. It was time to take the offense and drive the aliens away from Earth.

"On my mark, punch it," he ordered. He took a long breath. "*Now!*"

"Launching starfighters," Warner said. "Mass drivers online and firing...*now!*"

"Take us on a least-time course to Earth," Thaddeus added. "And prepare to launch the remaining starfighters on my command."

He sucked in his breath as his starfighter squadrons raced towards the alien observation squadron. He'd wracked his brains to find a way to dispose of the bastards without alerting their comrades, but there was nothing. The aliens had chosen their position well. They were close enough to keep tabs on Home Fleet's location, while far away enough to make it impossible for him to stomp on them easily. The alien commanders would know that Home Fleet was on the way.

"The starfighters are engaging the alien ships now," Warner reported. "They're taking them out, one by one."

And taking a beating too, Thaddeus thought. *Enterprise* quivered as she picked up speed, her flanking units spreading out around her. *Those cruisers were designed to deal with starfighters.*

"Ready a second strike," he ordered, curtly. "I want to dispose of the last of those cruisers before we reach the main body."

"Aye, sir."

Thaddeus leaned forward, watching grimly as the last of the alien ships vanished from the display. They were fast - he envied them their speed - but no match for a flight of starfighters. And while they *had* bled his pilots, they hadn't done any real damage to the fleet. They'd never had a chance to get within weapons range.

"Recall and rearm the strike force," he ordered. Choosing not to deploy the bombers had been a gamble, but it had paid off. "And then ramp up speed as much as possible."

He forced himself to lean back in his chair as the display updated, time and time again. The alien fleet had only two real options: fight or run. He wasn't sure which one the aliens would pick. Home Fleet had a major advantage - sixteen carriers to ten - but superior alien speed and firepower would even the odds. And they had their smaller ships too. Thaddeus had hoped to call on squadrons from Earth's defences to boost his forces, but it was clear that those pilots had taken a beating. At least a third of them were dead.

And they took out most of the lunar mass drivers, he reminded himself. *They'll have an excellent chance if they choose to engage us.*

He considered their possible options as the timer steadily ticked down to zero. The aliens *could* simply retreat at once and race for the tramlines. God knew he had next to nothing to put in their path, although the belters *might* give the aliens a fright if they passed too close to one of the fortified asteroids. Or they could seek open space and give battle there. Or - and worst, from his point of view - they could take themselves to Mars or Jupiter and lay waste to the facilities there. Home Fleet would have to give chase, which would mean engaging the aliens well away from Earth and Luna.

Or letting them lead us on a stern chase until they grow tired of it, he thought. *But they can't be sure when our reinforcements will arrive.*

"Inform Admiral Montgomery that we are coming in hot," he said, dismissing the thought with a bitter shrug. The aliens would have to show him their next move before he could respond to it. "And see if you can draw an update from Earth's defenders. If the aliens want to make a stand, I want Earth's remaining starfighters and bombers to reinforce us."

"Aye, sir," Warner said.

———

The Combat Faction was not afraid to die. Like the other factions, it was an ideal. Death - physical death - simply wasn't a real threat. But the prospect of being discredited was far worse. It had to concede, as the human fleet *finally* began its long-awaited movement, that it might have mishandled the battle. The humans hadn't - yet - matched them, not technologically. But they'd done enough to ensure that the Combat Faction couldn't smash their defences in a single short campaign and win the war.

Now, it considered a number of possible options. Pushing the offensive further against Earth was no longer in the Song, unless they chose to lay waste to the planet before the human ships arrived. The option danced through the various factions, only to be shortly dismissed by most of them. Retreat was a valid possibility - they'd already done a great deal of damage, admittedly at a significant cost - but it would leave the human fleet intact. And that would give the humans options for continuing the war.

That fleet must be destroyed, the Combat Faction decreed. *We must continue the engagement.*

The Song rose and fell. Given the damage to the human installations, it was quite likely the humans would need years to replace so many ships if they were lost. There was no way to be *certain*, of course, but it seemed logical. Besides, newer and better ships were already coming out of *their* shipyards. They hadn't gambled everything on one push against Earth, after all.

New orders flowed through the command net. The fleet slowly altered its position, turning away from Earth. Their remaining starfighters broke off their engagements and streaked back towards their carriers, reluctant to run the risk of being left behind. The humans held back, licking their wounds. Just for a long moment, the battle seemed to come to halt.

We will seek better ground, the Combat Faction announced. *And they will come to us.*

The sub-factions surveyed the system. There was no shortage of potential targets, even if the humans *did* seem to delight in putting colonies *everywhere*. The Tadpoles noted the terraforming project on the fourth world with bemusement. There was no shortage of habitable worlds beyond the tramlines either. Why the humans considered an attempt to reshape an old and dry world into something suitable for them was beyond the factions. It looked like an expensive and pointless project to them.

Let them waste their resources, if they must, one sub-faction stated. *It only weakens them.*

We will set course for the fifth planet, the Combat Faction said. There was nothing to be gained by trying to understand humans. They were alien beings. Their society and history spoke of nothing, but war. They were too dangerous to be allowed to infest space. *And they will follow us.*

Doubt floated through parts of the Song, but not enough to force a change. The fifth planet was a massive gas giant, one of the largest recorded. And the installations orbiting the giant planet were easy to identify. Cloudscoops and refineries...if they were destroyed, they'd hamper human reconstruction. It wasn't a direct way to win, but it would work. And it would force the humans to give chase. They'd have no choice.

And then we will win, the Combat Faction stated. *It will only be a matter of time.*

"They're pulling out!"

Ginny looked up in disbelief. The alien fleet was slowly turning away, redeploying its flankers to cover its retreat. Their starfighters were leaving too, breaking off their engagements and running for their lives. She felt a sudden rush of hope, mingled with fear, as the other starfighter pilots jeered the fleeing aliens. The battle hadn't been decided yet, had it? What were the aliens doing?

"Prepare to redeploy," the dispatcher ordered.

His voice brought Ginny back to herself with a bump. They were in trouble. Pournelle and several of the other installations were gone, which meant...she sucked in her breath. Could they survive long enough to find a starfighter berth? Could they land on a British or French flight deck? She was fairly sure of the former, but what about the latter? God knew she'd never tried to land on a Russian or Chinese flight deck.

And Home Fleet was coming...

She told herself to be patient. The aliens might be retreating, but they hadn't reached the tramline and vanished...not yet. There was a good chance she'd be called back to the fight, whatever happened. If, of course, she didn't run out of life support or simply collapse in her cockpit. She'd taken far too many drugs for her own peace of mind. The warnings the medics had given them, years ago, seemed a distant memory. Now, there was a faint fuzziness at the back of her mind that worried her.

"Hold position," the dispatcher ordered. "We're recovering the bombers first."

Ginny fought down a yawn. That made sense, she supposed. The bombers were far more vulnerable than any of the starfighters. But she couldn't help thinking that *her* squadron should have been recovered first. They'd been fighting for hours...she glanced at her watch, feeling cold. Two and a half hours. It felt like longer, much longer. She would have sworn a mighty oath that they'd been fighting for years.

She pushed the thought aside. There was no point in whining. She'd known the job was dangerous when she took it. And besides, she'd done well. They'd *all* done well...

Those who survived, she thought. Only four of her pre-battle squadron remained alive. She didn't want to *think* about how many other friends she'd lost over the last few hours. *And it isn't over yet.*

———

"Hold us within their blindspot," Captain Svetlana Zadornov ordered, quietly. The aliens were altering course at terrifying speed, coming about and setting course for Jupiter. She was tempted to order *Brezhnev* to go completely stealthy, long enough for the aliens to leave them behind, but she knew her duty. "Don't let them get a sniff of us."

She felt the tension rising on the bridge. The aliens hadn't noticed *Brezhnev*, but that might change as they passed far too close to her. There were too many starfighters and flankers moving past for her to feel *any* confidence in their stealth. And yet, the aliens had problems of their own. Home Fleet was bearing down on them and they were beating a hasty retreat.

No, she told herself, sharply. *They're heading for Jupiter.*

She cursed under her breath as she considered the implications. Every Great Power - and every nation that aimed at Great Power status - had an installation or two orbiting Jupiter. No sane power wanted to allow another power to control its supply of HE3. That was how OPEC had played the Great Powers for fools, before the Age of Unrest. Russia owned no less than *five* cloudscoops orbiting Jupiter, as well as three more orbiting Saturn. Losing them...she didn't want to think about the consequences.

New Russia gobbled up half our entire budget for space-based operations for the last twenty years, she thought. Her uncle and his comrades had backed the colony right from the start, insisting that Russia needed an entire star system of its own. *And now all that investment is lost.*

The alien craft passed closer to *Brezhnev* as they glided onwards. Svetlana held her breath, expecting to see the bridge explode around her at any moment. It felt weird to think that so many massive starships were so close to her, yet not seeing her...she couldn't even feel any trace of their passing. It reminded her of the time she would hide from her brothers on the estate, deliberately choosing the tiniest hiding place imaginable. They'd never quite believed just how small she could make herself, with an effort. Even as a teenager, she'd been better at hiding than them.

They would walk past me without noticing, she thought. She shivered, inwardly. One of her older brothers had died on a search-and-destroy mission, somewhere in Central Asia. The other was mustering forces on the ground to meet a potential invasion. *And the aliens are doing the same.*

"Keep us moving after them," she ordered, firmly. Home Fleet would need to overhaul the aliens, step by step, unless the aliens deliberately sought battle and slowed down. "Don't let them get too far ahead of us."

"We might have pushed our luck too far, Captain," Ignatyev said.

Svetlana smiled. She could hear a hint of grudging respect in his tone, even though she knew he would probably have denied it. *Brezhnev* had done well, all the more so as no one had expected them to do anything of the sort. Her ship had stayed close enough to the aliens to keep Earth informed, at great personal risk. She wondered, absently, how her detractors would feel, when they found out the truth. There weren't many commanders in any of the modern space navies who could make the same claim.

Not that it matters, if we don't get out of this alive, she reminded herself. *We could still be detected at any moment.*

"We have a duty," she said. She looked down at her pale hands for a long moment. She simply hadn't had enough sleep before she'd been woken, eight hours ago. "We cannot let them go back into stealth."

She glanced at him. Ignatyev looked like she felt, as if his greater age was finally catching up with him. Svetlana wished, suddenly, that she had a full crew - a *trustworthy* crew. She could have passed the bridge to an XO she trusted and got some rest, although she would have been in trouble if anything had happened while she was sleeping. Maybe her next command would be better, if she survived the battle. There was no way anyone could deny her a more significant command after *this*.

Assuming I survive, she thought. Her position was more dangerous than she cared to admit, even to herself. *Too many people would gain from my death.*

She studied the display for a long moment. "Keep Home Fleet appraised of the alien fleet's position," she ordered. "I want them to know every time the fleet twitches."

And keep them aware of my contribution to the battle, she thought, tiredly. She felt a stab of envy for her male counterparts. *They* didn't have to worry about being considered *mere* women. *It'll be harder for anyone else to claim the credit then.*

Her lips twitched, humourlessly. *The men do have to worry about someone else snatching the credit*, she thought, dryly. *But their critics have less ammunition.*

"The enemy fleet is picking up speed," Warner reported. "Sir...they're heading straight for Jupiter."

Thaddeus swallowed a curse. Jupiter...there wasn't any more important target in the entire system, save for Earth. Blowing up the cloud-scoops alone would be disastrous. They could be replaced - of course - but the knock-on effects would be bad. He had to stop them...

...And they probably knew it.

"Take us through the Earth-Luna system," he ordered. There was no point in trying to be clever. He certainly couldn't see any way to cut them off at the pass. The Io detachment was already reversing course, but they were badly out of position. "Inform the local defences that we will recover as many of their starfighters as possible."

"Aye, sir," Warner said. He paused. "What about Admiral Winters?"

Thaddeus glanced at him. "He's alive?"

"He's in a lifepod, according to the last update," Warner said. "I can't swear to it, sir, as there was a great deal of disruption, but he should have made it off Pournelle Base."

"Dispatch a shuttle to pick him up," Thaddeus ordered. He'd have to surrender command, of course...but Admiral Winters *was* the ranking officer. "Tell the crew that they are to bring him to *Enterprise* or take him to Nelson Base, depending on his decision."

And tell me, his thoughts mocked, *which decision would you want him to make?*

He sighed, inwardly. Command of Home Fleet was a dream come true - Home Fleet was the largest and most powerful fleet in the Human Sphere - but it was slowly turning into a nightmare. Part of him wished someone else could take the helm; the rest of him relished the opportunity. If Admiral Winters had stayed on Pournelle Base - and Pournelle Base hadn't been destroyed - the question would never have arisen. *He* would have stayed in command of Home Fleet.

And there's no time to worry about it now, he thought. *We'll need all the brainpower we can get.*

He keyed his console, bringing up the system display. The alien ships were picking up speed rapidly, forcing him to push his drives hard just to keep up with them. If they kept the range open, launching starfighter strikes would be difficult; if they reduced the range, he'd have to start worrying about what they might have in mind. And yet...

"Prepare to record a message," he ordered. There were *some* fixed defences orbiting Jupiter and her moons. Not enough to stand off the aliens, not until Home Fleet arrived, but enough to make a difference. With a little effort, they could be used to set a trap. "I want it sent directly to the Io detachment."

"Aye, Admiral," Warner said. "Ready to record."

Thaddeus took a breath. The aliens had lured them into a stern chase. *That* was impossible to ignore. And the wear and tear it would put on his drives was far from minimal. But it would cost them. He'd make sure of it.

"Record," he ordered. "Admiral Wright. The enemy is approaching your position..."

CHAPTER
TWENTY

Near Earth/Earth Orbit

"Now," Williams said. "*There* is a sight for sore eyes."

Ginny couldn't disagree as she guided her starfighter towards *Enterprise*. The giant carrier was clearly visible, even to the naked eye. Her sensors reported three squadrons of starfighters fanning out around the carrier, protecting her from a sudden attack, while nineteen more were covering the remainder of Home Fleet. She knew from New Russia that *Enterprise* and the other carriers were hellishly vulnerable to plasma guns, but it was hard to escape the sense that the carrier was invincible. She seemed so *solid*.

She braced herself as the starfighter flew into the landing bay and landed neatly on the deck, then sagged into her chair. The deck crew were already running forward, dragging the starfighter through a pair of air-lock hatches and into a pressurised bay. Ginny could barely move, even when the deck chief rapped sharply on her cockpit. Her entire body felt drained of energy.

Move, you silly bitch, she told herself.

It was hard, so hard, to pull herself up, then disconnect her flight suit from the seat. The tubes felt unpleasant against her skin, a grim reminder that she'd filled her urine bags sometime during the engagement. It was just a fact of life, but it still rankled. A smelly cockpit was a far from pleasant environment. She'd heard spacers joke about flyers who'd accidentally crashed their starfighters while fiddling with the bags, but she'd never found them very funny. It was one of the little details that somehow never got into the recruitment brochures.

She opened the cockpit and nearly toppled out of the starfighter. A deck hand caught her, a moment before she would have slipped and fallen; she leaned against him, just long enough to make it down to the deck. The racket was deafening: crews shouted to one another, airlocks opening long enough to admit the next set of starfighters...she couldn't even muster the energy to cover her ears as she stumbled towards the hatch. She hoped, desperately, that she wouldn't be required to fly for at least five or six hours. Her body was in no state for anything beyond a nap. She would have welcomed death if it meant an end to her suffering.

You're being stupid, she told herself, as the hatch opened. *Death would be the end, all right.*

A midshipman met her on the far side of the hatch and pointed her down towards the squadron room. Ginny winced as she saw him wrinkle his nose, trying to suppress her irritation. She probably stunk worse than a skunk. She almost giggled at the thought, then sobered as she remembered she was supposed to be in charge of the squadron. If there was anything *left* of the squadron. Chances were that she and any other survivors would be fitted into *Enterprise's* flight roster, if the ship went into battle. And it would.

The squadron room was empty. Ginny puzzled over it for far longer than she should before it dawned on her that the normal inhabitants were probably in space or waiting in the launch tubes. She stumbled towards the washroom, then stopped as she caught a glimpse of herself in the mirror. Her face was pale and sweaty, her hair damp, her flightsuit so badly rumpled that she looked a mess...she hoped, suddenly, that no one decided to carry out a snap inspection. Starfighter pilots got a great deal of latitude - they put their lives at risk every time they launched into space - but not *that* much. Any senior officer who saw her would probably faint on the spot.

She made her way into the shower compartment and stripped off her flightsuit, leaving it on the deck. She'd pick it up later, she told herself, as she turned on the shower. The water was lukewarm, but she didn't care. Just having the sweat and grime washed away felt heavenly, utterly heavenly. Her hands were trembling - the first sign that the stimulants she'd taken were catching up with her - but she found it hard to care. She'd survived a knife-range dogfight with alien starfighters. The risk of heart failure didn't seem quite so threatening.

The hatch opened. Lieutenant Bush Williams stepped into the shower. He didn't look any better than her, she noted. His face was haggard, as if he'd aged several years over the last few hours. The joker she recalled looked oddly subdued. She opened her mouth to reprimand him for dropping his flightsuit on the deck, then reminded herself that she'd done the same. They'd just have to draw replacements from the carrier's stores before they were ordered to return to the battle.

"Captain," Williams said. His voice was older too. "They've distributed the rest of the squadron over the carriers."

Ginny nodded. She wasn't too surprised. There just hadn't been time to organise the squadrons before Home Fleet resumed its pursuit of the alien ships. She was surprised they were still alone. They couldn't be the *only* pilots landing on *Enterprise,* could they? She hoped - prayed - that the others had been directed elsewhere. Foreign pilots wouldn't exactly be *encouraged* to wander around the ship, even if there *was* a war on.

"Fuck," she said. Counting her, five pilots had survived. The hell of it was that she knew she should be glad. Other squadrons had suffered far worse causalities during the opening weeks of the war. "Who else...who else survived? And where?"

"Sandra Woo was sent to *Kennedy*," Williams said. He stepped into the shower and washed, hastily. "I don't know where the others went."

Ginny sighed. Her body still felt as if she'd gone three rounds in the boxing ring, with her hands tied behind her. "Never mind," she said. "A few hours in the sleep machine will make us feel better."

Williams winked at her. "I know what *else* will make us feel better."

"Oh," Ginny said.

She found herself considering it, just for a moment. Williams wasn't unattractive...and besides, he was smart enough to keep his mouth closed afterwards. She was his commanding officer, but that wouldn't last long... he'd be promoted after the battle, if he survived. He'd done well enough to warrant a shot at squadron command for himself. It was still technically against regulations, but no one would give a damn. She could certainly rely on the other pilots keeping their mouths shut...

...But her body still felt like crap.

"The spirit is willing, but the flesh is weak," she managed, finally. Even lying back and thinking of America would cost her. "Maybe later."

She reached for a towel and dried herself hastily. Her body was covered in bruises, although she had no idea where they'd come from. Maybe she *had* picked a fight with a boxer after all. Or...she shook her head in wry amusement. The compensators were good, but far from perfect. Everything she'd put her starfighter through had probably worn them to a nub.

"The sleep machines are in the next compartment," Williams called after her. "I'll see you there."

Ginny nodded, forcing herself to pick up the dirty flightsuits and drop them in the basket to be cleaned. There was no way she could put hers back on, not now she was clean. She keyed the room's terminal, requesting a replacement flight suit from the ship's stores, then walked into the sleep machine room. The sleep machines looked like coffins - they *always* looked like coffins - but now they also looked welcoming. She hoped that wasn't a bad sign.

Getting woken up ahead of time would also be really bad, she told herself, dryly. Normally, that would guarantee a headache. Now, it would probably be worse. *This ship could be going back into battle at any moment.*

She climbed into the tube, pulled the lid shut and closed her eyes. A moment later, she was fast asleep.

———

"Welcome aboard, Admiral," Admiral Thaddeus Robertson said.

"Thank you," Jon said. He returned his subordinate's salute, then relaxed. The CIC looked very comfortable, all of a sudden. "It's been a long day."

"Not over yet, sir," Robertson said. He nodded towards the main display. "The aliens are steadily making their way towards Jupiter. They're also pulling ahead of us."

"Which may or may not be a good sign," Jon finished. He sat down at one of the consoles and studied the display. "Is there any suggestion that they are preparing another thrust at Earth?"

"If they are, we haven't seen any sign of it," Robertson said. "But they didn't get *everything* during their first sweep."

Jon nodded. The aliens had done a hell of a lot of damage, but Robertson was right. They hadn't finished off the orbital defences, let alone the industrial nodes. Sooner or later, they'd want to come back to finish the job...except Home Fleet was now between them and their target. Their ships were fast, but not fast enough to lure Home Fleet out of place and then dart back to Earth. Going after Jupiter made logical sense. Even if they abandoned the battle after smashing the cloudscoops, they'd do a great deal of harm.

And if they had another fleet in the system, they'd have attacked Jupiter earlier, he thought, grimly. The Tadpoles didn't seem to like complicated plans, although he did have a suspicion that the relative quiet between the battles of Vera Cruz and New Russia had been intended to lure the human forces forward into a trap. *But then, they know as well as we do that complex plans are practically guaranteed to fail.*

"We'll just have to hope that they have one fleet - one fleet alone - in the system," he said, nodding towards the red icons on the display. "You said you had a plan?"

"Yes, sir," Robertson said. "We'll use the Io detachment to make them reverse course, just long enough to let Home Fleet enter engagement range. At that point, we'll tear them to shreds with long-range fighter and bomber strikes. My starfighter pilots are relatively fresh, sir, and the newcomers are getting some rest now. We'll be ready to give them a kick in the nuts."

Jon gave him a sharp look. "Their pilots will be getting rested too," he pointed out. "And your ships will have to deploy significantly more fighters in a short space of time."

"It can't be helped," Robertson said. "Unfortunately, we didn't bring additional escort carriers with the fleet."

"They were needed elsewhere," Jon said.

He gritted his teeth, remembering a string of bitter arguments. Escort carriers were relatively cheap, although he - and the Pentagon - was uneasily aware of the knock-on effects of converting bulk freighters to escort carriers. But that very cheapness made them ideal for long-range raids into the enemy rear. Nothing as complex - or as dangerous - as Operation Nelson - but enough to hopefully knock the enemy off balance. And if the escorts were destroyed...well, at least the USN hadn't sacrificed a fleet carrier. He didn't like the logic - he certainly didn't like sending officers and men out *expecting* them to die - but there was no choice. The war could still go either way.

"Yes, sir," Robertson said.

Jon nodded, curtly. The latest stream of updates from Nelson Base were already on the display, waiting for him. Now the aliens were retreating, the defenders could turn their attention to smashing the pieces of debris that would otherwise hit the surface. It was a relief, yet there had already been far too many impacts. He hadn't dared look at the more detailed reports. He'd have to do that after the battle was over.

And then I'll have to brief the President and the Security Council, he thought, numbly. He'd have to give them an update, if nothing else. Chances were that the Security Council had been having problems following events beyond the upper atmosphere. And now, of course, they would be dealing with the aftermath of the battle. *They'll want proof the aliens can be beaten.*

He studied the tactical display for a long moment, silently weighing the possibilities. There was no way he could allow the alien fleet to proceed unmolested, even though there was a chance it *was* trying to draw Home Fleet out of position. No matter how he looked at it, there was no way to avoid the simple truth that letting the aliens devastate the facilities at Jupiter would put a severe crimp in humanity's ability to fight. And yet, Home Fleet might not be a match for a rejuvenated enemy fleet.

But they would have sent a stronger force, if they could muster one, he told himself. *Taking out Earth and the rest of the installations here would give them victory.*

He told himself, sharply, not to jump to unwarranted conclusions. The Tadpoles were *alien*, very alien. They might not *think* like humans.

For all he knew, this was their idea of a reconnaissance-in-force. And yet, the force they'd committed was far too large for anything other than a serious attempt to take out Earth. If they'd had more ships, they would have committed them.

Unless they threw the attack together at the last minute, he thought. *Did* Ark Royal *drive them to panic?*

There was no way to know. *Ark Royal* was hundreds of light years away, completely out of reach. She might have hit the alien homeworld or not, but *he* wouldn't know anything about it until a message reached home. There was certainly no point in hoping that *Ark Royal* would be back in time to affect the outcome of the battle. Jon and Home Fleet would win or lose without her.

"Continue the pursuit," he said. He hesitated. "I want you to remain in tactical command."

A flicker of relief crossed Robertson's face, mingled with concern. Jon didn't really blame him. The senior officer *should* have command, but Robertson had been in command of Home Fleet long enough to stamp his authority on the combined fleet. There was no point in risking the confusion that would follow - that would be sure to follow - if Jon assumed command. Besides, someone would probably complain that Jon *wasn't* the person who'd been placed in command of the fleet.

"I'll be here if you need me," he added. "Until then...do you have a cabin for me?"

"We've assigned a spare cabin in Officer Country," Robertson said. He looked oddly concerned. "It's a small space..."

"It will do," Jon assured him. He'd met admirals who'd pitch a fit if they weren't assigned cabins that fitted their status, but he'd never liked them. Besides, there *was* a war on - and he was exhausted. He'd happily sleep in a midshipman's bunk if it meant he got to *sleep*. "Can you assign cabins to the rest of my staff?"

"Yes, sir," Robertson said. "I'll have it done at once."

Jon rose. "Thank you," he said. "I'm very glad you came."

"Me too," Robertson said. "But it feels as though we didn't make it in time."

"We held," Jon said. "And that's all that matters."

―――――

"The alien fleet is gradually picking up speed," the helmsman reported. "They'll be inching ahead of us soon."

Svetlana nodded, curtly. The alien fleet carriers were fast, if the intelligence reports were to be believed, but their acceleration curves weren't much better than a human carrier's. They definitely weren't any better than *Brezhnev's*, although increasing her speed posed a significant risk. The aliens would be far more likely to catch a sniff of them if they forced their drives to work harder.

"Keep us here," she ordered. The alien carriers couldn't outrun *Brezhnev*. That was the important detail. "Time to Point Io?"

"Seven hours, assuming the alien speed remains fairly constant," the helmsman said, carefully. "However, I believe it will top out and steady eventually."

"Let us hope so," Svetlana said, dryly. If the aliens could keep ramping up their speed until they were pushing the light barrier itself, *Brezhnev* would be left in the dust. "Keep updating Pournelle...ah, *Nelson* Base."

She leaned back in her chair, fighting down a sudden wave of exhaustion. She'd expected a short, sharp engagement, not...not a long crawl across the solar system. She knew she'd done well - she knew her crew had done well - but she also knew they were pushing their limits. And they'd need to be fresh for the next engagement.

"Mr. Ignatyev, take the bridge," she ordered. It was unlikely anything would happen for at least six hours, unless the aliens detected *Brezhnev* before then. And if that happened, the ship would be blown to dust before they had a chance to realise that something had gone badly wrong. "Make sure that half the crew have a chance to get some rest for several hours."

"Aye, Captain," Ignatyev said.

Svetlana rose, taking the opportunity to look around the cramped bridge. She'd have to detox, then use a sleeping pill...she'd be vulnerable, if someone intended to try to stick a knife in her back. But now, with a battle still underway, it was unlikely that anyone would dare. Her enemies - her *family's* enemies - wouldn't support someone who put Mother Russia at risk. And the motherland was *still* at risk.

She walked through the hatch, keeping her head held high. It wasn't a sign of weakness, she told herself firmly. Male captains would need to rest too...not that they'd see it that way. And besides...she'd have to make sure that Ignatyev got some rest as well. He'd be tired too.

And he'd have to explain himself if anything happened to me, she thought. Ignatyev had no one to support him, if he was accused of murdering his superior officer. *He won't find that very pleasant at all.*

CHAPTER
TWENTY ONE

Sin City, Luna

Brian couldn't help feeling more and more uneasy as they made their way slowly towards the garage. Dead bodies lay everywhere, most of them wearing security or administration uniforms. What the hell had happened? If *he'd* heard the alert, the staff should have heard it too...they should have been encouraging the guests to abandon the card tables, gaming chambers and brothels and head straight to the nearest shelter. Had they really thought Sin City wouldn't be attacked? Or had they feared what would happen if hundreds of guests were forced to spend hours in the shelters?

He looked at Abigail as they reached the garage and opened the hatch. It was hard to be sure, but it looked as though a number of vehicles were missing. The main doors were open, revealing the cold grey landscape outside. Brian pursed his lips as he surveyed the remaining vehicles, wondering who had taken them and why. The tiny rovers were useless for what he had in mind, but the larger vans - were far better. He just hoped the ones left behind were in working order.

They used to do trips to the Apollo sites, he recalled. Sin City was hardly the *only* colony that handled such trips, but there was something special about theirs. The cynic in him wondered if they included orgies. *One of those vans would keep us alive long enough to reach safety.*

Abigail followed him as he walked towards the nearest van. "What are we going to do about the others?"

"I don't know," Brian admitted. He'd hoped to encounter other survivors as they neared the surface. Instead, Sin City appeared to be completely dead. "We'd need proper equipment to get back to them."

He opened the van and stepped into the airlock. The lights came on automatically, making him jump in surprise. He motioned for Abigail to remain outside, then cycled the airlock and walked into the interior. His suit checked the atmosphere and reported that it was breathable, something that worried him more than he cared to admit. If the van had been pressurised, why hadn't it been taken out of the garage? And yet, everything seemed to be working properly. The engine had power, the air cylinders were full and the navigation system was online.

Although half of the GPS satellites appear to be gone, he thought, as he put the system through a basic check. *Either the aliens took them out or they were shut down to keep from attracting alien fire.*

He called Abigail into the van, then activated the engine. The van hummed to life as he removed his helmet, taking a breath of dry air. There was enough life support to keep them alive for several weeks, he discovered as he explored the van carefully. The recycler would ensure they didn't run out of food, at least as long as they were careful not to think too hard about what they were actually eating...

"The suit was starting to smell," Abigail complained. "Can I get a shower?"

"Not yet," Brian told her. There *was* a shower in the back - and they *could* recycle the water - but he wanted her to stay in the suit. "We don't know what we're going to encounter on the surface."

He gunned the engine, moving the van through the doors and out onto the lunar soil. The navigation system seemed to be having problems picking out a safe place to go...he checked the radio and datanet, but found nothing. They couldn't be the last living humans on the moon, could they? It seemed impossible, but...he shook his head, angrily dismissing the thought. Humans had burrowed deep into the lunar surface over the last fifteen decades. The aliens would have had to shatter the moon into a whole new asteroid field just to slaughter every last human.

"There's a defence station nearby," he said. In hindsight, perhaps *that* had been what had drawn the alien fire. They might have assumed Sin City and the defence station were linked in some way. "There should be recovery crews there, if nowhere else."

Abigail looked downcast. "And what if there's nothing left, but a pile of rubble?"

"We have power and supplies," Brian told her. "We can head straight for another colony, if necessary."

The van hummed as it moved forward. Abigail sat quietly for several minutes, then stood and clumped her way to the rear. Brian felt a flicker of pity, mingled with irritation. Going to the toilet in a spacesuit was never fun, but...she should know better than to risk taking off her spacesuit. The van would normally have provided all the protection she needed, yet... there *was* a war on. Someone might just decide the van posed a threat and drop a missile on them.

Which would kill us both, spacesuits or no spacesuits, Brian reminded himself, dryly. *A KEW would smash us to atoms.*

"I made coffee," Abigail said, as she returned. "Do you take yours with or without sugar?"

"Black, no sugar," Brian said. He silently awarded her points as he took his mug. He hadn't thought to check for coffee himself. "How much coffee is there?"

"A couple of dozen cups," Abigail said. "I guess they don't trust the guests enough to give them coffee grains and powdered milk."

"They probably have a deal going with whoever produces the cups," Brian said. He sipped his coffee gratefully. "What else was back there?"

"Some ration bars," Abigail said. "I don't think they expected someone to take this van."

"Probably not," Brian said. He looked up. The stars were burning in the lunar sky, utterly unmoving. "Why did you run away?"

Abigail looked down. "Do we have to talk about it?"

"It's something to do," Brian said. He glanced at her, then returned his attention to the lunar surface. "You're not the first kid I've seen run away from home."

"I'm not a kid!"

"You're fifteen," Brian said. He kept his face expressionless. Had *he* been so convinced he wasn't a child when *he'd* been that age? Probably. "You won't even be old enough to *vote* for another six years."

"That's unfair," Abigail said. "I *live* on the moon. Why can't I vote?"

"Because you need some life experience to keep you from falling for the first idiot politico who promises you free lunches for the rest of your life?" Brian asked. "There ain't no such thing as a free lunch!"

Abigail snorted. "You see that written everywhere on the moon."

Brian sighed. "Most of the kids I saw who ran away had problems at home," he said. "Their parents were nasty, or drug addicts, or simply didn't know how to take care of them. Others...others thought they were grown up and that they could take care of themselves. They always managed to get themselves into trouble by the time the police caught up with them."

"My parents treated me like a child," Abigail said. "They...they think I'm still *five!*"

"I thought the same, when I was your age," Brian said.

"And I bet you found it just as maddening," Abigail said. Brian conceded the point with a nod. "Did you ever wonder how many of your friends weren't really *your* friends?"

"No," Brian said.

"My parents never let me do anything for myself," Abigail said. "I never got to go out of the mansion, unless I went straight to a friend's mansion. Even then, I was driven there by one of the servants, who would stay with me until it was time to go home. I never got to do anything!"

"There are people who would say that was heaven," Brian said, dryly.

"Not me," Abigail said. She crossed her arms. "I just wanted to get away and live my own life."

"And you ran right into trouble," Brian pointed out. "The world is a dangerous place."

"I never knew that," Abigail said. "Do you know...do you know what happened, when I reached Sin City? I was *mugged!*"

"Yeah," Brian said. "And I'll bet good money you weren't taking care as you walked around."

Abigail sneered at him. "What are you going to tell my parents?"

"The truth," Brian said.

"That's what always happens," Abigail said. "I tell the staff something... my mother hears it by the end of the day. I couldn't confide in *anyone*. And you're just the same! You're going to tell my parents what I told you and they won't *listen!*"

"You'll be an adult soon," Brian told her. "And you can make your own decisions."

"Except I just proved I can't," Abigail said.

The radio crackled. Brian glanced down at it in surprise, then peered out the window. A pair of men in spacesuits were walking towards the van, one of them holding a laser transmitter in his hand. Brian's eyes narrowed, a moment before he realised that they were both wearing military spacesuits. Behind them, he could see a Luna APV, barely visible against the grey landscape. It didn't look threatening, but that could change in a heartbeat.

"Open the hatch," the radio said. "Do not reply."

"They must be concerned about signal leakage," Brian said. It wasn't a good sign. His experience was police, rather than military, but even *he* knew that the high orbitals were insecure if people were worried about stray radio transmissions. "Stay here."

"Yes, boss," Abigail said, as Brian rose. "Should I put my helmet on?"

"Keep it on your lap," Brian said. He suspected it was pointless - if the soldiers wanted to punch through the van's thin armour, they could - but she was at least thinking along the right lines. "I'll cycle the hatch for them."

One man stayed outside, leaning against the van's sides. The other stepped through the airlock, removing his helmet as soon as he was inside the van. Brian allowed himself a moment of relief as he saw the Luna Federation Defence Force uniform, even though he still didn't know what was happening. The LFDF might want to confiscate the van for military use.

"I'm Corporal Littleton," the newcomer said. He looked younger than Brian had expected, although that probably shouldn't have surprised him on the moon. Abigail aside, children were expected to grow up fast. "And you are?"

"Brian Wheeler," Brian said. He dug into the suit for his ID. "We escaped from Sin City and came here."

"There's nothing left here," Littleton said. He scanned Brian's ID quickly, then frowned. "What's at Sin City?"

"The colony has been largely vented," Brian said. Their guest didn't seem to want to check Abigail's ID. That suggested the situation was worse than he'd feared. "There were some survivors in the shelters who need help."

"If there's anyone on hand to do it," Littleton said. "I'll pass the word, but right now we're pushed to the limit. I don't know if anyone can be spared to check Sin City."

He looked grim. "How long can you stay in this van?"

"Around six weeks, assuming nothing fails," Brian said. He had no idea if anything *would* fail. Sin City's maintenance definitely left something to be desired. "Why?"

"Right now, the whole situation is chaotic," Littleton said. "You would be well advised to find a quiet space and hunker down there and *wait*. The all-clear will be sounded once the system is clear."

Brian blinked, then looked up. "What...what happened up there?"

"Chaos," Littleton said, flatly. "Aliens attacked...two-thirds of the lunar defence stations are gone, apparently. The last report said that Earth itself was under attack. Right now, we have orders to keep radio transmissions to an absolute minimum. I couldn't swear to anything up there."

"Shit," Brian said. He looked up at the unblinking stars. "We could stay and help?"

"Probably not," Littleton said. He looked around the van, then shrugged. "Go find somewhere to hide and stay there. You'll hear the all-clear when it's safe to come out."

"We could drive directly to my parent's home," Abigail said.

Littleton gave her a sharp look, as if he hadn't noticed her until she opened her mouth. "I don't know what you'd find," he said, sharply. "How fast can this thing go, anyway?"

Brian nodded shortly, conceding the unspoken point. It would take weeks to reach Clarke Colony, assuming the wretched van held out that long. And there was no way to know what they'd find when they finally got there. He wanted to stay and help, but he rather suspected they'd just get in the way. Better to do as Littleton suggested and find a place to hide.

"Not fast enough," he said. "Do you have any links to the datanet?"

"Strictly for military use only," Littleton said. He turned back to the hatch. "I heard tell that Braidburn Colony was unharmed, but that was over two hours ago. I don't know if that's still true."

"I see," Brian said. "Thank you."

He watched Littleton jump down to the lunar surface, then meet his friend and walk back towards the APC. Braidburn Colony was only three or four hours away, depending on which route they took, but getting there might be difficult. A moving target was far more likely to be detected, if there were prowling aliens up there. And even if they *did* get there, getting the rest of the way to Clarke might be impossible. The inter-colony rail network was probably shut down for the duration of the emergency.

"We could start driving to Clarke," Abigail said. "It isn't *that* far."

Brian snorted. It *wasn't* that long a trip...in a railway car or on a spacecraft. But for the van, it would take at least five or six weeks to reach Clarke Colony. And all the problems about being a moving target would still apply.

"We'll do as he suggested and find a place to hide," Brian said. He started the engine, studying the map for possible hiding places. "And we'll listen for updates."

Abigail stared at him. "We can't just stay in the van!"

"There's no choice," Brian said. "Unless you can think of a way to get to Clarke Colony that doesn't run the risk of being detected by the aliens?"

"You don't *know* the aliens are up there," Abigail said. "They didn't kill us when we left Sin City."

"Point," Brian agreed. "But they might not be paying attention."

He shook his head as he put the van into gear. He didn't really blame Abigail for being frantic. There was no way *anyone* would want to spend a week or two in the van with a complete stranger, certainly not when there was a war on. But there was no alternative. He checked the map again, just to be sure, but he couldn't find anywhere that would provide a reasonable level of security that would probably also have escaped destruction. Going to Braidburn *might* work, yet without an update there was no way to be sure.

"And what do we do when we start running out of air?" Abigail asked. "Choke to death on our own flatulence?"

"We'll give it a few days," Brian said, patiently. He doubted choking to death was a possibility unless the air recyclers failed completely. If that happened, they were dead anyway. "And if we don't hear an update, we'll decide what to do then."

Abigail made a sarcastic sound, but said nothing as Brian drove the van away from the defence station. Brian kept his thoughts to himself too, concentrating on finding a good hiding place. He didn't want to be too far from the developed regions, but being too close might attract attention... thankfully, large swathes of the lunar surface were still completely undeveloped. As long as they were careful where they drove, they should have no trouble remaining out of sight.

Unless they take the high orbitals for good, Brian thought. He wished that he knew just what was happening in space, even if it was the worst case scenario. At least he'd *know. If they then start firing on everything that moves, we're dead.*

He found a suitable space and parked the van, then stood and walked to the rear. The sleeping compartment was clearly designed to introduce intimacy, although personally Brian would have suspected it was only for one full-grown adult. He'd have trouble sleeping in it alone, let alone sharing with his last girlfriend. Perhaps tourists weren't *meant* to sleep together in the van. It certainly seemed the most likely possibility.

"You can have the bunk," he called back. He checked the water supply, then nodded to himself. They had enough to keep them going for several weeks. "And you can have a shower too."

Abigail rose. "You mean I can finally get out of this suit?"

"You may as well," Brian said, after a moment. The suit wouldn't provide any protection against a KEW. "Just don't waste the water."

"I suppose you think I'm terribly spoilt," Abigail said. "Or a little brat."

"I think you're ignorant," Brian said. He wasn't about to tell her that he'd gone off the idea of having kids himself. "Ignorance isn't a sin, but it can be a capital offence. I thought lunar dwellers had that drilled into them at school."

Abigail flushed. "That's different."

"No, it isn't," Brian said. He walked past her. He'd kip in the driver's seat, far away enough to give her some privacy but close enough to respond to any problems. He hoped she wouldn't have a nightmare or two. "Ignorance can kill. You didn't know what you were getting into...and you were damn lucky to get out alive."

"But my parents could have taught me better," Abigail said, innocently. "They wanted me to remain ignorant."

Brian pointed a finger at her. "And now you know what you lack," he said. He understood why parents wanted to be protective, but there were limits. "Are you going to use this opportunity or waste it?"

CHAPTER
TWENTY TWO

London, United Kingdom

"Prime Minister?"

Andrew opened his eyes. He'd dozed off...when had he dozed off? It took several moments for his memory to return, reminding him that the solar system was under attack. He'd slept...how long had he slept? He wasn't sure of anything any longer.

He looked up. A pale-skinned girl was looking down at him, holding a mug of coffee. He forced himself to sit up, even though his body was aching painfully. Sleeping at the table hadn't been a good idea, it seemed. He took the coffee and sipped it gratefully, then glanced at his watch. It was 0500. He'd slept for nearly four hours.

And there are people out there who haven't had any sleep at all, he told himself, as he remembered the last reports. An endless liturgy of disaster: floods, riots, panic...troops and police on the streets, trying to contain the chaos. *All hell has broken loose and I can do nothing.*

"General Templeton suggested that you should have a shower and a change of clothes," the girl said. She pointed to a side door. "You'll find everything you need in there."

Andrew looked down at his rumpled suit. "Including clothes in my size?"

"We pride ourselves on being thorough, Prime Minister," the girl said. She gave him a shy smile. "There's something stored here for everyone."

"Thank you," Andrew said. He finished the coffee, then rose. "Can you bring me some more coffee while I shower?"

"Of course, Prime Minister," the girl said. "It'll be on your table when you come out."

Andrew nodded and walked through the door. The washroom was smaller than he'd expected, but laid out with military precision. He undressed quickly and stepped into the shower, sighing in relief as warm water flooded down and drove the last traces of sleep from his mind. He was tempted to stay in the shower forever - or at least for hours - but he knew he didn't have time. He turned off the water, dried himself quickly and then found a set of clothes. Someone had definitely been *very* through. The shirt and trousers were practically perfect.

They'd look bad in front of the television, he thought, wryly. *But otherwise they're perfect.*

General Peter Templeton was waiting when Andrew stepped out of the washroom, looking grim. Andrew cursed, inwardly. The last thing he recalled was that the aliens had been pressing the offensive against Earth, but that had been *hours* ago. Now...he didn't know *what* to expect. He supposed the aliens hadn't hailed Earth and demanded surrender - he'd have been woken for that - but what *else* had happened?

"Home Fleet forced them to retreat," Templeton said, bluntly. "But they're now *en route* to Jupiter."

"I see," Andrew said. He knew he should be concerned about that, but the battle in space was out of his hands. "And the situation on the ground?"

"It's bad, Prime Minister," Templeton said. He ran his hands through his hair. It dawned on Andrew, suddenly, that Templeton hadn't had any sleep at all. "We were spared any major direct impacts - unlike Russia - but tidal waves have been pounding our coastlines for the last few hours. We've lost dozens of seaside towns on the west and south coasts, Prime Minister; it was sheer luck that the east coast didn't take such a beating."

Andrew sucked in his breath. "How many dead?"

"We don't know..."

"*How many dead*?" Andrew repeated.

He caught himself. Templeton wouldn't know. Of *course* he wouldn't know. The national infrastructure that had been so painstakingly built over the last few centuries was completely overwhelmed. There was no way to know how many people might have been caught along the coastline, let alone what had happened to them. The records would be woefully inaccurate for generations to come.

"I'm sorry," he said.

"Don't worry about it," Templeton said. "Preliminary reports..."

He spoke rapidly, but his words started to blur together into a constant drone. Andrew couldn't begin to grasp what had happened, couldn't even come to terms with the scale of the disaster. *Nothing* he'd ever expected matched what had happened. Hundreds of thousands - perhaps *millions* - dead? He couldn't even begin...it was just *numbers*! There was no way he could put a name and a face to *all* of the dead.

"I want to see it," he said.

Templeton blinked. "Sir?"

"I want to see it," Andrew said. He *had* to see it. He *needed* to understand just what had happened. He had presided over Britain's single greatest disaster, in war or peace. Nothing, not even the Troubles, came close to it. "Get me a helicopter. There should be one on standby at all times."

"Yes, Prime Minister," Templeton said. He rose, his disapproval evident. "I'll make the arrangements."

He strode out of the room, leaving Andrew alone. Templeton *hadn't* been pleased...Andrew understood, all too well. The Prime Minister *had* to remain alive. He certainly shouldn't be placing himself at risk. But Andrew knew he *had* to see what had happened with his own eyes. He wouldn't be able to grasp it if he couldn't. The Deputy Prime Minister would take over if something happened to Andrew during the flight.

Templeton returned. "We've called in a stealth helicopter from RAF Northolt," he said, firmly. "It'll be here in twenty minutes."

"Thank you," Andrew said.

"We'll have to go to the roof to get onboard," Templeton said. He glanced at his watch. "I suggest you get something to eat. You'll need it."

Andrew nodded. "I will," he said. He couldn't bear the thought of eating anything, but he knew Templeton was right. "And thank you, once again."

"You're welcome," Templeton said. He looked down, just for a second. "I need to see it too."

The helicopter landed on top of the MOD building, rather than Ten Downing Street. Andrew hurried up the passageway from the bunker, then up a deserted flight of stairs. His escorts, a trio of burly SAS officers, insisted on going first, even though the building had been evacuated before the battle began. Andrew told himself, as he reached the top and clambered into the helicopter, that he shouldn't take it personally. The streets of London were no longer safe.

Dawn was glimmering over the horizon as the helicopter jumped into the sky. Andrew recalled, vaguely, that the pilots had been trained to get the Prime Minister - and other government officials - out of London at speed, on the assumption that any hostiles prowling the streets would have MANPAD weapons. He didn't think it had ever happened - certainly not in the last century - but he understood the need to be careful. His guards remained quiet as Andrew leaned forward, peering down. London...

He stared, unsure - just for a moment - if he really *was* looking at London. The skyline was different...no, it was just missing a number of buildings. They seemed to have vanished. He looked down and spotted the Houses of Parliament, with Ten Downing Street and Trafalgar Square nearby. But there were great pools of water everywhere. The Thames had broken her banks. Further to the south-east, he could see flooding...

"My God," he breathed. How many people lived there? The water would have driven them from their homes...or drowned them, if they hadn't fled in time. He swallowed, hard, as he tried to comprehend the scale of the disaster. "How many people are down there?"

No one answered as the helicopter drifted slowly east. Hundreds of people were walking south, as if they expected to find help and succour there. Andrew prayed, silently, that they would find *something*, although he had no idea what. Fires were burning out of control in a dozen places, the flames threatening to spread rapidly despite the flooded streets. The fire brigade couldn't get to them, Andrew guessed. Piles of rubble marked the spot where tall buildings had stood, before they'd been knocked down by the flood. He felt a pang of guilt as he recalled how the motion to replace those cheap buildings had been tabled, time and time again. How many people had died because the government had thought it had too many other problems that needed attention?

The helicopter rose still higher, jerking as gusts of wind battered the hull. Floods were everywhere, shimmering brightly under the early morning sun. Even the sunlight looked odd, as if it was diffused through an invisible cloud. The clouds seemed to be moving north, thickening rapidly. It looked like a scene from hell.

My God, Andrew thought, numbly. *How do we cope with this? Where do we even start?*

"We have strict orders not to fly too far from London, Prime Minister," the pilot said. "Where do you want to go?"

Andrew shrugged. He had no idea. He'd hoped he could grasp the disaster, once he saw it with his own eyes, but it was still beyond him. Britain hadn't had anything this bad for centuries, if at all. The Troubles, the Blitz...he had to look as far back as the Black Death before he could think of anything that might have had the same impact. He'd seen the plans for coping with a nuclear attack - there was always a fear that a terrorist group might one day obtain a nuke - but that would have remained confined to a single city. *This* was national in scope. He didn't even know where to begin...

The helicopter jerked, again. "We've got a sudden shift in the weather," the pilot said, sharply. "I'm going to have to put this baby back on the roof."

"Take us back," Andrew said. He fought despair as the helicopter turned and clattered back up the river. No matter what he did, hundreds of thousands - perhaps millions - of people were going to die. And there was nothing he could do about it. "I..."

He shook his head. Words seemed so...*inadequate*, somehow. The greatest disaster in living memory, perhaps the greatest disaster in Britain's long history...the thought kept rattling around and around his head. There was nothing he could do to save the people who'd elected him into office. He couldn't save *anyone*.

The helicopter landed. His escorts checked the rooftop, then led the way back down to the bunker. Andrew couldn't help thinking he smelled death in the air as he followed them into the building. Perhaps it was just his imagination, but...he shook his head, again. Death *was* in the air. And there was nothing he could do about that too.

Templeton met him when he entered the command chamber. "General Richardson has assumed command of the London District," he said. "He's requesting permission to burn bodies."

Andrew blinked. "Burn bodies?"

"A dead body will become a source of disease, Prime Minister," Templeton said. "And there are thousands of them out there, poisoning our water supplies..."

"Do it," Andrew said. "What else do you intend to do?"

"Set up refugee camps, then start pressing civilians into service," Templeton said. "We do have plans for something like this, Prime Minister, just..."

"Just not on such a scale," Andrew said. He sagged into his chair, feeling helpless. "I don't suppose there's any hope of international aid?"

"I doubt it, Prime Minister," Templeton said. "Anyone who might have been inclined to help has their own problems. The Yanks have lost San Francisco and several other cities along their west coast, the French have lost their south coast...there'll be a security nightmare too, depending on the situation in North Africa."

Andrew sighed. Normally, unauthorised ships trying to cross the Mediterranean were sunk without warning. The Age of Unrest had left scars deep within Europe's politics. But now, the naval patrols and orbiting laser satellites were gone. North Africa would be in a mess too, he was sure - the warlords had never been able to rebuild the long-gone states of Egypt, Libya and Algeria - but they might recover quicker. Who knew what would happen then?

Templeton sighed. "The Irish have already asked for our help," he added. "Their coastlines were battered too."

"Send them what we can spare," Andrew ordered. There *was* no one else who could help Ireland...no one else had either the motivation or the ability. "If we can spare anything..."

"We don't have enough for ourselves, Prime Minister," Templeton said. His voice was politely regretful. "I'm sorry."

"I know," Andrew said. He couldn't put Ireland ahead of Britain. The voters would crucify him, when - if - the next election was held. "I'm sorry too."

———

"Form an orderly line," Police Constable Robin Mathews bellowed, as civilians kept flowing towards the hastily-established registration centre. His body ached, but he forced himself to keep going. "Form an orderly line and wait your turn!"

He gritted his teeth. There was an ugly mood in the air, a sense that violence could break out at any moment. He'd sensed it before, back when a particularly important football match was on, but this was different. Yesterday, the civilians had had jobs, homes and lives; today, they'd lost everything, but their lives. He had no idea if the civilians would ever be able to go home...

The banks have been shut down, he thought, as he directed a nasty-looking man towards the line. So far, no one seemed to have thought of checking their bank balance. But that wouldn't last. *How long will it be before someone realises they've lost their money too.*

He kept one hand on his shockrod as more and more civilians appeared. Most of them looked shell-shocked, but a handful were definitely in a bad mood. They'd had expensive homes by the river, the river that had just broken its banks. He'd heard brief snatches of chatter on the radio that suggested it was far worse to the east. A number of shoddy buildings had come crashing down in rubble. God alone knew how many people had been killed.

"I'm a fucking taxpayer," a large man said. He was waving something around. Robin tensed until he realised it was a folder, rather than a weapon. The rescue worker who was trying to deal with him looked terrified. "Do you know how much I pay in fucking taxes? I demand you give me some fucking food, right now!"

Robin hurried over, drawing the shockrod and holding it behind his back. "Sir, please wait your turn," he said. There were only seventeen policemen assigned to the registration centre, most of whom had their own problems. A fight could turn into a mob riot very quickly, killing all of the policemen as well as some of the civilians. "The staff are already cooking the food."

"I pay half a million in fucking taxes," the man said. There was a vague murmur of agreement from some of the onlookers. "I pay your fucking wages, you..."

"Sit down," Robin ordered. He didn't want to shock the man, but he was already losing control of the situation. Unrest could easily turn to anger if he mishandled things. "Food will be provided as soon as possible."

He held the man's eye, trying to combine reasonableness with naked intimidation. If the man refused to cooperate...the man glared back at him, then sagged suddenly. Robin kept the relief off his face as he motioned the man into one of the lines, which was already picking up speed as the rescue workers smoothed out the process. Once registered and fed, some of the civilians would be marched south to the refugee camps and the others would be put to work helping to clear the streets. God knew they needed clearing. The floods had caused an awful mess. Cars had been overturned or simply smashed, trees had been torn out of the ground and thrown in all directions, windows and doors had been shattered...

A tiny hand caught his. He found himself looking down at a small girl in a red dress. "I've lost my mother," she said. "Where is she?"

Robin cursed under his breath. "I don't know," he said, looking around. He couldn't see anyone who looked like a plausible candidate among the crowd. "How did you get here?"

"Mummy told me to run," she said. Her face darkened, as if she were about to cry. "Where *is* she?"

"I don't know," Robin repeated. He led the girl to the front of the line and waved to the nearest rescue worker. "The nice lady here will take your name and address, then try to link you up with your parents."

He shivered as he looked away, wondering what had happened to the rest of his family. Or the girl's family...he'd be astonished if she was the only child who'd lost her parents in the chaos. They'd just have to hope that the registration system held up well enough to reunite parents and child, if the parents had survived. He didn't want to think about what might happen to the poor girl if her parents *hadn't* survived.

Normally, we'd find her a foster family, he thought, as he paced his way back to the end of the line. Another wave of civilians was approaching. *But now the vetting process will be utterly fucked.*

He looked up as he heard a rumble of thunder. Panic ran through the crowd - he could hear people muttering about aliens - as the skies darkened with terrifying speed. It was going to rain, and rain heavily...he gritted his teeth, cursing savagely. Of *course* it was going to bloody rain. What English crisis would be complete without rain?

And that'll make it harder to get anyone out of the city, he thought, grimly. The first water droplets were already splashing down. *God help us.*

CHAPTER

TWENTY THREE

Ward Mansion, Penzance, United Kingdom

Molly shifted, uncomfortably.

She'd grown used to sleeping poorly, ever since Kurt returned to the Royal Navy, but this was different. The bed felt hard, her sides were aching and...and someone had his arms wrapped around her. She tensed automatically, then opened her eyes. She was lying on a blanket in Ward Mansion. Sunlight was streaming through the windows, driving away the last residue of sleep...

Memory returned. *The kids!*

She sat upright and looked around. Garrison was lying next to her, snoring loudly. His jowls rose and fell as he breathed...she couldn't believe that, once upon a time, he'd been her lover. The room itself was a wreck, piles of books and damp flooring everywhere. Even finding the blankets had been a nightmare, she recalled. She listened, carefully, but heard nothing. There were no engines in the driveway, no voices calling...no birds singing in the trees. The world seemed almost *eerily* silent.

Garrison shifted against her. "Molly?"

"Time to get up," Molly said, firmly. She stood, looking down at her dress. It was torn and wrinkled, probably beyond repair. Somehow, she doubted the shop would replace it if she asked. The shop itself might no longer exist. "I can't hear anyone outside."

She walked to the window and peered down. The grounds had been ruined: the flowerbeds ripped to shreds, the trees and statues knocked to the ground, great pools of water lying everywhere...it was a nightmare. There was something odd about the sky, something she couldn't quite place. It was blue, but not the blue she knew. There were no signs of human presence, save for the two of them. She could almost believe they were the last humans left alive.

We can't be, she told herself. *Where are the staff?*

"There should be something to eat in the kitchen," Garrison said. He sounded tired and broken. His expensive suit was a write-off. "Have you checked your smartphone?"

Molly cursed herself under her breath as she pulled the device from her pocket and glanced at the screen. There was no signal, no connection to any local or national datanodes. There didn't even seem to be any updates from the government, no orders or reassurances for the civilians. She gritted her teeth, wondering what *that* meant. The entire country couldn't be gone, could it? She followed Garrison down the corridor, splashing through puddles of water as she tried to think. If they really were the last two people alive...

We are not, she reassured herself, again. *There will be others.*

She cursed again as they walked into the kitchen. It was a wreck too: pots and pans lying on the wet floor, storage cupboards torn open and their contents strewn everywhere. She had no idea how to use half of the equipment in the chamber, even if there was power...she looked around until she found a kettle, then tested it. There was no power. Even the emergency lighting was gone.

"No power," she said, grimly. "What do we do?"

"We look for stuff we can eat without power," Garrison said, dryly. He stepped through a half-open door into a darkened chamber. "I..."

His voice hardened. "Shit!"

Molly walked up behind him and peered into the semi-darkness. There was a hatch - no, a ladder - leading down into a basement. The basement was full of water...she recoiled in horror as she realised that there were *bodies* drifting within the water. She had to turn away to keep from being sick, her mind racing to try to understand what they'd found. The staff must have gone down to the basement in hopes of finding shelter, only to drown when the waters blasted through the hall. They hadn't even had a chance to escape.

Garrison slammed the door closed. "There's nothing we can do for them now," he said, harshly. "We have to find something to eat."

Molly nodded and joined him in searching the kitchen. The fridges and freezers were powerless, naturally, but the milk tasted all right when she tested it against her tongue. She hesitated, then drank as much as she could. Garrison found a box of cereal and passed it to her, ordering her to fill a bowl and eat it. Molly didn't bother to argue. She'd never been that fond of wholegrain cereal, back when she'd been at home, but it was all they had. She certainly didn't have anything *else* to eat.

She sat down on the damp chair and munched a second bowl of cereal, considering her options while she ate. No one knew where she was, at least as far as she knew. She'd certainly never told Gayle or the kids where she was going. And that meant...no one would be looking for her. She was sure that *someone* would check out the hall eventually, but when? The government might have other things to worry about. She certainly couldn't send a distress message to request help.

"There are several more bodies in the backroom," Garrison said. He walked back into the kitchen, carrying a box of milk chocolate bars. Molly could have kissed him as he offered her one. "And no sign of anyone living at all."

Molly met his eyes. "We're going to have to walk back to Woking," she said. "We don't have a choice."

"Penzance would be closer," Garrison pointed out.

"Penzance went dark," Molly reminded him. She shivered, remembering the dark waters snuffing out the town's lights. "There's no way to know when help will arrive, if it ever will."

"No," Garrison agreed. He looked back at her. "You do remember being told to stay put?"

"My children are in Woking," Molly said, sharply. She gritted her teeth. "I am going there, with or without you. Stay here if you want."

Garrison sighed. "I'll come with you," he said. "Just give me an hour to search the house for anything else we can use."

Molly nodded, unsure if she should be pleased or upset. She was starting to dislike Garrison, more than she cared to admit. Having him along might not be a wholly good thing...but at least he was company. She chewed her chocolate bar, telling herself she needed him. There would be time to dump him after she reached home.

"I'll find something better to wear," she said, looking down at the dress. "I...should we be worrying about paying for it?"

"Probably not," Garrison said. He looked grim, just for a moment. "Lady Penelope is dead."

Molly finished her makeshift breakfast, then searched through the bedrooms until she found the wardrobes. Lady Penelope hadn't been *that* much smaller than her, thankfully. She found a set of clothes that fitted, if poorly, then a coat that would hopefully provide her with some genuine protection from the elements. The air felt cold, yet gusts of hot and cold wind blustered against her as she walked outdoors. There was still no sign of anyone else, not even a plane flying overhead. The gardens were still drenched in water.

"Take this," Garrison said. He passed her a sharp knife, then a small bag of food and bottled water. "Unfortunately, I couldn't get into the weapons locker. Lady Penelope never gave me the code."

"It'll have to do," Molly said. She stuck the knife in her pocket. Lady Penelope had probably had a small collection of firearms, but there was no way to get them. Besides, she didn't know how to *use* a firearm. Military dependents had been offered training, but she'd never bothered to take the course. "Shall we go?"

"Let me check out the stables first," Garrison said. He led her towards a stone building at the rear of the hall. "The horses *might* be alive."

Molly felt a flicker of hope - she hadn't thought of horses - which died the moment they walked into the stable. The poor beasts were dead, their bodies lying in their stables...she recoiled in horror at the stench. Garrison held his nose as he checked the stables, one by one, then shook his head. There was no hope of riding out of the disaster area.

And I don't know how to ride either, Molly thought. *If I get home, I'm going to learn.*

She checked her bag as they made their way slowly down towards the gates. The driveway was a muddy track, fallen trees lying everywhere. It would have been impossible to get out of the estate if they'd had a car, she realised. The horses would have had trouble too. But she had a feeling she'd miss the car in an hour or so. Walking all the way to Woking would take *days*.

"We should encounter *someone* as we head east," Garrison said. They looked down the muddy road, lined with half-fallen trees. "There will be rescue missions underway, won't there?"

Molly nodded as she worked her smartphone. The GPS was offline - the satellites seemed to be missing - but she could still bring up a map and compass. It wouldn't be anything like as effective - map-reading had never been one of her skills - yet what else *could* she do? The sign marking the entrance to the estate lay in the mud, utterly useless. She couldn't help thinking that the flood waters had smashed every other street sign too.

"If we walk east, we should eventually cross the motorway," she said. It wasn't ideal, but it would keep them on the right route. They'd probably run into *someone* along the way too. "I think we should be able to get there without problems."

"Hah," Garrison said. He glanced up at the darkening sky. "Keep telling yourself that, if you like."

Molly scowled at him, then started to walk. She didn't bother to look back. If he decided he wanted to stay behind, he could stay behind. She had enough food and water to keep her going for a few days, as long as she was careful. Garrison...she didn't need him. His skills wouldn't be much use in the brave new world.

She wished, with an intensity that surprised her, that *Kurt* was with her. Kurt never gave up, Kurt never stopped...she wondered, suddenly, why that had irritated her, after they'd been married long enough for the shine to wear off. Kurt's skills would be useful in the new world, useful enough to make him a very important man. Garrison...he was a lawyer and an old lawyer at that. There wouldn't be any lawsuits in the near future.

And he might not even survive the next few days, she thought. A day ago, Garrison had been *connected*. Now, the aristocracy might no longer exist. *Can he keep up the pace?*

She heard him splashing through the puddles behind her and smiled, inwardly. Garrison was older than her, *much* older than her. Could he keep up with her? Did it matter if he could? If she hadn't accepted his invitation - knowing that she'd pay for it in his bed - would she be with her children now? Or would she have gone somewhere else instead? Perhaps she would, she admitted privately. She'd wanted to do something exciting with her life - and Kurt's share of the prize money - before she had to go back to being a housewife. She would have found some other way to get into trouble.

Her legs started to ache as the temperature rose rapidly. Sweat ran down her back, pooling in her knickers and trickling down her legs. The sky was darkening, turning a deep blue that spoke of rain and thunderstorms. She looked up for a moment, but forced herself to keep going anyway. Garrison wasn't the only one in bad shape, she told herself as the aches spread up into her chest. She hadn't been fit as a fiddle for years. Perhaps, in hindsight, she should have worked out more while the kids were at school. It wouldn't have done her any real harm.

And if I'd known this was coming, I would have stayed with the kids, she thought. *And done everything I should have done to keep us alive.*

"Something hit the water," Garrison called. She stopped and looked back. His face was red, his breathing came in ragged gasps. She wondered, morbidly, if he was on the verge of a heart attack. "That's what caused the tidal waves."

"I know that," Molly said. She'd seen the...*something*...hit the water. "I'm not stupid, you know."

Garrison took a deep breath. "The impact will have thrown a shitload of water into the atmosphere," he said. He sounded as though he was trying to talk down to her, but didn't quite have the energy. "What goes up must come down."

Molly looked at the looming cloud. It had been a long time - a very long time - since she'd sat through basic science, but she vaguely recalled that water vapour turned into water droplets in the sky and fell to the ground as rain. Or something like that...she'd never really *liked* basic science, not when she'd been a little girl. The teacher had been all too ready to send pupils to the headmaster for even the *slightest* infraction. She'd thought about trying to become a nurse, later in life, but her marks just hadn't been good enough.

"Are you saying it's going to rain?"

"Yes," Garrison said. He caught his breath. "And we have to find shelter."

"We have to keep walking," Molly said. The only shelter was the trees... and she didn't want to be under them if a thunderstorm broke out. She checked her smartphone, trying to estimate how far they'd walked. It didn't seem like more than a kilometre or two. "Come on."

The rain started twenty minutes later. Thunder and lightning flashed and boomed overhead while the rain fell so heavily that she felt as if someone had tipped a cosmic bathtub over her head. The road started to puddle over at once, the water growing deeper and deeper as the rain just kept falling. Molly pulled the coat around herself, but the water still leaked into her clothes. The wind was still blowing hot and cold. She shivered, helplessly, as she forced herself to keep going. There was nothing else to do.

At this rate, it'll take weeks to get home, she thought. She checked her smartphone once again, but there was still no signal. What was wrong with the network? She'd been told it couldn't be knocked down accidentally, even if terrorists took out a dozen nodes. But the government had turned it off. *Maybe we should try to find a shelter.*

The rain seemed to grow heavier, drenching her to the bone. She looked under the trees, but the ground was already muddy as hell. There was no way to escape the impression that the soil had turned into a swamp. If she stood under the trees, she might just get stuck even if she didn't get struck by lightning. Brilliant flashes of light danced overhead, followed immediately by peals of thunder. The storm had to be right overhead.

Garrison caught her arm. "We have to go back!"

Molly shook her head. There was nothing for her at the hall; nothing, apart from endless worrying about her kids. She couldn't go back, even though cold logic suggested there was no real choice. Besides, the dead bodies would get unhealthy in a hurry. She'd never studied more than the basics of first aid, but she recalled being told that dead bodies spread diseases or something along those lines. In hindsight, she wished she'd studied that too.

And then she heard a car horn.

She jumped and spun around. A minivan had sneaked up behind them, the sound of its engine drowned out by the thunder and rain. Three camper vans hid behind it, followed by a pair of cars and a tractor. She waved desperately, hoping - praying - that the drivers would give them a lift east. They'd been very lucky the drivers had even *seen* them in the storm.

The door opened. She pulled Garrison forward and climbed inside, heedless of the possible danger. The rain seemed to grow quieter as the door was slammed closed, although the drumming on the roof was terrifyingly loud. She caught her breath, then looked around the vehicle. Six children - the oldest around ten - and three adults, all looking grim. A school trip?

She caught her breath. "I'm Molly," she said. She hadn't been raised to trust strangers, but she had no choice. They weren't going to get back home without a vehicle and probably some help. "Where are you going?"

"Rosemary," one of the adults said. She sounded wary. "We're trying to get back to London. Where are you going?"

"Woking," Molly said. She looked back at the rest of the small convoy. "Can you give us a lift to" - she had to think for a long moment - "somewhere closer to my home?"

"You're welcome to stay with us," Rosemary said. "We'll drop you off somewhere closer to Woking, if we can get that far. Half the roads to the north are blocked, it seems."

She sighed. "What the hell happened?"

"Aliens," Garrison said. He introduced himself with a nod. "Where were you?"

"Camping trip," Rosemary said. "My brothers are in the military, so we took their kids into our home for the duration. And then we went camping and..."

"Next thing we know, the entire campsite is awash and the radio is prattling nonsense," another adult said. "This whole trip might have built someone's character, but it sure as hell hasn't built mine!"

"You were lucky," Garrison said.

"I know," Rosemary agreed. Her eyes narrowed. "Aliens?"

Molly nodded and started to explain.

CHAPTER
TWENTY FOUR

Luna

Brian was half-asleep in the cap when the radio bleeped. He jerked awake, one hand reaching for the pistol he wasn't carrying as he glanced around. The van was...the van was safe, he told himself firmly. It was just the radio. He looked at the timer - he'd been asleep for three hours - and then keyed the console. An all-clear message popped up, informing him that the alien fleet was now no longer in weapons range. Brian breathed a sigh of relief, then opened a direct link to the lunar datanet.

Half the nodes are no longer working, he thought, numbly. *But at least Braidburn Colony seems to be intact.*

He looked down at the console for a long moment, thinking hard. If the all-clear had been sounded - and it had - he had a duty to get in touch with the lunar authorities as soon as possible. If nothing else, he had to tell them that he was available to go into the personnel pool if necessary... and, of course, reunite Abigail with her parents. But if the alien fleet was still in the solar system, it might double-back at any moment. Going to Braidburn Colony might be enough to get them both killed.

Brilliant, he thought. *Make the wrong choice and we both end up dead.*

They *could* stay hidden for several days, he knew. The van could keep them both alive for weeks, although conditions would grow steadily more and more uncomfortable. And yet, he doubted Abigail had the ability to hide out indefinitely. There wasn't much to *do* in the van, save for chatting and - perhaps - playing computer games. He sighed, then started to power up the engine. If nothing else, they'd get a full update at Braidburn Colony. *That* would tell him what they should do next.

He heard a sound behind him as the van hummed into life. "Go back to bed."

"I couldn't sleep," Abigail said. She walked up to the front compartment and sat down next to him. "Where are we going?"

"The all-clear has been sounded," Brian said. "We're on our way to Braidburn."

"Thanks," Abigail said. She gave him a sidelong look. "Do you...do you *have* to tell my parents you found me?"

"I have to give them a full report," Brian said. "And no, I *won't* tell them you died at Sin City."

Abigail pouted. "They won't be pleased to see me again," she said. "I... does everyone *know* I ran off?"

"No," Brian said. "It was never advertised. Lucky, or one of your employers might have realised who he had working for him."

He cleared his throat. "And I think your parents *will* be relieved to see you again," he added, after a moment. "They wouldn't have spent so much money on tracking you down if they hadn't wanted to find you."

"I suppose," Abigail said. She leaned back into her chair. "Do you want me to make more coffee?"

"Please," Brian said. "It's going to be a long day."

The radio crackled, time and time again. Brian listened, carefully, as the lunar surface slowly came back to life, hundreds of small colonies and independent prospectors exchanging notes as they tried to put their lives back together. A number of colonies had been hit, apparently, along with two-thirds of the defence stations. Luna would never be the same again. Brian frowned as a couple of speakers discussed how the Great Powers might try to take advantage of the situation to eliminate all hopes of lunar independence. He doubted any of the Great Powers would have the time or resources to try - if Luna was battered, he hated to think what things must be like on Earth - but resolved to monitor the situation anyway. It might not be a good thing to be an Earther if the lunar population thought he was here to take over.

He took the coffee and sipped it, thoughtfully, as they found a well-travelled road leading towards Braidburn Colony. A handful of other vehicles joined them, exchanging brief signals as they came in from the cold. Brian wondered, absently, just how many of them had come from Sin City. He was still fairly sure that far too many of the staff had deserted, before or after the colony had been hit. The garage might have remained airtight long enough for the staff to board some of the vehicles and run for open terrain.

Abigail cleared her throat. "What are you going to do...I mean, afterwards?"

"I don't know," Brian admitted. He'd originally planned to head straight back to Earth, but *that* might no longer be possible. God alone knew when the regular Earth-Luna shuttles would recommence. "I might end up helping with recovery work."

"Oh," Abigail said.

Brian gave her a sharp look, then turned his attention back to the road as they approached Braidburn Colony. A long line of vehicles was waiting outside the garage, entering one by one. Brian hoped that meant the inhabitants were being careful, rather than limited interior space. He'd never visited Braidburn, but the colony's entry on the luna database suggested it was a fairly large - and independent - settlement. It *should* have facilities to cope with a sudden influx of refugees.

Assuming it doesn't get overwhelmed, he thought, coldly. *The Luna Federation never planned for a disaster on such a scale.*

He waited, as patiently as he could, as the line inched forward, vehicle by vehicle. The radio chattered from time to time, offering yet more updates. He listened, making mental notes as a speaker confirmed the destruction of Sin City. Apparently, no one was known to have survived. Brian was tempted to make a formal statement immediately, but held his tongue. It would probably be better to get Abigail back to her parents, *then* make a statement. Sin City's Management - if there was anything left of it - would be very interested in speaking to him.

They'll have to rebuild, somehow, he thought, wryly. *And I don't even know if they'll get the insurance to pay out.*

He guided the van through the doors, when their turn came, and parked in a massive underground garage. A trio of armed men entered the moment he stopped, searching the van and its inhabitants with swift and brutal efficiency. Abigail squawked in protest, but Brian said nothing. The locals had to be careful, if nothing else. Who knew what *else* might be travelling in the van? All the stories about alien infiltrators were nothing more than trashy nonsense - although Brian was fairly sure several of his teachers had been aliens in disguise - but terrorists could easily be trying to make the catastrophe worse.

"Walk straight to the gate and go through," the searchers ordered curtly, once they were finished. "Take your ID, but nothing else. We'll get your vehicle somewhere safe."

"Understood," Brian said.

He led Abigail across the garage and through the airlock. A line of people was waiting on the far side, seemingly bored as they waited for their number to be called. Brian took a ticket from a tired-looking administrator, then sat down to wait. Abigail sat next to him a moment later, closing her eyes as she leaned against him. Brian felt a flicker of envy as she started to sleep. The young were always much more resilient than they thought.

She hasn't done too badly, he told himself. *She'd do well with some proper training.*

He had to fight the temptation to fall asleep himself as minutes turned slowly into hours. The line was moving very slowly, even though the entry chamber was filling rapidly. It was unusual to have so many people trying to gain entry at once. Even a fully-loaded train wouldn't carry more than fifty passengers. And there was so much chaos that there was no way anyone's identity could be verified.

They might have to put us all up in a makeshift dome, he thought sourly, as their number was called. *That won't be pleasant either.*

He nudged Abigail, then helped her to her feet as their number was called again. The guard pointed them to a door, leading to a small office. A tired-looking bureaucrat was sitting on the far side, staring down at a computer screen. Brian would have thought he was being deliberately rude, if the man's head hadn't been nodding towards sleep. The poor man had had even less sleep than Brian himself.

"Good morning," the bureaucrat said. His voice was tired too. He pointed them to chairs with the air of a man who was too tired to play power games. "Name, ID numbers and places of origin?"

Brian had to think to come up with the answer. "We fled Sin City," he said. "But I came from Earth and she came from Clarke."

The bureaucrat looked puzzled for a moment. "Name and ID?"

"Brian Wheeler and Abigail Swansong," Brian said. He ignored Abigail's grunt of displeasure. Her name might get them better accommodation, if it didn't get them a flight to Clarke. "Here are our cards."

"I see," the bureaucrat said. He ran the cards through his reader, then frowned. "There's a missing persons advisory on both of you."

"My parents," Abigail said. "Does that mean they're alive?"

"I don't know," the bureaucrat said. "It was issued five hours ago, but it came from Swansong Enterprises rather than anyone in particular."

Abigail looked at Brian. "It does mean they're alive, doesn't it?"

Brian hesitated. As far as he knew, Abigail's parents *were* the only people who knew he was working for them, let alone that he'd gone to Sin City. But it was quite possible that they'd informed the rest of the company board or their lawyers. *Someone* would have to explain his disappearance, if he never returned home. It wasn't solid *proof* that Abigail's parents were still alive.

"It seems likely," he said, slowly. He looked at the bureaucrat. "What does the advisory actually *say*?"

"Just that you were missing," the bureaucrat said. He yawned, suddenly. "Excuse me."

"I feel the same way too," Brian said. "What do we do now?"

"I'll arrange for you to get a room - two rooms," the bureaucrat said. His hands danced over the computer console. "And then I'll inform the datanet that you two are alive. After that, I don't know. It may be some time before we can arrange a flight to Clarke."

"Understood," Brian said. He hesitated. "Are there any water restrictions?"

"Not at the moment," the bureaucrat said. He printed out two slips and passed them to Brian. "Go out the rear door, then ask for directions. Make sure you link your wristcom into the datanet. Someone *might* want to ask questions about Sin City."

"I understand," Brian said. "Did anyone send a recovery mission out there?"

"Not to the best of my knowledge," the bureaucrat said. "Sin City is very low on the priority list."

Brian nodded, then led Abigail through the door and down a long corridor. A grim-faced guardsman met them at the bottom, glanced at their slips and then pointed them towards a large building under the dome. The colony's park had been turned into a makeshift refugee camp, crammed with women and children. Brian couldn't help feeling a spark of guilt at how easily they - or, rather, Abigail's name - had managed to get a hotel room.

"It looks bad," Abigail said, softly. "Isn't there anything they can *do* for them?"

"It'll take time," Brian said. No one *starved* on the moon - mass-producing cheap food was easy, even if it *did* taste like something that had passed through a cow's digestive system - but it would take time to ramp up production. The Luna Federation hadn't planned for a disaster on such a scale. "Most of them will probably be moved out within the next few days."

Abigail gave him a sharp look. "Are you sure?"

"No," Brian said. They entered the hotel, passing a suspicious-looking bellhop. "But we have to hope for the best."

They made their way to their rooms and opened the doors. Brian checked Abigail's room carefully, then told her to get some sleep, before heading next door. He had a suspicion that Abigail would go straight for the shower, but he could hardly blame her. He'd been able to smell her ever since they'd entered the colony and he had a nasty feeling she could smell him too. God knew he needed a shower...but he'd feel guilty about using the water, even though he *knew* it could be recycled.

He checked his own room, then sat down on the bed and reached for the terminal. A new string of updates greeted him, all written in what might as well be baby talk. The aliens had been driven away from Earth, but they were still in the solar system...he shook his head in annoyance as he tried to read between the lines. No doubt the various governments believed the commoners would be happier - or at least calmer - if they were spoon-fed what the governments wanted them to know. The thought that not *knowing* would cause the commoners to jump to the worst possible conclusions probably hadn't occurred to them.

Idiots, he thought, morbidly.

The news from Earth was bad, although half the posts on the various datanet forums sounded like scaremongering. Thousands of pieces of debris - and alien weapons, if some of the reports were to be believed - had fallen into the planet's atmosphere, wreaking huge damage on the surface. Earthquakes, tidal waves...Brian had no idea how much to take seriously, but he knew that even a handful of relatively small impacts would be disastrous. It was starting to look as though he'd be better off staying on the moon.

If we can, he reminded himself. *I might not be allowed to stay.*

He keyed the terminal, bringing up the email datanode. It should have given him access to his email account, but it failed midway through launching. Brian cursed under his breath, then tried to open it again. This time, the node didn't respond at all. He swore, openly this time, then accessed a public email datanode. It was about as secure as a politician's mouth, but it would have to do. He wrote a brief report for his office back home - using a number of code words they'd planned for insecure communications - and then another one for Abigail's parents. There was no way to be sure they'd see the email - spammers used public email datanodes, so filters often wiped those messages sight unseen - but there was no other way to send a message. He rather doubted he'd be allowed to use the colony's link to the Luna Federation's military datanet.

Undressing rapidly, he climbed into bed and closed his eyes.

It felt like no time at all had passed before his wristcom started to bleep. Brian forced himself to open his eyes and glare at the device, then check the timer. An hour...he'd barely had an hour to sleep. He swallowed a number of curses as he keyed the wristcom, accepting the call. He'd have to keep his mouth firmly closed, just to keep from swearing at whoever had disturbed his sleep. The urge to commit a homicide gruesome enough to make the Britannia Serial Killer's look like a rank amateur rose within him. He fought it down as the connection opened.

"Yeah?"

"Mr. Wheeler, sir," a male voice said. He sounded disgustingly fresh. "We have been in touch with Swansong Enterprises. They have dispatched a lunar shuttle to retrieve you and your charge. They'll be here in thirty minutes."

Once, Brian knew, he would have kicked up a fuss. Abigail's parents were flouting all the rules and regulations, just to get their daughter home quickly. God alone knew how many parents were *also* missing their children...he shook his head, telling himself that he should be grateful that they'd responded so quickly. He'd be able to hand Abigail over to them, then go back home or...or what? He didn't even know what was waiting for him on Earth.

The voice cleared his throat. "Mr. Wheeler?"

"Thank you," Brian managed. He forced himself to sit up. A shower, a shave...he'd be something resembling human by the time the shuttle arrived. "Please inform us when the shuttle arrives."

He stood, feeling his legs totter underneath him. Everything was catching up with him now, steadily wearing him down. He'd sleep on the shuttle, if he didn't collapse before then. He wasn't a young man any longer. And besides, even as a young man, he'd have had problems coping with an alien attack. He'd been luckier than he'd deserved.

"Please also inform Abigail," he added. He needed the shower, desperately. "And then have coffee sent to the hotel room."

"Yes, sir," the voice said. "Good luck."

Brian staggered into the shower and turned the water on, twisting and turning until he felt clean again. He said a silent prayer of thanks as he reached for a towel. Showers were something people didn't really appreciate until they had to live without them. Being unable to wash...smelling was really the least of their concerns. Whoever had invented showers, back in the distant past, should be canonised. It was certainly a more important contribution to human life than many other achievements.

Get Abigail back to her parents, he thought, as he dried himself. *And then get a few days of rest before...*

He shrugged. He'd worry about that when the time came. Now...now, all he had to do was get her to the shuttle. After everything else, it should be a piece of cake.

And if it isn't, he thought, as he felt his head begin to pound, *I'll deal with it anyway.*

CHAPTER
TWENTY FIVE

London, United Kingdom

"The thunderstorms are growing worse, Prime Minister," Templeton said. "Right now, we have major floods developing everywhere in the south and south-east."

Andrew nodded, feeling another wave of guilt. He'd eaten well - the bunker staff included a chef, of course - but the people on the surface were drowning. Rainstorms were moving further and further inland, threatening to wash out the entire country. Roads were rapidly becoming impassable as floods or landslides blocked vehicles from moving from place to place. The rail network wasn't in any better shape.

He looked up at the general. How could the man be so calm? Templeton hadn't seen the floods, had he? He'd seen satellite images and the live feed from the remaining CCTV cameras, but he hadn't gone to see them in person. To him, the dead and drowning in London were just numbers. *Andrew* had watched, helplessly, as people struggled to cope with a disaster on a scale beyond human imagination.

"The rainstorms will have to come to an end soon," he said, plaintively. "Won't they?"

Templeton frowned. "The latest update from the meteorologists suggests that the rains will come to an end in a few hours," Templeton said. "There was so much water hurled into the upper atmosphere that it *has* to come down. But the weather patterns are likely to be unpredictable for days or weeks to come. We're already seeing patches of sunlight in the rainstorms that come and go, seemingly at random."

Andrew looked down at his hands. Very few people in Britain placed their faith in the meteorologists. Predicting the weather wasn't *easy*, even before the alien bombardment had thrown thousands of tons of water and dirt into the atmosphere. He supposed the rainstorms would have their limits - they'd eventually run out of water - but he had no idea how long it would take. He *certainly* wasn't sure he cared to trust any of the meteorologist's predictions.

"Fuck," he said, finally. "Is there anything we can do about it?"

"No, sir," Templeton said. "Realistically speaking, all we can do is wait for the rainfall to stop."

Andrew gritted his teeth. "Just how bad is it going to be?"

"Bad," Templeton said. "We've already had to ground all flights, civilian and military, over a large swath of the countryside. The atmospheric disturbances are interfering with radio communications...combined with damaged landlines, parts of the country are almost completely isolated from the rest. We're working hard to help as many people as possible, but..."

"But we can't save everyone," Andrew said.

He'd taken the opportunity to review more of the emergency plans, but none of them had offered any encouragement. Even a single nuke, the planners had noted, would push British resources to the limit. If a city were to be destroyed, they'd argued, the former inhabitants might not be worth saving. The ones who were badly wounded - who couldn't be saved easily - would have to be left to die. Andrew understood the logic, but it was sickening. He didn't know if he could give those orders...

I might be about to find out, he thought, numbly. Despair gnawed at his heart. *How many people will I have to kill to save the rest?*

"We are opening temporary refugee camps to the north and south of the Thames," Templeton told him. "We're converting schools, stadiums and parks into camps. They'll do for the next few weeks, once we get the roads reopened and food deliveries rushed into London. It should let us come to grips with the situation *and* start press-ganging young men into helping with the clean-up."

"*That* will go down well," Andrew observed, dryly.

"It will," Templeton said. "The men who work for us - and their families - will be put on top of the list for food and medical aid. It's harsh" - Andrew shot him a sharp look - "but it's the only way to get them to work in a hurry. I'd prefer to use different methods myself, Prime Minister, yet...I don't see any alternatives."

Andrew shook his head, slowly. "I know," he said. The sense of futility, the sense they were battling against an unbeatable foe, was growing stronger. How did one fight rain and thunderstorms? The devastation had only just begun. "Can you get them to work effectively?"

"We can," Templeton said. "I've got Civil Affairs teams already *en route*. They'll get the civvies working on everything from clearing roads to building flood barriers out of sandbags and whatever else comes to hand. We're damn lucky it's not winter, Prime Minister. I'll tell you that for sure."

"Because we'd have to worry about ice too," Andrew said. He studied the weather chart for a long moment. "What else do we have to look forward to?"

"I don't know," Templeton said. "The weather predictions suggest that the rainfall will stop soon, as I said, but beyond that...there are just too many variables. Adding so much water and dust to the atmosphere will probably have long-term effects...we just don't know what."

"As long as the dust doesn't block out the sun," Andrew said. He met the general's eyes. "And the situation in space?"

"Unchanged," Templeton said. "The aliens are continuing towards Jupiter. Home Fleet is in pursuit, keeping the range open enough to allow them to break off contact if necessary. I assume Admiral Winters has a plan, but he hasn't shared it."

He sighed. "Was there any word from the other world leaders?"

"No," Andrew said. He'd spoken, briefly, to a number of his counterparts, but the conversations had been very limited. None of them were in any position to do anything, either about the battle or the endless series of disasters sweeping the globe. "The Irish President repeated his request for assistance, but I had to tell him that we had too many problems of our own."

"I'm sorry, Prime Minister," Templeton said.

Andrew nodded, feeling bone-weary. It wasn't a physical tiredness, but a mental tiredness...something sapping at his very soul. He could go back to bed, if he wished - there was a bedroom for him - but it wouldn't help. There was nothing he could do about that too.

"It can't be helped," he said. He looked down at his hands. If he went to a refugee centre...he shook his head, again. He'd have to go with armed guards and *that* would draw resources from the recovery effort. And besides, it was unlikely that any of the civilians would want to see him. "Just...just keep me informed."

"I will," Templeton promised.

―――――

"Fuck," Constable Sally Fletcher said. "Is this rain ever going to end?"

Robin shrugged as they patrolled the streets. The rain had been falling steadily for the last couple of hours, turning the streets into rivers. He was uneasily aware that the Thames was probably on the verge of breaking its banks again and perhaps flooding more of the city, although the cynical side of him rather suspected that no one would notice. London was already awash. Hyde Park, according to the last reports, was steadily turning into a muddy swamp.

"It doesn't matter," he said. His waterproof jacket was waterlogged. He was tempted to make an official complaint about shoddy equipment, if things ever returned to normal. But then, London rarely saw *quite* so much rain. "We have to keep on alert."

He peered down the darkened streets. It was morning, according to his watch, but it looked more like twilight. The dark clouds blocked out most of the sunlight, casting the whole city into shadow. Anything could be out there, lurking in the darkness, and he'd never know about it. The endless drumming of the rain was playing merry hell with his ears. He kept thinking he was hearing things. There was no way to tell if they were *real*.

They might be, he thought, numbly. *But I don't know.*

A gust of cold air blew against him, making him shiver. His clothes were damp...he wished, suddenly, that they'd had a chance to change into something a little more watertight. He hadn't joined the River Police, after all...not that anyone would notice, after today. He'd heard that the River Police were boating through London's eastern streets, rescuing people from rooftops before the floodwaters dragged them to their graves. It certainly sounded plausible.

He looked up as a rumble of thunder split the air. Lightning flashed - for a moment, it looked as though the lightning was frozen in mid-air before it vanished - followed rapidly by more thunder. The sound echoed off the buildings, sending more shivers down his spine. He could hear lapping water in the distance, perhaps the first sign that the Thames was about to break its banks again. The wind was picking up, blowing against their exposed hands and faces. It felt like the end of the world.

His radio crackled. He keyed it, automatically. "Go ahead."

There was a screech of static, then nothing. He exchanged looks with Sally, silently cursing the procurement division under his breath. They could have issued the police with military-grade radios, couldn't they? God knew a handful of terrorists had managed to fuck around with police radios during the Troubles. But the more charitable side of his mind pointed out that no one had expected so much thunder and lightning. The military radios might be disrupted as well.

Sally coughed. "Do you think we should go back?"

Robin frowned. There was no reason to *think* there was anyone left in their sector. The first flood had been enough to convince everyone - shopkeepers and hotel guests alike - that they needed to seek higher ground in a hurry. But his superiors were adamant that the sector needed to be patrolled. The Met had learned harsh lessons about surrendering control of the streets, even if - technically - there was no one to surrender *to*. His superiors had no intention of leaving the streets unmonitored if it could be avoided.

"I think we should complete our route down to the river," he said. If nothing else, his superiors needed to know if the Thames *was* on the verge of breaking its banks. "And then we can walk back to the station."

He tapped his radio again, but there was nothing. He'd been told that the radios were supposed to be hardened against...well, everything. Clearly, there had been a failure of imagination somewhere in Scotland

Yard. They'd expected everything from EMP attack to virus infections, but not giant thunderstorms. They...

Glass smashed, not too far away.

"Shit," Sally muttered. She drew her pistol. "Can you get anyone?"

"No," Robin said. He reached into his pocket and removed the emergency beacon, carefully opening the cover and placing his finger over the button. Normally, activating it would bring every copper within five miles hurrying towards him - as well as armed tactical response teams - but now...now it was anyone's guess if the signal would be heard, let alone summon reinforcements. "We have to move in slowly."

He forced himself to think as he drew his pistol and inched down the street. There was a fancy store - a whole *set* of fancy stores - that normally catered for tourists. He'd never been in them, even when he'd been off duty. The prices had been so far above his usual range that there was no point. Now...he felt his heart starting to pound as he kept low, ducking from ruined car to ruined car. A small group of men were standing in front of the plate-glass windows, filling their rucksacks with expensive watches. Robin couldn't help a flicker of contempt. The watches were probably worthless at the moment. Coming to think of it, *money* was probably worthless too.

The beacon clicked as he pushed the button, then dropped it under a car. Hopefully, reinforcements would be on the way. Until then...he sucked in his breath as he heard someone cry out. The gang had a hostage or a prisoner or...he glanced at Sally, keeping his face low. He would have stayed back, if only watches were at risk, but a life...

He put his whistle in his mouth, then rose and blew as hard as he could. "Armed Police," he shouted. His voice echoed through the rain. "Put your hands in the air, now!"

The gangsters stared at him. A couple dropped to the ground, several more ran...and one produced a gun. Robin shot him instinctively. There was no way to know just how practiced the gangster was at using his gun, but a loaded weapon made things far too dangerous. The gangster dropped like a stone, his body hitting the ground like a sack of potatoes. Robin moved forward as the runners rounded the corner and vanished, fleeing for their lives. There was nothing he could do about them, unless he shot them in the back. He had a nasty feeling that some of his superiors would probably rather he did precisely that, just to make sure the looters didn't try to loot anywhere else.

"Keep your hands where I can see them," he ordered. The two gangsters on the ground were trembling. They didn't look very dangerous, but that meant nothing. Robin had seen enough suspects move from cooperative to violent in a split-second to know just how unpleasant things could become. "Cover them."

Sally nodded, wordlessly. Robin nodded in approval as he removed his plastic ties from his belt and hastily secured the first captive. Too many macho young fools believed that a female copper couldn't fight as well as a male for him to be entirely comfortable letting them know her gender. If they were stupid enough to think it was actually two-on-one rather than two-on-two...the gangsters didn't offer any resistance. Robin studied them for a long moment, then picked up and checked the fallen weapon. It *was* loaded.

Someone is going to be in trouble for this, he thought, as he put the safety on and stuck the weapon in his belt. *I wonder if they even reported the loss.*

He put the thought aside as he heard a whimper from inside the store. Carefully, he removed his torch and shone it into the building, bracing himself for anything from a shout to a shot. The torchlight would reveal his position to any watching eyes...nothing came at him, not even a scream. He glanced at Sally, silently indicating that she should stay back, then inched into the building. A dark shape was moving on the ground. He knelt and shone his torch towards him - no, her. A young oriental woman, her slanted eyes wide with fear. There was a nasty bruise on her cheek. Her shirt had been torn open, exposing a pair of small breasts; her hands were bound behind her back with duct tape. Robin shone the torch at his uniform, just long enough to let her recognise him as a police officer, then leaned forward to whisper in her ear.

"Is there anyone else in the building?"

She shook her head. Robin relaxed, very slightly. She didn't have to be lying to actually mislead him. He'd been in the force long enough to know that witness testimony was often the most unreliable bullshit in the world. A witness's version of the truth might have nothing in common with the *real* truth, insofar as it existed. He pushed the thought aside as he slipped further into the store, listening carefully. Apart from the drip-drip-drip of water, there was nothing. But *anything* could be hiding in there.

He inched back to the woman, then helped her up and half-carried her out of the store. Sally took her, cut the duct tape and helped her to cover herself up. Robin kept an eye on the two prisoners, while checking the dead gangster. He wasn't carrying any ID...

"They made me take them to the store," the woman said. She sounded as if she was on the verge of complete collapse. Her hands held the remains of her shirt closed, even as it clung to her skin. "They..."

Robin sighed. The reinforcements hadn't shown up. Of *course* they hadn't shown up. There was no way that two of them could search the store, even if they hadn't had two prisoners and an unwilling captive to supervise. They'd have to go back to the refugee camp and leave the store alone. The gangsters were probably watching from a safe distance, just waiting to come back to finish the job. Or maybe they'd target a food store or even one of the refugee camps...

"On your feet," he ordered the prisoners, yanking them up. "Let's go."

"We have rights," the first one said. He was trying to sound defiant, even though he had to know he was in deep shit. "I..."

Robin drew his pistol and shoved it into the man's face. "Martial law has been declared," he snapped. It was hard, so hard, to resist the temptation to just pull the trigger. Madness howled at the back of his mind. "You have no rights. Your only hope of survival lies in cooperation."

He shoved the man forward, then glared at his companion. There were always human locusts, weren't there? Coming out of the woodwork when society tottered, threatening to collapse...making it impossible to rebuild. He wanted to kill them, he wanted to just dump their bodies in the Thames...no one would know. They'd just be two more rotting bodies to be carted off and burnt. Sally would keep her mouth shut...

Society is three missed meals from collapse, he reminded himself. He had no idea who'd said that, but it was true. *And we're going to miss a great many more meals in the future.*

CHAPTER
TWENTY SIX

Near Townsend, United Kingdom

The rain didn't let off, even when the tiny convoy started to crawl up the hillside. Molly watched with growing horror as the waters ran faster and faster, carrying soil and mud down towards the sea. Branches floated in the water, suggesting that it was only a matter of time before there was a landslide. If they got stuck...she hated to think about what would happen.

"We need to stay as high as possible," Rosemary said, as she navigated her way along the road. Water flooded past the van, gliding across the road and splashing down the hill. Molly leaned forward as the visibility dropped and dropped again, making it harder to see. "It looks like Kuala Lumpur out there."

"Except colder," Garrison said. He sounded better, now they were in a vehicle. "I was there two years ago."

Molly sighed, inwardly. There had been a time when she'd liked that about him, hadn't there? International travel - at least outside France and the rest of Europe - had been well outside her budget. Kurt hadn't even been stationed in another *star* system...not that he would have been able to take his family with him. She felt a stab of envy, mingled with the grim awareness that she'd been foolish. Garrison wasn't the man she thought he'd been.

One of the kids coughed. "What was it like?"

"Hot and humid," Garrison said.

Molly half-closed her eyes as Garrison chatted, distracting the kids with a story that would have interested her too, once upon a time. Her body ached, demanding sleep, but she didn't dare close her eyes. She wasn't sure how far she trusted Garrison now...and she didn't know Rosemary at all. Society had probably already started to break down. Penzance could hardly be the only place to have been smashed flat by tidal waves.

There will have been strikes up and down the coastline, she thought. It wasn't something she'd ever had to consider before. Apart from a brief global warming scare during the run-up to the Troubles, Britain's weather had remained fairly consistent. Tidal waves had never been a concern when she'd taken her family to Scarborough or Portsmouth for summer holidays. *The entire coast might be flooded.*

The van lurched as it crested the hill and started down towards the road at the bottom. Molly fought the urge to close her eyes as the wheels started to slip before regaining their grip, even though she knew there would be nothing she could do if they tumbled down the hill. Water washed down beside them, moving so fast that she honestly wondered if Rosemary had accidentally driven into a river. It might not be too long, part of her mind warned her, before the water destroyed the road's surface and turned it into a *real* river. The roads were designed to cope with rain - Britain was *renowned* for its rain - but nothing like this.

This isn't a motorway, she told herself, firmly. The van lurched again, water splashing down on the rooftop. *We'll be safer once we reach the M5.*

Garrison nudged her. "If we get home," he muttered, "I'm going to learn how to drive my car."

"Good idea," Molly said. She carefully *didn't* mention that she had no intention of seeing him ever again. "I think everyone should know how to drive a car."

"Crap," Rosemary said, as they reached the bottom of the hill. "Look at that!"

Molly peered out the front window and swore. A handful of cars had come off the road, lying in a water-filled ditch with their windows smashed. Anyone inside would have drowned, she realised grimly. The driving compartments were already under water. It wouldn't be long before the rest of the vehicles were covered and lost forever, or at least until the water drained away. God alone knew how long it would be before anyone came to check out the wrecks.

"We should stop to help," Gordon said. He was an older man, related to Rosemary...somehow. Molly hadn't cared enough to listen to the explanation. "The people there might need us..."

"There's no sign of anyone moving," Garrison said, peering through the windows. "I don't think we *can* help them."

Molly followed his gaze. Water was splashing down around the cars, but nothing else appeared to be moving. The road still looked stable, but it was alarmingly clear that the ditch was growing larger as more and more water flooded down and eroded its banks. Rosemary evidently agreed. She carefully drove past the wreck, making sure she stayed in the centre of the road as more and more water flooded down. There was no time to stop and help.

"We can't do anything," Garrison said. "We can barely help ourselves."

Rosemary glared at him, then reached out and slapped the radio. It emitted a crackling noise, but nothing else. Molly looked down at her smartphone, constantly searching for an active datanode or even a low-level signal network. There was nothing. She'd grown up in a world where she could download an entire season of *Doctor Who* or *Stellar Star* in seconds, but now...now she felt isolated. There was no one around for miles. The trees - the dripping wet trees - appeared to be closing in.

"I thought the government would be making emergency broadcasts," Rosemary muttered, as she twisted the knob. The static grew louder. No matter how hard she strained her ears, Molly couldn't hear any voices within the storm. "We don't have any idea what's waiting for us."

"They might be concerned about attracting enemy fire," Gordon said. "When I was in the Rifles, we taught our enemies not to make radio transmissions unless they wanted to be thumped."

Molly gave him a sharp look. "You think the aliens *won*?"

Gordon jabbed a finger upwards. "I think there's no way to know," he said. "Anything could be up there, beyond the cloud."

"The defences are powerful," Garrison said, sharply. "Earth is heavily defended."

"Not heavily enough to keep the aliens from dropping rocks on us," Gordon countered. "The bastards might have done it deliberately, just to soften us up for when they land combat troops."

Molly swallowed. She was no expert, but the whole scenario made a great deal of sense. If the tidal waves had battered *every* coastline - and she had no way to know if they had - Britain's defenders would be in disarray. The government and military would be scattered, perhaps broken. No one, as far as she knew, had made any attempt to get on the airwaves and reassure the population that there *was* a government out there. For all she knew, the next thing they encountered would be an alien landing force.

We're staying off the beaten track, she told herself. *But that might change in a hurry.*

She leaned back in her seat as Rosemary led the convoy onto a main road, heading north-east. Molly keyed her smartphone, bringing up the map, but she was forced to admit she didn't have the slightest idea where they were. It had been far too long since she'd been in the Girl Guides and she hadn't been particularly good at reading maps, even with help from the rest of her squad. She didn't think they'd gone *that* far from Penzance, but there was no way to be sure. The rain made it impossible to pick out any local landmarks.

"We'll find a way onto the M5 in an hour, if we keep going down this road," Rosemary said, as they picked up speed. The rainfall seemed to be decreasing, although it was hard to be certain. Winds buffeted the van, blowing at random. "That should speed things up a little."

The rain stopped, with a suddenness that made Molly look up in surprise. The skies were still overcast - the deep blue clouds looked as if they were about to burst at any moment - but, just for a moment, the torrential downpour stopped. And yet, she could still hear thunder in the distance. She shook her head as she ran her hand through her wet hair. The temperature seemed to be rising rapidly, now the rain had stopped. She wondered, absently, if that was a good thing or not.

We might be able to get to Woking in a few hours, she thought. She couldn't ask Rosemary to go *that* far out of her way, but she knew people who would probably loan her a car in a couple of nearby towns. Or she could rent a car. She could easily find a car hire shop and pay over the odds, just to get home. *And then...*

She swallowed, hard, as she realised the possible implications. She'd made sure to carry her credit card as well as some paper money, but how much good were either of them now? At best, she might have to pay for the car on her knees; at worst, she wouldn't be able to get a car for love or money or even sex. Someone who owned a car might not want to trade it for *anything*. And they certainly wouldn't want to drive her home.

I could walk, she told herself, firmly. *At least I'd be closer to my home.*

"Shit," Rosemary said, as they neared the motorway. "Police!"

Molly looked up, sharply. Three police cars were blocking the slip road, their lights flashing blue and red in the half-light. She swallowed, hard, as she tried to decide what to do. They'd been ordered to stay put, after all. Most of the county had clearly obeyed orders...she glanced at Rosemary, who looked grim as she drove towards the blockade. A moment later, a pair of policemen waved the convoy down.

"Remain calm," Rosemary said, as she rolled down the window. The policemen were clearly armed. "Don't do anything stupid."

"Please get out of the vehicle," the policeman said. "And bring your ID cards with you."

Molly exchanged a look with Garrison, then opened the door and stepped onto the road. It was hotter than she'd realised, hotter than she'd expected...even for June. The air smelled of salt and mud and something she didn't want to identify. She stepped onto the kerb as the rest of the convoy pulled up, rapidly evacuating their vehicles. Molly sucked in her breath as she saw their full numbers for the first time. Seven adults, fifteen children. They really *were* in trouble.

At least my kids are at home, she thought, grimly. *Gayle is looking after them...*

She felt her blood run cold. What if Gayle *left*? What if she decided to go home? God knew she hadn't been hired for more than a day...what if she just left? Molly fought down panic as the awful realisation dawned. She could get home, only to discover that her kids had been abandoned. Percy was old enough to take care of his sister, she thought, but Penny probably wouldn't listen to him. She took too much after Molly for her mother's comfort.

The policemen checked their ID cards, one by one, then searched the vehicles with practiced ease. Molly watched, wondering what to expect. They *were* disobeying orders, but...but they had an excuse! Somehow, she doubted *that* would go down well with the cops. The age of excuses - the age when even the most vile crimes could be excused - was long since over.

"The M5 is closed," the lead policeman said, once the vehicles had been searched. Molly assumed they'd run the ID cards through the police network, although she had no idea if the network was working or not. "Where are you going?"

"London," Rosemary said. "We have..."

"All the roads heading in and out of London have been closed," the policeman told her. He didn't *sound* unsympathetic. "There's flooding in the capital, from what we've heard. You won't get much closer."

Rosemary sagged. "I have to get home..."

Molly leaned forward. "What about Woking?"

"I don't have any direct reports about Woking, but there are reports of heavy flooding in the Thames Valley," the policeman said. His eyes flickered over Molly, then looked away. "I believe a number of roads have already been closed."

"I have to get the kids home," Rosemary said. She sounded as if she was on the verge of crying helplessly. "Sir...I have to get them home."

"You might not *have* a home," the policeman said. "Look, where *were* you?"

"Camping," Rosemary said. She waved a hand at the vehicles. "We had to leave half of the equipment behind..."

The policeman glanced down at his terminal. "There's a B&B place a couple of miles up the road," he said. "It's marked down as an emergency refugee centre, but so far hardly anyone has been sent there. Go there now - the staff will make sure you have something to eat and drink while you wait for orders. It isn't much, but it will have to do."

Rosemary nodded, shortly.

"My kids are at Woking," Molly said. "I *have* to get there!"

"You and millions of others," the policeman said. "Half the roads are blocked; the remainder, I'm afraid, have been reserved for the emergency services. There is no way you can make it to Woking without being stopped and arrested. I understand your problem, but you *cannot* use the roads. It's just not *safe.*"

Molly felt her hands beginning to shake. She *had* to get to her kids. She *had* to go...

"I don't care about the risk," she said. "I have to get back home."

The policeman sighed. "You have a choice," he said, tiredly. It struck Molly, suddenly, that the policeman hadn't slept for hours. He might have been up all night, trying to cope with the sudden crisis. "You can go with your friends to the B&B, where you will get something to eat and a chance to rest, or I can arrest you now, which will save time because you *will* be arrested if you're caught on the roads. In that case, you'll be cuffed, chained to a work gang and forced to do hard labour. And that will make getting back to your kids *much* harder."

Molly stared at him for a long moment. A dozen arguments ran through her head - she was a taxpayer, her husband was in the military - only to be dismissed. The policeman was not going to budge. And she didn't want to be arrested, even if she was never brought to court and tried. She'd never live down the shame of it...

"Fine," she said, sourly.

She followed Rosemary back to the minivan and climbed into her seat, thinking hard. If there was a police checkpoint on *this* slip road, chances were there was a police checkpoint on *every* slip road. The M5 was no longer an option then, she thought, which meant...she looked back at the policemen and gritted her teeth. She had no choice. She *had* to keep going, whatever the cost. Garrison might not come with her, but...

Rosemary started the engine and drove off, following the side road. She looked worried...Molly wondered, suddenly, if she could convince Rosemary to continue heading south-east instead of finding the B&B. The countryside was *threaded* with small roads, roads she could use to get closer to Woking without ever driving onto the motorway. She could drive herself, if she took one of the cars.

But Rosemary won't agree, she thought, numbly. *She doesn't even know if she has a place to call home any longer.*

It was a grim thought. If London was flooded, that meant...she shivered. Rosemary wouldn't want to go any further, not when she had a place to stay. The skies were darkening rapidly, suggesting that it was about to start raining again. And that meant...

She forced herself to relax as the small convoy drove onwards. There was nothing she could do until they reached the B&B. And then...

"I'm sorry we can't get you any closer," Rosemary said.

"That's all right with us," Garrison told her. "We know you did your best."

Molly shot him a nasty look. Garrison should have stayed at the hall, even if that meant being stuck with the dead bodies. He would have been out of her hair, if nothing else. For all she knew, he was wishing that he *had* stayed at the hall. He would have had enough to eat and drink until *someone* arrived to find out what had happened to Lady Penelope and her guests.

But then I would have been alone, she told herself. *Who knows what would have happened then?*

She pushed her thoughts aside as Rosemary turned off the road. The B&B looked large: a dozen holiday cabins, a campsite that looked to be on the verge of turning into a muddy swamp and a BBQ site that was completely deserted, save for a pair of mangy-looking cats and a large dog. She looked around as the convoy pulled up in front of the main building, feeling nervous. There was no one in sight. The police had said the B&B was a refugee centre, but had they told the owners?

"There," Rosemary said. She opened the door as a couple of young men peered out of the main building. "I'll go speak to them."

Molly glanced back at the cars as Rosemary hurried away. She could drive them, if she had one of the keycards. There was probably a way to hot-wire them, but she didn't have the slightest idea where to begin. If she ever got home, she'd make sure to learn. In hindsight, she *really* should have paid more attention when she'd been in the Girl Guides, instead of ogling some of the hunkier Boy Scouts...

"I got us a set of cabins," Rosemary said. She held out a set of keys. "They should do, for the moment."

"Thank you," Garrison said. He took one of the keys. "We'll share, if you don't mind. It'll free up more room for the kids."

Molly scowled. She hadn't wanted that at all. But there was no way to argue.

"Fine," she said. She glanced at Molly. "But I need to talk to you later."

CHAPTER

TWENTY SEVEN

Clarke Colony, Luna

"My parents are going to kill me," Abigail muttered, as the shuttle dropped down towards a small dome to the south of Clarke Colony. "They're going to kill me for *life!*"

"I think it would be better to worry about being grounded for life," Brian pointed out, doing his best to conceal his irritation. At least Abigail's parents had survived...he'd be paid, assuming money was actually worth *anything* in the near future. "And they can't really ground you past the age of eighteen."

He peered down at the datanet, thinking hard. The Luna Federation *had* managed to get out a handful of updates, but most of them had been resolutely centred on Luna itself. Colonies that had been bombed, defence stations that had been wiped out...a list of people known to be dead or missing...as far as he could tell, Abigail and himself were the only people to have made it out of Sin City. And there was practically nothing on Earth, save for a handful of reports of pieces of debris hitting the atmosphere and extensive damage. None of them were particularly specific.

"You don't know my parents," Abigail said. "They'll be *mad* at me."

Brian rolled his eyes. "They clearly didn't keep a very close eye on you," he said. It wasn't *easy* to travel across the moon, not without passing through any number of checkpoints. In a sane world, Abigail would have been caught and returned to her parents a long time before she reached

Sin City. "And while I do think they'll be mad at you, they won't actually *kill* you."

He sighed. "My parents were stricter," he added. "You have *nothing* to complain about, really."

The shuttle tilted, slightly. Brian peered out the porthole, his eyes seeking the domes of Clarke Colony. Clarke had been founded by a colony of free-thinkers, if he recalled correctly: men and women seeking a way of life that was better than anything to be found on Earth. It was hardly the first colony bent on living according to its own rules, but it had definitely been one of the most successful. The early wave of immigration - almost entirely composed of rich and able men - had crafted a society that actually encouraged newer and better ways of thinking. Clarke had an enviable reputation, both as a place to live and as a place to follow one's dreams. A good third of the Luna Federation's corporate start-ups were founded on Clarke.

Such as Swansong Enterprises, he thought. Abigail's parents weren't just rich, they were *loaded*. The private dome alone would have cost them millions of lunar credits. *The ones who do well do very well indeed.*

He pushed the thought aside as the shuttle finally touched down, quivering slightly on the landing pad. He'd expected to drop down into a pressurised hangar, but instead an airlock tube moved towards the shuttle and mated with the hatch. It made sense, he supposed. The Luna Federation had put out a call for shuttles and everything else that could fly, up to and including private craft. Abigail's parents wouldn't want to risk censure after the fighting was over by withholding their personal shuttle.

"Come on," he said, standing. "Let's go."

Abigail hung back as Brian walked towards the hatch. Both airlock doors were open, revealing a man and woman at the far end of the tube. Abigail let out a little moan, then ran past Brian and into her mother's arms. Brian followed at a more sedate pace, pretending not to hear as Jacqueline Swansong alternatively praised and scolded her daughter. It didn't look as though Abigail had anything *real* to fear, although Brian knew she was in for a rough few days. He'd seen quite a few parents grow angry with runaway children, once the relief of their safe return wore off, but it normally came to an end. He hoped Abigail would learn from the experience. She might not realise it - yet - but she'd really been very lucky.

Although she couldn't have predicted the aliens attacking the solar system, he thought, sardonically. *I didn't predict it either.*

Galahad Swansong cleared his throat. "Mr. Wheeler," he said. "If you would like to come with me...?"

Brian sighed, inwardly. He *wanted* to go to bed. He wasn't fussy. He would happily sleep on a blanket under the stars if it meant being able to actually *sleep*. But he doubted he had a choice. He took one last look at Abigail, who was crying in her mother's arms, then followed her father down the corridor and out under the dome. The family's mansion rose up in front of him, glimmering faintly under the starlight.

It was an impressive sight, he had to admit. Galahad Swansong had copied a mansion from Earth - he thought he knew which one, too - but he'd built it out of grey lunar rock. Brian didn't even want to *think* about the cost, not when the dome alone would have cost millions of credits. And to think that Abigail had run away from *this*...he shook his head, grimly, as they walked through the doors. He wouldn't have blamed Abigail for running if she'd been abused, but there hadn't been anything to suggest that she *had* been abused. Her parents had merely been incredibly overprotective.

"We both owe you our thanks," Galahad said. They walked into a study. Galahad closed the door, then poured them both a shot of something expensive. "I didn't think to factor in an alien invasion when I hired you."

"I never expected it either," Brian said. He took the glass and sniffed it, carefully. Whiskey, the good - and expensive - stuff. It tasted smoky in his mouth. "I believe we were both quite lucky."

"So I hear," Galahad said. He motioned for Brian to take a seat. "The first reports came in from Sin City, only an hour ago. Apart from the two of you, there were no reported survivors."

"There *were* people who fled onto the surface," Brian said. "Haven't they reported in yet?"

"Not to my knowledge," Galahad said. He sat down himself, sipping his whiskey. "Unless they do, I'm afraid that you and our daughter will probably have to answer a great many questions. Sin City's surviving managers - who were lucky enough to be somewhere else when the rocks fell - are already trying to claim on the insurance."

Brian rolled his eyes. "Don't they have something more important to be doing?"

"You'd think," Galahad agreed. His face twisted into an odd smile. "Right now, they're arguing that Sin City is good for morale and therefore reconstruction should be an urgent priority. They won't get very far until the rest of the damaged colonies are inspected, but after that...well, they *might* get lucky. But their insurers might want to fight it out in court."

"Ouch," Brian said.

He'd hoped to get a flight straight back to Earth, but he suspected that was receding into the distance. There was a good chance that the insurance companies had already requested a court order preventing him from leaving the moon. It was what they would have done, under normal circumstances. He rubbed his forehead in annoyance. The circumstances were far from normal. Either no one would give a damn, allowing him to slip home without further ado, or they'd do everything in their power to get things back to normal as soon as possible.

"As of now, I don't know how it will shake out," Galahad said. "But you are welcome to stay here as our guest until matters get sorted out."

Brian frowned. "Have you heard anything from Earth?"

"A jumble of reports, ranging from the believable to the absurd," Galahad said. "I've got a team of staffers working on sorting out and verifying the different reports, but so far it's hard to say for sure what's happening. Earth's governments certainly aren't being very talkative at the moment. They're saying it's because there's an alien fleet in the system, but I suspect they're more concerned about secessionist sympathies on the moon."

"That's all we need," Brian said. "A civil war on top of an interstellar war."

"Let us hope not," Galahad agreed. "It will be weeks, perhaps months, before regular flights to Earth are reinstated."

He met Brian's eyes. "Before we go any further, I need a honest report," he said. "What *happened* to my daughter in Sin City?"

Brian took a moment to compose a reply. "She found work in a bar," he said, carefully. "I do not believe she was molested - she certainly doesn't *act* like she was molested. However, she had a rough time of it. Her... employer...didn't know who she was, let alone who her parents were. I didn't have any trouble convincing her to come back with me."

Galahad's eyes narrowed. "And did she say why she left?"

"She wasn't very clear," Brian said. Technically, he didn't owe Abigail any privacy. Her father was his boss, after all. He certainly didn't have any obligation to keep her secrets. But practically, he didn't want to tell him everything. "I think she wanted a little more freedom of her own."

"Which isn't the smartest thing to want," Galahad pointed out, stiffly. "She's the heir to my fortune - to *both* of our fortunes. She is one of the most...one of the children most likely to be kidnapped on the moon."

Then you should have invested in extra security, Brian thought. He kept that thought to himself. Abigail hadn't been kidnapped. She'd run away. *And you should have done something to keep her occupied.*

He took a breath. "May I speak freely?"

Galahad nodded.

"I've worked on close-protection details before," Brian said. It was technically true, even though he'd never been on a close-escort squad. "The principals - ah, the people who are the prime movers - normally understand the importance of being protected, even if they don't like it. Their companions, adults and children alike, are often less understanding. They don't like having to report to the police or private bodyguards, they don't like having their movements monitored, they don't like the absence of *freedom*. I've known children who have given their escorts the slip for a few hours, just so they can pretend to be alone for a while. It is stupid and dangerous and very human."

"Of course," Galahad agreed.

"Abigail isn't *you*," Brian added. "She grew up in a goldfish bubble - servants everywhere, bodyguards keeping an eye on her - and she grew to resent it. I don't think you ever gave her anything like enough freedom... even if you let her wander around the dome, she wouldn't meet anyone new. She couldn't even do anything without having it reported back to you."

"I didn't have the bodyguards keep *that* close an eye on her," Galahad said, sharply.

"I don't think she felt that way," Brian said. "And so she came up with a plan - a very clever plan - to get away from you. And it worked."

Galahad gave him a sharp look. "She managed to get to Sin City," he said. "How long would it have been before she was forced into a brothel?"

"I don't know," Brian said. The first part of Abigail's plan had worked perfectly. It was the second part that could have got her killed - or worse. "But you need to help her to grow and develop, rather than thinking she's still a child. She might be glad to be home now, but she's going to want to leave again soon if nothing changes."

"Parenting should be done by the professionals," Galahad said, wryly. His lips twitched. "I thank you, again."

Brian nodded. Abigail really *had* been lucky. No one on Sin City had known her true identity, let alone her age... And if the Management had ever found out, they might have seriously considered murdering Abigail and feeding her body into an incinerator rather than run the risk of being implicated. It hadn't been their fault that Abigail had reached Sin City, but it would have made them look bad regardless. And if Brian hadn't found her, she'd probably be dead now. She might not have been able to head for the shelters if she'd still been working in the bar.

"You are welcome," he said. He cocked his head. "And if you will put up with me long enough for things to start returning to normal, sir, I would be very grateful."

"You have a room here," Galahad assured him. He leaned forward. "Payment *might* be a problem, at least until the banks open again. The Luna Federation closed them when the alien ships were detected, preventing a bank rush. But we will pay you as soon as possible."

"I understand," Brian said. He wouldn't panic for a few weeks. He'd be happy enough with a room in the mansion, if he could just get some sleep. "I can wait."

"I'd also like to offer you a job," Galahad added. "Abigail...is going to need a new bodyguard. The old ones were...ah...let go."

Brian winced. He didn't really blame Galahad for being pissed at the old bodyguards. They'd fucked up and their charge had nearly died because of it. And yet, there weren't *many* precautions that could be taken against a principal deliberately *trying* to give her guards the slip. He rather doubted the bodyguards had been authorised to keep Abigail in cuffs and shackles all day. Even monitoring her datanet usage would be a stretch.

"You saved her life, several times," Galahad added. "And she might just have learnt to listen to you. She certainly never bothered to listen to the old guys."

"She might," Brian said. "I'd have to think about it."

He thought, rapidly. If the more alarmist reports were correct, there wasn't going to be much left for him on Earth. He might have real trouble finding a job, if he wasn't drafted into a recovery and reclamation project. There certainly weren't going to be many opportunities for a private investigator to find work over the next few years. A lot of people would probably go missing - there were quite a few people he knew who'd take advantage of the chaos to vanish - but finding them would be damn near impossible. God alone knew what would happen if hundreds of thousands of bodies were swept out to sea.

And Swansong Enterprises will be needed to help with the reconstruction, he thought. *I'd have a measure of job security.*

He contemplated the possibilities, grimly. On one hand, there would be a good job with a certain level of job security. It wasn't as if he *needed* to go back to Earth. On the other hand, he might have to answer a great many questions about Sin City...and, coming to think of it, take care of a teenage girl who'd already given an entire *team* of bodyguards the slip. But if he actually talked to her, instead of treating her as a baby...

"It sounds like a good idea," he said, finally. "But it would depend on the outcome of the battle."

"Life will go on, battle or no battle," Galahad said. He smiled. "If you will take on the job, we will be honoured. And if not...we will understand."

He nodded towards the door, which opened. A man wearing a butler's uniform stepped into the office. Brian kept his face expressionless as he assessed the man, silently noting all the hints pointing to SF training. The butler was a bodyguard as well as everything else, he guessed. It made a certain amount of sense. Galahad and his family *were* prime kidnapping targets, after all. Chances were that the rest of the staff had some combat training too.

"Please escort Mr. Wheeler to his bedroom and show him the facilities," Galahad said. "Mr. Wheeler, the upper two levels and the basement are closed to you. The remainder of the house is at your disposal. That includes the swimming pool, gym and bowling alley. I'll contact you when - if - I hear something."

"Thank you, sir," Brian said.

He relaxed, slightly, as he followed the butler out the door and down a long corridor. The walls were lined with famous paintings, including a number that had to be replicas. Brian had never been particularly arty - at school, he'd shared the opinion of most of his peers that art classes were boring and pointless - but even *he* recognised a couple that had been lost during the Paris Intifada. The rampaging mobs might even have *won*, from what little he recalled, if they hadn't stopped to plunder one of the most famous cities on Earth.

"This is your suite, sir," the butler said, opening a door. "This is the antechamber, with the master bedroom directly ahead of you. The bathroom is on the far side - just walk through that door. There's no water or food limits. Order what you want from the kitchens and it will be sent to you. The terminal is already unlocked, but you won't be permitted access to private household nodes."

He paused. "Do you require clean clothes?"

"It would probably be a good idea," Brian said. Did the mansion keep a spare set of clothes in every possible size, just in case they were needed? "Do you have clothes suitable for me?"

"Yes, sir," the butler said. He sounded vaguely offended. "I'll have them delivered and placed in the antechamber. You'll be called when Mr. Swansong wishes to speak to you."

Brian nodded. "Thank you."

He turned and walked into the bedroom. It was huge, easily large enough to pass for a five-star London hotel. The bed alone was big enough for five or six people to share, comfortably...

Taking off his boots, he lay down on the bed. They were safe at last, unless the aliens reversed course and attacked the moon again. Until then, he could rest. And the future could take care of itself.

He closed his eyes and fell asleep.

CHAPTER
TWENTY EIGHT

Near Townsend, United Kingdom

"Safe at last," Garrison said. "At least we're dry here."

Molly glared at him as she took off her sodden coat, hanging it on the hooks behind the wooden door. The cabin was meant for either lovers or children...probably the latter, as the beds were small enough to make a woman *her* size uncomfortable. Maybe they were meant to encourage romance. No one could share one of the bunk beds without being very - very - friendly. The constant drumming of rain above them didn't make her feel any better about the B&B.

"I have to get to my kids," she snapped, angrily. She'd give Rosemary a chance to settle in, then ask to borrow one of the keycards. Or maybe just take it. Rosemary would be able to say, if anyone asked, that Molly had stolen the car. "Maybe you can stay here..."

Garrison caught her arm. "You heard the policeman," he said. "The roads are either closed or blocked. There's nowhere to go!"

Molly yanked her arm free. "I'm not going to stay here while my kids are alone," she said, pacing the room. The thought of Gayle abandoning Percy and Penny refused to leave her mind. She just couldn't get it out of her head. "You can stay here if you like."

"Listen to me," Garrison said. "If they catch you again, they'll *arrest* you!"

"I'll take that risk," Molly said. She felt her temper begin to flare. "Stay here if you want. I don't care. But I am going after my kids!"

"You're not leaving," Garrison said. "You'll just get yourself killed or arrested."

Molly felt her temper snap. "And should I stay here with a cowardly little shit who is willing to leave two helpless kids alone...?"

Garrison slapped her, hard. Molly stumbled, falling to her knees. He was on top of her a moment later, shoving her back to the wooden floor. Molly yelped in pain as she banged her head against the wood, Garrison landing on top of her a moment later. His face was contorted with fury. Her head swam as she fought to keep her thoughts straight. Calling him a coward hadn't been a very good idea after all.

"You've been a fucking awful date," Garrison snarled. He stared down at her, his hot breath on her lips. "I didn't bring you to the party to *talk*."

"Get off me," Molly gasped. It wasn't the first time he'd been on top of her - she wanted to vomit as those memories rose to mock her - but this time he was trying to crush the life out of her. "Get off!"

Garrison caught her arm and forced it back. Molly had to bite her lip to keep from screaming. She did know a little about self-defence, but none of her instructors had ever covered what to do if she was pinned to the floor. Her legs refused to move as he pressed down hard, forcing the breath from her lungs. He was trying to kill her...

"All your little social pretensions," he hissed, pushing his face against hers. His lips crawled down her face, leaving a trail of slime behind them. "All your dreams of rising above your station...you're just a filthy little slut, aren't you? Trading her tits and ass and pussy and mouth for a chance at the golden ring? You never realised how much they were laughing at you?"

"Fuck...you," Molly managed.

Garrison's face darkened. "That's what you were brought to do," he said. "Or do you not remember what we did in the car?"

"The car you can't drive," Molly taunted. She'd always been good at pushing buttons. In hindsight, perhaps she'd pushed too many of Kurt's. "What sort of man can't drive a car?"

"Shut up," Garrison growled. He shoved her head back to the floor, keeping one hand on her throat. "You're going to fucking open your legs for me."

Molly gritted her teeth as his free hand reached into her blouse and groped her breast. She knew he had a point. She didn't want to admit it, but it was true. She *had* been willing to trade on her body, she had been willing to degrade herself in the hopes of finally enjoying the life she'd thought she was owed. She'd gone down on him - and more - in the naive belief he would push her up to a more suitable level. And now...

"You won't get away with this," she panted. His hand felt cruel as he pinched her nipple, hard. It was all she could do to keep from screaming. "The police..."

"The police are already overworked," Garrison said, unpleasantly. He moved his hand to her other breast. Molly cringed at his touch. "Hundreds of thousands of people have already died. Who's going to care about a middle-aged slut like you?"

Molly felt her blood run cold. He was right, again. She hadn't told the kids where she was going, let alone who she was going with. They wouldn't even know where to start looking for her. She *had* shown her papers to the cops on the roadblock, but she didn't think they'd actually scanned them into the datanet. It was quite possible that Garrison would just dump her body in a ditch somewhere, after he'd had his fun. The water would take care of the evidence. God knew no one was going to be looking for her.

And as long as he's got his hand on my throat, I can't get free, she thought. She felt oddly calm, even though his hand was making its way down to her knickers. *I have to get him to let go of me.*

"You're right," she said, lowering her eyes as much as she could. "I'm sorry..."

"You should have stayed with me, at the hall," Garrison said. He pushed at her trousers, trying to get them down. "Look where we are now."

His face twisted into a leer. "But I can do anything to you," he added. "Do as I say and I'll let you go."

Molly didn't believe him. Garrison couldn't let her go, not now. He'd gone too far. The police would arrest him, if they found out. England was in a bad way, but society hadn't collapsed completely. No, Garrison would have his fun and then kill her. No one else was coming to help her. She had to stop him.

I shouldn't have left the knife in my coat, she thought. His fingers were pushing her trousers down to her knees. *If I'd kept it with me...*

"I'll behave," she managed. "Just don't kill me."

"Good," Garrison said. He sat back, tugging her shoes and trousers off. "Open your legs, then..."

Molly drew back her legs, then kicked him in the groin as hard as she could. Garrison staggered, then toppled forward, groaning in agony. Molly forced herself to crawl back as he hit the floor, his face contorted by pain and rage. She forced herself to stand, then kick him in the throat. He gasped, then lay still. Molly kicked him again and again, her rage driving her on even though he was already dead. By the time she was finished, his throat was a bloody mess.

She sat down, hard. She'd killed someone. She'd ended a life. She'd...she had to fight, suddenly, to keep from throwing up. She'd never killed anyone before, never. It wasn't something she'd ever expected to have to do.

Dear God in Heaven, she thought, numbly. *I'm a murderess.*

She'd never killed anyone before, not ever. She'd never seriously hurt anyone before. She'd...her thoughts raced round and round in circles. She was a murderess and...

He was going to rape you, her thoughts reminded her. *And he would have killed you, afterwards.*

She forced herself to stand up and reach for her trousers. Thankfully, there were no visible bloodstains, even though she knew the blood would never wash off her hands. She pulled the trousers on slowly, fighting down the urge to shake helplessly. It wouldn't be long before *someone* came to check on them and then...she knew she could explain what had happened, but would she be believed? What if she *wasn't* believed? She was an adulteress as well as a murderer.

It isn't murder if you kill someone in self-defence, she thought, as she tied her shoelaces and grabbed her coat. *But you'd have to prove it was self-defence.*

She looked down at Garrison's body for a long moment, then checked his pockets. A smartphone...useless, without his fingerprints. She pressed it against his fingers anyway, but the sensors refused to accept his cold dead hands. They were more sensitive than she'd realised. A chunk of money and a handful of credit cards...she took both, hoping it would slow down identification. Rosemary didn't know her full name, did she? She'd have a chance to make it to Woking before it was too late.

I'll confess after I've checked on the kids, she thought, firmly. She checked his remaining pockets, then pulled her damp coat over her rumpled blouse. Garrison no longer needed his bag, so she slung it over her shoulder and carried hers in her hand. *And then take whatever punishment they have in store for me.*

The rain was still dripping down as she opened the door and stepped outside the cabin. She closed and locked the door behind her, then headed for Rosemary's cabin. The rainfall was deafeningly loud, the constant drumming broken by regular peals of thunder. No wonder no one had heard the fight, she thought, as lightning flashed above her. The weather was so loud it drowned out everything else.

She tapped the door and waited, hoping that Rosemary hadn't gone to sleep. She had her kids with her, didn't she? But she might have sent them to sleep too...thunder crashed, again and again, before Rosemary opened the door. She looked tired.

"I need to borrow one of the cars," Molly said. She hoped Rosemary didn't ask too many questions. No one had children - certainly not more than one or two children - without becoming very aware of when something was wrong. Rosemary's intuition *might* realise that Molly was in trouble. "I'll send it back to you as soon as I can."

"The roads are blocked," Rosemary pointed out.

Molly felt a hot flash of anger. Her hand reached out to touch the knife in her pocket. It would be so easy to stab Rosemary, to kill her...she'd already crossed the line once, hadn't she? Rosemary was in her way...she fought down the impulse, gritting her teeth. What would she do after she killed the older woman? Kill the other adults and children? Garrison had deserved to die. Rosemary had been nothing, but kind to her.

"I should be able to make it up using the smaller roads," she said. She lowered her eyes, just for a second. "Rosemary, my children are alone. I have to get to them."

"One moment," Rosemary said.

She closed the door. Molly let out a long breath, knowing the die was cast. Either Rosemary gave her the keycard or...or she didn't know what she'd do. Try to take another car, she supposed. She had no idea how to hot-wire one of the vehicles or she would have done it already. In hindsight, her education had *definitely* been lacking. Kurt would probably laugh at her, if they ever saw each other again. She'd assumed there was a good chance he'd die, out in the inky darkness of space. It had never occurred to her that *her* life was at risk.

Rosemary opened the door and held out a keycard. "It's the green car," she said. "Good luck."

"Thank you," Molly said.

She turned and hurried to the green car, opening the door with the card. The air inside smelled faintly of too many children in too close proximity - it had been years since either Percy or Penny had been carsick, but Molly's nose remembered the smell - but there was nothing she could do about that. She dropped the bags on the passenger seat, then slipped the keycard into the slot and started the engine. Someone shouted behind her, but she ignored it as she steered the car through the gate and onto the deserted road.

I have to keep heading south-east, she thought. *Once I get into the Thames Valley, I can head straight for Woking.*

She drove a mile away from the B&B, then pulled into a lay-by and activated the onboard map. The GPS was *still* down - she cursed the government under her breath - but it wasn't *that* hard to work out her precise location. She knew where they'd tried to get onto the M5, after all. The local maps weren't as detailed as she might have wished, but she should be able to keep moving as long as she didn't try to get onto the motorway. The only problem was the map trying to constantly steer her onto the motorway. It would have been ideal, if the motorways weren't closed.

Assume they found the body as soon as I left, she told herself. *How long will it take them to track me down?*

She considered the problem for a long moment, then dismissed it. Under normal circumstances, the police would connect the body with the stolen car and put out an alert for the vehicle as soon as possible. Coming to think of it, there might even be a radio transponder in the car...hell, they didn't *need* a radio transponder. She remembered reading, somewhere, that the GPS system could be used to track the vehicle if necessary.

But then...she shook her head, sourly. The situation was far from normal. Garrison's death was a minor footnote, one of millions. And the police didn't have time to start tracking her down.

The rainfall - somehow - managed to grow heavier. Visibility shrank to almost nothing as she reached a turning. The road led uphill, but water and mud - even some stones - were cascading down it, suggesting that the road was rapidly becoming impassable. She wished, suddenly, for an ATV as she considered the sight, then grimly decided to try to drive to the next road. The longer she stayed on *this* road, the greater the chance of being caught by the police, but there was no point in taking too many chances. Getting bogged down would be bad, yet being caught in a landslide would be far worse.

She keyed the radio as she drove onwards, hoping for an update, but there was nothing. It made no sense to her. The government *had* to want to speak to the population, if only to avert panic. What if there was *no* government? Who'd been giving the policemen their orders? Perhaps London had flooded so completely that the Prime Minister and the Members of Parliament had drowned. A few days ago, she would have thought that was a brilliant idea. God knew she'd had to surrender too much of Kurt's prize money in taxes. But now...

Lightning flashed, overhead. The rain splashed down, hitting her windscreen so heavily that she thought she was driving through a sandstorm. She gritted her teeth, then pulled the car to one side and parked, careful to keep her lights on. There was no way she could travel any further, not until the rain finally stopped. She activated her smartphone, scanning desperately for something - anything - but there was nothing. Molly ground her teeth in frustration. The smartphone was powered up - the battery should last for weeks - but it was effectively useless.

It was nearly an hour before the rain finally started to slow to a trickle, although the clouds were black with impending rain. Molly let out a sigh of relief and started the engine, driving down a road that had turned into a river. Water splashed up around her as she passed a farm, a handful of miserable-looking sheep turning their heads to look at her as she drove by. A farmhouse was clearly visible in the distance. Molly thought about trying to turn up the driveway and ask for help, but she doubted they'd loan her an ATV. The farmers would need everything they had just to tend to their sodden fields and drowning animals.

Poor little lambs, she thought. She'd thrown a fit when she'd finally made the connection between farm animals and the meat on her table. Her lips quirked. She'd been nine at the time, but she'd never realised just how tolerant her parents had been until Penny had done the same thing. *They'll be killed and eaten soon enough.*

Her heart raced faster as she followed the road up the hillside. The trees started to close in, again, as she climbed higher. She gritted her teeth as the car started to slip backwards, the wheels struggling to find purchase on a rapidly-decaying road. The farmer's track might be unwatched, she thought sourly, but it was dangerous. Her borrowed car was having real problems...she cursed out loud as she fell into a rut, gunning the engine desperately to get out. The car lurched backwards and forwards for a long moment before she finally managed to escape. There were so many ruts in the ground - all filled with water - that steering around them was almost impossible.

She guided the car around a bend in the road, then slammed on the brakes. A large tree was lying flat on the road, blocking her way east. Molly cursed, then looked up - sharply - as she heard someone shouting. Three men in striped uniforms were racing towards the car, their expressions hungry. Molly thrust the car backwards, only to crash into a rut. They caught up with her before she could escape, tearing the door open and throwing her onto the muddy ground.

"Food," one of them said. "She brought food!"

"How nice of her," another said. He yanked Molly to her feet. "We're *very* pleased."

Molly stared at him, numbly. Striped uniforms meant chain gang workers, if she recalled correctly. She'd had a friend at school who'd been given the choice between jail or the chain gang. He'd been a loudmouthed ass, but he'd come back a changed man. And he'd never really talked about it.

Fuck, she thought, as they frisked her roughly and then tied her hands. *What now?*

CHAPTER
TWENTY NINE

Interplanetary Space

The intercom beeped, once.

Captain Svetlana Zadornov jerked awake, one hand going to her pistol. She thought - she was fairly sure - that none of her crew would do something stupid during a battle, but there was no way to be certain. An engagement would make an ideal opportunity to do something stupid and cover it up, if the KGB didn't ask too many questions. She listened for a long moment, making sure she was alone, then sat upright and tapped her bedside terminal.

"Report," she ordered.

"Captain," the tactical officer said. His voice was artfully flat. No doubt he was relishing the brief opportunity to take command, with both the captain and XO resting. "The enemy fleet is reducing speed."

Svetlana frowned. "Are they still on course for Jupiter?"

"Yes, Captain," the tactical officer said. "They haven't altered course."

But they could be trying to lure Home Fleet into a knife-range engagement, Svetlana thought, as she swung her legs over the side of the bed. Her body didn't feel *that* refreshed. A quick look at the chronometer told her that she'd only slept for four hours. *If the fleet tries to catch the aliens too hard, it might actually succeed.*

"Keep us close to them," she ordered. In theory, Home Fleet had the edge; in practice, the odds might well favour the other side. "Is there any sign they've detected us?"

"No, Captain," the tactical officer said.

Of course not, Svetlana thought, coldly. She slipped on her jacket, then returned the pistol to her holster. *The first sign they've detected us would be a missile slamming into our hull.*

"I'm on my way," she said. "Have the steward bring coffee to the bridge."

"Aye, Captain."

Svetlana's lips twitched as the connection broke. Having coffee on the bridge would probably be taken as a sign of weakness, but she had no choice. The enemy fleet was reducing speed, which meant they were probably planning something...she'd need to be in her command chair, if all hell broke loose. Even if the aliens were rethinking their approach to Jupiter, Svetlana needed to stay close to them to keep Home Fleet abreast of the alien movements.

She checked her appearance in the mirror, then walked through the hatch and strode up to the bridge. The tactical officer was sitting at his console, rather than occupying the command chair. Svetlana's lips twitched in disapproval - whoever had the bridge was supposed to sit in the command chair, just to make it clear who had the conn - but there was no point in making an issue of it now. A fleet carrier would have a couple of dozen tactical staffers who could have handled the tactical console. *Brezhnev* did not. The tactical officer's three staffers lacked his experience.

"The aliens are still reducing speed," the tactical officer reported. "Home Fleet is steadily gaining on them. They'll be in starfighter range in forty minutes if the relative speeds remain constant."

Svetlana nodded, tartly. It did look as though the aliens wanted to lure Home Fleet into a dogfight, far enough from Jupiter or Earth that Home Fleet would have to stand and fight alone. But the aliens were *alien.* It was possible they were reconsidering the rush to Jupiter or even contemplating immediate withdrawal from the system. They had to be concerned about reinforcements rushing to Earth from Washington or Britannia.

"Keep us in their blindspot," she ordered. She sat down in her chair, silently contemplating the problem. The hell of it was that she didn't know if the aliens still *had* a blindspot. They certainly weren't trying to *hide* any longer. Their active sensors were sweeping space near their hulls with a thoroughness she could only admire. "Are they launching starfighters?"

"No, Captain," the tactical officer said. "They've rotated around five or six squadrons through their CSP, but they haven't made any attempt to launch their remaining craft."

Not that they'd need them to deal with us, Svetlana thought. *A handful of missiles would be more than sufficient.*

She took a mug of coffee from the steward and sipped it, gratefully. It was thick, more like sludge than actual liquid. There had been a time when she'd detested naval coffee, but she'd grown to like it over the years. American or British coffee just didn't have the same kick. It was a shame the steward hadn't added a shot of vodka or even shipboard rotgut, but she knew better than to drink on duty. She had to set a good example. Alcoholism was a chronic problem in the Russian Navy - all the more so after the Battle of New Russia - but it couldn't be allowed to interfere with operational readiness. She'd have flogged anyone stupid enough to drink on duty to within an inch of his life, then send him back to Earth with a blistering report that ensured he spent the rest of his life counting trees in Siberia.

The vectors weren't hard to follow. Assuming the aliens continued at their current speed, they'd reach Jupiter in ninety minutes. The Io Detachment was waiting for them, according to the last update, but Svetlana doubted the squadron would do more than slow the aliens down. The handful of mass drivers on Io, Ganymede and Europa would probably do more damage, if the aliens came within effective range. But they'd be watching for mass drivers now they knew how dangerous they could be.

And if they keep reducing speed, they'll come to a halt within thirty minutes, she thought, running through the calculations in her head. *And that will force Home Fleet to decide if it wants to push the issue or not.*

She scowled. The idea of leaving a formidable alien force *alone*, as it skulked around the single most important system in the Human Sphere, didn't sit well with her. She couldn't imagine any halfway competent commanding officer thinking it was a good idea, either. And yet, she had to admit it did have its advantages. The aliens presumably couldn't lurk in the solar system forever.

They wouldn't have to, she thought. *They'd wear us down just by sitting there.*

She finished her coffee, passed the mug back to the steward with a nod and then leaned forward. "Keep a passive sensor watch on them," she ordered. "And prepare to yank us back if they start to reverse course."

"Aye, Captain."

Svetlana nodded, then sat back to wait.

———

The Combat Faction was, for the first time since encountering the armoured carrier, unsure how best to proceed.

The advantages of attacking and destroying the human facilities orbiting the gas giant - and the ground-based installations on its moons - remained obvious. Much of their earlier logic remained intact. The war might be won if they smashed the cloudscoops, then retreated before the humans could catch up with them. And yet, the enemy force was pursuing the fleet with a single-minded obsession that the various factions found more than a little disquieting.

They may be trying to drive us against the gas giant's defences, one analyst faction insisted.

It is impossible to assess the strength of those defences, another faction added.

They may not exist at all, a third faction countered. *The humans were not expecting to fight a major war.*

They prepared for a civil war, the first faction pointed out. *Surely, their factions would have assumed that their enemies would strike at the gas giants?*

The Combat Faction seethed with displeasure. Humans were...*alien*. They settled disputes between their factions by force, rather than talking them out. The whole idea of 'nations' bemused the Tadpoles, leaving many of the analyst factions to wonder if their translations were rather less accurate than they'd assumed. All the human wars seemed petty and pointless, the atrocities they committed on each other even more so. It was a grim reminder of the reason behind *this* war, if nothing else. The idea of sharing the galaxy with a race as violent and fundamentally aggressive as humanity was *not* pleasing.

But it still found itself in a bind. Pushing the offensive seemed the smart choice, yet...yet it could be a trap. Moving carefully seemed the best solution, but the human fleet was snapping at its rear. There was no *time* to move carefully, which might be what the humans wanted. A mistake now could cost too many ships that couldn't be replaced in a hurry.

We could turn and engage the human ships, the analyst faction pointed out. *They would suffer worse losses.*

The Song rose as the idea grew stronger. Reversing course and engaging the human ships seemed a good idea. The humans were good - better than the factions had realised, when they'd made the decision to go to war - but it would take years to replace their carriers, if they were destroyed. Or would it? What if they were wrong? Taking out the cloudscoops might seem to be the better idea after all.

We will alter course, marginally, the Combat Faction decided. *And allow them to catch up with us, if they wish.*

———

"They're reducing speed, but continuing on a direct route to Jupiter," Admiral Robertson said, as Admiral Jonathan Winters strode into the CIC. "I think they're trying to lure us into a close-range engagement."

"Which would give them the edge," Jon said. He felt better, after several hours of sleep, but the battle wasn't over yet. "Do you want to reduce our own speed to keep the range open?"

He felt a flicker of sympathy for Admiral Robertson. Engaging the aliens would give him a chance to break their fleet - and, perhaps, allow him to score a decisive victory - but it also ran the risk of immense losses. They were still too far from Jupiter for the mass drivers to play a major role in any engagement. The aliens might even know they were there, he considered. Reducing speed would make it easier for them to detect and avoid any incoming projectiles.

"I think we have no choice, for the moment," Admiral Robertson said. "We don't want to engage them without support from Jupiter."

"If the aliens reverse course, you won't have a choice," Jon pointed out. "Or if they circle Jupiter and then try to rush back to Earth."

"I doubt they have the speed to do that in any meaningful sense," Admiral Robertson said, wryly. "Hiding behind Jupiter isn't going to work, even if they didn't have to worry about the mass drivers taking pot-shots at them."

Jon nodded, slowly. "That gives them only two options," he said. "Plunge into orbit or try to hurl KEWs from outside the mass drivers' effective range."

He keyed the console, running a handful of simulations. The cloudscoops were fragile, but heavily protected with a combination of passive and active defences. The aliens wouldn't find it *easy* to score a direct hit, not with every eye orbiting Jupiter watching them. Jupiter was surrounded by debris, from chunks of ice to metallic asteroids that were slowly being mined for resources, but nowhere near enough to blind watching eyes. *That* didn't happen outside bad movies. There were enough installations orbiting Jupiter and its moons to ensure that the defenders saw everything approaching their system.

Admiral Robertson scowled as the simulations came to an end. "They can be fairly sure of scoring hits if they take up position and just keep firing," he said. "But that would expose them to us."

"Yes," Jon said. "And they'd know it, too."

What would he do, he asked himself, if *he* was in such a situation? He'd certainly try to force the enemy into a fleet action, knowing there was a reasonable chance of victory. But there was no way to know if the Tadpoles agreed. He cursed, not for the first time, the sheer lack of intelligence on their foes. How badly would they be hurt, really, if this entire fleet was smashed?

"The enemy fleet is reducing speed again," Admiral Robertson commented, grimly. "I'll reduce our own speed to match."

Jon opened his mouth to countermand him, then closed it without saying a word. He hadn't assumed command of Home Fleet, after all. Besides, Admiral Robertson might not be *wrong*. He was the only man in the solar system who could lose the war in an afternoon, if he pushed the offensive too hard. But letting the aliens waltz around the solar system wasn't an option either.

They may be hoping that we'll pull our ships from the front, he thought, although he doubted it was probable. *And that would allow them to open up other routes to Washington, Terra Nova and Earth herself.*

He shook his head, dismissing the thought. The Tadpoles might be alien, but they weren't stupid. They couldn't handle a simultaneous offensive across multiple star systems...could they? There was no sign they could communicate at FTL speeds, any more than their human opponents. But they might have told their commanders to watch for an opportunity for some aggressive raiding at their own discretion. And yet...

"We might want to prepare for starfighter strikes," he said. "We *should* have a numerical advantage. It's high time we used it."

"If they weren't concealing more starfighters inside their carriers," Admiral Robertson said, dryly. He smiled. "But that doesn't seem *too* likely."

Jon nodded. Starfighters that were held back, when their mothership was destroyed, were no good to anyone. It was why fleet carriers practiced launching all their fighters as fast as possible, even when there was no *apparent* danger. God knew there was no evidence the Tadpoles disagreed. The combination of Home Fleet's own starfighters and the starfighters they'd recovered from Earth *should* give them an advantage. But he would have hated to take it for granted.

"Hold back a sizable reserve," he advised. "They'll try to strike back at us."

"We'll let them get closer to Jupiter first," Admiral Robertson said. "The Io Detachment should be in position by now."

Should, Jon thought, grimly. Coordinating an operation across interplanetary distances wasn't exactly impossible, but it was difficult. Too many things could go wrong. *I guess we're about to find out.*

———

Captain Ginny Saito opened her eyes.

For a moment, she was utterly disoriented. She was in a sleeping tube... but not the one she used on Pournelle Base. Where *was* she? And then she remembered. The Tadpoles had attacked Earth, Pournelle Base had been destroyed and she'd landed on *Enterprise*. She'd fought a long battle...

She fumbled for the opening switch and keyed it, breathing a sigh of relief as the tube opened without hesitation. She'd been locked in one during basic training, an exercise that straddled the borderline between extensive testing and outright sadism. It was important to find out if a pilot suffered from claustrophobia, she'd been told, but a starfighter cockpit allowed its occupant to see out. The tubes were isolated and sealed.

"Welcome back," a voice said. "Did you have a good nap?"

Ginny sat upright and looked around. A dark-skinned man wearing a pilot's uniform was sitting next to the tubes, reading a magazine. She resisted the urge to cross her arms over her bare breasts - she'd grown far too accustomed to her squadron mates, rather than starfighter pilots in general - as she climbed out of the tube. Her nude body felt refreshed, if nothing else. She breathed a sigh of relief as she saw the neat pile of clothes next to the tube, waiting for her.

"It could have been better," she said. She smiled wryly as she snapped on her bra, then reached for the trousers. Williams had propositioned her, hadn't he? "What's the situation?"

"You're to report to the briefing room, once dressed," the man said. He rose and stuck out a hand. "Captain Jeffers. *Enterprise-A*."

Ginny shook his hand firmly. "Thank you for letting us use your squadron room," she said, seriously. She knew he wouldn't be *too* pleased about it, but she found it hard to care. There was a war on. She didn't have time for petty bullshit. "We needed a shower and a rest."

"So I heard," Jeffers said. He turned away as she finished dressing. "There are some ration bars in the next room. I suggest you eat now. We may be launching soon."

"Understood," Ginny said. She wasn't sure which of them was actually the senior officer, but it was *his* squadron room. "Have we been reassigned?"

"I think you're being lumped in with all the other guests," Jeffers said. He sighed. "But the higher-ups keep changing their minds, so you might end up being thrown in with us instead."

"As long as I get a crack at the enemy," Ginny said. It would be a climb down, after commanding a squadron, but she'd just have to put up with it.

The USN wasn't going to assign her to squadron command if they needed her to be a pilot instead. "Some of those bastards are good."

"So I hear," Jeffers said. "Do you have any advice?"

Ginny hesitated. "Watch yourself if they lead you into a chase," she said. "Those little bastards can turn on a dime."

"They must have fiddled with their compensators," Jeffers mused. "I'm surprised they don't blow up their own starfighters if they do that regularly."

"We couldn't be that lucky," Ginny said.

She followed him into the ready room and took a ration bar from the table. A large pot of coffee sat next to the ration bars, just waiting for her. Ginny poured herself a cup and drank it rapidly. It tasted foul, but at least it drove the last traces of sleep from her mind. Williams appeared a moment later, looking wretched. Ginny hoped he'd slept for the full four hours rather than trying to chase skirts on the carrier. There just wasn't time for fun.

"Grab your coffee and come with me," Jeffers ordered. A low hooting ran through the giant ship. "The shit might be about to hit us again."

CHAPTER
THIRTY

Near Townsend, United Kingdom

"You could have brought us more food," one of Molly's captors said. He looked around eighteen, although it was hard to be sure. There was a wild look in his eyes that Molly didn't like at all. "Why didn't you pack more shit?"

Molly tried to force herself to remain calm. It wasn't easy. There were three of them, all young and strong and her hands were tied behind her back. She tested her bonds as surreptitiously as she could, but they refused to budge. There was no way to break free, not with all three of them watching her. The hungry expressions on their faces chilled her to the bone.

"I didn't know I'd be feeding you," she managed, finally. She looked from face to face, trying to understand them. Would it be better to appear defiant or crawl on her belly in front of them? Anyone who'd been sent to a chain gang wouldn't be anything like as socialised as her son and his friends. "If I'd known, I would have brought more."

"There's fuck-all in here, Dave," another captor said. "Just a bunch of shitty children's toys."

"Keep your mouth shut, Colin," Dave snarled. He glared at Molly as if she'd personally offended him. "Where the fuck were you going?"

"Home," Molly said. She had a nasty feeling she wouldn't see home in a hurry. The hungry looks were scaring her. "I was driving to Woking..."

Dave snickered. "You're lost," he said. "I *knew* women couldn't read maps!"

Molly flushed with anger, but said nothing. Mentioning the police wouldn't make things any better. Dave and his two companions had abandoned a chain gang, which meant...she suspected it would probably mean a return to jail, if they were caught. The country was in a mess, coming to think of it. There was a good chance they wouldn't be caught for years, if they were careful. The police had more important things to worry about.

Dave reached forward and touched her cheek, lightly. Molly had to fight to keep from cringing back. "You're coming with us," he said. He gripped her arm and marched her off the road. "Try to keep up."

The rain started to fall again as Dave half-pushed her up a hidden track. Molly wondered, numbly, just when the three of them had escaped the chain gang. During the battle...or earlier? There would have been a manhunt for him, if they'd escaped even a day ago...she didn't recall *hearing* anything about a manhunt. But that meant nothing. She'd been too busy planning her time at the party to bother to watch the BBC. Perhaps, if she had, she'd have thought better of *going* to the party.

Dave leered nastily at her as her wet clothes started to cling to her skin, exposing all of her curves. Molly shuddered as she tried - desperately - to think of a plan. She'd killed Garrison, hadn't she? But Garrison had been twenty or more years older than her *and* she'd caught him by surprise. Now, there were *three* young men escorting her...

She tested her bonds again, trying to think of a way to get her hands free. But even if she did, she knew it wouldn't be easy to get far without being stopped. Dave and his comrades *knew* they were dead meat, if they were ever recaptured. The best they could hope for was a speedy transfer to a penal colony or an isolated island somewhere up north. Now, with martial law declared, they might just be shot out of hand by the police. God knew they'd broken the terms of their parole when they'd fled the chain gang.

And they've got nothing to lose, she thought, numbly. Dave's leers were *far* from reassuring. The other two weren't much better. *And when Garrison thought he had nothing to lose, he tried to rape me.*

She sucked in her breath. She'd been offered courses on what to do if she was kidnapped, back when Kurt had been on active service. She hadn't thought much of it at the time - no one in their right mind would kidnap the wife of a military officer, not when the police would do everything in their power to catch the bastards - but now...now she wished she'd taken the course when it was offered. What *should* she do? Try to befriend them or keep herself aloof?

Her mind raced. The coastline had been devastated. Every town along the shore had probably been wiped out. The remaining population would have too many other things to worry about...no one would be looking for the chain gang. Or her...Rosemary was the only person who knew she'd taken the car and *she* had her own problems. God alone knew what she'd do when she discovered Garrison's body. She certainly wouldn't think that Molly might have walked from the frying pan into the fire.

"Blair, check around the fence," Dave ordered. "And then come inside."

Molly looked up. They were approaching a house in the woods, a little holiday cabin...it would have been charming, if a dead body hadn't been lying outside. She shivered as Dave pointed to the body, then drew a finger across his throat. He'd killed a man...Molly reminded herself, again, that Dave had nothing to lose. Murder would get him transported or hung for sure.

"Our little home from home," Dave said. He pushed open the door, then shoved Molly into the cabin. "Honey, we're home!"

"Put her in the backroom," Colin said. "We need to talk."

Molly forced herself to look around as she was shoved towards a rear door. The interior was larger than she'd expected, resembling a farmhouse kitchen from any number of movies and TV shows that extolled the virtues of living on a farm. And yet, it was just too perfect to be real. It was a *holiday* home, she told herself. The people who came to live on the farm could pretend, just for a while, that they were farmers too. She couldn't help noticing that there were plenty of mod cons too.

Dave opened the door. "We're home," he called. "Hi, there!"

The room was dim. Molly looked up - there was a skylight, but the clouds were blocking most of the sunlight - then down towards the bed. A dark shape lay on it, unmoving. Dave flicked a switch, turning on the light. Molly recoiled as she saw a young girl - no older than Penny - lying on the bed. Her hands were tied firmly behind her back and her legs were chained to the bed. She could barely move.

Shit, Molly thought. The girl's eyes were wide with fear. *What did they do to her?*

"We'll be back soon," Dave promised. He shoved Molly onto the bed. "Try not to have *too* much fun without us."

He chuckled, then turned and walked out of the room. Molly heard him slam the door closed, but she didn't hear a lock...it didn't matter, anyway. There was no way out of the backroom, unless they managed to somehow open the skylight and climb onto the roof. She looked up, silently considering their chances. They *had* to get out before it was too late.

The girl coughed. "Who...who are you?"

"I'm Molly," Molly said. She looked down at the girl. "Who are you?"

"Fran," the girl said. Her voice was trembling. "What...what are they going to do to us?"

Molly sighed. "I think we'll find out soon," she said. "How did they catch you?"

"Dad and I were on holiday," Fran said. She gulped. "We...we had planned a weekend away before I went to university. This place...it was awesome. And then it started to rain and *they* showed up. Dad..."

The body, Molly thought. She felt a sudden flicker of envy for Fran, mixed with fear. *Her* father had never taken her on a private holiday. *They killed her father and dumped him outside.*

She forced herself to think. "What happened to your mother?"

"She died when I was seven," Fran said. "Dad...he never wanted to marry again."

Molly shivered. Fran was tall and thin, with long brown hair...she really looked more like Penny than Molly cared to admit. It looked as though she hadn't been molested - yet - but Molly knew that was just a matter of time. Dave certainly didn't *look* the type to wait long before taking what he wanted. God knew he'd managed to escape the chain gang in the chaos.

Fran stared at her. "How do we get out of this?"

"I don't know," Molly said.

She looked up at the skylight. If she stood on the bed, she could open it...and then what? She didn't think she could climb up and out onto the roof. Perhaps if she put the chair on the bed...her wrists twanged uncomfortably, reminding her that her hands were still tied behind her back. She twisted her head, trying to see the knots. Maybe she could work her hands free, now they were alone.

If I get out of this alive, she promised herself, *I'll study everything from martial arts to escapology.*

The rope resolutely refused to budge. Molly cursed, forcing down the wave of bitter frustration that threatened to overcome her. She'd watched hundreds of TV shows where the heroines always managed to escape, after they'd been tied up by the moustache-twirling villains of the week. How had *they* done it? She couldn't help thinking that they'd had help from a patriotic scriptwriter. The real world was nowhere near so obliging.

She eyed Fran for a long moment. "Was this your room?"

"Yeah," Fran said. "Dad slept on the couch outside."

Molly nodded. "Did you have anything sharp with you?"

Fran hesitated. "I had a makeup knife," she said. "It was in my bag. I don't think I had anything else."

Molly forced herself to stand and walk around the bed. A large suitcase was lying on the floor, the contents scattered across the room. Molly felt an uneasy twinge of fear as she realised that Fran and Penny had a *lot* in common. Her daughter had always left her room a mess too, no matter how much Molly nagged. Kurt wasn't any help, either. Molly had always thought that a military officer would be neater, but he hadn't seemed to care.

Or maybe Dave and his pals searched the bag, just to be sure there was nothing dangerous here, she thought. *Did they expect Fran to escape while they were gone?*

She looked up. "How many of them are there?"

"Three," Fran said. She paused. "At least...I *saw* three."

Molly nodded, slowly. It wasn't easy to dig through the bag's contents with her feet, but she managed it somehow. The box of cosmetics was larger than it should have been, her maternal instincts insisted. She'd certainly never allowed Penny to spend so much money on makeup and perfume. No wonder Penny had been so irked, when she'd realised that Molly was buying expensive dresses and handbags. She'd thought her mother was being a hypocrite.

And I was, Molly conceded, grimly.

The guilt was almost overpowering. The conclusion was inescapable. She'd been a complete fool. Worse, she'd been a bitch. She'd made the decision to abandon her husband and children for an older man who'd treated her as his personal whore and planned to abandon her when her tits started to sag. Or when she became inconvenient. Kurt was a war hero, after all. Garrison might have got into some trouble if he'd been caught seducing a war hero's wife. Better to end the affair before the war ended, leaving Molly in the cold. No doubt he'd have picked up some even *younger* girl to warm his bed for the rest of his life.

And now he's dead, Molly thought. Tears prickled at the corner of her eyes. *I've fucked up everything.*

Fran shifted. "Are you all right?"

Molly forced down the urge to cry - or to laugh, hysterically. Was she all right? Of *course* she was not all right. She'd betrayed her husband, abandoned her children, killed her lover...and now she was the captive of a bunch of thugs who probably planned to rape her before they cut her throat. Or maybe even keep her prisoner for months, perhaps years. Molly had heard more than a few stories about people being kidnapped and held captive indefinitely, even in suburban Britain. The police had far too many problems to worry about three runaways, even if they knew the chain gang had escaped in the first place.

"No," she said. "I'm not all right."

She twisted until she was in position to use her fingers to open the box. A handful of makeup pens fell out of the box, landing with a clatter on the floor. Molly tensed, expecting Dave to break down the door, but nothing happened. She listened, carefully...there was no sound on the far side of the door. Had they slipped out? Or had they fallen asleep? She wondered if she dared open the door. But with her hands bound, there was no way she could sneak around without making a sound.

"Footsteps," Fran hissed.

Molly pushed the box under the bed, an instant before the door opened. Dave was standing there, an unpleasant expression on his face. His eyes went wide when he saw Molly, sitting by the suitcase. He reached forward and yanked her to her feet, then scooped up a pair of frilly panties.

"I don't think they'll fit you," he said, nastily. He caught her arm and shoved her towards the door. "The others will take care of you."

Molly gritted her teeth as she stumbled through the door. Colin caught her and pushed her into an arm chair, slapping her ass as she fell forward. Molly landed badly, grunting in pain; Colin laughed, then helped her to sit upright. Behind her, Dave half-carried Fran through the door. The younger girl was staring around wildly, perhaps looking for her father's body.

"So," Dave said. His eyes travelled over Molly's breasts, leaving a trail of slime in their wake. "What *were* you doing in that car?"

Molly forced herself to keep her voice level. "I was going home," she said. She'd told them that already, hadn't she? "I have to get to Woking..."

"No, you don't," Dave said. "You're *ours* now."

Fran whimpered. Dave smirked as his hand crawled towards her chest. Molly wanted to look away, but Colin held her head still. She didn't want to know what he'd do if she tried to close her eyes. And yet, Fran was *far* too much like Penny for her peace of mind. She didn't want to see Fran degraded and humiliated, then raped and perhaps murdered. Dave's hands were already playing with Fran's shirt buttons...

"Don't," Molly said.

Dave leered at her. "And why should we not?"

"We haven't had any pussy for months," Blair put in. "You think we get to fuck on the chain gang?"

Molly took a breath. "Do you really want to add rape to your list of offences?"

Dave laughed. "Do *you* really think they'll let us off with a slap on the wrist?"

No, Molly thought. She had no idea what they'd done to get themselves assigned to the chain gang, but it hardly mattered. Dave and his friends had escaped custody *and* murdered an innocent man. That was a hanging offence, whatever else they did. It wasn't as if they could be hanged twice, either. *They have nothing to lose.*

Her blood ran cold. They could do anything to her...

"We could hide the body," she offered. She didn't know if they'd go for it, but it was worth a try. "Fran and I will keep our mouths shut..."

Dave lunged forward and slapped her, right across the face. Molly reeled back, tasting blood in her mouth. The pain was overwhelming, but the humiliation was worse. She was utterly helpless, unable to say or do anything that might change their minds. They could gang-rape Molly and Fran until both women were bleeding, then kill them...they could do anything they liked. Society was breaking down.

"Women always lie," Dave snapped. He tugged at his striped uniform. "Do you know how I got sent to prison? Some bitch *lied* about me! She came on to me, but when I kissed her back she screamed *rape*! Why the fuck should we believe a pair of bitches like you?"

Molly lowered her eyes as he glared at her. Her cheek hurt, the throbbing pain making it hard to concentrate. One of her teeth felt loose...the taste of blood was getting stronger. She could feel it dripping out of her mouth. She was a prisoner...

She looked up. "Don't touch her," she said. It was desperate, but she saw no choice. At least Fran would be spared, for a while. "Take me instead."

Dave snorted. "We can take both of you," he said. His hand grabbed Fran's breast and squeezed, hard. "What do you have to offer?"

"I'm an experienced woman," Molly said. It was *all* she had to offer. "I won't just lie there while you have your fun. Leave her alone and I'll...I'll do anything."

"Very well," Dave said. He shoved Fran back in the backroom and closed the door, then started to unbuckle his pants. "But you'd better be very good."

Molly tried, as he advanced on her, to pretend he was Kurt. Or even Garrison...someone he'd chosen. She couldn't afford to have him think she wasn't living up to her side of the bargain. She *had* to pretend she wanted him and his friends...

It didn't work.

CHAPTER
THIRTY ONE

London, United Kingdom

Ten Downing Street was a mess.

Andrew walked slowly through the building, ignoring the increasingly anxious looks from his close-protection detail. Ten Downing Street had been designed to stand up to anything short of a nuke or a KEW strike, but the floodwaters had still managed to smash down the doors and cascaded through the lower levels. The library was soaked - a number of books donated by various Prime Ministers were probably beyond recovery - and the civil servant offices were ruined. Water still dripped from the ceiling as he made his way to the entrance hall and peered up the stairwell, wondering if he wanted to see what had happened to the master bedroom. Or the handful of other rooms he'd been allowed to personalise...

"The building is not safe," Sergeant Howe told him. The burly SAS sergeant gave Andrew a sharp look. "I wouldn't care to swear to anything right now."

Andrew nodded, mutely. He'd seen the building plans, when he'd moved in. Ten Downing Street - the new Ten Downing Street - was meant to be tough, but no one had predicted a massive flood. Or alien attack, for that matter. The Troubles had been bad, yet...they hadn't been *that* bad.

"There were people working in the building," he said. He could have kicked himself. He should have thought to ask earlier. "What happened to them?"

"I believe most of them were moved to the emergency evacuation point, then taken out of London to the Alternate Government Post," Howe said. "The building has been searched twice, since the bombardment. No bodies were discovered within the governmental centre."

Andrew nodded, then stepped through the open door and onto Downing Street. A cold air blew through the street as he looked up and down, sending shivers running down his spine. The policemen who should have been on duty outside the building were gone, but a number of policemen in bright yellow jackets could be seen at the gates. Andrew wasn't sure if that was a good thing or not. It was hard to imagine anyone actually trying to *rob* Downing Street, while the policemen could have been of use elsewhere.

He tasted salt water in the air as the wind blew harder, mocking him. He'd seen report after report of anarchy in the UK, everything from looters robbing food stories to countless reports of rapes and murders. Society was breaking down, it seemed. People were falling back on their own resources, sometimes even lashing out at the police. There was even a vague report of the owners of a food shop shooting at the police when they came to requisition food. It wouldn't be long before the rumours got out of control, even though large chunks of the datanet were still down. Thankfully, most of the population had too many other things to worry about...

It only takes a handful of people to cause a riot, he thought. *And stopping them means diverting police and soldiers from other places.*

He pushed the thought to the back of his mind as he walked down towards the gates. The rain had stopped, for the moment, but water droplets lingered in the air. Giant puddles of murky water lay everywhere, a grim reminder that London's sewage network was flooded out. London got plenty of rainfall, but it had never been so bad before. Some of the grimmer reports warned of disease outbreaks, even if the dead bodies were rapidly removed from the city and incinerated.

A car was waiting for him, as he'd ordered. He felt a twang of guilt as he climbed into the back, his escorts mounting motorbikes so they could respond to any threats before they turned into a real problem. The car was warm, waterproof as well as bulletproof...he was protected, just because he was Prime Minister. And he was drawing men and equipment away from the public, just because he wanted to visit a refugee centre.

I have to see, he told himself. It had only been a day - less than a day - but he felt as if he'd spent *years* in the bunker. Years of briefings, years of endless prattle, years of knowing that nothing he said or did would actually matter. He was Prime Minister, but his title was practically meaningless. The briefings meant nothing. *I have to know what's going on.*

He pressed his face to the window as the car began to move, the outriders fanning out around the vehicle. Normally, London would be jam-packed with traffic, despite endless government attempts to convince people to take the tube or use taxis. Now, the streets were almost eerily deserted. A handful of work gangs could be seen picking up bodies and carting them off to the disposal sites, but little else. London seemed to have collapsed into a handful of safe zones, surrounded by chaos. Andrew couldn't help feeling another flicker of bitter guilt. He'd given the orders himself.

The damage was immense, he realised as the car headed south. The floods had broken into hundreds of buildings, smashing windows and drenching floors. Hotels, corporate offices, shops and tourist traps...the damage was almost beyond his comprehension. He'd thought himself hardened to horror, after all the reports had started to blur together, but now...now he knew he had never really grasped what horror was.

He gritted his teeth as the car moved past a large pile of bodies. A handful of men in MOPP suits were picking them up, one by one, and tossing them into a refuse lorry. Andrew wanted to order them to stop, to order them to treat the bodies with respect, but he knew there was no point. The bodies were already rotting, the damp air speeding up the process. They had to be burnt before they started to turn London into a disease-riddled hellhole. And yet...

You wanted to be Prime Minister, his thoughts mocked him. *Did you ever really understand what the job actually meant?*

It wasn't a pleasant thought, but it had to be faced. He'd assumed leadership of the Conservative-Unionist Party after his predecessor had managed to lose the trust of the Tory backbenchers. The poor man had been too willing to please, too willing to dicker with the other parties...

he hadn't shown himself possessed of the strong character the Tory Party wanted from its leaders. Andrew had put his name forward, when the party had started looking for a new leader. He *had* led them to victory, but now...

I'll be lucky if I last long enough to see the next election, he thought. The Tory Party was historically unwilling to unseat Prime Ministers, but *no* Prime Minister had presided over such a disaster. *The bastards will need to find a scapegoat fast enough to save their own asses.*

It was a bitter thought. There had been no way to predict that humanity would encounter aliens, let alone that the aliens would be hostile. God knew there were no alien bodies in the MOD basement, no alien flying saucers in RAF bases that weren't on any civilian maps. The conspiracy theorists could talk all they liked, but no one in authority had known about the Tadpoles before Vera Cruz. They would have taken more precautions if they had, Andrew knew. *He* sure as hell would have fortified all the approaches to Vera Cruz and New Russia before the Tadpoles showed their hand.

But he hadn't known. And he would be made to pay for his ignorance.

He sat back in his chair as the car picked up speed, fighting the urge to brood. Prime Ministers had been sacked before, after they lost the confidence of their MPs; Prime Ministers had lost votes of confidence or frantic bids for re-election...but none of them had ever been blamed for a disaster that hadn't been their fault. *Andrew* would be the first Prime Minister to be kicked out of office for a disaster he hadn't seen coming, a disaster that would have been very hard to handle even if he *had* seen it coming...

The car came to a halt. Andrew looked outside and froze. The stadium was full of people, mainly women and children. They looked miserable, drenched to the skin despite hastily-erected shelters. Many of them were injured, sitting on the ground while a handful of medics walked from patient to patient, trying to decide who could be saved with the limited resources imaginable. They were suffering...

Andrew swallowed, hard, as the door opened. The stench of blood and piss and shit and stuff he didn't want to identify reached his nostrils. It was a refugee camp...he'd seen others, camps established near the handful of Great Power military bases in the Middle East, but this was in the heart of London. Yesterday, everyone in the camp had been living in apartments near the heart of the city; today, they were struggling to survive. A handful of policemen stood guard, their weapons clearly visible...

It was all he could do to force himself to climb out of the car. He'd been to rallies and protest marches where the protesters had hated him and everything he stood for, but this was far worse. A despondency infested the air, draining the energy from everyone...a handful of kids were kicking a ball around, listlessly, but even they looked tired. Andrew met the eyes of a young woman - a young professional woman, he was sure - who barely seemed capable of meeting his eyes. Her blonde hair was a horrific mess, but she didn't seem to care. She'd lost the ability to take care of herself.

"Prime Minister," a sharp voice said. Andrew turned to see an older, grey-haired woman holding a terminal in one hand. "Why did you come?"

Andrew had no good answer. "I had to see," he said, finally. The wind shifted, blowing the stench of garbage into his face. "What is...?"

"This way," the woman said. She led the way towards a set of tents, speaking in a curt monotone. "This stadium was designed to hold 10'000 people, all sitting on chairs. Right now, we have over 30'000 men, women and children registered here. The menfolk have largely been assigned to work gangs, save for the ones who are injured or too old to work effectively. Even with that, we're pushing the limits. We need to move as many people out of London as possible before it's too late."

Andrew nodded. "I..."

"You'd better get the army moving fast," the woman added, cutting him off. She opened one of the tents. "I don't think we can feed everyone for more than a day or two. The police have been opening up food stores for us, but half the supplies they found were drenched and inedible."

She nodded as Andrew followed him into the tent. "As you can see, we have a serious public health problem."

Andrew followed her gaze, trying not to be sick. The tent was crammed with wounded men, women and children. They were lying everywhere - on makeshift beds, on blankets, even on the cold floor - gasping and moaning as they struggled to survive. Andrew swallowed, hard, as he saw a man with a broken arm. No one had even bothered to make him a splint, let alone try to repair the damage. Beside him, a girl scratched her eyes until blood flowed from under her nails. Andrew didn't even want to *know* what was wrong with her.

"We're already out of most kinds of medicine," the woman informed him. It dawned on Andrew that she hadn't even bothered to introduce herself. "The police dug up painkillers and other supplies from the stores, but most of them are of limited value. Some bastards looted the nearby hospital for drugs during the night, damn them. There are people here who would be a great deal better off if we could give them a shot of morphine, but all we can really do is make them comfortable as they wait to die."

She shook her head. "And that's just the physical trauma," she added. Her voice darkened as she led the way through the tent. "There are several hundred people - so far - who simply haven't been able to cope with...well, everything. They've completely zoned out, as far as we can tell. They just sit there and do nothing. We've not been able to do anything for them either, Prime Minister."

Andrew looked at her. "Is that normal?"

"It depends," the woman said. She peered down the tent. "The way people respond to disaster is inherently unpredictable. Some people don't cope very well when they're yanked from a world they understand and dumped into a disaster area. They struggle to cope, they try to bargain with the new rules, they...sometimes, they just zone out. It would be better, I suspect, if people were more aware of how quickly things could change, but..."

"They're not," Andrew finished.

He gritted his teeth. Britain was safe. No, Britain *had* been safe. The crime rate had been low, the threat of foreign invasion or civil war practically non-existent, the threat of natural disasters even less...Britain had been safe. He - and the rest of the population - had grown up in a bubble, protected from even the *prospect* of massive upheaval. They'd thought themselves safe. They'd thought that disasters were things that happened to people in other countries. And they'd been wrong.

The woman sighed. "The rapes are even worse," she added. "We've had at least fifty reports since we opened the centre, Prime Minister, and we suspect a number have remained unreported. Normally, we'd take semen samples from the victims and try to match them against our records, but now...we don't even begin to have the resources. We certainly can't give the women the support they need."

Andrew winced. "I'm sorry."

"So you should be," the woman said, sharply. "I think a great many people are going to have to come to terms with their trauma on their own. And as for the people who zoned out...we can't do much for them either."

She reached the end of the tent and pushed open the flap. Andrew hesitated, looking back. A young boy was sitting on a blanket, looking at nothing. His face was scarred, a crude bandage wrapped over one eye. Beside him, a girl who couldn't be more than a year or two older was crying silently. Andrew felt his heart go out to her as he forced himself to turn away. He couldn't bear to watch.

A convoy of buses had arrived outside, the soldiers speaking rapidly to the policemen before starting to load the women and children into the buses. Andrew watched, silently grateful for being ignored, as some of the women tried to argue, insisting that they should wait for their husbands or search for their missing children. The soldiers were polite, but firm. They needed to move as many people out of the city as possible before it was too late.

"Too many people have filed missing persons reports," the woman said. Her voice was very soft. "My husband is missing too..."

Andrew opened his mouth, but said nothing. What was there to say? What *could* he say? He had never been particularly good with words, not when he'd had speechwriters to turn his original concepts into something he could say with confidence. Now...he found himself utterly lost for words. The woman's husband was gone, yet she was still carrying on. The entire country needed to carry on.

"I'm sure he'll turn up," he said, finally. "I think..."

"I don't know," the woman said. She waved a hand to the west. "They're moving bodies out of the city, you know. My husband could be among them. So could the other missing people. And I will never know."

"I am sorry," Andrew said. "But..."

"I know you're sorry," the woman said. "But does it make a difference?"

She cleared her throat. "Go back to your office, Prime Minister," she said. "Get us all the support we need. And understand that nothing will ever be the same again."

"I will," Andrew said.

"I doubt it," the woman said. "This isn't something that can be fixed in a day. The country took one hell of a beating."

Andrew nodded, tersely. "How do *you* manage to cope with it?"

"I deal with it, one problem at a time," the woman said. She smiled, humourlessly. "You know, that's all you can do. Put one leg forward, then the other...keep going until you get through, instead of getting bogged down. And brace yourself for the discovery that there is no perfect solution after all."

A helicopter clattered overhead, heading south. Andrew looked up, wondering if it was safe to fly now. Aircraft were still grounded over much of the countryside, but the SAR flights had to go on. He'd seen reports of SAR helicopters being blown out of the sky by freak winds and forced to ditch in the ocean. He hoped the helicopter crews made it out, but he didn't give much for their chances.

"I'll go," he said, quietly. "What's your name?"

"It doesn't matter," the woman said, flatly. She waved a hand at the growing crowd of refugees. Lines were forming outside the buses as the soldiers struggled to keep track of who was going where. "Just get these people the help they need."

"I will," Andrew promised. The woman should get a medal. But she probably didn't want one. He'd look up her name later, when he had time. She'd be listed in the emergency register. "And thank you."

The woman gave him a sharp look. "For what?"

CHAPTER
THIRTY TWO

London, United Kingdom

"This isn't safe," one of the men muttered. "You should get trained people to do it."

"And you're all we've got," Robin snapped. He'd never liked the idea of conscripting civilians for recovery work and this was why. They either didn't know what to do or they grumbled as they did it. "So do as you're told."

He walked up to the storefront and opened the door. "You know what to look for," he said, curtly. "Fill the shopping trolleys, then take them out onto the street and wait. Remember to put the alcohol and medical supplies in separate trolleys."

The store had already been looted, he noted as he paced the aisles. Someone - rather less intelligent than the average criminal - had been trying to force open the tills, while others had been stealing alcohol and cigarettes. Robin was privately relieved, although he was fairly sure the stolen alcohol would cause problems later. The civilian recovery workers were already grumbling about the shortage of anything to drink.

But we need the alcohol to clean wounds, Robin thought. He wasn't sure *just* how effective cheap red wine would be at cleaning wounds, but medical supplies were already terrifyingly low. *And we need to keep the refugees from getting drunk and starting fights.*

"Put the medicine in the medical trolleys," he ordered, as he passed a young man removing boxes of painkillers from the shelf. "And make sure it's covered. It won't be long before it starts to rain again."

"Yes, boss," the young man said. He pointed a finger at a red notice. "Should we be taking more than two?"

Robin snorted. Legally, a person could only buy two packets of painkillers at a time. It was supposed to keep people from overdosing, he'd been told, but it was pointless. Anyone intent on buying a few hundred painkillers could walk down the street, buying a couple of packets in every shop. They'd have enough to kill a dozen people by the time they reached the end, all perfectly legal. Someone who wanted to commit suicide wouldn't have any problems with skirting the law.

"Take them all," he said. The painkillers were meant to deal with everything from headaches to menstrual cramps, not broken bones and starvation. But they would have to do. "And make sure you take the rest of the supplies as well."

He moved to the next aisle, where a team was rapidly stripping the store of baby food and supplies. The women and children were supposed to be be moved out of the city by early afternoon - he'd heard that buses were already arriving from depots outside London - but they'd need *something* to feed their children. Hardly anyone had thought to grab nappies when they fled their homes, let alone anything else. The baby food wasn't ideal - he'd always preferred home-cooked food when he'd been a child - but it would have to do. They were running out of other options.

Sally joined him as he reached the bottom of the store. "Who do you think is going to pay for all this?"

Robin shrugged. "I have no idea," he said. Looting stores didn't sit well with him, even though it was perfectly legal. Martial law had been declared. "I doubt the insurance will pay for all the damage, let alone requisitioned goods."

"That might cause other problems," Sally said. "What happens if the economy collapses into rubble?"

"Right now, it's the least of our problems," Robin said. The government had closed the stock market and ordered the banks to limit withdrawals before the bombardment had begun, but now...now people had more important things to worry about than trying to withdraw money from their bank. "We have to keep as many people alive as possible."

He peered past her, watching as the remaining wine shelves were emptied into trolleys. "And it won't be easy," he added. It didn't *look* as if the workers had helped themselves to a couple of small bottles, but it was hard to be sure. "Some of them will be fighting us all the way."

"Yeah," Sally said.

The radio crackled, loudly. "All units, be aware of gunfire on Salvation Road," the dispatcher said. "Armed officers are on the way."

Robin tensed. They were some distance from Salvation Road, but he'd been in the police long enough to know that trouble could move at ter- rifying speed. The radio network might be coming back up, yet it was far from perfect. He'd bitched and moaned about its weaknesses back before the bombardment, but now he would have sold his soul for the network he'd had yesterday. Had it really been less than a *day* since all hell had broken loose?

Only nineteen hours, he thought, checking his watch. *And the world is now a fucking mess.*

He touched his holster, silently reassuring himself that his pistol was still there. The thought of using it - of using it *again* - chilled him to the bone. And yet, he knew he might need it before too long. None of the workers looked as if they were going to turn violent, but that could change in a hurry too. People became dangerously unpredictable when they were in mobs.

The skies were starting to darken again as he led the workers back outside, suggesting that it wouldn't be long before it started to rain again. Water was still running down the streets, bubbling up from sewer grates... he wrinkled his nose as he saw pieces of rubbish and debris floating down towards the river. The stench of human waste was growing stronger, warn- ing him that the sewer network was on the verge of collapse. He shud- dered, helplessly. He'd seen the emergency toilets at the refugee centre. They were a breeding ground for diseases that hadn't been seen in over a hundred years.

Not in Britain, he thought. There had been a time when everyone was vaccinated against everything, once vaccines had been developed and made safe. The threat of bio-terror had demanded the harshest measures to keep diseases from spreading. But now...he sucked in his breath as he saw a dead cat, floating in the gutter. Now, far too many people lacked even the most basic protections against disease and tainted water. *It won't be long before people start to die.*

He pushed the thought out of his head as he shouted orders, leading the way up the road. The sight would have been surreal, once upon a time: a policeman, leading a dozen men pushing shopping trolleys...shopping trolleys that had effectively been stolen. Now...it was just another sign of desperation. Robin liked to think that the police had it under control, but he knew that wasn't the case. There were entire sections of London that had effectively been abandoned altogether.

Nineteen hours, he thought, numbly. *That was all it took for the city to collapse.*

The wind blew stronger as he walked. He pulled his coat tighter around himself, careful to keep his pistol within easy reach. A helicopter clattered overhead, heading south. He wondered, absently, where it was going. It didn't look like a police helicopter or a military machine...it looked more like a private corporate aircraft. Perhaps it had been pressed into service. Nothing civilian should be flying, certainly not near London. He'd heard rumours of hypersonic jets blown out of the air by sudden, shocking turbulence. The stories might be exaggerated - he knew they were exaggerated - but he was glad he wasn't flying. He hadn't missed the shortage of aircraft flying over the city.

"The army's arrived," Sally said, as they approached the refugee camp. "They're in force."

Robin nodded. A dozen commandeered buses were parked outside the camp, women and children being escorted inside by grim-faced squaddies. The soldiers looked nervous, half of them holding their weapons at the ready. Robin scowled at them - they were making the civilians nervous too - even though he understood their concern. London had turned into hostile territory, all of a sudden. They didn't know when or where they might be attacked.

Particularly as martial law has been declared, he thought, grimly. *The looters know they won't get mercy if we catch them.*

He saluted Detective-Inspector Doyenne as he arrived. "Sir," he said. "We found enough food to keep us going for a few hours."

Doyenne nodded, barely lifting his head from his terminal. "Put whatever you found in the stores, then report to the kitchen for some grub," he said, absently. "You'll be going back out soon."

Robin groaned, inwardly. He'd been awake for over a day. His body was insisting on reminding him that he wasn't a young man any longer. But there was nothing he could do about that, not now. He'd sleep when he was dead.

"Follow me," he ordered. "There'll be some food afterwards."

The cooks had worked wonders, he discovered, as they joined the line for food and drink. They'd taken over a school kitchen, but somehow managed to produce edible food. It was a minor miracle, Robin decided, although he was hungry enough to eat reconstituted ration bars and drink tasteless water. The plates, cutlery and glasses were all plastic, probably taken from one of the nearby stores. It felt like attending a BBQ - a handful of disposable BBQs were cooking meat before it went off - but far grimmer. There just wasn't enough food and drink for everyone.

He scowled as he caught sight of a handful of bureaucrats, making their way through the crowd. They were checking some of the refugees, making sure they were registered and matched to lost friends and relatives. But few of the working refugees looked happy to speak to them. They'd been working hard and now they needed a rest before they went out to search for more food. They were just lucky they weren't further to the east. Robin had heard that everyone who could carry a sandbag was being pressed into service to build barricades before the tide rose again.

And there's a cheerful thought, he told himself. *Who knows what will happen here when the tide rises again?*

He reached for his pistol as he heard a handful of gunshots, not too far away. The crowd tensed, uneasy murmurs running from person to person as it sank in that the gunfire really *hadn't* been that far away. Robin glanced at Sally, then led her towards the edge of the refugee camp. The soldiers were already deploying, half of them taking up firing positions as if they expected to be attacked and overrun at any moment. The remainder were hurrying the rest of the evacuees into the buses.

"They'll have to watch their route out of the city," Sally said. She was staring at the soldiers, her face unreadable. "I heard there's a block on the road to Heathrow."

Robin shrugged as the sound of gunfire faded away. "They're the lucky ones," he said, as the buses roared to life. "They'll get to sleep somewhere out of the city tonight."

"Unless they get attacked on the route," Sally offered. "The soldiers might not be enough to save them."

Robin glanced at her. Handguns weren't uncommon in London - although there was a very strict set of requirements for anyone who wanted to own one - but assault rifles and antitank weapons were almost unknown. Offhand, he couldn't imagine anyone outside the military or private bodyguards who'd even have a *shot* at getting the licences. Shotguns and hunting rifles were very common in the country, but bringing them inside the city limits was a serious offence. The soldiers would almost certainly be better armed than anyone they might have a reasonable chance of encountering...

Unless an army unit goes rogue, he thought. *Or someone starts improvising weapons.*

He scowled as the radio summoned him to the makeshift HQ, along with a handful of other officers. He'd watched historical documentaries about the Troubles, when policemen had faced screaming mobs, improvised weapons and horrific terror tactics. The streets had run red with blood, back then. There had been times when the army had been deployed to restore order, whatever the cost. But now...this time, the problem couldn't be solved by mass deportations and heavy repression. Anyone who turned feral would have to be thrown into a detention camp until the crisis was finally solved.

"We've identified a number of food stores that have yet to be looted," Doyenne said. He sounded more alert now, although he was still keeping an eye on his terminal. Robin couldn't help wondering if his superior was having problems coming to grips with what had happened to his city. "You'll take the lead in securing them. I'll have work gangs dispatched to strip them within the next hour."

Robin groaned, inwardly. He wanted - he needed - a rest. But there was no choice.

"Yes, sir," he said.

He checked the map. The food stores were several miles from the refugee centre, near Tottenham Court Road. He'd been there, in happier times. It was a shopping district, but it normally sold fashionable clothes, expensive pieces of crap and cheap junk for the tourists, not food. No wonder the food stores hadn't been looted. It wasn't where people normally went to buy food.

Not that that will last forever, he thought, as the rain started to fall again. *The looters will be getting more and more desperate.*

Water ran down the streets as they walked up through Soho, keeping a wary eye out for trouble. It was normally peaceful, but now...now anything could happen. More helicopters buzzed over the city as they walked, barely visible against the increasing gloom. Robin peered down a side street, remembering when the street had teemed with life. The cheap Chinese buffets had once been good, if one didn't mind a lack of sophistication. Now, they were as dark and cold as the grave. The line of gay bars looked to have been looted. A handful of bodies lay on the street outside, already cool to the touch. Robin winced as he recognised one of the bartenders. He'd died defending his bar.

He frowned as he saw a handful of soldiers on guard duty near the underground station, looking thoroughly drenched. They waved cheerfully to the policemen, then resumed their silent watch. Robin puzzled over it for a moment before remembering that they'd be watching the road south. The army would probably wind up using it for supply and evacuation convoys.

"It's been quiet up here," the leader said. He was a lieutenant, if Robin read his stripes correctly. He looked far too young to shave, let alone be in command of five men. "We haven't seen anyone for the last hour."

"Good for you," Robin said. He glanced at the soldiers. It was hard to be sure, but he rather suspected they weren't impressed with their commander. "Can you...?"

He broke off as he heard the sound of breaking glass, coming from the nearby shop. He drew his pistol in one smooth movement, then led the policemen towards the building. The soldiers followed, weapons at the ready. Robin held up a hand as they reached the edge of the shop, then slipped forward and peered inside. A small mob of young men was ransacking the place, stuffing hundreds of expensive watches into bags and baskets.

"Armed Police," he shouted, as he stepped into the light. "Put your hands..."

One of the looters drew a gun at terrifying speed. Robin jumped to one side a second before he fired, the bullet snapping through the air far too close to him for comfort. The soldiers rushed forward a second later, slamming into the looters and knocking them to the hard ground. Moments later, they were cuffed and helpless.

"Get them up against the wall," the army lieutenant ordered. He sounded pissed. Robin didn't blame him. The looters had somehow slipped into the store without being noticed, which would be a black mark on the lieutenant's record. Or it would be, if so much else hadn't gone wrong over the last twenty hours. The odds were good that no one would notice, as long as it wasn't brought to their attention. "Prepare to fire."

Robin stared at him. "Are you mad?"

The lieutenant rounded on him. "I have authority to shoot looters," he snapped. His face was red with fury. "These goddamned cockroaches..."

"You don't *have* to shoot them," Robin said. Only one of the looters had been armed, for crying out loud! Looking at them, it was easy to tell that most of the youngsters had been dragooned into looting. "They can go to the detention camps!"

"I have authority to shoot them," the lieutenant repeated. Sweat was beading on his brow as he glared at Robin. "They won't loot again if I kill them."

Robin met his eyes. "If you do, I'll arrest you for murder," he snapped. He understood the lieutenant's problem - he was worried about showing weakness in front of the men - but he didn't really care. Murder was murder. "They don't deserve to die."

He took a breath. "Call them in, get them sent to the chain gangs," he added. "They can do something useful and if they try to escape, they can be shot *then*!"

The lieutenant scowled. "On your head be it," he said, finally. He turned and walked towards the door, holding himself ramrod straight. "Follow me."

Robin allowed himself a sigh of relief as the soldiers trooped out of the store. The lieutenant *had* had authority to shoot...but he hadn't had the *obligation* to shoot. And the looters had learnt their lesson.

I hope, he thought, as he keyed his radio. The prisoners could be held until they were picked up and put to work. They didn't have to die. *And if I'm wrong, I'll have to deal with it.*

CHAPTER
THIRTY THREE

Near Townsend, United Kingdom

"Fuck," Fran said, as Molly was shoved back into the backroom and the door slammed closed. "What...what happened?"

Molly barely heard her. Her entire body was throbbing in pain. Their captors had *had* her in ways she hadn't known were possible, not without bending her arms and legs in ways that threatened to break them. She'd had them in each and every one of her orifices, often two or three at once. Dave, Colin and Blair had been starved for female companionship for months, she realised now. She was honestly surprised they'd honoured their side of the deal.

Dave won't, she thought. The other two had just wanted sex - they'd even been happier when she'd cooperated - but Dave had wanted it to hurt. He'd smiled as he'd pinched her skin, making her yelp in pain...she knew, as surely as she knew her name, that he'd rape Fran eventually, no matter what Molly did. *He'll come in here soon enough and take her.*

"Don't worry about it," Molly said. "Just...just don't."

She shivered. Dave had gloated, mocking her for her submission... and talking about ways he could take advantage of the chaos for himself. He'd told her that there was a girls' school nearby, one he intended to raid; he'd told her that he intended to free others from the chain gangs and turn them into an army. And, all the time, he'd been hurting her, watching her grunt and screech in pain. He'd *enjoyed* himself, the bastard. Molly didn't think that he'd be able to turn most of his plans - hell, *any* of his plans

- into reality, but she didn't doubt he intended to try. It wasn't as if there was anyone in place to stop him.

And he can still kill us, she thought, morbidly. Dave was mad enough to cow the other two, as long as he was careful. *He can do whatever he likes to us.*

It was a grim thought. She'd considered trying to turn her captors against one another - Stellar Star had done that in one of her many movies - but she hadn't had the slightest idea where to begin. Dave and his friends were *dependent* on each other. And besides, they were willing to share. Molly could hardly deny them anything they wanted, if it kept Fran relatively unharmed. She didn't have any leverage she could use to manipulate them.

Society is breaking down, she told herself. *And all the old certainties are gone.*

It was a grim thought, an epiphany that she'd had time and time again. Garrison had been manipulative and demanding, but he hadn't tried to *rape* her until society had collapsed. And then...she shuddered, remembering his touch. And Dave and his friends...they'd just taken her, as if she was nothing more than an object. They hadn't given a damn about her, not really. They hadn't given a damn about anything beyond their own pleasure. Her opinions didn't matter to them.

She felt sick as she lay on the floor. She'd known that Kurt was stronger than her, but he'd never raised a hand to her, even when they'd had *nasty* fights. And if he had, she would have had no difficulty in getting a divorce. No court would have sided with him if he'd beaten her to within an inch of her life. But now...was she at his mercy, if he ever came home? Or at the mercy of her brothers or eldest son? Did the strong rule now? Did the weak just have to bend over and take it? *She'd* bent over and taken it...

Molly retched. She'd enjoyed Kurt's strong arms, years ago. There had been something *comforting* about them, even though she'd been reluctant to admit it. Now...those strong arms could beat her into submission...and the only thing *stopping* them from doing just that was her husband's good nature. All of a sudden, the horror stories she'd heard about women in the Middle East and Central Asia made sense. The poor women had grown up in a world where they could be beaten to a pulp if they said or did the wrong thing. Of *course* they were submissive. No one would come to their defence if their husbands beat them. Their society told them that being beaten was natural and right.

She retched again. *Dave* had hurt her...he'd *break* her, if she gave him the chance. And she knew she couldn't hold out indefinitely. He'd have her, again and again; his friends would have her...sooner or later, she'd forget herself. She *had* to get out. Whatever it took, she *had* to get out.

Move, you stupid bitch, she told herself. Her body's aches seemed to grow worse. It was all she could do to get her arms to move. *Get up!*

She twisted, struggling to stand up. They'd torn off her clothes at some point - she wasn't sure exactly *when* - and then freed her arms. The only saving grace, as far as she could tell, was that they hadn't bothered to tie her up again afterwards. Maybe they thought she was too badly hurt to do anything, but lie there. She didn't want to consider that they might be right.

Blood trickled down her legs, a grim reminder of Dave's power games. He'd cut her skin in a dozen places, pressing a knife against her bare flesh until the others had told him to stop before he actually *killed* her. She wiped the blood away as best as she could, then forced herself to walk up and down. Her body felt like a mass of bruises, but nothing was actually broken. She rather suspected the only reason they hadn't crippled her was because they wanted to use her again, when they recovered.

And if they keep using me like this, she thought darkly, *they'll cripple me anyway.*

Bile rose in her mouth. She swallowed hard, telling herself that there was no time to panic, let alone curl up into a ball and shake. Dave would be back soon enough, ready to use her again...or take Fran. They *had* to get out before it was too late. She looked up at the skylight, silently judging how best to open it. It was too high for her, but if she mounted a chair on the bed...

"Thank you," Fran said. Her eyes were crawling over Molly's body, lingering on the cuts and bruises. "I..."

Molly eyed her. Fran's face was pale, consumed with a mixture of relief and guilt that Molly knew all too well. Someone else had taken the bullet for her...and, while Fran was relieved, she also knew Molly had paid dearly. Molly had felt the same, back at school when her boyfriend had taken the blame for something she'd done. She hadn't had the nerve, then, to go to the headmaster and confess. And yet, she'd known she *should* have confessed...

"Stay very quiet," Molly ordered, finally. Fran was *far* too much like Penny for Molly's peace of mind. She wondered, sourly, if Percy had ever taken the blame for something Penny had done. "Don't say a word."

She fumbled through Fran's suitcase, looking for something she could use to clean the blood from her body. Fran had packed only a handful of clothes, as far as Molly could tell, all of which were too small for Molly to wear. Molly wiped her body with a shirt that had probably cost Fran her entire allowance, then tried to put on a pair of frilly panties. But they were definitely too small.

Penny bought something like this once, she thought, as she discarded the panties in annoyance. *But I made her take them back to the shop.*

The memory made her frown in disgust. She'd known her daughter had become a woman, but still...she didn't want to *think* about Penny having a boyfriend, let alone going all the way with him. Penny was *her* little girl...she shuddered, again, as she realised what could happen to Penny in the new world. Would Percy look after her? Or would he be knocked aside by gangsters and rapists, all eager to have their way with his sister?

I have to get back, she thought. *I have to.*

She tiptoed over to the door and listened. There was no one outside, as far as she could tell, yet the door was locked. She considered a number of possible ways to open the door, but came up with nothing. Besides, anything she did would run the risk of waking them...if they were asleep. She didn't know *what* they planned to do in the future...hell, she wasn't sure they'd even thought that far ahead. They might just be enjoying their freedom without giving any thought to what would happen when - if - the government reasserted control.

"Keep *very* quiet," she whispered, as she picked up the makeshift knife and cut the ropes around Fran's wrists. "If they ask, tell them you're trying to help me."

Fran nodded, her eyes wide with fear. Molly sighed inwardly, then picked up the chair and placed it on the bed. It didn't look very stable, but she couldn't think of any other way to reach the skylight. She motioned for Fran to hold it as she clambered onto the chair, bumping her head against the glass. It was higher than she cared to think about, but at least she could reach the latch. She forced herself not to look down as she fingered the latch, bracing herself. They'd be committed the moment she opened the skylight.

I should have spent more time learning to climb, she told herself, as she undid the latch carefully. It moved smoothly, much to her relief. *And more time learning other things too.*

The skylight opened. Rain drizzled down on her head. Molly breathed a sigh of relief, even as cold water splashed down on her nude body. So far, so good. She braced herself, resting her hands on each side of the skylight, then pushed herself upwards as hard as she could. It wasn't anything like as easy as she'd expected. She had to struggle to get her legs up and into the open air, then roll over until she was lying on the wet roof. It wasn't *that* high - the cabin was nothing more than a small bungalow - but getting down would still be a problem.

She peered down into the room. "Come on up," she whispered. Fran was staring at her in disbelief. "Hurry!"

Fran drew back. "I *can't!*"

Molly felt a rush of pure rage. Fran...Fran was doomed, if she stayed in the backroom until the men returned. How stupid *was* she? Did she believe Dave would keep his word? Or was she too scared to resist, even though she *had* to resist? Molly found it hard to care. Fran *wasn't* her daughter and if she was too stupid to take advantage of a chance to get out...

"Get onto the chair, then climb out," Molly ordered. She wanted to shout. It was all she could do *not* to shout. She had to fight to keep her voice low and even. "If you don't get up now, *you'll* have them up your cunt and ass and mouth and..."

She would have slapped Penny for being so crude, but it seemed to work. Fran rose and clambered onto the chair, looking terrified. Molly didn't really blame her for being nervous, but falling onto the floor - and perhaps cracking her skull - would be a better fate than letting Dave have her. But then, Dave would probably have his way with her corpse. Fran struggled, almost tumbling as she fought to get through the skylight. Molly had to catch hold of her and pull her up...

Fran's foot struck the chair as she clambered out. It tottered, then fell to the ground with a crash. Molly swore, inwardly. If their captors heard that...

"Come on," she hissed. She didn't know *what* was behind the holiday cabin, but the boys had been in the front room when they'd finished with her. "Hurry!"

She heard someone moving below as she crawled to the edge of the roof and peered down at the ground. The ground was muddy, but she doubted it was soft enough to break her fall if she jumped. She'd break her legs if she wasn't insanely lucky. Instead, she glanced around until she spotted a pipe and scrambled down it. Fran watched her, then tried to follow in her footsteps. Molly had to catch Fran to keep her from slipping and falling to her death.

Penny is the better athlete, Molly thought, with a flicker of satisfaction. Her daughter did well in gym class, even though Molly had never considered it particularly lady-like. But then, *her* gym mistress had been a tyrant of the first order. *Fran will have to work harder.*

She caught Fran's shoulder as she heard someone shouting, inside the cabin. "Get into the woods," she snapped. Dave was shouting...she was sure it was Dave. "Run!"

Her feet started to ache as she ran across the field, but there was no time to search for shoes or something else. The noise from inside the cabin was growing louder. Dave was screaming, shouting orders at his two friends. Molly gritted her teeth and forced herself to run harder, despite the growing pain in her body. She *had* to keep moving, whatever happened. Dave wouldn't let her bargain a second time.

And they'll probably see my body vanishing into the woods, she thought. The sky was turning dark again - the rain was growing worse - but she was naked. Her pale skin was probably too visible for her to escape easily. She didn't think they'd beaten her *that* black-and-blue. *I wonder if I should have a mud bath.*

She caught Fran's arm. "Do you know where the nearest town is?"

Fran shook her head. "There was a farmhouse back there," she said, jerking her hand towards the cabin. "The farmer there owns the land."

Molly gritted her teeth as she tried to think. Dave and his friends *had* to stop them before they made their escape. They didn't have a hope of hiding if the police mounted a full-scale manhunt. Indeed, their only *real* hope lay in the police - and everyone else - believing they'd died during the alien attack. And that meant they *had* to keep their prisoners from getting away.

Think, she told herself. Her thoughts ran in all directions. *What would you do if you wanted to recapture two prisoners? How would you look for them?* She scowled as the rain came down, drenching her naked body. Her feet were torn and broken, the pain making it hard to think clearly. She'd assume the worst - she'd assume that the prisoners knew *precisely* where to go - and then try to block them. Or was she giving them too much credit? Master criminals never ended up on chain gangs. Dave's tale of minor sexual assault didn't make him sound like a criminal mastermind.

"We have to keep going," she said. "They'll expect us to head to the farm."

And perhaps get the farmer killed too, she added, silently. *He won't be expecting three criminals to attack him, will he?*

Fran stared at her. "But where can we go?"

Molly frowned. Fran was breathing heavily, her clothes so drenched that they revealed every last one of her curves. Her nipples were hard, clearly visible against the cloth. Dave and the others wouldn't hesitate if they recaptured her, not now...Molly clenched her teeth, silently vowing that Fran would get away. But how...?

"Good question," Molly said. Dave had taken her smartphone, of course. But even if he hadn't, she still wouldn't have been able to find her location. She was hopelessly lost. Unless the network was back up...she shook her head. There was no point in worrying about it. "If we keep heading north, we're bound to come across something eventually."

She glanced behind them as the rain continued to fall. It was hard to see more than a few metres, but the sound of crashing and thudding could be heard in the distance. Wild animals...or Dave and his friends? She had no way to know. Chances were that any foxes or whatever had hunkered down, trying to stay out of the rain. Only desperate men would be insane enough to run in the semi-darkness.

Fran caught her arm. "What if you're wrong?"

Molly felt her patience snap. "You can try to loop around and get to the farm if you like," she snarled. There *were* limits, after all. Fran was being an ungrateful bitch...she cursed herself, a moment later. Fran wasn't any more accustomed to the brave new world than Molly herself. She'd grown up in relative safety. "But there's a very good chance you'll be caught."

She swallowed, hard, as the rain fell harder. Was this what it was going to be like from now on? Running and hiding, fearing rape or enslavement or death...would she ever see her kids again? She told herself that things would return to normal, eventually, but she didn't really believe it. The country had taken one hell of a battering. God alone knew if things would ever return to normal.

Something moved, in the twilight. Molly tensed.

"Keep moving," she ordered, sharply. Her feet screamed in protest as she started to move, insisting that she couldn't walk another metre. She ignored them, concentrating on putting one foot in front of the other. "And don't look back."

CHAPTER
THIRTY FOUR

London, United Kingdom

"It looks as though the aliens will be in position to engage the Jupiter installations within the next thirty minutes," Admiral Cathy Mountbatten said. Her image fuzzed slightly, bearing mute testament to the battering the secure datanet had taken over the last twenty hours. "I believe that Admiral Winters and Admiral Robertson have already deployed the Io Detachment to delay the enemy."

"You believe," the French President said. He looked as exhausted as Andrew felt. The hologram wasn't hiding anything. "Are you not *sure?*"

"The time delay between Earth, Home Fleet and Jupiter is increasing," Cathy said. Her voice was very calm. "It is impossible to follow operations with any degree of immediacy."

"And the battle will be decided before we hear that it has fairly begun," Andrew injected, sharply. "Can you update us on the orbital situation?"

"Yes, Prime Minister," Cathy said. "Tactical command, as planned, has devolved on Nelson Base. Local space appears to be clear, although we have not dropped our guard. Indeed, we are mounting continuous long-range starfighter patrols to ensure the aliens don't sneak up on us while we're distracted. In the meantime, the remaining orbital and ground-based defences have been destroying pieces of debris on re-entry trajectories."

She took a breath. "SAR teams have recovered all of the lifepods from the destroyed military and civilian installations, including Pournelle Base," she added. "Not counting the damage to the various lunar stations, we're prepared to go on the record and state that over two hundred thousand civilian and military personnel were killed during the battle."

Andrew swore under his breath. He'd known it would be bad, but two hundred *thousand*? It was sheer luck that a number of installations had been evacuated, their personnel dispersed elsewhere, when war broke out. And yet, many of the destroyed installations had been economically important. The long-term effects were likely to be bad.

The American President frowned. "And the lunar stations?"

"We don't have a precise headcount yet," Cathy told him. "The Luna Federation has started full-scale disaster-recovery procedures, but their command-and-control network has been shot to hell. I've assigned a number of frigates to serve as signal relay stations until the ground-based relays can be repaired."

"Ah," the Russian President said. "And why did you think you had the authority to issue such orders?"

Andrew groaned. He'd expected *some* dispute over command, now that Admiral Winters was heading away from Earth on *Enterprise*, but he hadn't expected *this*. Politics, of course. Russia wasn't the Luna Federation's strongest supporter, not after a number of Russian miners had escaped the Russian colonies and fled to Luna City. The Russians would want to extract a price from the Luna Federation for their help.

And they might just drag the rest of us along with them, Andrew thought. Britain wasn't too fond of the Luna Federation either. *We might get stampeded into doing something we'll regret later.*

"I have authority as the current commander of Earth's defences," Cathy said, with frightening evenness. "And I believe, given that we are still in a state of alert, that rebuilding the lunar network should be given priority. Their mass drivers accounted for a number of alien starships."

She went on before anyone could raise another objection. "So far, installations outside Earth-Luna have not been touched," she added. "A state of high alert remains in being across the solar system. We won't relax until the enemy fleet withdraws completely."

"Very good," Andrew said. "I believe there is nothing to be gained by trying to micromanage the fleet, is there?"

"No, Prime Minister," Cathy said.

Andrew cleared his throat. "Then we thank you," he said. "Dismissed."
He watched Cathy's image vanish, then turned his gaze to the other
world leaders, silently trying to gauge which way they'd jump. The Great
Powers hadn't *needed* each other for nearly a century, even though they'd
been locked in a semi-alliance against the rest of the world. Now...their
power was truly threatened for the first time since the Age of Unrest.

"This cannot go on," the American President said. "The cost in lives
is appalling."

Andrew nodded. The Americans had lost nearly their entire western
coastline. Tidal waves had drowned San Francisco and battered a number of other cities. Others had struck all the way down to Peru, smashing
the Panama Canal beyond easy repair and threatening the foundations
of the orbital tower. He didn't want to think about how many Americans
had been killed, but he had a nasty feeling that Britain had got off lightly
compared to the United States. France and Russia had been battered too.

So has most of Europe, he thought. *And they still haven't found the
Japanese Premier.*

"Unless you want to surrender, there seems to be no way to convince
the aliens to stop," the Chinese President said. China had gotten off relatively lightly, according to the reports, but MI6 was already predicting
civil unrest. "They don't respond to any of our messages offering talks,
even concessions."

"You would surrender New Russia just to gain peace," the Russian
President snapped. The Sino-Russian alliance seemed to be a dead letter.
"I think you would sing a different tune if one of *your* colonies was groan-
ing under the alien jackboot."

"Right now, we do not have the power to recover it," the Chinese
President countered, sharply. "We have *one* effective fleet carrier, just one.
The others might as well be sitting ducks!"

"We *have* improved the armour on their hulls," the American
President said.

"They're still vulnerable," the Chinese President said. "How long will
it be before we can churn out an improved armoured fleet carrier?"

Andrew winced, inwardly. The Royal Navy had hastily redesigned
two carriers in the pipeline for armoured hulls and plasma weapons - and

then started work on an entirely new class of armoured carriers - but it would be at least a year before the first of the modified carriers came out of the shipyards. The newer designs would take even longer.

"Nine months," the American President said. "And that assumes we don't lose the war before then."

"Longer than that for us," Andrew said. Parliament had approved the military's budget, back before the war, but no one had realised that Britain needed *armoured* carriers. In hindsight, that had been a serious mistake. "And bolting armour to the carrier hulls has its limits."

The Russian President cleared his throat. "We have a proposal," he said. "It should be possible to use the...ah, the alien captives to produce a workable bioweapon."

Andrew sucked in his breath. "A bioweapon."

The French President was blunter. "Are you *mad*?"

"No," the Russian President said. His voice was very calm. "Let us be blunt. None of us seriously expected to have to engage in a *long* war. We believed, not without reason, that any conflicts between us would be handled by the diplomats. There was a great deal to lose and very little to gain by fighting to the finish."

He paused, dramatically. "Now, all of our cheerful assumptions have been up-ended. We are locked in a fight to the death with an alien power that refuses to talk to us, that refuses to even accept surrender. We don't know what they want, we don't know just how powerful they really are... all we really know about them is that they launched an unprovoked invasion of our space *after* carefully making sure we wouldn't be able to offer real resistance. Their weapons were *perfectly* calibrated to beat our most advanced starships at minimal cost. I don't think there can be any doubt that this was a pre-planned invasion."

Andrew nodded, tersely. There was nothing *new* in what the Russian was saying. MI6 had said the same, following the Battle of New Russia. The Tadpoles had planned their invasion carefully. They weren't responding to a provocation, they weren't taking urgent action to push humans away from their worlds...they'd cold-bloodedly planned and carried out a full-scale invasion of human space. Whatever they wanted, it didn't include coming to terms with human governments. Their actions ever since the war had begun suggested a frightening lack of concern for human casualties.

"And now, we have our homeworld bombarded," the Russian President said. "Millions of people are dead, or injured, or homeless. That is bad enough. But what is worse is the damage they have caused to our industrial base. My staff have yet to determine just how badly we have been hurt, but it was *bad*. Our very ability to continue the war lies in doubt."

He took a breath. "I submit to you that survival should be our first priority," he concluded, firmly. "And if the choice boils down to them or us, I suggest it should be us."

"We made that choice before, during the Crazy Years," the American President said.

"Yes, we did," the Russian agreed. "And we survived."

"At a price," the American President said.

The Russian snorted, rudely. "You *Americans!* The only reason you get to beat yourselves up over stealing your homeland from its *original* owners is that you won the wars to *get* it and *keep* it! The only reason you get to feel guilty about driving out the infidels is because you drove out the infidels! Do you think they'd have been any kinder to you, if things had gone the other way?"

His image thumped the table. "We cannot keep fighting at our current level," he said, sharply. "We cannot convince them to come to the negotiation table even if we offered to concede New Russia and all the other colony worlds. And we cannot even *surrender* to the bastards! I say to you that we need to use each and every weapon at our disposal, including a bioweapon!"

"Bioweapons have gotten out of control before," the French President said, sharply. "What happens if *this* one gets out of control?"

The Russian President picked up a terminal. "I'll send you a copy of the report from *Biopreparat*, but the principle point is simple. There is no way a virus designed for the Tadpoles will spread into the human population. They are *not* our brothers and sisters under the skin, but a whole new order of life. We could dust their worlds and watch their populations die without fear of losing our own people as well."

"You're talking about genocide," Andrew said. He felt sick. "You're talking about exterminating an entire *race*!"

"I'm talking about survival," the Russian President snapped. "We have a duty to our populations - to *Earth* - that goes beyond any obligations we might have to *them*. No one will be happier than I if we manage to talk them into peace, but we have to assume the worst! Peace is not possible - and either we wipe them out or they wipe *us* out!"

"They haven't moved to slaughter colonists on New Russia," the French President said, coolly.

"They might be waiting until they actually *win* to proceed with the genocide," the Russian President said.

The Chinese President cleared his throat. "Leaving aside the...ah, *morality* of plotting the destruction of an entire sentient race, there are practical issues to consider. Infecting Earth with a horrendous bioweapon would *not* automatically wipe out the remaining colonies. The same might well be true of the Tadpoles. There would be no guarantee that infecting their homeworld, wherever it is, would infect the rest of their domain. We might slaughter billions, but the remainder would come after us with blood in their eyes."

"We can use the weapon to demonstrate that we *can* wipe them out," the American President said. "It *might* bring them to the negotiation table."

"And surrender any chance of surprise," the Russian sneered. "I for one don't think we should waste this chance. The entire human race depends on us finding a way to win."

Andrew leaned forward. "Do we actually *have* a working bioweapon?"

"*Biopreparat* is working on it," the Russian President said. "They think they can put together a working model within four months, perhaps less."

"Shit," the American President said.

Andrew felt cold. Bioweapons had always terrified him. They'd been deployed enough, during the Age of Unrest, for humanity to have a deep-seated fear of weaponised disease. The idea of being infected with a targeted bioweapon, one designed to kill people for having the wrong skin or hair or eye colour, was utterly terrifying. He'd read enough reports, when he'd been elected into office, to know that such terror weapons were only the tip of the iceberg. The government had worked hard to keep some of the *really* dangerous concepts out of the public imagination, knowing there would be utter panic if the truth ever got out...

And yet, he couldn't deny the truth behind the Russian President's words. Humanity was losing the war. The Tadpoles had inflicted a mortal wound, one that might win them the war...one that *would* win the war, if humanity couldn't find a way to force them to *stop*. The thought of using a bioweapon disgusted him. And yet, he knew there might be no choice.

"Four months," the Chinese President said. "We *might* be able to deploy it before the end of the year."

"No," the American President said. "We're talking about genocide!"

"Us or them," the Russian President said. "Whose side are you on?"

He smiled, coldly. "Why don't you ask the citizens of San Francisco which way *they'd* vote, if they were offered the choice."

"I understand the opportunity," the French President said. "But I also understand the dangers. How could we *guarantee* the infection of every last colony, space station and starship? We could slaughter them in their billions and *still* lose the war!"

"Doing nothing guarantees that we *will* lose the war," the Russian President said. "Russia has been invaded before. We understand that we cannot avoid war. We understand, even if you do not, that victory comes with a heavy price. And right now, we understand that we are locked in mortal combat with an enemy we cannot even *surrender* to!"

He paused. "I will not allow your *morality* to keep me from deploying every weapon in my arsenal to fight the foe," he added. "Do *not* misunderstand me. Russia is committed to the alliance, but - beyond that - Russia is committed to survival! And so are all of you!"

"I understand your position," the French President said. "However..."

Andrew cut him off. "I think we have time to consider the issue later, before the weapon is ready," he said. He'd have to have a long chat with the experts from Porton Down. If nothing else, he needed to know if there *was* a realistic chance of producing a bioweapon or if the Russians were just blowing smoke. Either way, it was going to be bad. "Right now, tempers are flying too high for us to have any serious discussions."

"Right now, our people are dying," the Russian President said. "I can't forget that. Can you?"

"No," Andrew said. He looked from face to face. "I suggest we revisit the issue after the battle is over. By then, we may have a better idea of just how bad things have become."

"Agreed," the American President said. "I'm expected to address the nation in an hour."

Andrew nodded as, one by one, the images vanished. *He* had to address the nation too, although he was damned if he knew what he'd say. What *could* he say to a population facing the greatest disaster in British history? He certainly *couldn't* tell them that they'd been one of the luckier nations. God knew *that* wouldn't go down very well.

He leaned forward, resting his head in his hands. The bioweapon was tempting - as horrifying as it was, he had to admit it was tempting - but it was also a nightmare. He couldn't believe that *all* the Tadpoles would be infected, not unless the disease took years to move from infectious to deadly. The survivors would want revenge, of course. They could render humanity's worlds just as lifeless as their own if they wished. It wouldn't be *that* hard.

And we don't even know if it will work, he thought, numbly. He'd heard too many promises from the boffins, great ideas that had somehow never panned out in the real world. The Russians probably had the same problem. *What if it doesn't work?*

And yet, his thoughts asked, *what if it does?*

He'd always considered himself a good man. He'd always promised himself that he wouldn't abuse the power of his office. God knew, there were enough checks and balances written into the British constitution to make it difficult for any Prime Minister to go off the rails, although Sir Charles Hanover *had* been on the verge of madness. But now...the humanist side of him insisted that a bioweapon was neither a practical nor moral solution to the war, while the practical side wondered if it could be gotten to work. Britain was on the edge of defeat...

Humanity is on the edge of defeat, he corrected himself. This wasn't just a British war. *And what will we do to stave it off?*

It was a chilling thought, one he didn't want to face. But he'd seen refugees on the streets of Britain, men and women driven from their homes by the war. Nothing like it had been seen for over a hundred and fifty years. Even if the war ended tomorrow, it would take years to repair the damage, years to rebuild the nation. And the war would *not* end tomorrow. He had no doubt it would continue until one side broke under the strain.

What would Churchill do? What would Thatcher do? What would *Hanover* do?

No, Andrew thought. Those Prime Ministers were *long* dead. *What will* I *do?*

But he knew, all too well, that he had no answer.

CHAPTER

THIRTY FIVE

Interplanetary Space, Near Jupiter

Admiral Johan Wright was not pleased.

It was bad enough to be caught out of position when the alien fleet was detected, ensuring that the Io Detachment was unable to rendezvous with Home Fleet before it moved forward to drive the aliens away from Earth. But it was far worse to be grimly aware that the titanic mass of the alien fleet was heading straight towards Jupiter, forcing him into a battle against overwhelming odds. The Io Detachment had three escort carriers and thirty frigates, stacked against ten fleet carriers and fifty-seven smaller ships. It was true, Johan knew, that some of the alien carriers were damaged. He doubted they were damaged anything like enough to give his formation a fighting chance.

"Start deploying pods," he ordered. The tension in the CIC was so thick he could cut it with a knife. His personnel had been watching the aliens crawling towards their position for hours. "Prepare to activate them on my signal."

He gritted his teeth as he looked down at his dark hands. Surprise and unconventionality would be the order of the day, the only thing that would keep his ships and crew from a very short and exciting life. In an ideal world, he would have fallen back on the Jovian mass drivers and dared the aliens to follow him, but there was too much junk floating around the gas giant for him to have any hope of scoring enough hits to matter. Besides, the aliens could sit outside his engagement envelope and start firing KEWs at the cloudscoops. It would only take one hit to smash a fragile cloudscoop beyond repair.

And Admiral Winters has a plan, he thought. *It might just work.*

"Pods deploying now, sir," his aide said. "The engineers report they need at least ten minutes to get all the pods out into space, then activate the control links."

"Tell them they've got five," Johan said. The alien ships were growing closer. It wouldn't be long before they detected his ships, if they hadn't already detected them. God knew they had no *reason* to change course, even if they *did* know he was waiting for them. The chance to smash an isolated detachment was worth a certain amount of risk. "And activate the control links in seven minutes, regardless of the deployment status."

"Aye, sir," his aide said.

Johan nodded, curtly. Jupiter's mini-system of moons and asteroids had been heavily colonised, once the human race had started expanding into outer space. There were over five million men, women and children living on a handful of moons and orbital installations, along with a significant industrial base. They'd hunkered down as best as they could, according to the last set of reports, but he had no illusions about what would happen if the aliens rampaged through the defences and attacked the colonies themselves. Even Ganymede, the most habitable of Jupiter's moons, was far from terraformed. It would be centuries before she could support life outside the domes.

And there will be no place to hide if the aliens claim the high orbitals, he thought. *That would be the end.*

The aliens were coming closer, their fleet carriers fanning out as they launched a new flight of starfighters. They'd been playing games for the last two hours, increasing and then reducing their speed as the whim struck them. Johan wasn't sure if the aliens were hesitating, uncertain if they wished to proceed, or if they were just tormenting their human enemies, but it hardly mattered. They'd still have plenty of time to destroy his fleet and ravage the human colonies before Home Fleet caught up with them.

And then they could accept or avoid action as they pleased, he thought, sourly. *They could force Home Fleet to chase them all over the solar system.* it was a galling thought. home fleet was the most powerful formation the human race had ever produced, yet the wear and tear on its hulls and personnel was undeniable. the longer the chase continued, the weaker home fleet would become...a problem made worse by inventory shortages because no one had seriously planned for a full-scale war. in the future, he promised himself, he'd make damn sure the politicians didn't forget just how close humanity had come to defeat. a strong defence rested on more than just starships and starfighters.

Assuming we win, he reminded himself. *This could end very badly.*

The console chimed. "The majority of the pods have been deployed," his aide reported, slowly. "Primary control links are going active...now."

"Tie in the secondary control links as soon as the primary network is up and running," Johan ordered. The risk of being detected would go up sharply, but it was a gamble they had to take. Besides, the aliens had an excellent chance of detecting them anyway. "Time to certain detection?"

"Nineteen minutes," the aide said.

"Prepare to activate the first set of pods," Johan ordered. "On my mark..."

He braced himself. The aliens *had* to be surprised. And yet, the closer they came, the greater the chance of pushing them into doing something stupid...assuming, of course, they didn't detect his ships first. The timing was everything. He'd run through a hundred simulations over the last few hours, but none of them had been very illuminating. There were too many factors that were outside his control. War was a democracy. The enemy got a vote in proceedings too.

And we can't limit their options too much, he thought, grimly. *They can break contact any time they like.*

"Activate," he snapped. Most of the pods were in space. They *might* have a chance to deploy the remainder before the aliens recovered themselves. Even if they didn't, the aliens were still going to get one hell of a fright. "And then prepare to activate the *second* set of pods!"

"Aye, sir," the aide said. He ran his hand down the console. "Pods going active...*now!*"

"Launch fighters," Johan ordered. "And remind them that this is *not* the time to seek engagement."

"Aye, sir."

————

The Combat Faction flinched.

There really was no other word for it. One moment, space ahead of them had been empty; the next, space was filled with twelve human fleet carriers and a multitude of smaller warships. A handful of starfighters were already deployed, sweeping space ahead of them; the remainder, no doubt, were already readying themselves for deployment. The fleet was caught between two fires.

Reverse course, the Combat Faction ordered. It was hard to focus, but it had to be done. *And launch starfighters.*

The analysts hastily updated their assessments. Two human fleets... the fleet might prevail against one, but the other human fleet would be in a perfect position to crush the invasion force. Indeed, the timing had been almost perfect. If the fleet didn't manage to evade, the two human forces would unite and bring their superior firepower to bear.

Attack wings will assault Force Two, the Combat Faction ordered. It wasn't perfect, but it was their only hope. Crushing Force Two was probably beyond them - at least without Force Two crushing them in turn - but they could cripple its carriers. It might just give them a chance to either spar with Force One or break off and escape to the tramline. *Defence wings will prepare for counterattack.*

The Song wavered as dissent washed through the factions. Some factions and sub-factions wanted to break off the engagement immediately. Their arguments were compelling, the Combat Faction agreed, but based on wishful thinking. The humans had a massive firepower advantage, all of a sudden. There was no way they would *not* push their advantage while it lasted. Escape would be difficult, if not impossible. Human starfighters would harry them all the way back to the tramline.

The attack wings must push the attack as hard as possible, the Combat Faction said. The first starfighters flew out of their carriers and launched themselves towards Force Two. Force One was already picking up speed, but their timing was off. *And then return to their motherships.*

There was a moment of relief as more and more starfighters piled out into open space. The timing had been good, but not good enough. There was still a chance to win, to inflict horrendous damage on the human fleets. Taking out half of their carriers would practically guarantee overall victory. And if it came at the cost of the entire fleet...

The war can still be won, the analysts agreed. *And we must press our advantages as hard as possible.*

———

"The enemy fleet is launching starfighters," the tactical officer said. "They're flying straight towards the Io Detachment."

Svetlana nodded. The display was showing a massive fleet bearing down on the enemy ships. She *knew* the ships didn't exist and yet her sensors insisted they did. It was something to contemplate, later. *Brezhnev's* sensors had been upgraded repeatedly in the days after Vera Cruz, although she'd always been on the bottom of the priority lists. And yet, they were being spoofed. Svetlana would have to warn her relatives about that, when she returned home. The Americans had clearly made a major breakthrough in ECM.

"Alert Home Fleet," she ordered. Home Fleet would probably see the launch for themselves, but it paid to be sure. "And inform them that we are ready for phase two."

"Aye, Captain."

Svetlana gripped her command chair, bracing herself. Too much could go wrong - or go right - in the next hour. Even if everything went perfectly, there was too great a chance of being detected and blown away. And then...

You wanted to sit in the command chair, she reminded herself. *And you got it. Stop complaining and get to work.*

———

"The enemy ships have launched starfighters," Jon noted. "Well called."

"They'll see through the deception sooner rather than later," Admiral Robertson said. "The question is just how much time it will take."

Jon nodded, shortly. The latest ECM - straight from Area 51 - had been designed, but not yet put into production before the war had begun. *That* was a stroke of luck - the analysts assumed the Tadpoles would have studied the remains of destroyed human starships, giving them insights into humanity's technological development - yet getting some of the drones into service had been a nightmare. Hell, the vast majority of the drones had been given to *Ark Royal* shortly before she left the Solar System. The remainder had been assigned to Home Fleet.

"We launch in two minutes," Admiral Robertson said. "And then we kick their asses."

Let us hope so, Jon thought.

Admiral Robertson smiled. "Do you want to address the fleet?"

Jon shook his head. He had no doubt that *someone* would put a rousing speech in his mouth, when the official accounts of the battle gave way to telemovies and original fiction, but there was no point in making a speech now. The crews knew what was at stake. They knew what had to be done. And they *didn't* need a pompous ass in an admiral's uniform distracting them from their duty.

"No," he said. "Give them hell."

Admiral Robertson raised his voice. "All fighters, launch," he said. "I say again, all fighters launch!"

———

"Go, go, go!"

Captain Ginny Saito gritted her teeth as her starfighter blasted out of the launch bay, followed by hundreds more. Her HUD updated, time and time again, as new alerts flashed through the network, keeping her aware of what was going on. *Enterprise's* fighter wings were already forming up into their strike groups, but the ramshackle squadrons were finding it harder to get organised. Ginny wasn't too surprised. The hasty reorganisations hadn't given her any time to get to know the pilots under her command, let alone take them through the simulations.

"Form up on me," she ordered. She was relieved she'd managed to keep Lieutenant Williams. The other survivors from her original squadron had been parcelled out to fill holes elsewhere. "Prepare to engage."

She felt a cold smile form on her face as her starfighter picked up speed. The aliens had been tricked into sending most of their starfighters towards the Io Detachment, leaving their hulls largely undefended. They must have panicked, she thought. A more rational commander might have settled for altering course and trying to evade *both* human fleets. But then, having no less than twenty-three fleet carriers bearing down on them had to be more than a little intimidating.

Should have taken the chance to get laid after all, she thought. *It might have been the last time.*

The alien carriers were coming closer, their escorts swinging about to cover their hulls. She could see just how neatly the aliens had been trapped in a dilemma. If they recalled their starfighters, they'd be chased all the way back to their carriers...except they wouldn't be, because those twelve fleet carriers didn't exist. What choice would *she* make, she asked herself? She thought she'd recall her starfighters, even knowing the risks.

"Engagement in two minutes," the dispatcher announced. The alien CSP was moving to challenge the bombers, ignoring the starfighters. It was about the only move they could make, Ginny thought, but it was going to cost them. "Group One, target the carriers; Group Two, target the smaller ships; Group Three, engage the enemy starfighters."

"You heard the man," Ginny said. "On my mark, break and attack."

Her HUD flashed up an alert as the alien frigates opened fire. The odds of scoring a hit were minimal, but they were spewing out one hell of a lot of fire. Their starfighters opened fire a second later, forcing the bombers to fall out of formation and snap into evasive action. Ginny felt her heart twist in pain as four bombers vanished, picked off by the enemy craft. She pushed the thought aside as she opened fire herself, scattering the enemy starfighters. They recovered quickly and came after her.

"Your target is Alien #45," the dispatcher said. "Good luck."

"Noted," Ginny said. "All starfighters, follow me."

The alien frigate grew larger and larger on the display as the starfighters closed to attack range. Her HUD painted an odd picture, a starship that looked oddly *melted*. And yet, there was no mistaking the sheer number of plasma guns on its hull. The only saving grace was that the frigate didn't seem to have the ability to shoot plasma from *anywhere* on its hull.

"Fire at will," she ordered, switching her guns to automatic fire. "Give them hell."

She yanked her starfighter through a series of unpredictable movements as her guns opened fire, pounding the alien hull. The aliens, unsurprisingly, had armoured their starships - they'd known what they might be facing - but they couldn't protect their weapons and sensor blisters from being blown off the hull. Worse, their craft was too small for an inner layer of armour that would provide additional protection. Ginny couldn't help a savage whoop as plasma bolts dug deep into the alien hull, giving them - finally - a taste of their own medicine. It was all she could do to break away before the craft exploded into a ball of superhot plasma.

"Target destroyed," she said. An alien starfighter lunged towards her and she blew it away without a second thought. "I say again, target destroyed."

"Noted," the dispatcher said. "The enemy starfighters are returning."

Ginny nodded, curtly. She flew straight for a long second, just long enough to assess the situation. Home Fleet's starfighters had given the aliens one hell of a beating; one of their carriers had been destroyed, while two more were badly damaged. And their starfighters were still out of position. They'd be tearing into the human craft in a few minutes, but...

"Regroup on me," she ordered. Three of her pilots were dead. She couldn't help a pang of guilt. She'd never met them in person. She hadn't even seen their deaths. They were faceless...she pushed the thought aside, grimly. There would be time to mourn later, if there *was* a later. "Prepare to cover the retreating bombers."

The aliens were *pissed*, she thought, as she angled her starfighter to block the alien advance before they could reach the bombers. They came straight at her, firing savagely as they darted from side to side. She was surprised that none of them tried to turn the encounter into a dogfight, even though it would have given them the upper hand. A dozen enemy starfighters died, but the rest blew through and hurled themselves on the bombers. They didn't seem to care about their own lives as long as they could take out a bomber or two before they died.

She swung her starfighter around and blasted two alien craft in the back. Their wingmen altered course, dropping into an evasive pattern that remained focused on the bombers. It looked as though they were ready to chase them all the way back to their carriers, she noted absently. Perhaps they were. Alien starfighters could tear their way through a human carrier like paper, if they wished.

"Keep hounding them," she ordered. Another alert blinked up on her HUD, informing her that she'd just lost another pilot. "Don't let them have a free hand!"

"The alien carriers are altering course," the dispatcher warned. "They're coming about."

Right down our throats, Ginny thought. An alien pilot lunged at her, then flipped over and vanished into the distance. She had no idea what *that* was about. A coward? Or someone who'd just received new orders? *They can hammer us with their ship-mounted weapons if they wish.*

She pushed the thought aside. It didn't matter, not now. All that mattered was killing the enemy.

And if we don't kill them, she thought as she gunned her drives once again, *they'll sure as hell kill us.*

CHAPTER
THIRTY SIX

Interplanetary Space, Near Jupiter

Tricked.

The Combat Faction cursed its own mistake as the human starfighters tore through its capital ships, trying to inflict as much damage as they could before the hastily-recalled starfighters could drive them away from the fleet. They'd been tricked. Force Two didn't exist, save for a handful of starfighters and escort carriers; Force One was the *real* threat. And it had done far too much damage, when given the opening. The fleet was in serious danger of losing the engagement.

We should retreat, one sub-faction suggested. *We have already inflicted significant damage on the human industrial base.*

But that would give the humans a victory, a second sub-faction insisted. *We still have a significant edge.*

The Combat Faction ignored the bickering. One fleet carrier had been destroyed and two more had been significantly damaged, reducing the number of starfighters and ship-mounted weapons they could bring to bear. And yet, their carriers were superior to human designs...they still had *some* advantages. But they had been tricked. They needed time to think and plan for the next encounter.

Drive the enemy starfighters back to their carriers, the Combat Faction ordered. The Song grew louder as the various factions braced themselves for the fight. *And then engage their carriers.*

The analyst factions assessed the situation quickly. There was no way to ignore the fact that the humans had inflicted significant damage, but the fleet still possessed considerable firepower. And the human fleet was still isolated from the planetary defences...it would be ship on ship and starfighter on starfighter, rather than duelling with ground-based weapons. The prospect for a major victory could not be discounted.

Bring the fleet about, the Combat Faction added. *Prepare for a major engagement.*

———

"Here they come," Admiral Robertson said, quietly.

Jon nodded, forcing himself to watch as the alien starfighters fell on Home Fleet like ravenous wolves on sheep. They split into two formations: one set hunting the bombers, the other harrying the carriers themselves. Damage started to mount up, rapidly, as plasma bolts slammed into hulls, even though the new armour seemed to be holding.

And we also added more damage control teams, he thought, as red lights flashed up on the display. *They're very motivated to patch up any damage as quickly as possible.*

"*Washington* has taken heavy damage," Commodore Warner said, quietly. "*Mao* has been destroyed. *Inflexible* may go the same way if she doesn't receive any support."

"Order the CSP to detach reserve squadrons to cover her," Admiral Robertson said. His voice was very calm, even when an alien squadron strafed *Enterprise.* "And warn her CO to be ready to pull back, if necessary."

Jon nodded, but said nothing as a stream of alien starfighters swept over *Washington* and blew her to hell. A fleet carrier, over five thousand officers and men...just gone. He forced himself to push his regrets to the back of his mind, silently promising himself that their sacrifice would not be forgotten, after the war. The aliens were regrouping, reforming their squadrons just out of weapons range. It wouldn't be long before they resumed their attack.

"The bombers have been rearmed, Admiral," Warner said.

"Get them out there," Admiral Robertson snapped. "Give the bastards something else to think about!"

"Aye, sir," Warner said.

"And bring up the frigates to cover our hull," Admiral Robertson added, as *Enterprise* shuddered alarmingly. "We can't take many more hits like that!"

———

Ginny gritted her teeth as she zoomed towards *Enterprise*, trying to blast the alien pilots who seemed intent on using the fleet carrier for target practice. The aliens were good, she acknowledged sourly; they twisted and turned, evading her fire even as they pumped plasma fire into *Enterprise's* hull. And as the range closed, their fire would become more and more effective. Atmosphere was already streaming from a dozen places on the carrier.

And that will be the least of her problems, if they take out the drives, Ginny thought. One alien pilot died, picked off by her guns, but the remainder ignored it. They weren't even turning to swat her before she could kill more of them. *We can't afford to lose more fleet carriers.*

"Hit the bastards," she snarled. She jammed her thumb down on the trigger as the aliens altered course, pouring fire into the carrier while skimming her hull. "Die...!"

"Got one," Williams said. He sounded as pissed as she felt. "And you..."

Ginny swore as the alien pilot spun around, coming right at her. She hit the firing key an instant before it was too late, blowing the alien pilot into a fireball. His companions were already gone, either picked off or fleeing as fast as they could. No doubt they had orders to regroup before pressing the offensive again. She forced herself to give chase, barking orders to the rest of the squadron. If they could scatter the alien fighters, they could keep them from concentrating their forces and taking out another carrier.

More alerts flashed up in front of her. The bombers were redeploying, heading out to hit the alien fleet again. New orders followed, instructing her to cover the bombers. She nodded, fighting down her frustration as a string of missiles flashed past her. Shipkillers wouldn't be *that* effective against starfighters, but if they were keyed for proximity detonation...

We might just take out a handful with a single missile, she thought. It wasn't much, but...but it would have to do. *And even if we don't, we'll make them jumpy.*

The alien carriers were closing the range, she noted. She'd been taught that carriers shunned fleet engagements, but the aliens had clearly read a different tactical handbook. Pressing the offensive against Home Fleet made no sense, unless they were confident their speed and firepower advantage would give them the edge. She pushed the thought aside as she forced her starfighter to fly faster, ignoring the risk of overheating her drives or plasma guns. The bombers *had* to be covered.

"The alien frigates are deploying to stop us," Williams said. "This is not going to be pretty."

"Home Fleet is launching missiles to compensate," Ginny told him, after a brief glance at her HUD. Hopefully, the aliens wouldn't realise the danger before it was too late. A handful of bomb-pumped lasers would really ruin their day. "Let them go through, then follow them."

"Understood."

She felt sweat trickling down her back as the massed squadrons approached the enemy formation. The Tadpoles really *had* done their homework, she noted coldly. Their frigates provided so much cover for their carriers that they could afford to detach almost all of their starfighters. But they clearly weren't completely sanguine about their chances. They were already recalling some of the squadrons bedevilling Home Fleet.

At least we took some of the pressure off, she thought. *We bought Home Fleet some time.*

"Missiles will enter attack range in twenty seconds," the dispatcher said. "Be ready."

"Yeah," Ginny said. She checked her squadron's status, then nodded to herself. "I'll be ready."

Enemy bombers are mounting a renewed offensive, a sub-faction noted. *Their numbers have been significantly reduced.*

A flicker of satisfaction ran through the Song. The human bombers had proven themselves dangerous in large numbers, but they'd already lost dozens of craft in the engagement. They simply didn't have the numbers to break through the frigates and attack, not now. They'd be so brutally winnowed by the frigates that the survivors would be picked off effortlessly as they tried to get into attack range. And then the fleet would pound the human fleet to scrap...

ENEMY MISSILES, another faction screeched. *WARNING!*

The Combat Faction recoiled. Hundreds - no, *thousands* - of enemy missiles had appeared, heading straight for the frigates. They couldn't be real. There was no *doubt* that most of them - perhaps all of them - were little more than sensor ghosts. And yet, just for a second, the point defence network was utterly overloaded. The Combat Faction worked desperately, hurling new orders through the datanet, as the human missiles drew closer. They couldn't afford to assume that *all* the missiles were fake...

Too late, a faction noted.

The Combat Faction seethed in annoyance. Seven frigates had been blown out of space, with nine more heavily damaged. The human starfighters and bombers now had a clear path to the fleet carriers, even though the remaining frigates were hastily moving to close it again. Once again, the outcome of the battle was in doubt. There was still too great a chance of losing.

We should withdraw, one faction insisted. *Prolonging this engagement may cost us the entire fleet.*

The opportunity to cripple the human fleet should not be missed, another faction countered, clearly preparing to rehash the entire argument once again. *We would still have the edge even if we lose the entire fleet.*

But it will take us time to reassess the situation, the first faction reminded the others. *The Heart of the Song will not know what has happened to us.*

A picket will carry word to them, a third faction stated. *The outcome will not remain a mystery for long.*

The Combat Faction brushed the matter aside as the human bombers slipped into attack range. A handful fell to point defence fire, but the remainder managed to salvo their missiles and then retreat as the point defence concentrated on the incoming threat. Deliberately or otherwise, the humans had managed to damage several point defence grids, weakening the carriers badly. The Combat Faction conceded, grimly, that the humans were still a very effective threat. A third fleet carrier had been badly damaged, along with the frigates.

This battle will be won by whichever side suffers the least damage, the first faction said. *It may not be us.*

The starfighters are to intercept the bombers on their way home, the Combat Faction ordered, ignoring the dispute. There was no *time* for an argument. *The bombers are not to have a chance to return to their motherships.*

It focused its collective intellect on the problem. The humans had inflicted serious harm, but they'd taken damage themselves. Four of their fleet carriers were gone, along with a number of smaller ships. The odds were still in the Combat Faction's favour, as long as the humans didn't produce more surprises. But it had to admit that the odds of *that* were incalculable.

For the first time, it gave serious consideration to simply breaking off the engagement. The humans were in no state to give pursuit, even if they *could* cross the weaker tramlines. It was fairly certain that the humans would take the opportunity to lick their wounds, rather than harass the fleet as it tried to withdraw. But it couldn't surrender the chance to destroy such a large chunk of the human fleet. The numerical advantage was still on their side.

Assuming the humans don't manage to launch any new starships of their own, it told itself, grimly. *If they do, all calculations may have to be reconsidered.*

It watched as the fleet steadily approached its target. One way or the other, it would all be over soon.

———

"They're passing right through our position," the tactical officer said. "I don't think they've seen us."

Svetlana nodded. *Brezhnev* was in an excellent position to engage the enemy, if they'd carried enough weapons to make a difference. She thought they could hit one of the alien carriers, at the cost of being detected and blown to atoms. Home Fleet would probably consider that a worthwhile trade, she thought, but her orders still held. *Brezhnev* had to watch the aliens until they were detected or the aliens broke off the engagement.

"Hold us steady," she said. There were enough starships, starfighters, missiles and drones flying through the combat zone to hide any betraying flicker from *Brezhnev*, as long as they were careful. "Don't let them get too far away."

"Aye, Captain."

"*Putin* has taken heavy damage," the communications officer said. "She's sending out a general distress call."

Svetlana winced, inwardly. She remembered, all too well, *Putin's* XO. He'd had opinions on the proper place for women, all women. Svetlana pitied his wife *and* his endless string of mistresses. She even pitied *Putin's* captain. His XO would stick a knife between his ribs sooner or later, perhaps not metaphorically. And yet, the fleet carrier didn't deserve to die because her XO was an asshole of the highest order. Mother Russia simply didn't have many fleet carriers left.

"There's nothing we can do," she said, quietly. She ignored the sharp look *her* XO shot in her direction. "Just...hold us here."

"Picking up orders from the flag," the communications officer said. "We're to prepare ourselves for Contingency Alpha."

Svetlana sucked in her breath. The odds of survival had just gone down, again.

"Very well," she said. "Tactical?"

"The systems are online, Captain," the tactical officer said. "We're ready."

"Inform Home Fleet," Svetlana ordered. "And now, we wait."

———

"They're giving the bombers a pounding," Admiral Robertson said.

Jon nodded, curtly. Home Fleet's bombers had trained - and trained hard - to face the aliens, but none of the simulations had really come close to the reality. The aliens had planned countermeasures of their own. They'd kicked hell out of the second flight of bombers, which meant the *third* would be considerably less effective. And then...

"Redeploy starfighters to chase the enemy craft away," he suggested. It wasn't really his *place* to offer suggestions, but they didn't have time for a discussion. "And then recover the bombers as fast as possible."

We need to start adding torpedoes to starfighters, he thought. *The Tadpoles' armour gives them a slight edge. But we could get a torpedo or a missile through it if we could somehow slip past their point defence.*

He pushed the thought aside as he assessed the odds. Home Fleet had taken one hell of a beating - and it wasn't over yet. Four fleet carriers gone, three more heavily damaged...he'd long since lost count of just how many starfighters had been blown to atoms. The only consolation was that the enemy had taken a pasting too, but even *that* was tempered with the grim awareness that there was no way to know just how many ships the enemy had in total.

At least we're wearing down their starfighters, he told himself.

It was a reassuring thought, reassuring enough that he knew to be wary. He'd seen a couple of enemy craft show signs of tiredness, although he was honest enough to admit that it could have been wishful thinking. One of them had crashed into a frigate, but that could easily have been deliberate. The Tadpoles hadn't had a habit of suicide attacks, yet they might have decided to change that policy if they thought they were losing.

But they're not losing, he thought. *The outcome is still undecided.*

"Signal from Admiral Wright, sir," the communications officer said. "The Io Detachment is ready to activate the second set of pods."

Admiral Robertson glanced at Jon. "Now?"

"Yeah," Jon said. The timing was already bad, but they were running out of options. A knife-range fight would be far better for the Tadpoles than Home Fleet. "Order him to activate the pods as planned."

And hope to hell the aliens don't see the trap opening in front of them, he added, in the privacy of his own mind. *They can't be allowed the time to react.*

———

"*Now* what's happening?"

Lieutenant Geoff Willis resisted - somehow - the urge to look upwards and ask God *precisely* how he'd managed to piss off the XO. Whatever he'd done, he couldn't imagine it being so bad that he *had* to be assigned to babysit Tanya Crompton. And to think that the other lieutenants had been *jealous*. Tanya was beautiful, with long dark hair and a sultry face, but anyone who spent more than five minutes on the receiving end of one of her interrogations would forget her looks and start trying to find a way to get *out*. She was one of the lead reporters for FOX-CNN and she never let anyone forget it.

"The bombers are returning to the carrier," he said, carefully. Tanya was recording everything and, despite strict censorship, he wasn't convinced that she *didn't* have a way of slipping recordings past the security teams. "They'll be going out again as soon as possible."

Tanya looked at him. "And when will that be?"

Geoff groaned. He didn't know. And even if he had known, he wasn't sure he'd be allowed to tell her. The USN took a dim view of reporters, particularly after a handful had been tried and executed for treason during the Crazy Years. He wasn't sure if Tanya knew that or not, but if she did she didn't seem to care. She'd already driven too many officers mad with her theory that the Pentagon had known about the Tadpoles years before Vera Cruz.

"I don't know," he said, finally. Perhaps one of the other officers would swap with him. Or perhaps he should just grovel in front of the XO. Taking a walk out the airlock was starting to seem a good idea. "I think they'll be launched as soon as possible."

"But there are only a handful of bombers left," Tanya said. "Doesn't that mean they're going out there to die?"

They're going out there to defend a bitch like you, Geoff thought.

He didn't say it. Tanya would use it against the USN and *he'd* get the blame. The XO would *not* be amused, nor would the captain. By the time the shit reached him, it would have already covered everyone two or three steps up the rank chart. He'd be lucky if he was *merely* skinned alive.

"Yes," he said, instead. "But they have to try. Everything depends on them."

The display changed. Tanya leaned forward. "What is that?"

"I don't know," Geoff said. What *was* it? "But I think we're about to find out."

CHAPTER
THIRTY SEVEN

Interplanetary Space, Near Jupiter

"Activate the second set of pods," Johan ordered.

"Aye, sir."

Johan leaned back into his chair as the pods started to activate, launching their cargo into space. The whole concept had come out of a lab during the desperate search for something - anything - that might give human navies a fighting chance against the Tadpoles. It had never been deployed in combat before and might well never be deployed again. Too much could go wrong for the concept to work more than once.

They'll know what we did the moment they see it, he thought. The Tadpoles hadn't had a chance to drop a hammer on his force before they recalled their starfighters, but they wouldn't give him a second chance. *And they won't let us do it again.*

"The pods have finished launching their cargo," his aide said. "And the ECM platforms are standing by."

"Switch them to cover mode," Johan ordered. "And then prepare to fall back on Jupiter."

"Aye, sir."

He forced himself to relax. The die was cast. Either the aliens would be caught by surprise or they wouldn't. And then...his detachment was too small to alter the outcome as the aliens converged on Home Fleet. They'd just have to watch and wait to see what happened.

And pray, he thought. *There's nothing else we can do.*

———

The Combat Faction silently assessed the situation as the two fleets continued to close. Its starfighters had taken heavy losses, but so had the humans'. The Combat Faction still had an edge, particularly as the human capital ships could not escape engagement. It didn't *look* as if any of them were carrying mass drivers either. Surely, they would have started firing long ago if they *had*.

There is still the risk of being surprised, one faction insisted. *We should not let them get any closer.*

But pushing the offensive will bring us victory, another faction countered. Voices rose and fell as dozens of speakers switched sides. *Let us break this force and then withdraw in victory.*

The Combat Faction recalculated the odds, again and again. There was no way to deny that the humans had a slight numerical advantage, but it would count for nothing. Their carriers lacked heavy armour, antiship weapons and mass drivers. And their escorts lacked the weapons necessary to cover the carriers against the Combat Faction's fleet. Victory would be costly - there was no point in trying to hide from that fact - but it would come.

We proceed, the Combat Faction announced.

New prospects raced through the Song. The humans would have to withdraw ships from the front, allowing other elements of the Combat Faction to push the offensive...further weakening the human defenders. And then, another offensive against Earth. It would bring the humans down, allowing the last of their starships to be destroyed. And then...

Well, *that* would have to wait until the end of the war.

———

"The alien fighters are regrouping," Admiral Robertson commented. "And they're out of our range."

"At least we taught them respect," Jon said. He glanced at the timer. "There's no point in trying to retreat, of course."

"None," Admiral Robertson agreed. "Unless, of course, we wish to play Taffy-3 all the way back to Earth."

Jon nodded. The battle could still go either way, but the sick feeling in his gut made him wonder if humanity was about to lose. A knife-range fight would be utterly disastrous for both sides, yet...humanity would take the worst of it. Home Fleet just wasn't equipped for a confrontation that might as well have come out of the wet-navy battleship era.

At least they're not that much better off, he told himself. *We'll claw them good before they destroy us.*

"Try to open the range," he urged. "We'll need more time to fly bombers into the teeth of their fire."

He tried to think of other options, but none came to mind. There were starfighters and bombers on Jupiter Station, yet there was no way to get them to Home Fleet. They were well out of range. The same could be said for the defenders of Mars or the starfighters they'd left behind at Earth. Home Fleet was on its own, facing an enemy force that seemed willing to accept mutual destruction. They might just have led their fleet to ruin.

"We will also need to order the starfighters to engage the enemy capital ships directly," Admiral Robertson said. "And *that* will be costly too."

The display flickered and updated. A stream of red icons altered course, falling on Home Fleet; a cloud of green and blue icons moved to meet them, looking pathetically inadequate against the alien storm. It wouldn't be long before the alien craft blew through the defences and attacked the carriers directly. And then...

"Make it so," he ordered, quietly.

He looked at the timer, again. There might *just* be enough time.

* * *

"Captain," the tactical officer said. "I have the missile control links up and running."

Svetlana allowed herself a moment of hope. She'd gone through one of the most intensive training courses in the solar system. She *knew* just how much could go wrong, particularly when they hadn't planned or trained for the manoeuvre. And yet, it looked as though they'd managed to pull the first stage off.

"Very good," she said. There was no way they could use lasers to instruct the incoming missiles. They'd have to use radio...and pray, desperately, that the aliens wouldn't notice until it was too late. She hadn't even had time to deploy a remote relay platform! "Have you set up the targeting matrix?"

"Aye, Captain."

Svetlana exchanged a glance with Ignatyev. They were committed now...no, they'd been committed the moment they received their orders. The Io Detachment had launched the missiles, hoping - believing - that Svetlana and her crew would be in position to guide them to their targets. She was damned if she would let them down now.

"Then relay the targeting matrix to the missiles," she ordered. "And then order them to bring up their drives."

She leaned back in her command chair, trying to ignore the sweat running down her back. It had seemed simple, when she'd received their orders. The missiles would be launched on ballistic trajectories, almost completely undetectable as long as the aliens didn't look for them with active sensors. Ideally, the alien ships would have impaled themselves on the missiles, but the human race hadn't been *that* lucky. Their steady acceleration would have removed them from the danger zone if they'd started earlier.

"The missiles are coming online," the tactical officer reported.

"Then bring up *our* drives and get us out of here," Svetlana snapped. There was no point in trying to hide any longer. Even if the aliens had missed the radio transmissions, there was no way they could miss the missiles themselves. "Boost us right out of their range."

"Aye, Captain."

"They've seen them," the tactical officer said. "But Home Fleet is already deploying its fighters to cover them."

"Then keep us moving," Svetlana ordered. The missiles no longer needed her. They could find their own targets, if their primary objectives were lost. "And deploy all of our remaining decoys."

———

For far too long, the Combat Faction refused to accept what it was seeing. Missiles. Missiles from behind the fleet. Missiles coming right at them, picking up speed at a terrifying pace. It wanted to believe that the missiles were *more* sensor ghosts, like the non-existent enemy fleet, but it couldn't. The humans could not have created an ECM system capable of producing such an effect. If they had, they would have already won the war.

It struggled to determine a response as it realised that the human starfighters were spinning around, going on the offensive one final time. The conclusion was inescapable. The humans had trapped it, again. There was no way to deal with one threat without allowing the other to do real damage. And the combination of sensor ghosts and previous battle damage made it impossible to be entirely sure what it was facing.

This situation must be reassessed, it announced. The missiles were closing in now, preparing to detonate. It could not be allowed. The human fondness for bomb-pumped lasers had already proven far too costly. And yet, there was no way to *prevent* the missiles from detonating. *We are trapped.*

Then we must retreat, one sub-faction insisted. *The battle is lost. But the war is not yet over.*

Consensus was reached with striking speed. New orders flashed through the command network, instructing the fleet to alter course and beat a hasty retreat towards the nearest tramline. Other orders followed, directing the starfighters to cover their retreat. And...a new awareness flashed through the Combat Faction as it detected a human starship far too close to the fleet. The human must have shadowed them for quite some time.

A flicker of admiration lingered in the Song for a long moment. The humans were remarkable. They were at a serious disadvantage, yet they still fought. The Combat Faction couldn't help but respect the human reluctance to give in to the inevitable. Perhaps, just perhaps, they could fend it off until it was no longer inevitable.

And then new orders were issued.

———

"Captain, they just locked sensors on our hull," the tactical officer snapped. "Their starfighters are already closing in for the kill."

"Target their carriers and open fire, all weapons," Svetlana ordered. She doubted she'd do more than scratch their hulls, but it was better than doing nothing. Besides, the alien ships were already taking a beating from the missiles. "Engage the starfighters with point defence when they enter range."

She forced herself to appear calm as the alien starfighters zoomed closer. *Brezhnev* was armoured, but not *that* armoured. There was no way her ship would stand up to the alien craft, once they opened fire. The only real hope was staying alive until the aliens had to break off and rejoin their motherships, but that wasn't likely to happen. Her family might even be pleased, she thought. She'd be feted as a hero, once she was dead. And she wouldn't be embarrassing them any longer.

"The enemy carriers are in full retreat," the tactical officer added. "But their starfighters are entering attack range...now!"

"Open fire," Svetlana ordered. She keyed her console. "All hands, brace for impact!"

———

"They're running," Williams said.

"Concentrate on our orders," Ginny snapped. The alien carriers *were* retreating, unless it was another trick. They were fast, damnably fast. It was easy to imagine them trying to loop around Home Fleet and race back to Earth. And yet, they'd been winning. There was no *need* to break off. "We have to save that ship!"

She forced herself to concentrate as the squadron raced towards the Russian ship. It was tiny, yet heavily armoured. The alien plasma bolts glanced off its armour, rather than burning their way into the ship. She felt a moment of hope, which died as she realised that the ship wasn't *completely* armoured. The aliens *were* slowly tearing her to shreds.

"Follow me," she snapped.

The first alien pilot died before even realising he was under attack. Ginny barely noted his passing as she yanked her craft around, searching for the next target. The rest of her squadron followed her, driving the aliens off the Russian starship. Ginny couldn't help a moment of envy as she saw the scorched paint on her hull. An American destroyer - a *modern* American destroyer - would have been blown to flaming debris in the first pass.

"They're breaking off," Williams carolled. "I think we won!"

"Don't jinx it," Ginny snapped. The last of the alien starfighters turned and fled, hurrying back to its carrier. She fired a stream of plasma after it, but the tiny craft was already well out of range. "Remain focused on the issue at hand."

She studied her HUD for a long moment. The alien carriers were picking up speed, heading straight for the tramline. It definitely *looked* as though they were running, as though they'd had enough. Their remaining starfighters were already being recovered. And yet...

"Attention," the dispatcher said. "All starfighters are to return to their carriers. I say again, all starfighters are to return to their carriers."

"Understood," Ginny said.

She suddenly felt very tired as she spun her starfighter around and gunned the engine, heading straight back to *Enterprise*. The carrier looked a mess, but she was intact. Ginny sucked in her breath as she saw the scorch marks on *Enterprise's* hull, yet it was clear that the makeshift armour had actually stood up to the challenge. Damage-control teams were already going to work, sealing off the damaged areas and patching cracks in the hull.

"What a mess," she muttered.

The landing deck was intact, thankfully. Ginny was surprised the aliens hadn't concentrated fire on it, although she supposed their plasma weapons were designed to pummel the main hull itself. They'd change their tactics, once they realised that humanity was armouring their hulls. She wondered, as the deck crew helped her out of her craft, just what that would mean for the future. Humanity might have won the battle, but had it won the war?

Williams met her on the far side of the hatch. "There's a privacy tube just down the corridor," he said. He lowered his voice, even though they were alone. "Do you want to join me?"

Ginny stared at him for a long moment. She was alive. She wanted to *celebrate* being alive. It was suddenly very hard to care about regulations. The thought of taking him to bed, of fucking him senseless...it was tempting. She wanted to feel him inside her...she wanted to feel *alive*, to feel that there was something beside an endless series of battles until her luck finally ran out...

And yet...she glanced at the wall-mounted display. The all-clear had already been sounded. They'd be expected to rest as *Enterprise* made her way back to Earth. God knew what they'd do after they made it home.

She smiled. "Why not?"

———

"We lost one drive unit and five pieces of armour," Ignatyev reported. "Right now, we can barely make enough thrust to take us back to Earth."

"Then set course for Earth," Svetlana ordered. They were in no condition to continue the fight, even if the aliens *hadn't* been retreating. Besides, she didn't want to push her luck any further. The damage could easily have been fatal. "And make sure you inform Home Fleet of our condition."

"Aye, Captain."

Svetlana smiled at him, then picked up her datapad. She'd have to write the report herself, just to make sure it reached the right people without being tactically edited somewhere along the way. She didn't lack for enemies in the naval hierarchy...hell, her *family* had plenty of political enemies. Someone would probably try to play down her achievement if she gave them half a chance.

And we ensured that the enemy fleet was driven off, she thought. It was a Russian achievement, one that couldn't be denied. She couldn't help wondering if some of her enemies would prefer to throw the glory to the Americans or British rather than let her take the credit. But she had no intention of letting them bury her. *There's no way they can take that from us.*

"Home Fleet is preparing to return to Earth too," the communications officer said. "They're offering us a tow."

"No," Svetlana said. She barely looked up from the datapad. The first reports would already be heading back to Earth. She'd have to get hers in quick before someone else took control of the narrative. "We can get back under our own steam."

"Aye, Captain."

———

"I think we won," Admiral Robertson said.

Jon nodded. Home Fleet would continue to monitor the alien fleet, of course, but it definitely *looked* like the aliens were running for the tramline. He wondered, absently, just which factor had made them decide to break off and retreat. The missiles? The prospect of a mutually-destructive engagement? Or something alien, something no human could hope to understand. He had a feeling he'd probably never know.

He looked over at Warner. "Damage report?"

Warner glanced at Admiral Robertson, who nodded. "Five carriers destroyed, sir; two more heavily damaged," he said. "The remaining carriers all took *some* damage, but their commanders believe they can be repaired fairly quickly. Their landing decks are still intact and the remaining starfighters have been parcelled out. Ah...national formations are now hopelessly jumbled."

"I dare say we'll survive," Jon said. Right now, it was the least of their problems. "It'll do wonders for international cooperation, if nothing else."

Admiral Robertson snorted. "Do you want to write the report for Earth?"

Jon looked at the timer. Earth wouldn't know - yet - that the battle had been joined, let alone won. They'd certainly have problems following the engagement from such a distance, although they *might* see the remaining alien ships running for the tramline.

"Tell them we won," he said, finally. His body was insisting, loudly, that he needed a shower and sleep. He felt as though he'd drunk enough coffee to float a battleship. "I'll write a full report later."

"Yes, sir," Admiral Robertson said. He looked doubtful. "Just that?"

"Right now, that's all they'll want to know," Jon said. "We won."

And yet, we took a beating, he thought as he headed for the hatch. Home Fleet had been battered into near-uselessness. Far too many trained pilots and spacers had been killed. The cost of replacing them - in time as well as money - would be staggering. *We may still lose the war.*

But he kept that thought to himself. It would only have upset people.

Let them enjoy the victory while they can, he told himself. *We'll have to return to battle soon enough.*

CHAPTER
THIRTY EIGHT

Near Townsend, United Kingdom

The rain fell ever harder, as Molly led Fran through the woods, but she could *still* hear someone chasing after them. Dave - she was *sure* it was Dave - seemed to have an unerring sense of direction, even in the pouring rain. Visibility was pathetic, yet he was still following them. And he was gaining on them.

We have to keep moving, Molly thought. Her bare feet were aching. Blood welled up from a dozen scratches and cuts. *Maybe he's following the blood.*

She glanced down, but the rain seemed to be washing the blood into the soil too quickly for anyone to see the stain. Or so she hoped. Did Dave have a dog with him? She'd read a dozen stories where hunting dogs had been put off the scent by pepper or wading through rivers, but she didn't *have* any pepper. And the rainfall should be enough to obscure her scent. She cursed herself as she forced her aching limbs to keep moving. She didn't even know if Dave *had* a dog.

The ground grew steeper, water splashing down as they clambered up a hill. She tried to picture the map in her mind before dismissing it as hopeless. There was no way to know where they were, let alone where they were going. Something *crashed* through the undergrowth behind them, spurring her on. Dave - or his friends - were far too close to her for comfort.

We could hide, she thought. But she was naked. Her pale body would stick out like a sore thumb. *What else can we do?*

Fran stumbled as she tripped, nearly landing on her face in the mud. Molly caught her arm and yanked her onwards, even though she knew Fran might have twisted her ankle. They didn't have *time* to stop. Fran limped after her, grunting in pain. Molly was just glad she hadn't screamed. If Dave was close enough for them to hear him, he was certainly close enough to hear them.

"I can't go on," Fran gasped. Her breathing was ragged, as if she could no longer take deep breaths. "I honestly can't go on."

"You must," Molly snapped. She kept hold of Fran's arm, forcing her to keep moving. "You don't want to be caught."

She looked around as the hillside grew steeper, prickly bushes appearing amidst the trees. It was growing harder to keep climbing, yet...she wasn't sure she dared try to head either left or right. Dave might change his own path to intercept them. She shivered as more water cascaded over her body, reminding her of her vulnerability. Dave wouldn't be remotely merciful if he caught them. Molly would probably have to watch as he raped Fran before being raped herself.

Fuck, she thought, numbly. Her limbs were starting to feel cold. *What do we do?*

There were plenty of tree branches within sight, but she had no illusions about her ability to turn them into improvised weapons. Dave was stronger than her, faster than her and nastier than her. And she'd proved she could plan and carry out an escape. She doubted he'd let her close to him without beating her to a pulp first. Playing helpless and dumb wasn't going to work a second time. Trying to ambush him was probably futile.

But we'll run out of hillside, sooner or later, she thought. *And what happens then?*

She tried to think of something, but nothing came to mind. There was no way to know what - if anything - was in front of them. They could be running further and further *away* from help, instead of towards it. Dave's friends might already have circled the hill, trying to get in front of them. They'd catch her when she reached the bottom of the hill. Or they might be heading the other way as fast as possible, leaving Dave alone. She wouldn't have blamed them for abandoning their monstrous friend.

"I can see you," Dave's voice called. It echoed oddly between the trees. "Come out now and I won't hurt you."

"Don't say anything," Molly hissed, sharply. She looked behind her. Visibility was still poor, mist slowly forming between the trees. There was no sign of Dave, but she could hear *something* moving towards them. She didn't understand how he could see them...he *couldn't* see them. He was hoping they'd shout back and reveal their position. "Keep moving."

Fran looked unsure. "What if...?"

"Ungrateful brat," Molly snapped. "Just move!"

The crashing sound grew louder as they picked up speed, scrambling up the rocky hillside. Water cascaded down, making it harder and harder to climb without using both hands and feet. Molly gritted her teeth as she cut her leg on a stone, hoping - praying - that Dave really *didn't* have a dog. Her thoughts refused to let go of the possibility. The water *might* wash the blood away or it might not. If it didn't, Dave could probably tell she was wounded. It wouldn't be long before her feet gave out completely.

Thunder crackled, high overhead. Molly glanced up at the gloomy sky, silently willing the rain to fall harder. It was cold and wet - she knew she'd be shivering helplessly if she hadn't forced herself to keep moving - but it was the only cover they had. Dave might find it harder to track them if the water obscured their path, hiding the signs of their desperate flight from him. She wished, not for the first time, that she'd paid more attention to outdoor sports. Her old gym mistress would have outraced Dave by now...

And probably kicked his ass, Molly thought. Her memories of the gym mistress made the wretched woman into a giant, although she probably hadn't been *that* much larger than her charges. *She never gave any of us any mercy.*

Fran grunted in pain. "I...I don't know how I can go on."

"Think of what he'll do to you," Molly advised. It was becoming increasingly obvious that Fran couldn't go on for much longer, if at all. "Do you really *want* to be raped and murdered?"

"I should never have come here," Fran said. "Maggie wanted to go to the city farm instead..."

Molly scowled. "Stop whining," she said. "Just keep moving."

Fran shot her a betrayed look, but Molly ignored it. She had too many regrets of her own to give much of a damn about Fran's. Her kids were still hundreds of miles away, without even the slightest idea where to start looking for their mother. If they were still alive...the policeman had talked about flooding in the Thames Valley. Percy and Penny might have been forced out of their home by now. And Gayle...

She wasn't paid to stay with them during a full-scale emergency, Molly thought. She'd certainly never anticipated the possibility. *She might have gone straight home.*

Dave was coming closer. She could hear him. And that meant...

He's far too close, Molly thought. *We're not going to get away.*

Cold ice congealed around her heart. Dave and his friends had...had *used* her, with as much consideration as they would have used a blow-up doll. She wouldn't have willingly gone back to them even if they'd showed her any *real* consideration. Now, after she'd escaped, they'd do much worse. And they'd rape Fran too. And then...

She caught Fran's eye as they pressed onwards. "When I tell you, I want you to hide in the undergrowth," she said. "I'll lead him after me. You stay put until he's gone, then creep back the way he came. Walk around the cabin, just in case they've gone back there, and head to the nearest farm."

Fran stared at her. "But he'll catch you!"

"Perhaps," Molly said. She was fairly sure Dave *would* catch her. And she was *very* sure she wouldn't survive the experience. But at least Fran would have a chance. Molly just hoped she'd make the most of it. "When you find the police, tell them..."

She shook her head. Fran didn't need to be burdened with a final message from Molly, not when she had too many other problems. Just getting away would be hard enough. She'd have to be very careful. There was no way to know where the other two thugs had gone. If one of them was following Dave, Fran would be in deep shit.

"Get under cover," she snapped, pointing to the left. There were enough bushes to hide Fran, if Dave didn't have time to look. "And don't come out until you're sure he's following me."

Fran nodded. "I..."

Molly hurried onwards, concentrating on making as much noise as she could. The rain would bury most of it, but she'd already decided that Dave had very good ears. He'd certainly managed to chase them, despite the poor visibility. She wondered, absently, if he'd found a pair of hunting binoculars. A pair might well have been stored at the cabin. She'd never been hunting, but she'd heard that rich people liked to do it.

Garrison never took me hunting, she thought, as she clambered up the trail. The noise behind her was growing louder. *Perhaps it was out of his price range.*

The thought would have made her smile, if she hadn't been so tired and sore. She'd been a damn fool. There was no point in disputing that, she thought. She'd betrayed her husband and children...for what? For a dream of a life amongst the Quality? For a dream that would fade when the money ran out? She'd been ripe for exploitation and Garrison had exploited her. And then Dave...the only real difference between Garrison and Dave, she decided, was that one was cruder than the other. Garrison had masked his bad intentions. Dave hadn't bothered to try to hide them.

And he will kill me, if he has half a chance, she thought. *And...*

She ran through a pair of bushes and skidded to a halt, just in time to keep herself from running over a cliff. Rainwater cascaded down towards a churning river, heading eastwards...she looked east, but saw nothing beyond the mist. The wind blew stronger, sending shivers down her spine...she looked left and right, yet there was nowhere to go. She peered down, hoping to see a way to get down to the river, but there was nothing. It was a sheer drop.

Trapped, she thought. *Fuck.*

The noise of someone coming towards her grew louder and louder. She could hear his heavy breathing...she hoped, desperately, that he would run right over the cliff. Because if he didn't...she looked around, frantically. Someone had designed the whole area as a lover's meeting place, she decided. There was only one way in or out that didn't involve pushing through thorny bushes and stinging nettles. And Dave was coming right up it.

I'm sorry, Kurt, she thought. *I...I don't know what to do.*

————

Dave knew, as he scrambled after the wretched bitch, that he'd made a mistake. It was something he never should have done, but he'd been tired and content after he'd had his way with her. He'd enjoyed watching her submit to him, he'd enjoyed watching her make the choice to do *anything*, rather than let the younger girl be taken in her place...it had never occurred to him, afterwards, that she would somehow manage to escape. And now everything was in jeopardy.

The cops hadn't managed to pin more than a fraction of his crimes on him, thanks to an expensive lawyer and some nifty witness intimidation. Being forced to work on the chain gang - suffering the hoots and hollers of every well-bred nincompoop with a car - hadn't been fun, but at least it had been better than summary execution or permanent exile. He'd promised himself that he would be more careful, once he was released; he certainly wouldn't leave the bitches alive afterwards. And when the chance to escape had come, he'd taken it without a second thought.

He'd dreamed, just for a while, that he could build a fiefdom of his own. Law and order had broken down spectacularly, perhaps completely. Whoever built an army might just be able to take the country, or at least a small fraction of it. Besides, he had nothing to lose. If he was recaptured, he wouldn't be put back on the chain gang. He'd be lucky if he wasn't simply marched to the nearest wall and shot. Escapees did not get second chances.

They should have been able to hide forever, he told himself. The cabin was isolated, the nearest farm quite some distance away. They could raid for food, then enjoy themselves with the girl. They could even go looking for *more* girls. There *was* a boarding school nearby, if nothing else. Farm girls were likely to prove too independent for his tastes. But instead, they'd captured an older woman...

It had been a mistake, he told himself. They should have ignored her, or killed her, or kept her tied up. Instead, he'd allowed her a chance to get away. His lust for dominance, for forcing her to surrender herself, had overwhelmed his common sense. It would have been easy to tie her up or break one of her legs or even make very sure she couldn't get out of the room. But he'd been too satiated to care.

And now the others have fled, he thought, darkly. They'd decided to run before the police arrived, as if there was anywhere they could hide. *And all my plans have come to naught.*

He smashed through a set of bushes and came to a halt. There was nowhere to go. The older woman - he'd never bothered to learn her name - was standing by the edge of the tiny clearing, watching him warily. Her naked body was streaked with blood, water splashing down from high overhead to wash her clean; her tits shook with fear, drawing his attention to her hard nipples. Dave snarled at her, feeling the lust return as she cringed back. This time, he didn't have to worry about keeping her alive. This time...

A thought struck him. "Where's the other bitch?"

The woman pointed to the cliff. "She fell down."

Dave glanced behind him. Water churned down, splashing up as it hit the rocks at the bottom before running down to the sea. The river hadn't been *that* impressive a few hours ago, when they'd scouted around the cabin, but the heavy rainfall had turned it into a torrent. If the younger bitch *had* fallen down, it would have killed her. And her body would be beyond recovery.

"What a shame," he said. He'd been looking forward to breaking the younger girl, but there was no point in crying over spilt milk. "I'll have to make do with you, won't I?"

He sneered at the older woman. He'd always wanted an older woman, ever since he'd learnt that scoring with one was better than luring a girl his own age into bed. The boys at school had bragged about their sexual conquests with older women, chatting about just *what* an experienced woman could do. And *this* one hadn't been a disappointment. She'd been as horny as them, by the time they'd finally tired of using her. She'd known things his companions hadn't known were possible.

He allowed his leer to grow wider. Women were always the same. Strong and proud, as long as they had a protector to look after them. When they were alone, when there was no one to trade sex for protection, they crumbled. The girls at his school had laughed at him because they'd thought he was too scared of their fathers and boyfriends to lay a finger on them, no matter how they displayed themselves before him. He'd taught some of them better, when he'd grown older. They'd paid for laughing at him.

They begged for mercy, he thought, remembering the first girl he'd lured into his clutches and raped. The slut hadn't even remembered him, damn her. *But I showed them who was boss.*

"Come here," he said. He tapped his groin. "You've got a lot of work to do."

———

Molly felt an odd calm descend on her as she faced him, one final time. She knew, all too well, that there was no way out. Dave was blocking the only way to escape - the only safe way. Even if she started to push through the thorns, he'd be on her before she managed to get very far. And she knew better than to expect mercy. Dave was sick in the head. It was a surprise he'd even bothered to honour his original agreement.

The others probably forced him to keep his word, she thought. *But that wouldn't have lasted long.*

She took a step forward, silently bidding farewell to everyone. To Kurt, to Percy and Penny, to all the friends she'd known...she'd been a damned fool. She hadn't anticipated the alien attack, of course, but she'd been riding for a fall anyway. Perhaps Garrison would have turned nasty, even if Earth hadn't been attacked. Perhaps...

The world had changed. And she didn't want to live in it.

"Come here," Dave repeated. He tapped his groin, again. "I won't ask a third time."

Molly gritted her teeth, then forced herself forward one final time. Dave's eyes widened, a second before she slammed into him, forcing him back and over the cliff. He let out a scream as he plummeted, Molly tumbling over the edge and following him down...

Fran will have a chance, she thought. The calmness didn't fade, even though she knew she'd killed herself, killed them both. *And I ...*

...And they both fell onto the rocks below.

CHAPTER
THIRTY NINE

Luna City, Luna

It's only been two weeks since the battle, Brian Wheeler thought, sourly. *You'd think they'd have something more important to talk about.*

He'd never really felt *sorry* for someone sitting in an interrogation cell, not until now. He'd been a cop long enough to be fairly sure that anyone unfortunate enough to be bandying words with a police interrogator had probably done something to deserve it. It was amazing just how many good-hearted citizens who just happened to have been in the wrong place at the wrong time were hauled into the station for questioning. The fact that most of them had been arrested in suspicious circumstances, to say the least, never seemed to matter.

But now...

He forced himself to keep his voice under tight control as the *third* set of lawyers fired an endless series of questions at him. Sin City's Management wanted to claim on the insurance and get the colony repaired as quickly as possible, even though Sin City was very low on the Luna Federation's agenda. The insurers, on the other hand, were looking desperately for an excuse to deny the Management's claim. They were already paying out more money than anyone cared to think about and Brian suspected, reading between the lines, that they were running out of cash. Their policies hadn't excluded alien attack.

"Do you believe," a lawyer asked, "that Sin City was well-prepared for the attack?"

Brian ground his teeth. He'd been over that point time and time again. They could read the transcript, if they cared enough to download it. He couldn't help feeling that the lawyers were merely stalling for time. The Luna Federation had been considering a temporary moratorium on paying insurance claims - another reason for Sin City's Management to want to move quickly - and if the insurers stalled long enough, the problem might just go away.

"No," he said, trying hard not to show his irritation. Or the headache that was pounding away inside his skull. "The colony was hit once, with a KEW strike. Emergency procedures should have kept the lower levels relatively safe. Instead, the entire complex vented, save for a handful of emergency shelters. Furthermore, a number of staffers deserted their posts instead of attempting rescue operations."

Another lawyer eyed him. "And do you believe that Sin City is responsible for protecting its guests?"

Brian met her eyes. "I was given to understand that all colonies within the Luna Federation are required to uphold a certain minimal standard of safety," he said. "Sin City clearly neglected its safety precautions."

"Sin City had no reason to predict an alien attack," a third lawyer added. "They may have taken all *legal* precautions, but found them insufficient."

There was a pause. Brian said nothing. They might expect him to speculate, but he knew better than to give them unnecessary ammunition. His speculations might be turned against him, if there was a legal dispute over just how much obligation Sin City's Management had actually *had*.

The lawyer cleared his throat. "Do you believe that Sin City took a reasonable set of precautions?"

Brian sighed. It was now harder to avoid answering.

"No," he said. He was tempted to force the lawyer to ask for more details, but it would be pointless. "Sin City took one hit. It should have been able to isolate the lower levels long enough for recovery missions to begin. Instead, the entire complex vented. That suggests either a very low level of readiness or outright sabotage."

He took a breath. "And while I understand that you have to keep asking these questions," he added, "I think you should know that they have already been answered."

The lawyers exchanged glances. "Thank you," one of them said, finally. "We may recall you if we have more questions."

Brian decided that was a dismissal and rose. He'd never liked lawyers, although the idealist in him knew they were necessary. Too many of the lawyers he'd met in the police force had been nothing more than hired guns, defending the guilty and persecuting the innocent as their paychecks dictated. And the lawyers he'd met on the moon had been no different. One set wanted to deny the claim, the other wanted to get it approved...and *both* of them were seeking evidence to bolster their side. Right or wrong didn't come into play.

He strode through the door, feeling his headache fading away as he saw Abigail waiting for him. *She'd* been interviewed too, but *her* lawyer - her family's lawyer - had managed to ensure that she didn't have to answer too many questions. He was apparently also working to get her testimony stricken completely from the record, although Brian doubted he would succeed. Too many people had an interest in using it against Sin City's Management.

They allowed an underage girl to live and work in Sin City, he thought, wryly. *And that will raise questions they won't want to answer.*

"Brian," Abigail said. She rose, smoothing down her skirt. "Can we go home now?"

"Of course," Brian said. Escorting Abigail everywhere hadn't been *that* challenging, although - with travel still heavily restricted - she hadn't been able to go very far. It would be harder, Brian was sure, once the travel restrictions were removed. "The shuttle is waiting on the pad."

"My father says he'll arrange for me to take up an internship when I turn sixteen," Abigail said, as they walked down to the shuttlepad. "Is that a good idea?"

"It would give you some useful experience," Brian said. It wouldn't be *easy*. "What *sort* of internship?"

"He said I could choose," Abigail said. "Where should I go?"

Brian considered it. "Somewhere that will teach you what is really important," he said, after a moment. "Not an office, not somewhere where your face is known..."

"I could join a mining crew," Abigail said. "Or ship out to the asteroids."

"That might not be a bad idea," Brian said. "But you'd need to get a spacer's cert before you could join an asteroid miner's crew."

Abigail gave him a sharp look. "Is that a good idea?"

"It would certainly teach you what you need to know," Brian said. He opened the hatch, then motioned for her to precede him into the shuttle. "And you'd be in a much better position to understand what is actually *important*."

He smiled at her as he closed the hatch. "You're in a position to take a shot at just about anything," he added. A merchant crew might be willing to take on an untried spacer, if she had the proper certification. "And you have plenty of time ahead of you."

"Thanks," Abigail said. "Do you think anyone will *want* me?"

Brian walked to the cockpit and took the controls. "I think you will have to work for it, if you want it," he said. "But it's worthwhile."

He lifted the shuttle into the air and set course for Clarke Colony. The Luna skies were full of shuttles, worker bees and other recovery vehicles, trying to patch together some of the damaged domes before the aliens returned. Brian had heard - from Abigail's father - that the Luna Federation was working desperately to rebuild the mass drivers, with help - for once - from the Great Powers. There was no choice. Earth and Home Fleet had taken one hell of a beating. Luna would be on her own if the aliens returned.

And they will, he thought, sourly. *And when they do, we will be ready for them.*

———

"Uncle Sasha," Svetlana said, as she stepped into his office. "I'm surprised you came all the way to the moon."

"Our offices here will allow for a private chat," Sasha Zadornov said. He stroked his white beard as she took a seat. "We are very pleased with you, of course."

"Thank you," Svetlana said. She met his eyes. "And the motherland?"

"A mess," Uncle Sasha said. "The Tadpoles devastated much of our territory, as you should be aware. If the other Great Powers hadn't been devastated themselves, we would be far more concerned. As it is...we may have problems continuing the war."

Svetlana kept her face impassive. Uncle Sasha might be her father's elder brother - and her favourite uncle, the one who'd always been kind to her - but she knew better than to underestimate him. Or to doubt him. If he said there would be problems, there would be problems. She'd heard next to nothing through the official channels, but she'd heard enough rumours to know that *mess* was an understatement.

"I see," she said. "I trust that my service has been of use?"

Sasha nodded, curtly. Svetlana hid her relief as best as she could, even though she suspected the old goat could see it. She existed for the motherland and the family - she'd had that drummed into her head since she'd been a little girl - and she *had* to be of use. Giving her a starship had been a gamble, one that had paid off in spades. Now, she had to find a way to capitalise on it before her superiors forgot what she'd done for them.

"I believe a better command will be in your future," Uncle Sasha said. "You have been awarded a number of medals from the Great Powers. It would be...*impolitic*...to deny you a new command. Unless you want to take a desk job..."

"No, thank you," Svetlana said, quickly. A desk job would destroy her. Worse, it would make her out to be nothing more than a common secretary. It wouldn't be long before her superiors decided she was nothing more than just another woman, rather than a person of consequence. "I want a carrier."

Uncle Sasha lifted his eyebrows. She didn't blame him for being surprised - or at least *pretending* to be surprised. Carriers were still the most prestigious commands in the navy, but they were also the largest targets. He had to be concerned about the prospect of putting her on a ship that would draw enemy starfighters like shit drew flies.

He didn't say that to her. Instead, he merely smiled. "Do you believe you *deserve* a carrier?"

"Yes," Svetlana said, flatly.

"Maybe you do," Uncle Sasha said. "And do you believe the family should spend the political capital to get you a carrier command?"

"Yes," Svetlana told him.

"Ah," Uncle Sasha said. His eyes lit up, challengingly. "And why, precisely, should we do that?"

Svetlana took a moment to compose her thoughts. Uncle Sasha had *never* treated her as anything less than one of the boys. He'd forced her to think - to defend herself - in the same way he'd challenged his sons and nephews. And she knew, all too well, that he wouldn't be swayed by anything less than a solid argument. Feminine wiles and tears would mean nothing to him. They'd just confirm prejudices that ran through the motherland, even though the rest of the world had long-since discarded them.

"Right now, I am the most successful commanding officer in the Navy," Svetlana said. She made a mental note to look up the medals she'd been given. There weren't many officers, apart from Theodore Smith, who'd won such an international collection of medals. "And we have had very few successes over the past year. You have to make the most of it."

"We could also have you paraded through the cities," Uncle Sasha pointed out, mildly. "It wouldn't do your reputation any good if you were killed on your next deployment."

"Then you'd have to explain why you weren't giving me another chance to save the motherland," Svetlana said. She had faith in the Kremlin's ability to bolster her reputation at the cost of everyone else who'd fought in the recent battle. It wouldn't fly outside Russia, but hardly anyone in the Kremlin cared about *that*. "Giving me a carrier, on the other hand, would bolster morale at home. And you need that, particularly now."

She leaned forward. "And my success will boost the family," she added. "If you don't capitalise on it, people will start wondering *why*."

Uncle Sasha nodded, slowly. "A compelling argument."

Svetlana smiled. It was more than *just* a compelling argument. She'd always been aware - all too aware - that she was an embarrassment to her family as well as an asset, but the embarrassment was gone now. Or it should be gone. There were people in her family with social attitudes so outdated that they would probably have done well for themselves in the courts of Peter the Great or Ivan the Terrible. *Their* reaction to her saving the family - and the motherland - would probably include snide remarks about how a man could have done it better.

"Yes," she said. She cocked her head. "No one will question it, now."

"True," Uncle Sasha agreed. "And the risk of being the lone woman on a starship, Svetlana *Zadornova?*"

"I have coped with that already," Svetlana said. Dropping the feminine convention for her surname had been a minor issue, after everything else she'd done. There were traditionalists who'd pitched a fit, but mostly after they'd *met* her. They never seemed to have the sense to check her *first* name before boarding her ship. "And a carrier command is worth any price."

"Don't say that to Ivan," Uncle Sasha said. He smiled, rather coldly. "I'll discuss the issue with my supporters, then take it to the *politburo*. And you *will* be expected to help keep up morale, I'm afraid. The kissing of babies is in your future."

Svetlana nodded, trying to hide her delight. Uncle Sasha was a powerful man - and she was famous. She was sure he was already exploiting his niece to bolster his - and the family's - position. If he wanted her to have a carrier command, she'd have a carrier command. And he could make life easier for her in a multitude of other ways too.

"I think I can cope," she said. She'd have to make sure her XO and other loyal officers were rewarded. No one reached flag rank without a patronage network of their own. A carrier XO would have more prestige than a frigate commander. "And so can you."

"We shall see," Uncle Sasha said. "We shall see."

He reached for a bottle of vodka and poured them both a generous measure. "And now *that's* over," he said, "I want to hear the whole story from your mouth."

"They blew up Sin City," Williams said. "Those bastards! They blew it all to hell!"

Ginny rolled her eyes. Two weeks in orbit - endless debriefings, followed by endless training simulations - had worn them both down. She hadn't argued when Williams had proposed booking rooms in Sin City, even though it was a risk. Going together might have been far too noticeable for their superiors to ignore. And then...

"It's shut down completely," Williams said. "Where will we go *now?*"

"There is more than one colony on the moon," Ginny pointed out. There had been over a thousand major colonies, before the war. *Most* of them were relatively intact. "I'm sure there's somewhere else to go."

Williams looked despondent. "They won't be as nice as Sin City." He made a show of tossing the datapad against the nearest bulkhead. "Those bastards did it on purpose!"

"I think those bastards don't give a damn about human sexual activity," Ginny said. She didn't have access to most of the reports from the xenospecialists, but some details had leaked into the datanet. The Tadpoles reproduced like frogs, not humans. "They certainly shouldn't have wasted a single missile on Sin City when there were actual targets of *military value* to destroy."

"That's my point," Williams said. "My morale has shrunk to the size of..."

"Your cock?" Ginny asked. She smiled at him before he could take offense. "There are other places to go, once the travel ban is lifted."

She sighed. Home Fleet had been in orbit for two weeks, but hardly anyone had been permitted to go down to Earth. She'd seen too many officers and crew walking the decks with haunted expressions, as they came to terms with the fact they'd never see some of their friends and families again. Millions of Americans - millions of *humans* - had died in the bombardment. Countless others would never be seen again, their fates unknown.

At least my family is safe, she thought. Tidal waves had battered Texas, but her family lived hundreds of miles inland. *And they're well, if wet.*

It wasn't a pleasant thought. Her father hadn't said much in his message, but she'd been able to read between the lines. The weather had changed, perhaps permanently. Texas would never be the same, any more than the rest of the world. The ranch might have to close if the downpour did permanent damage to the soil. God alone knew how bad it had been for the rest of the world. Japan and Australia had both taken heavy damage.

Williams sighed. "They did it on purpose," he said. He picked up the terminal and passed it to her. "I'm sure of it."

Ginny stuck out her tongue. "I think we should find a hotel somewhere else," she said sardonically, as she checked the terminal. Armstrong City was probably out - a lot of refugees were being hosted there until their colonies were repaired - but Clarke Colony or Luna City still had listings. The residents were clearly trying to get the interplanetary tourist trade up and running again as fast as possible. "Or we could head to L5 or L4."

"Perhaps," Williams said. He still looked despondent. "But it won't be the same."

"Cheer up," Ginny told him. "We *won!*"

"Yeah," Williams said. It was strange to see him so down. The jokester who'd fought beside her was gone, replaced by a stranger. "But at what cost?"

"We won," Ginny repeated. The cost had been high. She had a feeling that her squadron was going to be disbanded, sooner rather than later. With only two of the original pilots left, she doubted anyone would argue to keep it. She'd probably be reassigned to another squadron as the USN struggled to patch the holes in its formation. "We won."

She rested a hand on his shoulder. "And that," she added, "is all that matters."

And she wondered, as he leaned in for a kiss, just how many times she had to say that before she believed it herself.

CHAPTER
FORTY

London, United Kingdom

"It was our longest day," the Prime Minister said. His voice boomed over Hyde Park. "Our country - our *planet* - faced the gravest threat in our long history. And we rose to the occasion..."

Police Constable Robin Mathews kept his face expressionless, somehow, as the Prime Minister droned on and on. Whoever had written the Prime Minister's speech should be shot out of hand. He'd somehow dragged in quotes from Churchill, Wellington and a dozen other politicians, but failed to turn them into a coherent narrative. Indeed, as the droning went on, Robin was starting to think that shooting was too good for the speechwriter. Perhaps something lingering in boiling oil instead.

He sighed, inwardly, as he surveyed the crowd. There weren't *many* people in Hyde Park, two weeks after the war. Central London had been completely evacuated, save for the government ministers and their staff. A ring of steel kept looters and stragglers away from the site, but he knew the government was jumpy. Someone had fired on the Deputy Prime Minister's motorcade as he returned to Whitehall, yet somehow managed to escape detection and capture. The country was not pleased. If so many people hadn't been killed or displaced - or lost without trace - he would have expected a revolution.

And the PM probably doesn't have a hope of winning the next election, he thought. *Whoever takes over will have to clear up the mess.*

Sally nudged him. "How long can that man talk?"

"Too long," Robin muttered. The reporters seemed willing to listen, if nothing else. But then, they'd probably expected a long speech. "It'll be over soon."

"It will not be easy to recover from this disaster, to rebuild what we have lost," the Prime Minister said. His voice *sounded* confident, at least. "But I pledge to you that we *will* rebuild, we *will* recover. We will meet this challenge and we will overcome it."

Robin resisted the temptation to roll his eyes. The Prime Minister was safe and well-fed, spending his nights in a warm and secure location somewhere within London. *He* could talk all he liked about overcoming challenges. The refugees, scattered over a thousand makeshift camps and clearing houses, were suffering. Robin had never seen anything like it. Food and drink were in short supply; the supply of homes, tents and bedding was even more limited. Getting refugees to work was a very short-term solution. It had its limits.

The Longest Day, he thought. Some idiot in the Prime Minister's PR department had come up with the name. It would probably catch on, too. But the battle was over, while the scars remained. *It will never come to an end.*

The reporters clapped listlessly as the speech finally concluded. Robin wondered, absently, if the reporters intended to produce a honest version of the speech or not, then decided it probably didn't matter. The government had officers in each and every media outlet across the land. Bad news was ruthlessly played down, while every little scrap of *good* news was broadcast far and wide. Robin had no idea if it was good for morale or not, but hopefully it would keep the lid on for a while longer. Too many refugee camps had already collapsed into chaos.

His radio buzzed. "Escort the reporters back to their buses, then report back," the dispatcher ordered. The skies were already darkening. The rainfall had lessened, over the last week, but it was still raining heavily. "You'll be going east this afternoon."

Robin sighed. There was no end to it. And there never would be.

"Understood," he said. "We're on our way."

Admiral Jonathan Winters frowned as the small collection of reporters turned and headed as one towards the buses. He'd expected more, somehow. The services in Westminster Abbey had been far more dignified, even though it seemed that nearly everyone in Britain was mourning a family member who'd been killed in the bombardment. But the Prime Minister's speech had been dull and depressing. The man had aged twenty years over the last two weeks.

But that is true of all of us, Jon thought, as the Prime Minister approached him. *The President is already talking about not seeking re-election.*

"Prime Minister," he said. "I'm sorry we didn't have a chance to talk earlier."

"My schedule is very busy," the Prime Minister said. He nodded to the nearby car. "If you'd care to join me...?"

Jon followed him into the car, shaking his head inwardly. Normally, any meeting between a senior American naval officer and a foreign leader would require weeks of preparation...and all the *real* work would be done by subordinates. Now...knocking down a few of the barricades between the people in question and actual *work* could hardly be a *bad* thing, even if the diplomats did worry about their superiors going off-message.

"I haven't had time to see the latest reports," the Prime Minister said. "How bad is it?"

"Home Fleet is down to *three* effective carriers," Jon said. "Two more will be repaired in the next month, if we have time, but that might not be on our side. We've recalled three carriers from the front, yet that will weaken our defences..."

"And they might punch through the gap," the Prime Minister said. "Do they *know* how badly they hurt us?"

"Their fleet will have a pretty accurate count," Jon confirmed. "The forces they have facing us will be aware, sooner rather than later."

"Which will give them incentive to attack," the Prime Minister said. "Can we stop them?"

"I don't know," Jon said. He wondered, grimly, just what the British Admiralty had told the Prime Minister. *Ark Royal* had boosted their confidence, but the Battle of Earth had knocked it back down again. "We lack hard data on their true numbers."

"They could be weak too," the Prime Minister said. He sounded like a man grasping at straws. "We might be able to bring them to the bargaining table."

"Or they might still be bringing their forces to bear against us," Jon said. He hated to say it, but there was no choice. It was his duty to keep his superiors informed of such matters. "In that case, the odds will shift rapidly against us."

The Prime Minister nodded. Jon eyed him, wondering if the Prime Minister was on the verge of zoning out completely. The Vice President had been hospitalised after a nervous breakdown, while the Speaker of the House had committed suicide. America hadn't been hurt so badly since the Civil War, well outside living memory. Britain hadn't been battered so badly *ever*. And far more of their population lived on the coast.

"Then we have no choice," the Prime Minister mused. He sounded as though he was talking to himself. "We must find a way to end the war."

His terminal bleeped. "Yes?"

"*Ark Royal* has returned to the solar system," a voice said. Jon felt his heart leap, even though he knew it wasn't good news. *Ark Royal* was one ship. She couldn't have stopped the alien attack on her lonesome. "She's sent a datapacket for your consumption."

"Understood," the Prime Minister said. "I'll return to the bunker now." He looked at Jon. "You'll be coming with me?"

"If I can," Jon said. He wasn't due to return to orbit until evening. He'd planned to visit the Cenotaph to pay his respects, if the Brits could scrounge up an escort, but it wasn't set in stone. "I'm looking forward to hearing their report."

And maybe we can send them out again, he thought, grimly. *Hitting the aliens in the back may be the only way to win the war.*

"So it's confirmed," Andrew said, two hours after he'd returned to the bunker. "There *is* a second alien faction."

"Perhaps more than one," the French President said. "But is it - are *they* - potential allies?"

Andrew peered down at the report. "They *were* fired on by the other aliens," he said. *Ark Royal* had witnessed the whole affair, but she'd been too far away to intervene. "And they *were* trying to talk to us when they were destroyed."

"It could be a trap," the Russian President grunted. "Would *we* fire on one of our vessels in support of an alien power?"

"I like to think not," the American President said.

Andrew kept his face expressionless. MI6 had run up a number of scenarios where the aliens made common cause with a human power, perhaps more than one, but he'd never found any of them particularly plausible. A human power would have to be insane to trust aliens, even if they hated and feared their fellow humans. There would be no way to predict what the aliens would do after the war was over.

He leaned forward. "Don't you see? This is a chance to actually *talk* to them!"

"And perhaps sail right into a trap," the Chinese Premier said. "The aliens might be baiting us, after smashing so much of Home Fleet here."

"They don't *need* to bait us," the French President said. "Look at the timing. There is no way they *could* have known the outcome of the battle here when *Ark Royal* saw the...the encounter. They *couldn't* have known. There is no reason to think that this isn't a valid attempt to open communications."

"Except for the simple fact that they've had plenty of opportunities to talk to us," the Russian President snapped. "And they only do it *now*?"

"We don't *know* they had plenty of opportunities," the American President pointed out. "For all we know, this *was* their first chance to speak to us."

"But we *don't* know," the Russian President said. "We should work on deploying the bioweapon immediately."

Andrew held up a hand. "There is a certain level of risk in attempting to open communications," he said. "But I thought it was agreed that we could *not* hope for the bioweapon to infect *all* of their worlds before it went active. There is no way we could be sure of a clean sweep."

"We'd hurt them," the Russian President said.

"Perhaps," the American President said. His voice was very calm. "And perhaps we would just make them *really* mad."

"Yes," Andrew said. He closed his eyes for a long moment. "Let us try to open communications. And if it fails, we can move ahead with the bioweapon."

"Agreed," the French President said.

Andrew leaned back in his chair as the vote was taken. He'd never really expected to have to deploy a weapon of mass destruction, let alone a bioweapon. And yet...Britain was on the edge. *Earth* was on the edge. Victory - even a compromise peace - seemed less and less plausible with every passing day. A second alien thrust, aimed directly at Earth, would be decisive. It would end the war.

All in favour, he thought, numbly. *God help us.*

The discussion ended. Andrew watched the four images vanishing, wondering just what they were thinking. They'd agreed, in confidence, to sentence a sentient race - the only other one known to exist - to death. And they'd made the decision for everyone, without consulting with the rest of their governments. Andrew understood the logic - there was no way he could discuss it with his Cabinet, let alone the Houses of Parliament - but he hated it. The decision wasn't one he wanted to make on his own.

And yet, I have no choice, he thought.

He picked up his datapad. The records lay open in front of him, mocking him. Over two million confirmed deaths, with a further six million unaccounted for; millions of injuries, millions of pieces of property damage...and an economy that had slumped badly. It was the greatest disaster in British history. There was no way to sugar-coat it. Nor was there any way to make it just...*go away*.

And if they invade a second time, he reminded himself, *we will lose the war.*

"God help us," he said, quietly.

The End

APPENDIX:
GLOSSARY OF UK TERMS AND SLANG

[Author's Note: I've tried to define every incident of specifically UK slang in this glossary, but I can't promise to have spotted everything. If you spot something I've missed, please let me know and it will be included.]

Aggro - slang term for aggression or trouble, as in 'I don't want any aggro.'

Beasting/Beasted - military slang for anything from a chewing out by one's commander to outright corporal punishment or hazing. The latter two are now officially banned.

Binned - SAS slang for a prospective recruit being kicked from the course, then returned to unit (RTU).

Boffin - Scientist

Bootnecks - slang for Royal Marines. Loosely comparable to 'Jarhead.'

Bottle - slang for nerve, as in 'lost his bottle.'

Borstal - a school/prison for young offenders.

Compo - British army slang for improvised stews and suchlike made from rations and sauces.

Donkey Wallopers - slang for the Royal Horse Artillery.

Fortnight - two weeks. (Hence the terrible pun, courtesy of the *Goon Show*, that Fort Knight cannot possibly last three weeks.)

'Get stuck into' - 'start fighting.'

'I should coco' - 'you're damned right.'

King's Shilling - Army Pay. 'Taking the King's Shilling' means joining the army.

Kip - sleep.

Levies - native troops. The Ghurkhas are the last remnants of native troops from British India.

Lifts - elevators

Lorries - trucks.

MOD - Ministry of Defence. (The UK's Pentagon.)

Order of the Garter - the highest order of chivalry (knighthood) and the third most prestigious honour (inferior only to the Victoria Cross and George Cross) in the United Kingdom. By law, there can be only twenty-four non-royal members of the order at any single time.

Panda Cola - Coke as supplied by the British Army to the troops.

RFA - Royal Fleet Auxiliary

Rumbled - discovered/spotted.

SAS - Special Air Service.

SBS - Special Boat Service

Spotted Dick - a traditional fruity sponge pudding with suet, citrus zest and currants served in thick slices with hot custard. The name always caused a snigger.

Squaddies - slang for British soldiers.

Stag - guard duty.

STUFT - 'Ships Taken Up From Trade,' civilian ships requisitioned for government use.

TAB (tab/tabbing) - Tactical Advance to Battle.

Tearaway - boisterous/badly behaved child, normally a teenager.

Torch - Flashlight.

Tories/Tory Party - slang for the British Conservative Party.

Walt - Poser, i.e. someone who claims to have served in the military and/ or a very famous regiment. There's a joke about 22 SAS being the largest regiment in the British Army - it must be, because of all the people who claim to have served in it.

Wanker - Masturbator (jerk-off). Commonly used as an insult.

Wanking - Masturbating.

Yank/Yankee - Americans

CPSIA information can be obtained
at www.ICGtesting.com
Printed in the USA
FSOW03n2054021217
41964FS